A TEXT BOOK OF

MATERIAL SCIENCE

FOR

SEMESTER - I

SECOND YEAR DEGREE COURSE IN MECHANICAL & AUTOMOBILE ENGINEERING

Strictly According to New Revised Credit System Syllabus of Savitribai Phule Pune University
(w.e.f June 2016)

(Also Useful for SE Production and Industrial Engineering)

ADVAIT S. GHOLAP

M. Tech. (Mate. Tech.), I.I.T. Bombay,
Formerly, Lecturer in Metallurgy,
Mech. Engg. Deptt.,
Maharashtra Institute of Technology,
Pune.

DR. MILIND S. KULKARNI

M. Tech. (Mate. Tech.), I.I.T. Bombay
Ph. D. (Texas A & M University,
College Station U.S.A.)
Formerly, Lecturer in Metallurgy,
Maharashtra Institute of Technology, Pune.

SANGRAMSINH S. GHORPADE

M.E. (Mechanical)
Assistant Professor, Mechanical Engg. Deptt.,
Sinhgad Academy of Engineering,
Kondhava (BK), Pune.

NIRALI PRAKASHAN
ADVANCEMENT OF KNOWLEDGE

N3534

MATERIAL SCIENCE (SE MECH. & AUTO. ENGG.)

ISBN 978-93-86084-08-8

Second Edition : **June 2017**

© : **Authors**

Published By :   POLYPLATE

NIRALI PRAKASHAN

Abhyudaya Pragati, 1312, Shivaji Nagar,
Off J.M. Road, Pune – 411005
Tel - (020) 25512336/37/39, Fax - (020) 25511379
Email : niralipune@pragationline.com

☞ **DISTRIBUTION CENTRES**

PUNE

Nirali Prakashan : 119, Budhwar Peth, Jogeshwari Mandir Lane, Pune 411002, Maharashtra
Tel : (020) 2445 2044, 66022708, Fax : (020) 2445 1538
Email : bookorder@pragationline.com, niralilocal@pragationline.com

Nirali Prakashan : S. No. 28/27, Dhyari, Near Pari Company, Pune 411041
Tel : (020) 24690204 Fax : (020) 24690316
Email : dhyari@pragationline.com, bookorder@pragationline.com

MUMBAI

Nirali Prakashan : 385, S.V.P. Road, Rasdhara Co-op. Hsg. Society Ltd.,
Girgaum, Mumbai 400004, Maharashtra
Tel : (022) 2385 6339 / 2386 9976, Fax : (022) 2386 9976
Email : niralimumbai@pragationline.com

☞ **DISTRIBUTION BRANCHES**

JALGAON

Nirali Prakashan : 34, V. V. Golani Market, Navi Peth, Jalgaon 425001,
Maharashtra, Tel : (0257) 222 0395, Mob : 94234 91860

KOLHAPUR

Nirali Prakashan : New Mahadvar Road, Kedar Plaza, 1st Floor Opp. IDBI Bank
Kolhapur 416 012, Maharashtra. Mob : 9850046155

NAGPUR

Pratibha Book Distributors : Above Maratha Mandir, Shop No. 3, First Floor,
Rani Jhanshi Square, Sitabuldi, Nagpur 440012, Maharashtra
Tel : (0712) 254 7129

DELHI

Nirali Prakashan : 4593/21, Basement, Aggarwal Lane 15, Ansari Road, Daryaganj
Near Times of India Building, New Delhi 110002
Mob : 08505972553

BENGALURU

Pragati Book House : House No. 1, Sanjeevappa Lane, Avenue Road Cross,
Opp. Rice Church, Bengaluru – 560002.
Tel : (080) 64513344, 64513355,Mob : 9880582331, 9845021552
Email:bharatsavla@yahoo.com

CHENNAI

Pragati Books : 9/1, Montieth Road, Behind Taas Mahal, Egmore,
Chennai 600008 Tamil Nadu, Tel : (044) 6518 3535,
Mob : 94440 01782 / 98450 21552 / 98805 82331,
Email : bharatsavla@yahoo.com

niralipune@pragationline.com | www.pragationline.com

Also find us on 🪧 www.facebook.com/niralibooks

PREFACE TO THE SECOND EDITION

We are glad and excited to announce that the First Edition of this book received an overwhelming response from the engineering student community, compelling us to release its **Second Edition** within a very short period of time.

This thoroughly revised **Second Edition** has been updated with additional matter, many solved problems, including solutions to Numerous Exercises and University Question Papers (December 2013 to May 2017) for practice.

Special care has been taken to maintain high degree of accuracy in the theory and numericals throughout the book.

We take this opportunity to express our sincere thanks to Dineshbhai Furia of Nirali Prakashan, a reputed pioneer in the publication field. Our special thanks to Jignesh Furia for their effective cooperation and great care in bringing out this revised edition. We also appreciate the efforts of M. P. Munde and the entire staff of Engineering Books Deptt. of Nirali Prakashan namely Mrs. Deepali Lachake (Co-ordinator) for bringing this book to the students in a timely manner.

We sincerely hope that this "**Second Edition**" will also be warmly received by all concerned as in the past.

Valuable suggestions from our esteemed readers to improve the book are most welcome and highly appreciated.

Pune   **Authors**

PREFACE TO FIRST EDITION

It gives us great pleasure in publishing this text book on **"Material Science"** for the Students of Second Year Degree Course in Mechanical and Automobile Engineering. This book is strictly written According to New Revised Credit System Syllabus of Savitribai Phule Pune University (2015 Pattern).

As per the policy of the University, Engineering Syllabi is revised every five years. Last revision was in the year 2012. New revision is coming little earlier, as university has introduced **Online** system of examination from year 2012.

As per the New Credit System, the **In Sem (Online – 50 Marks) Examinations** (Combined Phase-I and Phase-II) will be conducted based on first, second, third and fourth units. The **Online** examinations will have objective types of questions with multiple choices. **End Semester Examination (Theory Paper 50 Marks)** will be based on all the six units and that will be conducted in traditional way and the theory course will have 4 credits.

We have given Free Separate book of Multiple Choice Questions (MCQ's) which will be very useful to the students, especially for Online Examinations.

We take this opportunity to express our sincere thanks to Shri. Dineshbhai Furia, Shri. Jignesh Furia, MRs. Nirali Verma and Shri. M. P. Munde and entire team of Nirali Prakashan namely Mrs. Deepali Lachake (Co-ordinator), Mr. Bharat Jadhav who really have taken keen interest and untiring efforts in publishing this text.

Finally, we express our gratitude to our family members for their continuous support and encouragement, thanks to all.

We have no doubt that like our earlier texts, student's community will respond favourably to this new venture.

The advice and suggestions of our esteemed readers to improve the text are most welcomed, and will be highly appreciated.

18th June 2016   **Authors**

Pune

SYLLABUS

Unit I: Structure of Metals and Materials   (6 Hrs)

Basic concepts of Crystal structures, Types of crystal systems, Crystal structure of metals (BCC, FCC and HCP systems), ceramics and molecular arrangement of polymers, Miller indices, indexing of lattice planes and directions, Lattice parameters (coordination number, no. of atoms per unit cell, atomic packing factor, density).

Unit II: Mechanical Behaviors of Metal and Materials   (6 Hrs)

Introduction to Crystal imperfections and Classification, Crystal imperfections : point defects, line defects- edge and screw dislocations, surface defects, volume defects, Mechanism of Elastic and plastic deformation (slip and twinning),Theory of dislocation, deformation of single crystal by slip, plastic deformation of polycrystalline materials, work hardening theory, Changes in properties due to cold working and hot working.

Unit III: Destructive and Non-Destructive Testing   (8 Hrs)

Study of destructive testing, Tensile test, engineering stress-strain curve, true stress-strain curve, types of stress-strain curves, Numerical based on Evolution of properties, compression test, different hardness tests-Vickers, Rockwell, Brinnel, Poldi, Micro Hardness Test, Durometers, Impact test, fatigue test, creep test, Erichsen Cupping Test.

Non Destructive testing: Principals and procedure, advantages, disadvantages and Industrial applications of NDT, such as Visual Inspection,Liquid /dye penetrate test, Magnaflux test, Eddy current test, Sonic and Ultrasonic testing and Radiography testing.

Unit IV: Metals Corrosion and its Prevention   (4 Hrs)

Classification of corrosion : Dry corrosion and wet corrosion, Mechanism of corrosion,Types of corrosion : Pitting corrosion, stress corrosion, season cracking, cavitation corrosion, caustic embrittlement, intergranular corrosion, crevice corrosion, erosion corrosion, uniform corrosion, galvanic corrosion, Corrosion prevention methods : classification of different methods, e,g, inhibitors, cathodic and anodic protection, internal and external coatings, Low and High temperature corrosion. Design against corrosion.

Unit V: Surface Modification Methods   (6 Hrs)

Importance of surface modification, classification of different methods and factors affecting: electroplating, PVD, CVD,IVD, powder coating, shot blasting, ion implantation, plasma nitriding, anodizing, Surface preparation before coating and coating defects.

Unit VI: Powder Metallurgical Technology   (6 Hrs)

Basic steps of powder metallurgy process, classification and methods of powder manufacturing, characteristics of metal powders, Conditioning of metal powders (Screening, Blending and mixing, annealing), Compaction techniques (cold compaction, hot compaction, Isostatic compaction and powder rolling), mechanism and importance of sintering, Pre-sintering and sintering secondary operations Advantages, limitations and applications of powder metallurgy. Production of typical P/M components (with flow charts), self lubricated bearing, cemented carbides, cermets, refractory metals, electrical contact materials, friction materials, and diamond impregnated tools, friction plate, clutch plate, commutator brushes.

CONTENTS

B. Non-Destructive Testing

✠ ✠ ✠

STRUCTURE OF METALS AND MATERIALS

STRUCTURE OF MATERIAL AND PLASTIC DEFORMATION

1.1 INTRODUCTION

Various properties of metals are governed by their crystal structures. Broadly speaking, the crystal structure is a definite arrangement of atoms. It is also referred as atomic structure of metals. All metals and their alloys are crystalline solids.

Crystal structures are studied by their atomic arrangements in particular planes and directions. The density of metal depends upon packing factor of atoms. The plastic deformation property of metals depends upon the number of atoms in a typical plane.

Crystalline solids are never perfect in nature. They show some imperfections, which are termed as crystal defects. Crystal structures are studied by using x-ray diffraction and electron microscopy.

A metal can be deformed elastically or plastically. Plastic deformation takes place by slip, twinning or both. Metal can be deformed plastically by hot working or cold working.

1.2 STRUCTURE PROPERTY RELATIONSHIP

Broadly, the structure of a material can be classified on three levels as

1. Crystal structure
2. Phase
3. Microstructure.

Crystal structure is a specific arrangement of atoms in ordered condition. A phase is a structurally homogeneous part of a system. The arrangement of grains, its size, orientation and non-metallic contents comprise the microstructure of a metal. Various properties like mechanical, thermal, electrical, magnetic, electronic and optical are directly dependent on the structure of materials. By modifying the microstructure, the properties of materials can be altered.

Features

- F.C.C. crystal structure has more slip systems than B.C.C. crystal structure. Therefore, metals with F.C.C. crystal structure (e.g. copper) are more ductile than B.C.C. crystal structure (e.g. Mild steel).

- Cold worked copper with deformed grain structure shows less electrical conductivity than the annealed and equiaxed grain structure of copper.

- Fine grained metal has higher strength and toughness.

- Creep resistance of coarse grained structure is always higher than fine grained structure.

- Highly stressed and distorted grain structure of austenitic stainless steel reduces its corrosion resistance.

- Two phase structure (e.g. alpha-beta brass) shows higher hardness and strength than single phase structure (e.g. alpha brass).

- Composite materials have two or more phases, which can give optimum physical, chemical or mechanical properties (e.g. fibre glass reinforced plastics).

1.3 CRYSTAL STRUCTURE

Crystal: A crystal is defined as a solid in which a definite arrangement of atoms is observed in three directions. Due to fixed positions of atoms, a crystalline solid is considered as a three dimensional network.

Unit Cell: It is defined as the smallest arrangement of atoms which is a true representation of the crystal structure and repeats in all possible directions.

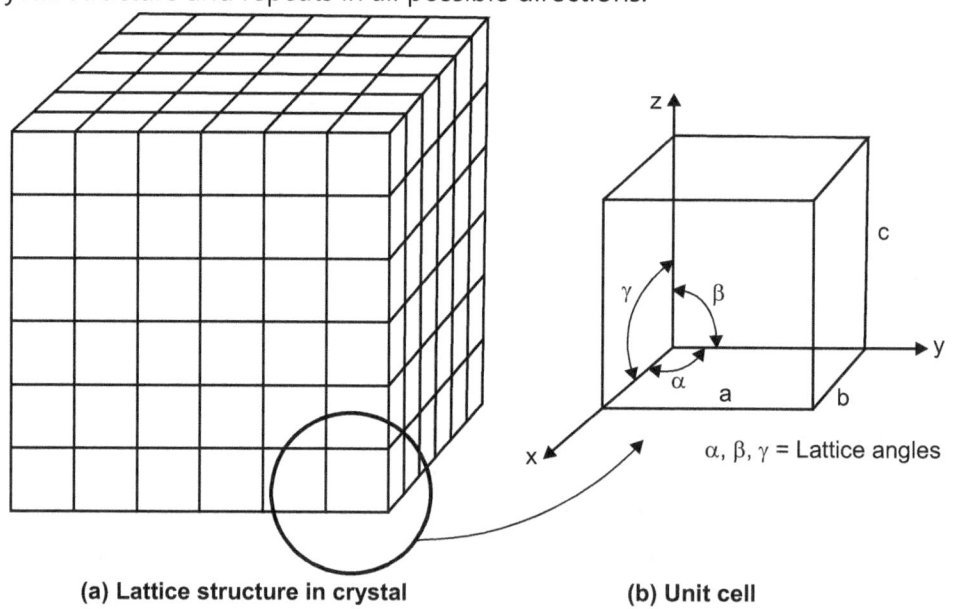

(a) Lattice structure in crystal   **(b) Unit cell**

Fig. 1.1: Space lattice

Space Lattice: It is defined as a three-dimensional network of imaginary lines connecting the atoms [Fig. 1.1 (a)].

Lattice Parameter: The distance between the centre of two atoms is defined as lattice parameter. It is also defined as the length of a unit cell.

Lattice Angles: These are defined as the angles between the edges of a unit cell.

Fig. 1.1 (b) shows a typical unit cell. In this unit cell, a, b and c are the lattice parameters, while α, β and γ are the lattice angles. This unit cell is situated at the origin of crystallographic axes x, y and z, mutually perpendicular to each other.

The various crystal systems that are commonly observed are tabulated in Table 1.1 and shown in Fig. 1.2

Table 1.1: The Crystal Systems

1.	Cubic	$a = b = c,\ \alpha = \beta = \gamma = 90°$
2.	Tetragonal	$a = b \neq c,\ \alpha = \beta = \gamma = 90°$
3.	Hexagonal	$a = b \neq c,\ \alpha = \beta = 90°,\ \gamma = 120°$
4.	Triclinic	$a \neq b \neq c,\ \alpha \neq \beta \neq \gamma \neq 90°$
5.	Monoclinic	$a \neq b \neq c,\ \alpha = \gamma = 90° \neq \beta$
6.	Orthorhombic	$a \neq b \neq c,\ \alpha = \beta = \gamma = 90°$
7.	Rhombohedral	$a = b = c,\ \alpha = \beta = \gamma \neq 90°$

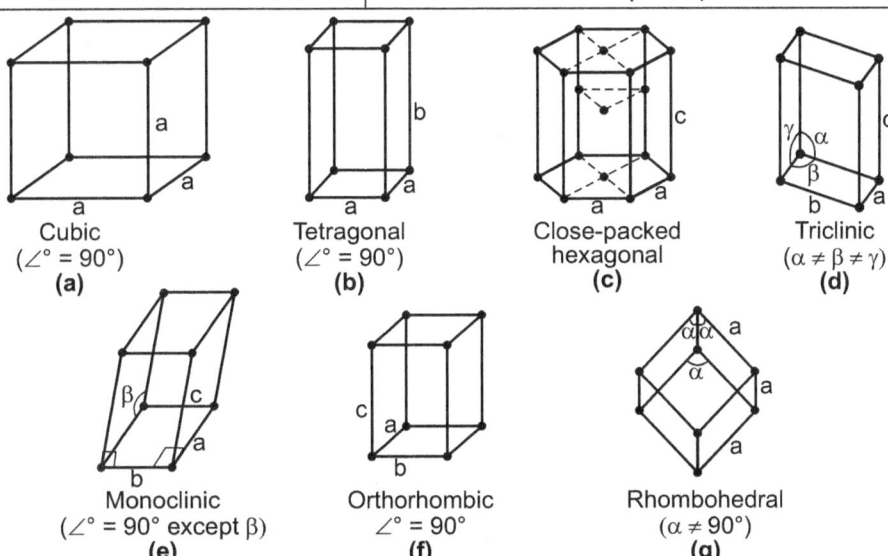

Fig. 1.2: Typical crystal structures

1.4 INDEXING OF LATTICE PLANES AND DIRECTIONS

(Nov. 16, May 17)

The indexing pattern of planes and directions is called as Miller indices.

Indexing the Planes: Consider a unit cell situated at the origin of crystallographic axes X,Y and Z. The planes of the unit cell makes an intercept on one or more axes. The Miller indices for a plane are given as the reciprocals of intercept made. The plane parallel to axis is considered as zero intercept for that axis e.g. in Fig. 1.3 (a), the plane makes an intercept equal to an unit length of X axis. This plane does not show intercept on Y and Z axes. In other words, the plane is perpendicular to X axis and parallel to Y and Z axes. So, the Miller indices for this plane are simply (1 0 0). In Fig. 1.3 (b), the plane intersects Y axis and parallel to X and Z axes. Its Miller indices are (0 1 0).

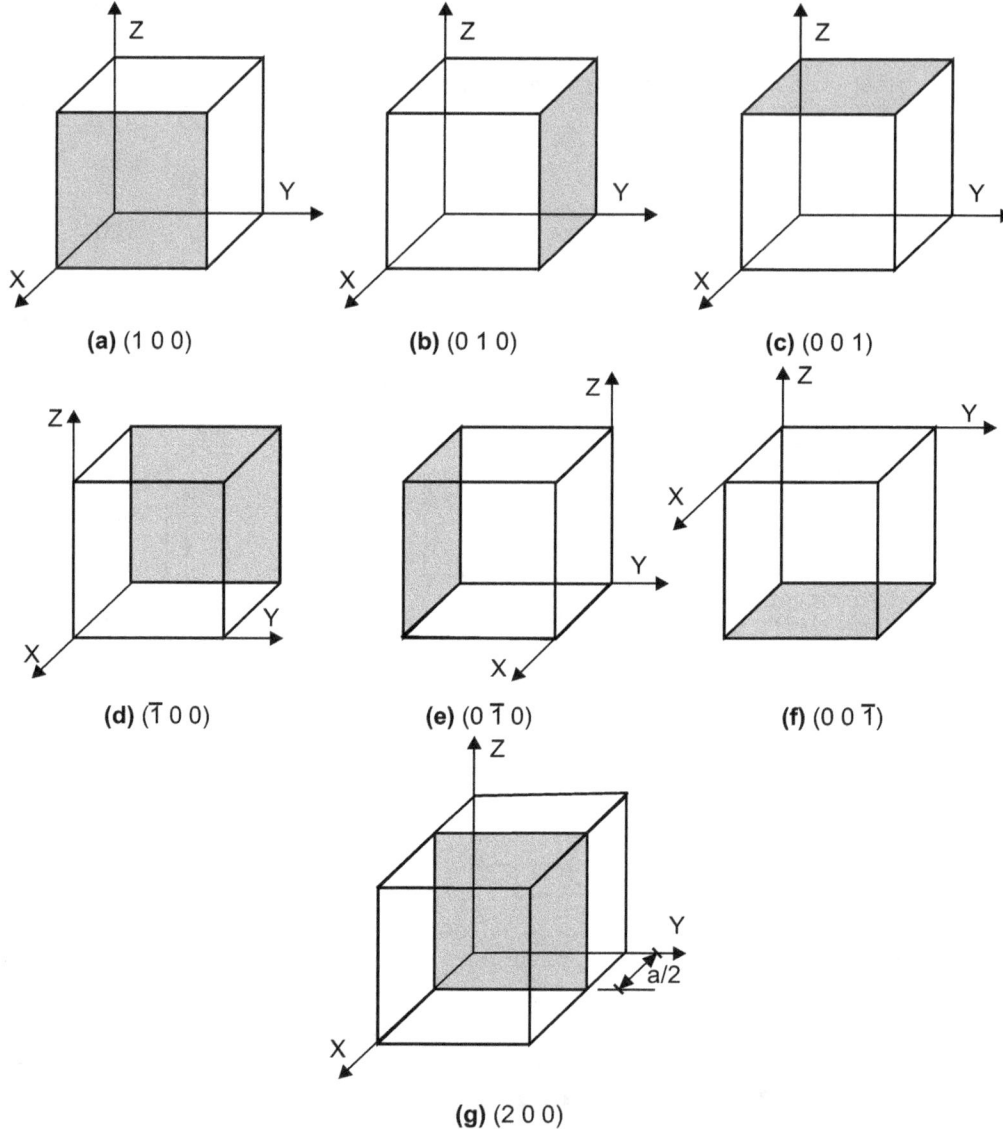

(a) (1 0 0) **(b)** (0 1 0) **(c)** (0 0 1)

(d) ($\overline{1}$ 0 0) **(e)** (0 $\overline{1}$ 0) **(f)** (0 0 $\overline{1}$)

(g) (2 0 0)

Fig. 1.3: Miller indices of various planes in a cubic system

In Fig. 1.3 (c), the plane intersects Z axis and parallel to X and Y axes. Its Miller indices are (0 0 1).

Above three faces i.e. planes shown in Fig. 1.3 a, b and c are front planes. For determining the Miller indices of the opposite planes, the origin is shifted. This makes the plane to intersect the axis in the negative direction. To indicate this, a negative sign (called bar) is placed above the reciprocal of the intercept e.g. in Fig. 1.3 (d) the plane makes an intercept equal to a unit length on a negative X-axis. This plane is parallel to Y and Z axes. The plane has Miller indices as ($\bar{1}$ 0 0) ($\bar{1}$ read as bar one). Similarly, in Fig. 1.3 (e) and Fig. 1.3 (f) the planes have miller indices (0 $\bar{1}$ 0) and (0 0 $\bar{1}$) respectively.

A six faced cube, thus, shows indices for all faces as follows

   (1 0 0), (0 1 0), (0 0 1) and ($\bar{1}$ 0 0) (0 $\bar{1}$ 0) (0 0 $\bar{1}$)

All these planes are collectively shown as {1 0 0} .

Now, consider Fig. 1.3 (g). If the intercept of the plane on X-axis is equal to half of the lattice parameter of the unit cell, then the Miller indices are (2 0 0). Similarly, a plane having intercept on X-axis as one third that of lattice parameter is indexed by (3 0 0) and so on.

Various planes and their indices are shown in Fig. 1.4.

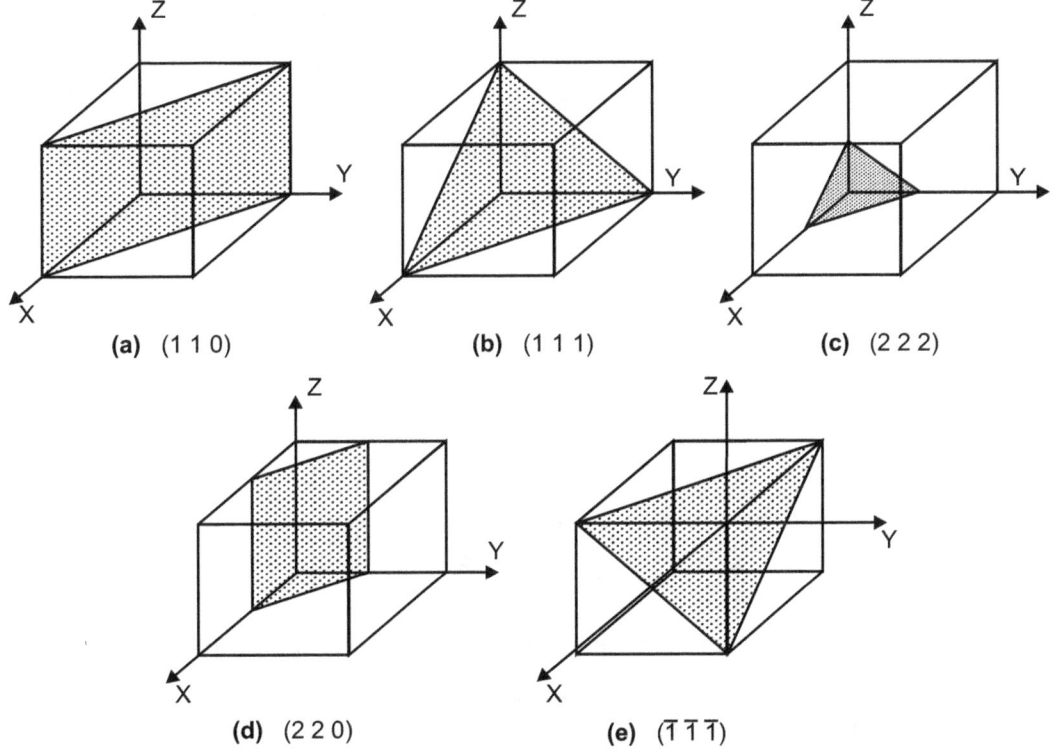

(a) (1 1 0)   **(b) (1 1 1)**   **(c) (2 2 2)**

(d) (2 2 0)   **(e) ($\bar{1}$ $\bar{1}$ $\bar{1}$)**

Fig. 1.4: Miller indices of some planes in a cubic system

Indexing the Directions: The direction has the same indices as of the plane to which it is perpendicular. The directions start from the origin. For example, in Fig. 1.5 (a) the direction starts from the origin and is perpendicular to plane (1 1 0). Therefore, it has indices [1 1 0].

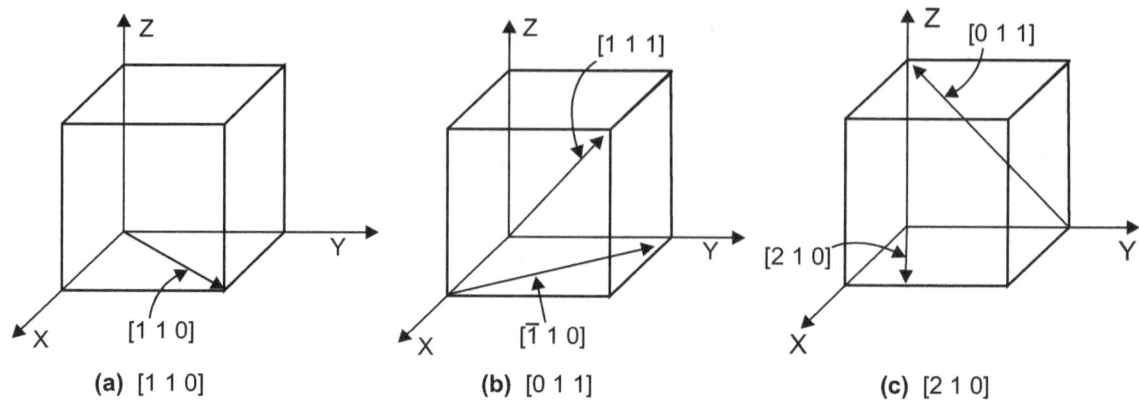

Fig. 1.5: Miller indices of crystallographic directions in cubic system

Similar to that of planes, the negative directions are indexed by shifting the origin. Some of the directions are shown in Fig. 1.5 (b and c). Directions are indexed by using a square bracket. Directions of the same atomic distribution are said to be of the same form. A set of symmetrical directions is represented by an angular bracket. For example, [1 1 0],

$[1\,0\,\bar{1}]$, $[0\,\bar{1}\,\bar{1}]$ etc., are shown as < 1 1 0 >.

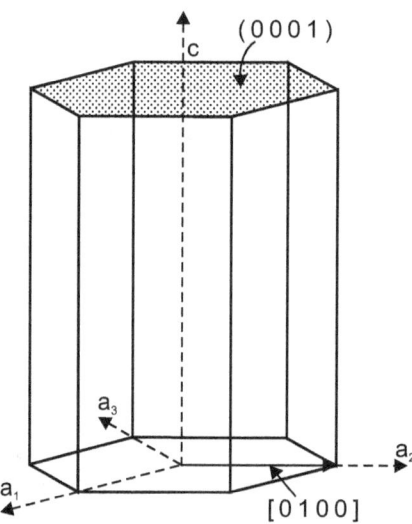

Fig. 1.6: Plane and directions in a hexagonal crystal structure

The above planes and directions are considered for a cubic structure. For a hexagonal close packed structure, four co-ordinates are used, e.g. the plane has indices (0 0 0 1) and direction as [0 1 0 0], as shown in Fig. 1.6.

1.5 AVERAGE NUMBER OF ATOMS PER UNIT CELL   (Dec. 10)

For a cubic unit cell, the number of atoms is eight (8) i.e. one atom at each corner. But, in a space lattice, a number of unit cells are present. Therefore, each corner atom is shared by other eight adjacent unit cells. Hence, for a unit cell, only 1/8th of the corner atom is available. Similarly, an atom on face of a unit cell is also shared by another unit cell; so a face atom per unit cell is only 1/2. The atom at the centre is not shared by any other unit cell. Thus, the average number of atoms per unit cell can be given as

$$N = \frac{A}{8} + \frac{B}{2} + \frac{C}{1}$$

where,   N = average number of atoms per unit cell,

              A = Total number of atoms at corner of a unit cell,

              B = Total number of atoms at face of a unit cell,

and   C = Total number of atoms at centre of a unit cell.

1.6 BASIC TYPES OF CRYSTAL STRUCTURES

Following are the basic types of crystal structures

   (a) Simple cubic crystal structure (S.C.)

   (b) Body centered crystal structure (B.C.C.)

   (c) Face centered crystal structure (F.C.C.)

   (d) Hexagonal close packed structure (H.C.P.)

   These are explained as follows

(a) Simple Cubic Crystal Structure

*   In this crystal structure, the atoms are situated at the corners of the unit cell i.e. one atom at each corner as shown in Fig. 1.7.

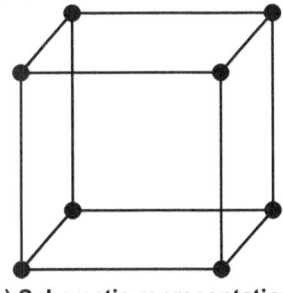 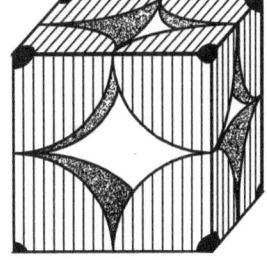

(a) Schematic representation   **(b) Actual stacking**

Fig. 1.7: Simple cubic structure

*   This crystal structure does not have atoms at the faces and at the centre of the unit cell. A simple cubic crystal structure has a total number of atoms equal to eight. As we know,

   Average number of atoms per unit cell

$$= \frac{A}{8} + \frac{B}{2} + \frac{C}{1} = \frac{8}{8} + \frac{0}{2} + \frac{0}{1}$$

$$= 1 + 0 + 0 = 1$$

*   Therefore, the average number of atoms per unit cell in a simple cubic crystal structure is one. Although simple cubic arrangements of atoms do not ordinarily exist in engineering materials, they are used to introduce the crystal structure subject because of their simplicity.

(b) Body Centred Crystal Structure (B.C.C.)   (May 13)

- This type of crystal structure is slightly complex compared to the simple cubic structure. In this crystal structure, one atom is placed at each corner of the unit cell. In addition to this, there is one atom at the centre of the unit cell (See Fig. 1.8).

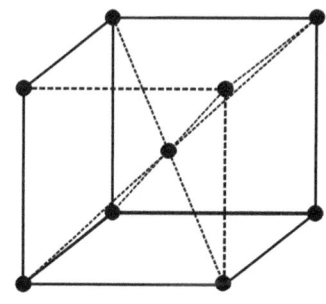 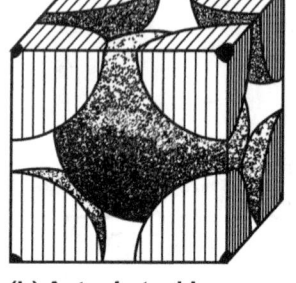

(a) Schematic representation   (b) Actual stacking

Fig. 1.8: Body centred cubic structure

- The corner atoms are shared by other eight unit cells, while the centered atom remains unshared.

  Average number of atoms per unit cell

$$= \frac{A}{8} + \frac{B}{2} + \frac{C}{1} = \frac{8}{8} + \frac{0}{2} + \frac{1}{1}$$

$$= 1 + 0 + 1 = 2$$

- Therefore, the average number of atoms per unit cell is two. This type of crystal structure is found in the following metals

  Li, Na, K, V, Ta, α - Cr, Mo, α - Fe etc.

(c) Face-Centred Cubic Crystal Structure (F.C.C.)   (Nov. 16)

- In this crystal structure, one atom is placed at each corner of the unit cell (i.e. eight corner atoms) one atom at each face centre (i.e. six atoms). It does not have any atom at the centre (Fig. 1.9).

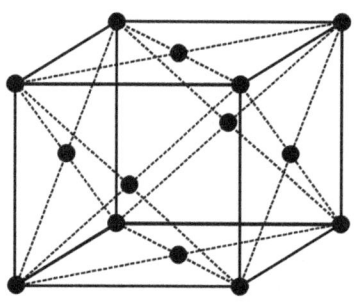 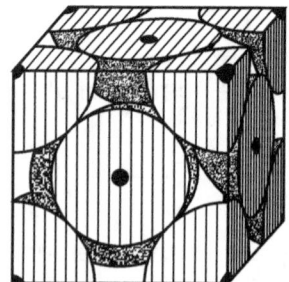

(a) Schematic representation   (b) Actual stacking

Fig. 1.9: Face centred cubic structure

- The corner atoms are shared by eight unit cells, while the face centred atom is shared by two unit cells.

  Average number of atoms per unit cell

  $$= \frac{A}{8} + \frac{B}{2} + \frac{C}{1} = \frac{8}{8} + \frac{6}{2} + \frac{0}{1}$$

  $$= 1 + 3 + 0 = 4$$

- Therefore, the average number of atoms per unit cell is four. This type of crystal structure is found in the following metals

  Cu, Ag, Au, Ca, Al, Pb, γ - Fe, Pt etc.

(d) Hexagonal Close Packed Structure (H.C.P.)   (May 13)

- This crystal structure shows one atom at each corner of the hexagon. The total corner atoms are thus 12. Each corner atom is shared by six unit cells. There is one atom on each hexagonal face centre (Fig. 1.10).

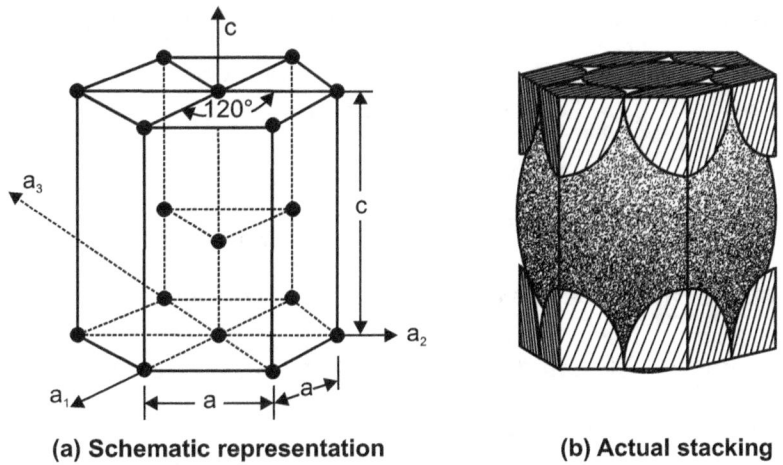

(a) Schematic representation	(b) Actual stacking

Fig. 1.10: Hexagonal closed pack system

- It is shared by two unit cells. The three atoms at interior remain unshared.

  Average number of atoms per unit cell

  $$= \frac{A}{6} + \frac{B}{2} + \frac{C}{1} = \frac{12}{6} + \frac{2}{2} + \frac{3}{1}$$

  $$= 2 + 1 + 3 = 6$$

- Therefore, a hexagonal closed pack structure has an average number of atoms per unit cell is equal to six. This type of crystal structure is found in the following metals

  Be, Mg, Ca, Zn, Cd, Co.

1.7 CO-ORDINATION NUMBER (CN)   (Nov. 16)

It is defined as the number of atoms surrounding and touching a central atom under consideration. It decides the packing density. The packing factor is smaller, if the co-ordination number is less. The co-ordination number is also called as **ligancy number** or simply ligancy. Co-ordination numbers of a typical crystal structure are given in Table 1.2.

Table 1.2: Co-Ordination Numbers for a Typical Crystalline Structure

Crystal Structure	Co-Ordination Number
S.C.	6
B.C.C.	8
F.C.C.	12
H.C.P.	12

1.8 ATOMIC PACKING FACTOR (APF)   (May 17)

It is the ratio of the volume occupied by the atoms to the volume of the unit cell.

$$APF = \frac{\text{Volume of atoms in a unit cell}}{\text{Volume of the unit cell}}$$

$$= \frac{\dfrac{\text{Average no. of atoms}}{\text{per unit cell}} \times \text{Volume of an atom}}{\text{Volume of the unit cell}}$$

The average number of atoms per unit cell is calculated previously.

The volume of an atom is calculated by the formula $\frac{4}{3}\pi r^3$, where r is the effective radius of an atom calculated by situation of the atom.

The values of APF for typical crystal structures are given in Table 1.3.

Table 1.3: APF Values for a Typical Crystal Structure

Crystal Structure	APF
S.C.	0.52
B.C.C.	0.68
F.C.C.	0.74
H.C.P.	0.74

From this table, it can be observed that the metals with a higher atomic packing factor are more dense. For example, the F.C.C. metals show more density than the B.C.C. metals.

SOLVED EXAMPLES

Example 1.1: Calculate the atomic packing factor (A.P.F.) for the B.C.C. unit cell, assuming the atoms to be hard spheres.

Solution: $\text{A.P.F.} = \dfrac{\text{Volume of atoms in B.C.C. unit cell}}{\text{Volume of B.C.C. unit cell}}$

Let 'R' be the radius of each atom and 'a' be the length of one side of the cube.

Since there are two atoms per B.C.C. unit cell,

$$\text{Volume of atoms} = (2) \times \left(\frac{4}{3}\pi R^3\right) = 8.38\ R^3$$

$$\text{Volume of unit cell} = a^3$$

The atoms are closely touching to each other in the diagonal of the cube in BCC structure.

Length of diagonal in the cube $= \sqrt{3}$ a. The same length is having one atom at the centre and two fragments of diagonally opposite atoms of corners touching to each other.

Hence, $4R = \sqrt{3}\ a$ (Length of diagonal in cube)

$\therefore$ $a = \dfrac{4R}{\sqrt{3}}$

$$a^3 = \dfrac{64R^3}{3 \times \sqrt{3}} = 12.32\ R^3$$

$\therefore$ $\text{A.P.F.} = \dfrac{8.38\ R^3}{12.32\ R^3} = \mathbf{0.68}$

Example 1.2: Calculate the atomic packing factor (A.P.F.) for the F.C.C. unit cell, assuming the atoms to be hard spheres.

Solution: $\text{A.P.F.} = \dfrac{\text{Volume of atoms in unit cell of F.C.C.}}{\text{Volume of F.C.C. unit cell}}$

There are 4 atoms per unit cell of F.C.C. Let 'R' is the radius of each atom and 'a' be the length of one side of cube.

$$\text{Volume of atoms per F.C.C. cell} = (4) \times \left(\frac{4}{3}\pi R^3\right) = 16.76\ R^3$$

The volume of unit cell $= a^3$,   where 'a' is a lattice constant.

The relation between 'a' and 'R' can be obtained in F.C.C. structure. Consider a diagonal on any face of the cube which contains one atom at centre and fractions of atoms at corners touching to the central atom.

Hence, diagonal on face is $\sqrt{2}$ a.

Hence, $4R = \sqrt{2}\ a$

$\therefore$ $a = \dfrac{4R}{\sqrt{2}}$

$a^3 = \dfrac{64\ R^3}{2\sqrt{2}} = 22.63\ R^3$

A.P.F. $= \dfrac{16.76\ R^3}{22.63\ R^3} =$ **0.74**

1.9 CERAMICS

Ceramics are in use from stone age to space age. The word ceramic is derived from the Greek word 'Keramos'. It means improving properties of material by heating to high temperatures. **Traditional ceramics** are clay, china, porcelein, tiles and glasses. Ceramics are combinations of metallic and non-metallic elements. Metal oxides, nitrides, carbides and silicates fall in the group of ceramics. High performance ceramics are used in structural, aerospace, electrical and communication applications. Ceramics have structures complex than metals. Ceramics are characterized by higher hardness, brittleness, wear resistance and creep. At room temperature, most of the ceramics are brittle and have low fracture strength. Ceramics are stronger in compression. Due to their inferior mechanical and fabrication properties than metals, ceramics find limited use in structural applications. However, ceramics are superior than metals for applications requiring dielectric, magnetic and optical properties. Ceramics have softening and melting points as high as 2000 - 3000°C.

Some of the engineering ceramics are

Magnesia,	Alumina,	Glass,	Silicon carbide,
Titanium carbide,	Silicon nitride,	Clay,	Cement etc.

Ceramic components are fabricated by casting process.

Recently, various hightech ceramics are invented and studied. They find applications in superconductors, nuclear applications, magnets, semiconductors and lasers.

Refractories are one of the important type of ceramics. These can withstand very high temperature without softening or degrading. They are inert to most of the environments. They are thermally insulative and wear resistant. They find applications in lining of furnaces. Refractories are classified according to their chemical content. Fire clay, silica, basic refractories and zirconia are few examples of refractories.

Abrasive ceramics find major applications in engineering, for grinding or cutting. They have high hardness, wear resistance and toughness. Diamond, silicon carbide, tungsten carbide etc. fall in this group. These abrasives are coated on papers or wheels or used in suspension for grinding. Tungsten carbide tipped tools and various abrasive ceramic coated tools are used in machining.

1.9.1 Applications of Ceramics

Table 1.4: Ceramics and their Applications

Ceramics	Applications
1. Silica, alumina, zirconia	Furnace lining
2. Silicon carbide, zirconia, Molybdenum bisulphide	Heating element
3. Barium titanate	Capacitors
4. Tin oxide, zinc oxide	Gas sensors
5. Alumina	Spark plug, Biomaterial
6. Iron based ceramic	Magnets, transformer
7. Sodalime glass	Optical, laser windows
8. Alumina, magnesia	Corrosion resistant lining
9. Uranium	Nuclear use
10. Silicon carbide, Tungsten carbide	Cutting, machining

1.10 POLYMERS　　　　　　　　　　　　　　　　　　　　(May 14)

Now-a-days, polymers are one of the major group of materials used for domestic and engineering applications. They offer versatility in their performance, properties and applications. Natural polymers like wood, cotton, silk, wool and leather are derived from plants and animals. Many of our useful plastics and rubbers are synthetic polymers. They are hydrocarbons. They are formed by process of polymerisation.

Polymer is a long chain structure having repetition of a simple chemical unit for a very large number of times.

Polymers are recognized by their thermal properties,

e.g.　　**1.　Thermoplastic polymers**

　　　　2.　Thermosetting polymers.

1.　Thermoplastic Polymers　　　　　　　　　　　　　　　(May 11)

Thermoplastic polymers are the polymers, which become plastic (soft) when heated. Due to their high plasticity, they can be shaped easily. They have low hardness, strength, low softening and melting temperatures. Thermoplastics can be recycled. Some of the typical examples of thermoplastic polymers are - polystyrene, nylons, polyester, polyvinyl chloride and polyethylene.

2.　Thermosetting Polymers　　　　　　　　　　　　　　　(May 11)

Thermosetting polymers are polymers, which set, when heated. They can be moulded once only. After moulding they become hard and strong. Their shape cannot be changed during reheating. They cannot be recycled. They have improved hardness, strength and good scratch resistance. Some of the typical thermosetting polymers are - phenolic resins, urea, melamine resins, epoxy resins and silicones.

Polymers are formed by the process called polymerisation. It is either addition or condensation polymerisation. Polymer exhibits linear, branched or network structure.

Natural rubber is soft and less strong. Its proper ties can be improved by the process of vulcanization. It is a process of adding sulphur to rubber during heating.

Polymers can be deformed elastically or plastically. The properties of polymers are affected by the nature of monomer, chemical composition, structure, molecular weight, processing type and density.

Polymers

Poly means many and mer means a unit in Greek. Polymer consists of thousands of manomers bounded by a chemical reaction. There are two main types of polymers plastics and elastomers. Plastics have bean divided into two classes – thermo plastics and thermosets. Elastomers are elastically deformed to a large extent after applying force on them and come into original shape after withdrawing the force.

Polymeric materials are light in weight with sufficient strength i.e. showing high strength to weight ratio. They can be easily fabricated and have food corrosion resistivity. Unfortunately many polymeric materials are not biodegradable and possess poor high t°C properties.

Differences between Thermoplastics and Thermosets

- Thermoplastics are linear polymers and thermosets have 3d network.
- Thermoplastics are held together by weak secondary vander waal's bond and thermosets by primary covalent bonds.
- Thermoplastics can be recycled while thermosets can not be recycled.
- Thermoplastics have less hardness and brittleness then thermosets .
- Examples of thermoplastics are PVC, nylon, Teflon, etc. thermosets are epoxy, phenolics, etc.

1.11 TYPES OF POLYMERIZATION

- In a polymer, molecules of ordinary size are combined into long chains and networks in which throusands of original molecules may be involved. This process is called polymerization and the original molecule is referred as monomer.

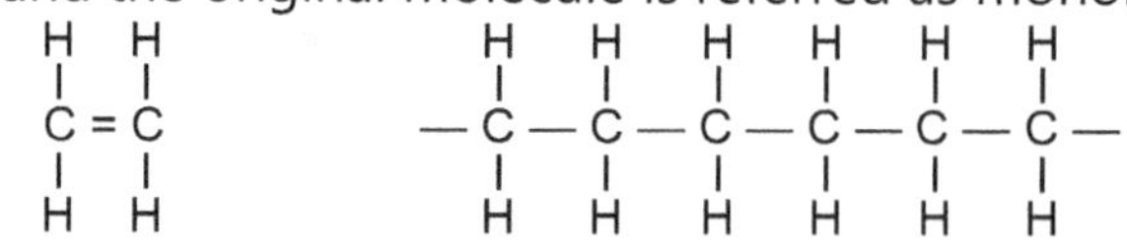

Monomer   Polythene chain molecule

(a)   (b)

Fig. 1.11

- The monomer is bifunctional as it can open to both forward and rear coupling. When several of such monomer add to form longitudinal chain as shown in Fig. 1.11 (b), the reaction is known as addition polymerization.

- The addition polymerization does not take place automatically, it has to be initiated, propogated and then terminated. The addition polymers are concerned with only one type of monomers.

- A single polymer may contain monomers of more than one type, this kind of polymerization is called co-polymerisation. For example a polymer chain containing monomers of vinylchloride and vinylacetate as shown in Fig. 1.12.

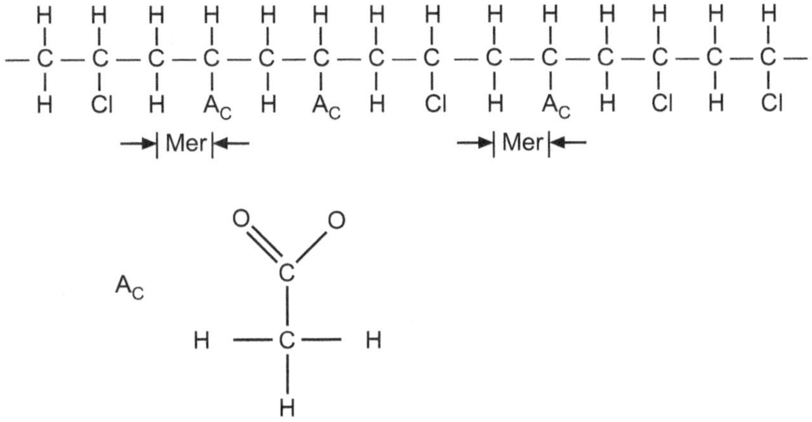

(c)

Fig. 1.12

- If in a polymerization reaction a second non-polymerisable molecule is produced as a by product then it is known as condensation polymerization. Usually the product is water or HCl or CH_3OH.

1.12 ELASTOMERS

- These are natural and synthetic rubbers showing more than 200% of elastic deformation. Rubber bands, tyres of automobiles, O-rings, insulation for electrical wires are a few examples of it. Elastomers are amorphous polymers and do not crystallize easily during processing. They have low glass-transition t°C and molecules can be easily deformed elastically.

- The molecular structures of elastomers are lightly cross-linked. The cross linking process in elastomers is called vulcanization, which uses sulfur atoms. Strands of sulfur atoms link the polymer chains as the polymer is processed and shapes at elevated t°C (around 150°c). This process was discovered by C. Soodyear in 1839.

- Modulus of elasticity T.S. and resistance to degradation by oxidation are improved by vulcanization. Usually vulcanised soft rubbers contain 3 percent sulfur by weight. More amount of sulfer decreases flexibility.

- Polyisoprene is a natural rubber. Neoprene is used for electrical insulation. Many of the synthetic rubbers are copolymers.

- Butadience styrene rubber (BS) is used to make automobile tyres. Butyl rubber is used to make inner tubes for tyres.

- Silicones (polysiloxanes) have high creep resistance and can be used at the temperature of 300°C.

- Base of chewing gum is made from natural rubber either polyvinyl acetate or styrene butadience.

1.13 POLYMER PROCESSING

- The magnitude and distribution of attraction forces between molecules determine the strength of polymers. These forces are due to chemical bonds. The long chain polymers exhibit strength along their length only, if chains are short the polymers are oils or crystalline solids, such as paraltin. The molecular weight of a polymer is controllable by changing the weight fraction of constituents and chain length. The long chain molecules may arrange in following possible ways amorphous wherein the molecules are randomly arranged, crystalline polymers in which molecules are arranged in the matrix of amorphous polymers. Groups of crystalline arrangements are known as crystallites. Crystallinity evolved in the processing of polymers as a result of t°C changes and applied stress.

- As the average molecular weight increases the melting t°C also increases and this makes the processing more difficult. [Toughness, strength, wear resistance also get increased with increase in molecular weight or degree of polymerization.] Having a mixed structure of crystalline and amorphous nature may improve the impact strength and flexibility both. Another method of improving the flexibility of crystalline polymers is the addition of plasticizer. Plasticizers like oils, resinous materials of low molecular height are effective in reducing intermolecular forces in a crystalline polymer, thus making their relative movement easier. One has to remember that this increase in flexibility and plasticity is at the cost of tensile strength. i.e. strength is reduced.

- The temperature at which the molecules of an amorphous polymer reversibly change their mobility such that, above this temperature polymer behaves rubbery and below this temperature it behaves glassy or more rigid, is called glass transition temperature. Mechanical properties of amoribous polymers degrade near this temperature.

1.14 MANUFACTURING PROCESS

There are two types of manufacturing processes

(1) Injection moulding   (2) Compression Moulding.

(1) Injection Moulding

- It is one of the important manufacturing method for forming thermoplastic materials.

- Modern injection moulding machines make utilization of reciprocating screw mechanism for melt injection.

- Feed plastic granules into the barrel. As the granules move along the rotating screw they start to melt and flow towards mold cavity.

- The screw bamel injects melted plastic through an opening with a plunger like motion, into a runner-gate system.

- Melted plastic is then injected into close mould cavity through runner gate system.

- Screw shaft maintains pressure on the material fed into cavity, till it becomes solid.

- Mould is then water cooled and opened to eject the part.

- Complex parts with good surface finishing at a fast rate can be produced. However it is not economical to produce big and large parts.

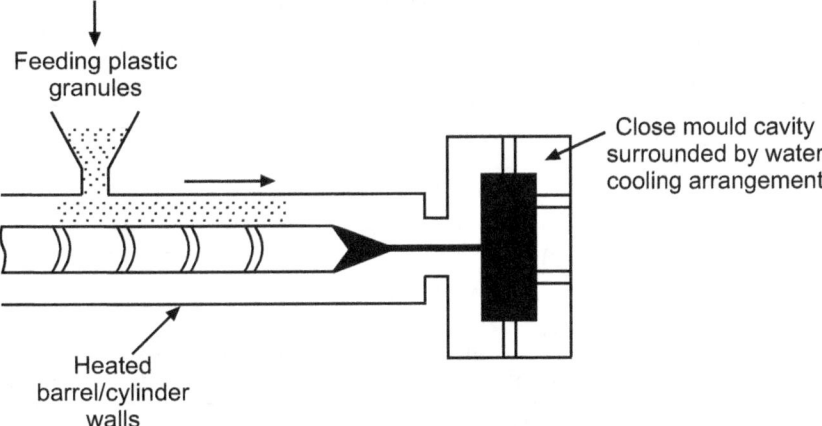

Fig. 1.13

(2) Compression Moulding

- It is an important manufacturing method to produce parts of thermosetting materials.

- Preheated plastic resin is loaded into the mould cavity and force is applied on the resin.

- Due to heat and pressure plastic melts and flows into the cavity. After a few minutes the part is ejected from mould.

- Process is applicable to manufacture large parts also.
- It is simple and economical.
- Surface finishing (quality) is fair.
- Complicates parts are difficult to make.

1.15 PROPERTIES AND APPLICATIONS OF ENGG. POLYMERS

Polymer	Properties	Applications
Polyethylene (PE)	Excellent corrosion Res. and insulating properties	Containers and electrical insulation
Polycinyl chloride (PVC)	Resistance to chemical attack, high strength.	Pipes, furniture, shoes
Polypropylene	Resistance to heat, andmoisture	Bottles, battery housing
Styrene-Acryonitrile (SAN)	Rigid, tough	Support panels for automobiles, syringes.
Acrylonitrile, butadience and styrene (ABS)	Impact and heat resistance	Door and inner liners in automobile and fridge.
PTEE (Teflon)	Low coefficient of friction	Non stick coating and bearings
Liquids crystals polymers	Resistance to flame and high impact strength	Laptop, computers, digital watches
Ultrahigh molecular weight polyethylene	High resistivity to impact and wear	Bullet proof vests, biomedical prostheses
Silicone	High resistance to low temperature and high temperature	Insulation, seals
Acrylonitrile	Resistance to oils	Gasoline and oil hose pipes
Styrene butadience	Abrasion resistance	Tyres of automobiles

1.16 PROPERTIES AND APPLICATIONS OF CERAMICS

- WC, TiC, Al_2O_3 etc. ceramics show same common properties like electrical insulation, abrasion resistance, high temperature strength high melting point, hardness etc.

- Alumina (Al_2O_3) ceramic is made from bauxite ($Al_2O_3 . 2H_2O$). There are a number of applications of Al_2O_3 insulators in spark plug and electronic packaging, container for molten metal, rocket nozzles, etc. Most of the ceramics can not be used for structural purposes due to having poor tensile and impact strength but Al_2O_3 is suitable for making supporting members in electrical devices and for any type of load bearing application. Shapes are generated by molding (compacting) or by machining in green state and then sintering. The size change occur in sintering are accomodated by machining with diamond grinding wheels. Al_2O_3 is also used as a refractory for steel making. Its properties are M.P. = 2050°C, T.S. at room t°C = 210 MPA, Comp. st. = 2750 MPa, hardness = 2100 kg/mm^2.

- Tungusten carbide and titanium carbide are normally not used as solid sintered ceramics as are Al_2O_3, MgO, etc. because of their high brittleness. WC, TiC, are used as composites bonded with a metal binder like Ni, Co, Cr, Mo, etc. such type of materials or composites of ceramic and metal are termed as cermets. Sometimes cermets are also known as metal bonded carbides or cemented carbides. These are mostly used as a cutting tool material due to having high hardness, wear resistivity, cutting ability even at high temperature. WC has M.P. of 2850°C and hardness of 2000 kg/mm^2 while TiC has M.P. 3120°C and hardness of 2500 kg/mm^2. Carbides are harder than any tool steel but they are very brittle so metal binder is added to improve impact resistance.

- WC is also used as an abrasive material for grinding and polishing operations. Ceramic materials melt at high t°C and are brittle in nature under tension so casting and mechanical working can not be applied in processing of ceramics. Since melting and mechanical working (like torging, rolling, etc.) are not suitable options; ceramics have to be processes into useful shapes starting with their powders.

Flow Chart of Processing Ceramics

Powder manufacturing

↓

Blending

↓

Green ceramic manufacturing by compaction

↓

Sintering

- Prepare ceramic powders using conventional crushing, milling or chemical processes.

- Subject it to screening to sort out the particles of desired size and shape.

- Mix them thoroughly with suitable additives.

- Press them to give desired shape. It is termed as green ceramics.

- Consolidate the green ceramics into a dense, monolithic object using sintering.

- As per need secondary operations like grinding, cutting, polishing are done.

Cermet (ceramics + metal = composite) may also be processed in a similar way, e.g. WC – Co cutting tool bits. One of the most cost effective ways to produce thousands of relatively small, simple shapes (less than 15 cm) is compaction and sintering.

WC is hard, stiff high melting t°C ceramic. To improve toughness, WC particles are combines with cobalt powder and pressed into power compacts. The compacts are heated above the melting point of cobalt. Cobalt helps to bind the solid WC particles together and provides good impact resistivity, other carbides such as TiC may also be included in the cermet.

Details of processing of cermets have already been discussed in powder metallurgy.

Example 1.3: Calculate the density of the cermet containing 10% cobalt, 80% WC and 10% TiC by weight. Given that densities of cobalt, WC and TiC are 8.8 gm/cm^3, 4.9 gm/cm^3 and 15.8 gm/cm^3 respectively.

Solution: Volume fraction of WC,

$$V_{WC} = \frac{80/15.8}{80/15.8 + 10/4.9 + 10/8.8} = 0.61$$

Volume fraction of TiC,

$$V_{TiC} = \frac{10/4.9}{80/15.8 + 10/4.9 + 10/8.8} = 0.24$$

Volume fraction of Co,

$$V_{CO} = \frac{10/8.8}{80/15.8 + 10/4.9 + 10/8.8} = 0.14$$

From the rule of mixtures,

The density of composite is

$$e_c = 0.61 \times 15.8 + 0.24 \times 4.9 + 0.14 \times 8.8$$
$$= 9.6 + 1.17 + 1.23 = \textbf{10.77 gm/cm}^3$$

KEY NOTES

1. Structure directly influences the mechanical behavior of the materials.

2. A specific arrangement of atoms in ordered condition is known as crystal structure.

3. FCC metals like Al, Ag, Cu shows more ductility than BCC metals like Fe, W due to having highest number of slip systems. Combination of slip plane and slip direction is called slip system.

4. Properties may differ when measured along different directions or planes within a crystal, such type of crystals are termed as anisotropic. If properties are identical in all the directions, the crystal is termed as isotropic.

5. Ratio of atoms contained in a plane to the area of the plane is called planar atomic density or area density.

6. Ratio of height of the unit cell to the size of base is called c/a ratio. It is unity (one) for SC, BCC and FCC and 1.63 for HCP.

7. Examples for BCC are Fe, Cr, W.   Examples for FCC are Al, Cu, Au.   Examples for HCP are Zn, Mg, Cd. Example SG is Po.

8. Broadly materials useful for engineering applications are classified as metals, ceramics, polymers and composites.

9. Ceramics are inorganic crystalline materials. Resistance to damage at high temperature, high strength, and good electrical thermal insulator are their main characteristics.

10. Polymers have low strength but high corrosion resistivity. The process by which organic molecules are joined into polymers is called polymerisation.

11. Polymers are of two types-Thermoplastics and Thermosetting. Polymers such as polyvinyl acetate (PVA) are water soluble.

12. Aramids are examples of liquid crystalline polymers. These are used as a reinforcing fibre in composites and to make electronic displays also.

13. The ratio of average molecular weight of polymer to molecular weight of repeated unit (mer) is called as degree of polymerisation.

14. At very high temperature, the bonds are destroyed and polymer may burn on char. This temperature is known as the degradation or decomposition temperature.

15. Fire retardant additives such as lime stone, alumina are added to thermoplastics to absorb heat and protect the polymer matrix.

16. Crazing occurs in thermoplastics when localised regions of plastic deformation occur in a direction perpendicular to that of applied stress. Craze is not a crack, however it may lead to brittle fracture of polymer.

17. Elastomers are known as rubbers. They sustain elastic deformation more than 200%.

18. Advanced polymeric materials are ultra high molecular weight polyethylene, liquid crystal polymers and thermoplastic elastomers. Liquid crystals can possess some of the qualities of both liquids and crystals. Under an electric field long chain molecules can mesh into a crystalline array and on removal of electric field, molecules become disordered by thermal motions. Properties (like in light refraction and reflection) are different of crystalline and liquid varients, thus it is possible to design digital displays e.g. watches, calculators, etc.

19. Alumina is a ceramic material having a mixture of covalent and ionic bonding. Structure of alumina (Al_2O_3) is basically HCP. It has very high M.P. 2050°C.

20. WC, TiC are mainly used in making composites. These are the ceramics showing high temperature resistivity, abrasion resistivity and hardness. These are used in making abrasives and cutting tools.

21. Inclusions, pores and flaws are inherently present in ceramic materials that so why they are brittle as these all act as stress raisers inviting most of the stresses to be concentrated there.

22. Advanced ceramics are used in housings for computer chips and sensors. New processing techniques help to improve the resistivity to fracture and thus making them suitable for load bearing applications also in few cases such as impellers in turbine engines.

23. Composites are made from different types of materials; they provide unique combination of props. which are not found in a single material.

24. SAP (Sintered Aluminium Powder) composites, TD (Thoria Dispersed)-Ni are the examples of dispersion strengthened composites or MMC. Reinforced mild steel bars in concrete is also an example of dispersion strengthening but here the matrix is cement concrete and reinforcement is of mild steel bars.

25. Carbon-Carbon composite i.e. matrix as well as reinforcement are of carbon is an example of ceramic matrix composite (CMC). This composite can sustain temperature up to 3000°C. It is used in parts of space launching vehicles, racing cars, aircrafts, etc.

26. Alclad is an example of Laminate/Laminar composite. It is metal-metal clad composite, in which pure Al is bonded to Al alloy. Other such an example is Cu cladded stainless steel as an utensil.

27. The properties of a composite is a function of volumetric fraction of each phase of the composite, is a Rule of mixtures .

REVIEW QUESTIONS

1. Define the following terms:
   (a) Crystal.   (b) Unit cell.
   (c) Space lattice.   (d) Lattice angles.

2. Explain the indexing method for planes and directions.

3. Calculate the average number of atoms for the following structures.
   (a) S.C.,   (b) B.C.C.,
   (c) H.C.P.,   (d) F.C.C.

4. What is atomic packing factor ? What is its importance ?

5. Represent following planes and directions within a cubic unit cell $(\bar{2}10)$, (113), $[1\bar{1}1]$, $[012]$.

6. Obtain effective number of atoms per unit cell for cubic unit cell and state its significance.

7. What is a polymer ? Describe properties of polymer in general.

8. Distinguish between thermoplastics and thermosets.

9. What are different types of polymerization reaction ?

10. What is an elastomer ? How is the strength of natural rubber is increased?

11. Additives incorporated in a polymer, enhanced its performance by improving certain properties. Explain it in brief.

12. What is glass transition temperature Tg ? Why polymers degrade near this temperature range.

13. What is the difference between copolymerization and polymer alloy?

14. Compare the ceramics and polymers in light of their properties, advantages and applications.

15. What is Alumina ? It is suitable for structural applications ? Comment in brief.

16. What is MMC ? In what respects it is different from a fiber reinforced plastic?

17. Write short note on
    (i) Polymer processing (ii) Ceramic matrix composite
    (iii) Dispersion strengthened composite (iv) Engineering polymers

18. State whether True or False and justify:
    (a) Refractories are ceramics.
    (b) All plastics can be deformed by heating.
    (c) RCC is a composite.
    (d) Twinns are observed in cold worked and annealed brass.
    (e) Cold working increases the hardness of metal.

    Ans.:

(a) True	(b) False	(c) True	(d) True	(e) True

19. Give some typical compositions and applications of following materials:
    (a) Ceramics   (b) Polymers

20. What are abrasive ceramics ?

21. What is Teflon ?

22. Give reasons: 1. Aluminium shows higher ductility than steel.

UNIVERSITY QUESTIONS

DECEMBER 2013

1. Differentiate between thermoplastic and thermosetting polymers.   **[2]**

2. Explain any one method of polymer processing, with suitable diagram.   **[4]**

MAY 2014

1. Write short note on ceramic materials.   **[4]**

2. What is role of dislocation in the plastic deformation of metal.   **[4]**

3. Explain how engineering materials are classified. Explain in brief thermoplastic and thermosetting polymers.   **[4]**

4. Explain elastomers.   **[4]**

DECEMBER 2014

1. Sketch within a cubic unit cell the following planes :
   (100), (110), (111) and (011).   **[4]**

2. The planes in a crystalline solid intersect the crystal axes at
   (2a, 2b, c). (2a, b, 2c) and (a, b, c:). Calculate the Miller Indices of this plane.   **[4]**

MAY 2015

1. What do you mean by the term 'Unit Cell' ? Define various lattice parameters.   **[4]**
2. What do you mean by the term polymer? Explain with types, characteristics and applications.
3. What do you mean by the term 'ceramic'? Explain with types, properties and application.   **[4]**

NOVEMBER 2015

1. Show that the atomic packing factor for BCC crystal is 0.68.   **[4]**
2. Derive linear density expression of FCC [100] and [111] directions in terms of the atomic radius R.   **[4]**

MAY 2016

1. What do you mean by space lattice ? Write any three imperfections in crystals/lattices with example of each.   **[4]**
2. What do you mean by the term 'Polymer' ? Differentiate between Thermoplastic and Thermosetting polymers.   **[4]**

NOVEMBER 2016

1. Show the following planes on a cubic cell (222), (110).   **[4]**
   [**Ans. :** Refer article 1.4]
2. Define the following :   **[4]**
   (i) Co-ordination number
   [**Ans. :** Refer article 1.7]
3. No. of atoms per unit cell in FCC metal is 4 explain with mathematical proof.   **[3]**
   [**Ans. :** Refer article 1.6]
4. What is Polymer and how its molecular structure is different than metals? Explain.   **[3]**
   [**Ans. :** Refer article 1.10]

MAY 2017

1. Calculate atomic packing factor for BCC and FCC crystal structure.   **[6]**
   [**Ans. :** Refer article 1.8]
2. What do you mean by the tern "Miller Indices"? Explain the procedure and determine the Millar indices for plane (111)   **[4]**
   [**Ans. :** Refer article 1.4]
3. What makes ceramics different than polymers with respect to properties?   **[2]**
   [**Ans. :** Refer articles 1.9, 1.10]

✠ ✠ ✠

MECHANICAL BEHAVIORS OF METAL AND MATERIALS

2.1 IMPERFECTIONS IN CRYSTALS (Dec. 10, May 11, Nov. 16)

Theoretically, it is assumed that the atomic structure of a crystalline material is perfect. This is based on the definition of crystal structure which is a definite arrangement of atoms observed in three directions. However, crystallographic study shows that crystals are rarely perfect. The defects in atomic structures and arrangement are called imperfections. Mechanical forming and heat treatment of metals is possible due to presence of defects.

Imperfections are classified according to geometry of defects as follows

- Zero dimensional defects – Point defects.
- One dimensional defects – Line defects.
- Two dimensional defects – Surface defects.

The above defects are discussed in this section.

2.1.1 Point Defects (Dec. 09, 10)

It is a localised defect. Major point imperfections are

- Vacancy,
- Self-interstitial atom,
- Substitutional impurity atom and
- Interstitial impurity atom.

Vacancy is a defect occurred due to missing atom in an atomic structure plane. Vacancies results during solidification and due to atomic vibrations or thermal disorder. This causes displacement of atoms from their usual lattice location. When an atom leaves its site and gets placed in the interstitial sites of atomic structure, a self interstitial atom defect occurs. Refer Fig. 2.1 for various point defects.

An impurity or foreign atom, which is in the location of base atom is called substitutional impurity atom. If such impurity atom occupies interstice between the atoms, it is termed as interstitial impurity atom.

(a) Self-interstitial   (b) Vacancy   (c) Interstitial impurity atom

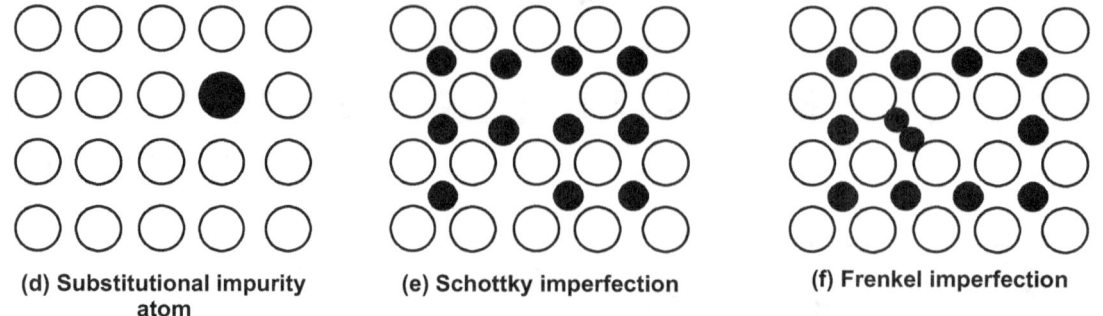

(d) Substitutional impurity atom   **(e) Schottky imperfection**   **(f) Frenkel imperfection**

Fig. 2.1: Point defects in the crystal structure

Frenkel Imperfection: In a regularly ordered crystal structure, if an atom leaves its place, creating vacancy and places itself intersticially in the structure, the related vacancy and interstitial atom is called as Frenkel imperfection.

Schottky Imperfection: Vacancies occur in pairs within an ionic solid to maintain a charge balance. In such cases, a cation vacancy balances an anion vacancy. The imperfection occurring due to this is called a Schottky imperfection.

2.1.2 Line Imperfections or One Dimensional Defect   (Dec. 10, May 11)

The line imperfections are directly related to the plastic deformation of metals. The plastic deformation corresponds to the net movement of large number of atoms as a result of applied force. The plastic deformation occurs due to motion of line or defect is called a dislocation. The crystalline structure-mechanical property relationship depends on these dislocations. Basically, dislocation is a line imperfection, around which some of the atoms are misaligned.

Two types of dislocations are observed as follows

1. Edge dislocation
2. Screw dislocation

1.   Edge Dislocation   **(Nov. 16)**

*   It consists of an extra half plane of atoms in the crystal structure. This dislocation corresponds to the row of mismatched atoms along a straight edge or line. The atoms on one side of the dislocation line get squeezed together and those on other side are pulled apart.

*   The magnitude of these lattice distortions decreases with increasing distance away from dislocation line. Edge dislocation is represented by the symbol ⊥. This indicates the position of the dislocation line. If the extra half plane of atoms is in the bottom part of crystal, its symbol is a T. When a shear stress is applied in a direction perpendicular to edge dislocation line, the edge dislocation moves.

*   Dislocation motion is analogous to the motion of a caterpiller.

2. Screw Dislocation

- If the atomic planes of atoms follow a spiral or helical path that is traced around the dislocation line, it is due to screw dislocation. The direction of movement is perpendicular to the shear stress direction.

- Screw dislocations are denoted by symbol or. In screw dislocation, the upper front region of the crystal is shifted one atomic distance to the right, relative to the bottom portion. Burger's vector is a unit vector required to close the loop around a dislocation. It indicates how much and in what direction the lattice above the slip plane appears to have been shifted with respect to the lattice below the slip plane. Refer Fig. 2.2.

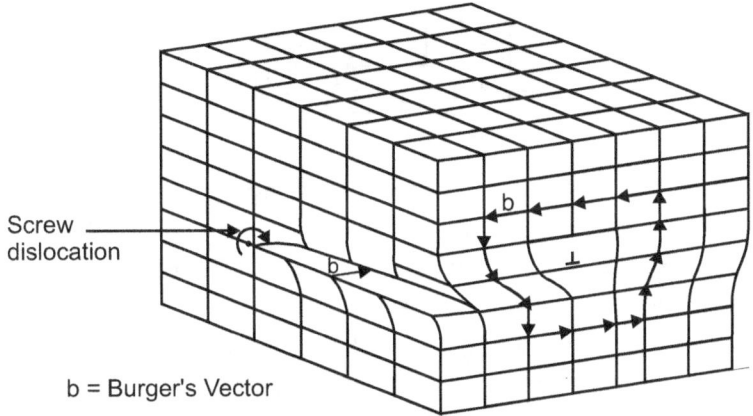

Fig. 2.2: Burger's vector of screw dislocation and edge dislocation

- Practically, pure edge or pure screw dislocations does not exist. They are in combined form called mixed dislocations. **Dislocation density is the total dislocation length per unit volume or number of dislocations per unit area.**

2.1.3 Surface Defects or Planer Defect (Two Dimensional Defect)

(May 13, Dec. 14)

A change in stacking of atomic planes across a boundary results in surface defects. Following are types of surface defects

1. Grain boundaries
2. Twin boundaries
3. Low angle boundary
4. Low angle filt boundary
5. Low angle twist boundary and
6. Stacking fault.

- Grain boundaries are observed in polycrystalline solids. These are the surface imperfections, which separate crystals of different orientations.

- Twin boundaries are those surface defects, which separate two orientations that are mirror image of one another. Twins are formed during solidification or plastic deformation. If the angular misorientation is less then the surface defect is called as low angle boundary. Refer Fig. 2.3.

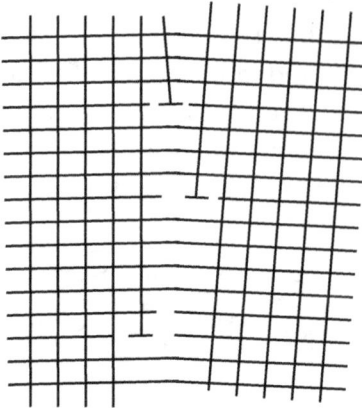

Fig. 2.3: Simple tilt boundary

- The low angle tilt boundary is observed, when edge dislocations lie one above the other in the boundary. Similarly, the low angle twist boundary is observed, if atleast two sets of parallel screw dislocations are lying in the boundary.
- Stacking fault is related with the stacking of atomic planes over one another. It results; when the stacking of one atomic plane is out of sequence on another, e.g. If there are 3 atomic planes over each other as PQR then in a defect free stacking, order must show PQR PQR PQR; while a stacking fault will show PQRQPRPQ.

2.2 PLASTIC DEFORMATION

When a metal is stressed, two types of deformations occur

(a) Elastic deformation   (b) Plastic deformation.

(a) Elastic Deformation

- Elastic deformation disappears after removal of external load.
- Elastic deformation is defined as the temporary deformation in a metal caused due to application of external load and which disappears after removal of the load. In the elastic deformation, the metal regains its original dimensions.
- Elastically deforming property is useful in the applications such as springs, while plastically deforming property is useful in fabrication processes such as rolling, drawing, forging etc.

(b) Plastic Deformation

- Plastic deformation is defined as the permanent deformation caused in a metal due to application of external load and which does not disappear after removal of the load. In the plastic deformation, the metal does not regain its original dimensions.

- Usually, a less stress is required for elastic deformation than for plastic deformation. Plastic deformation takes place by slip twinning or by both. The deformation of single crystal is different from that of polycrystal.

- This section also describes cold working and hot working principles with mechanisms of plastic deformation.

2.3 MECHANISMS OF PLASTIC DEFORMATION   (Dec. 10, 12, Nov. 16)

Plastic deformation takes place due to the following methods

 (a) Slip,

 (b) Twinning or

 (c) Combination of slip and twinning.

(a) Plastic Deformation by Slip   (Dec. 10)

Slip is defined as a irreversible shear displacement of one part of a crystal relative to another in a definite crystallographic direction and on a specific crystallographic plane.

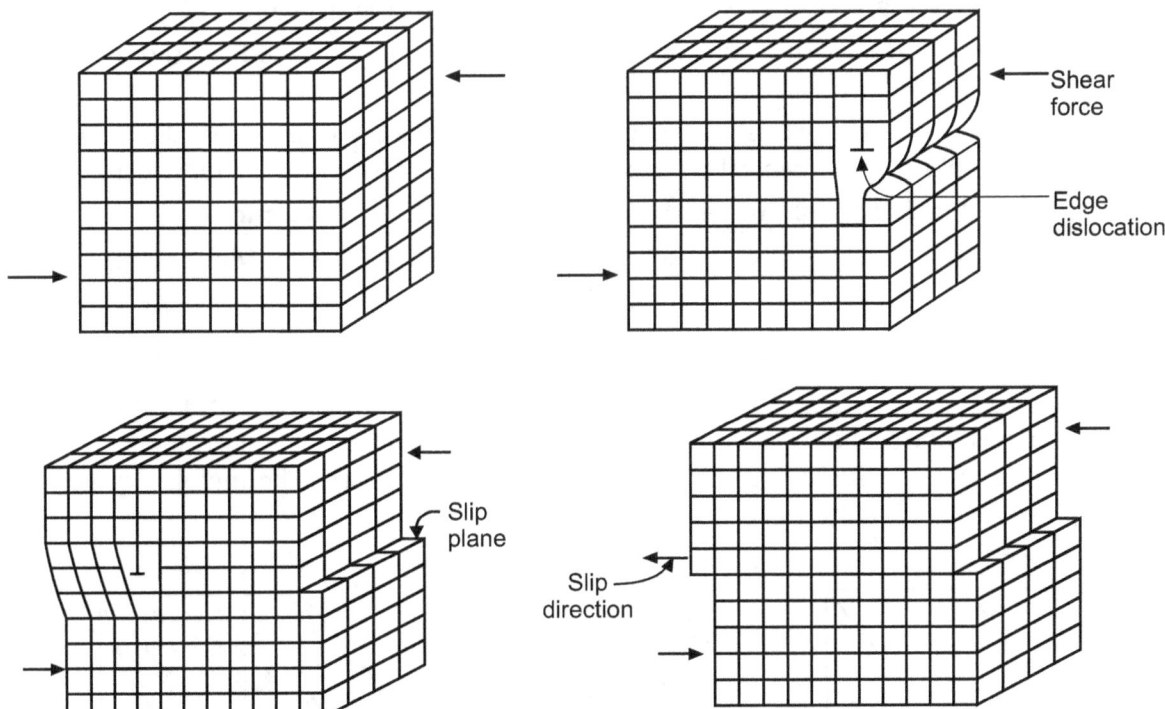

Fig. 2.4: Pure-edge dislocation movement 'a' through 'd', causing slip

As shown in Fig. 2.4, a block of crystal is moved over the remaining block by slip. It can be observed from the same figure that the slipped portion remains undistorted. A crystal structure consists of parallel planes of higher atomic density. The slip takes place at these planes. The planes on which slip occurs are called as slip planes [Fig. 2.5 (a)]. The slip motion is accelerated with increasing distance between slip planes. Slip takes place as a result of simple shear stress. Slip occurs in the directions in which the atoms are most closely packed. Due to such close packed plane, less energy is required for movement of slip.

As the interplaner distance between most closely packed plane is more, slip movement becomes easy.

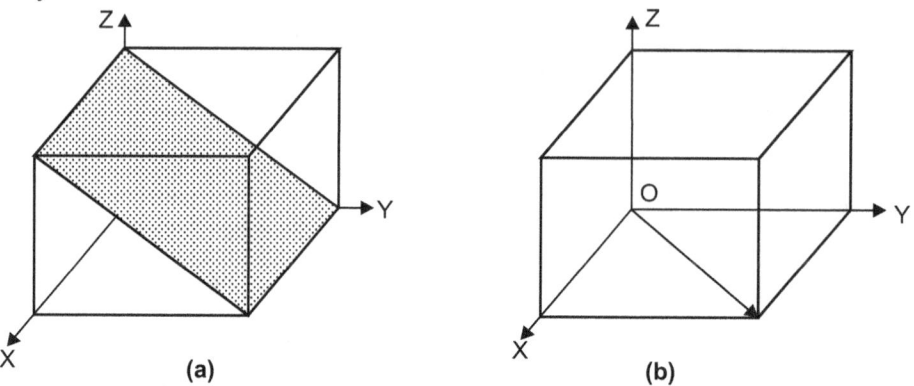

Fig. 2.5: Slip plane (a) and Direction (b) in crystal structure

A definite crystallographic direction along which slip occurs is called as slip direction. Fig. 2.5 (b).

If the direction of applied stress is parallel or perpendicular to the direction of slip plane, slip cannot occur. Table 2.1 gives typical slip planes and directions for basic crystal structure.

Table 2.1: Slip planes and directions for basic crystal structure

Crystal Structure	Slip Plane	Slip Direction	Metal (e.g.)
1. F. C. C.	(1 1 1)	< 1 1 0 >	Cu, Al
2. B. C. C.	(1 1 0)	< 1 1 1 >	Fe, Mo
3. H. C. P.	(0 0 0 1)	< 1 1 2 0 >	Mg, Co

F.C.C. metal has four sets of (1 1 1) planes and three close packed directions in each plane. Therefore, the number of slip systems is 12. This is the reason, why the metals like Au, Ag, Cu, Al; show higher ductility.

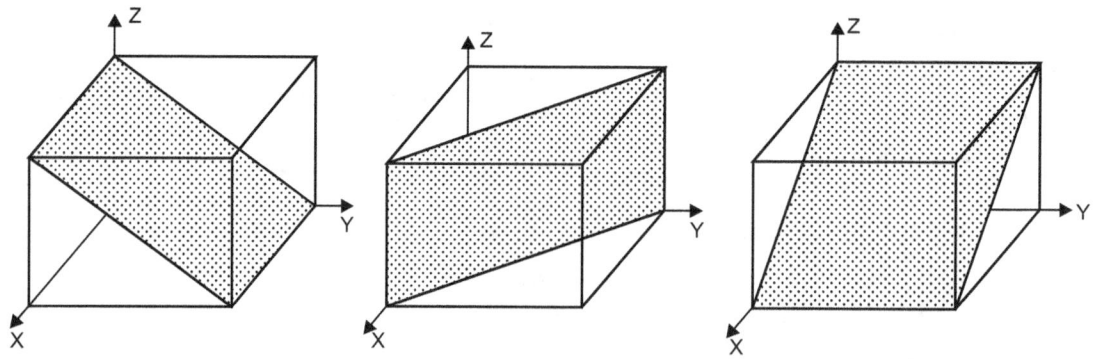

Fig. 2.6 (a): Slip planes in a B.C.C. crystal structure

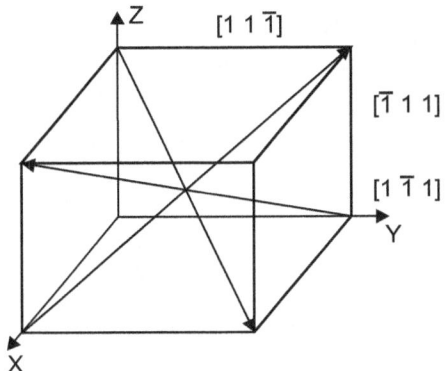

Fig. 2.6 (b): Slip directions in a B.C.C. crystal structure

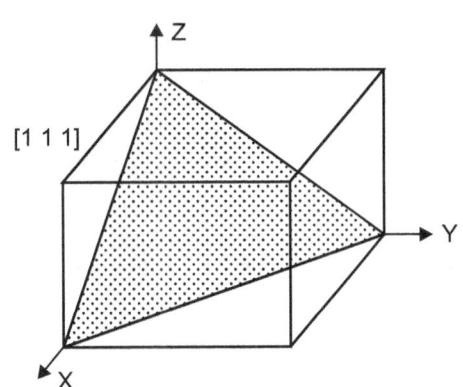

(a) **Slip planes in a F.C.C. crystal structure**

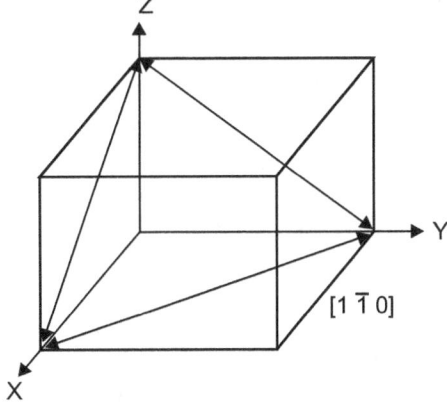

(b) **Slip directions in a F.C.C. crystal structural**

Fig. 2.6 (c)

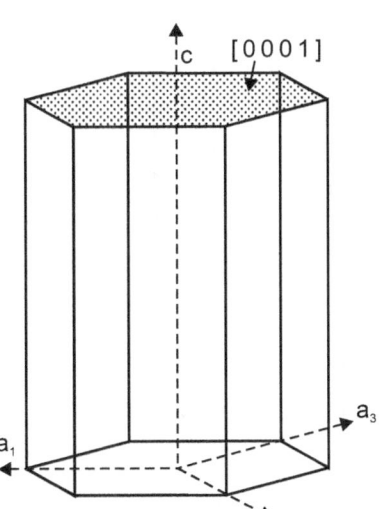

(a) **Slip planes in a H.C.P. crystal structure**

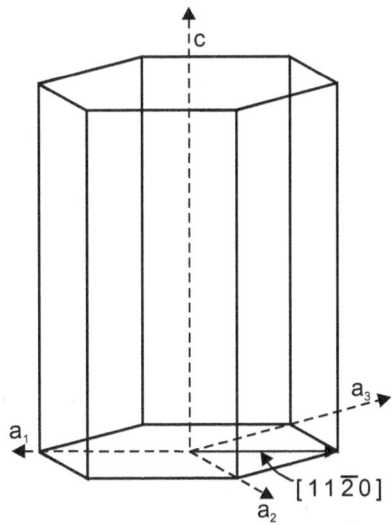

(b) **Slip directions in a H.C.P. crystal structure**

Fig. 2.6 (d)

The average number of atoms per unit cell in a B.C.C. crystal structure is less. B.C.C. metals do not have a well defined slip system. They do not have a true close-packed plane. The slip lines in B.C.C. metals are wavy and irregular. These metals require a high stress due to lack of closed packed plane. Due to this, B.C.C. metals show a less plastic deformation e.g. Mo, W, Fe.

The H.C.P. metal e.g. Cd, Mg, Co have only one plane of higher atomic density with 3 directions. This structure does not have a number of slip planes like F.C.C. metal. Therefore, H.C.P. metals show intermediate plasticity compared to that of F.C.C. and B.C.C. metals.

Slip planes and directions for B.C.C., F.C.C. and H.C.P. crystal structures are shown in Fig. 2.6.

(b) Plastic Deformation by Twinning:

Twinning occurs, when a crystal is subjected to stress. In this process, the atoms in the portion of crystal arrange themselves so that the deformed portion becomes mirror image of the remaining crystal portion. The crystal portion in which the original orientation of atoms is constant is termed as parent, while the deformed portion is termed as the twin.

Twinning plane is defined as the plane across which twinning occurs.

The axis around which the portion of crystal twins or rotates is called as twinning axis. Most of the h.c.p. metals undergo twinning during their plastic deformation. The movement of each atom in the twinned portion is proportional to its distance from the twinning plane. Twinning is shown schematically in Fig. 2.7.

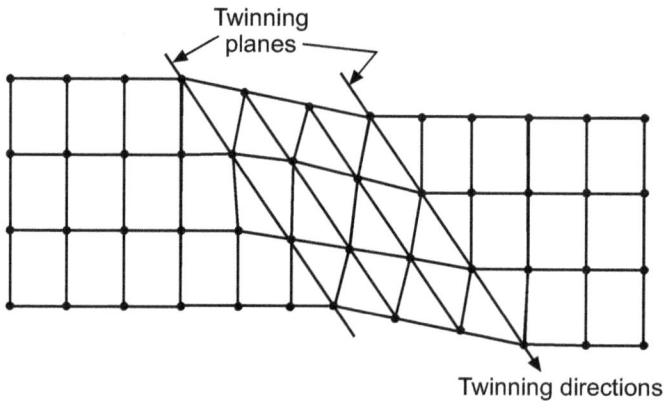

Fig. 2.7: Schematic diagram of twinning

The twinning planes and directions may not be similar as those for slip.

Twinning occurs in the following two cases

(a) Mechanical twins,

(b) Annealing twins.

(a) Mechanical Twins: Occur usually during plastic deformation of metals. It is also called as deformation twinning. It is observed in H.C.P. metals like Mg, Zn and B.C.C. metals like W, α-iron etc.

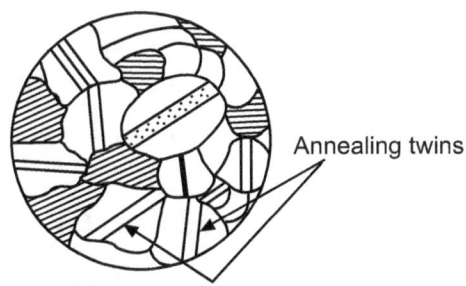

Annealing twins

Fig. 2.8: Microstructure of alpha brass, showing annealing twins

(b) Annealing Twins: Occur during a thermal treatment to the previously worked metals. If a metal is cold worked, it gets strain hardened. Annealing is done to relieve internal stresses of such metals. In this process, the cold worked metal is reheated at a higher temperature followed by very slow cooling. Because of this, twins are formed. A cold worked and annealed single phase brass (Cartridge brass) shows a typical twin structure (Fig. 2.8). The twins appear as parallel lines within the individual grains.

Table 2.2 gives most probable twin planes and directions for typical crystal structures.

Table 2.2

Crystal Structure	Twin Plane	Twin Direction
BCC	(1 1 2)	[1 1 1]
FCC	(1 1 1)	[1 1 2]
HCP	(1 0 1 2)	[1 0 1 2]

The slip and twinning can be differentiated on the following points -   **(May 10)**

Slip	Twinning
1. The stress required for initiation of slip is less.	1. The stress required to initiate twinning is more.
2. More stress is required for propagation or continuation of slip.	2. Less stress is required for propagation or continuation of twinning.
3. Slip involves movement of atoms at a same distance in slip plane.	3. Twinning involves movement of atoms at a distance proportional from twinning plane.
4. The slipped portion has the same orientation of atoms as that of the original portion.	4. The twinned portion shows mirror image of the untwinned portion.
5. Microscopically slip appears as a thin line.	5. Microscopically twin occurs as a broad line or parallel lines or band.

Slip	Twinning
6. Slip line disappears after polishing the surface of the metal.	6. Twins remain after surface polishing.
7. Slip lines are observed only after plastic deformation.	7. Twin lines are also observed after mechanical working and annealing.
8. Slip is more common in B.C.C. and F.C.C. metals.	8. Twinning is more common in H.C.P. metals.

2.4 DEFORMATION OF SINGLE CRYSTAL BY SLIP　　(May 10, 12, 13)

The process of deformation by slip can be easily explained by a single crystal deformation. Consider a cylinder shaped single crystal subjected to a tensile load F. The load is acting at the direction of axis. This load is resolved in the following

(a) a force normal to the slip plane and

(b) a shearing force in the slip plane.

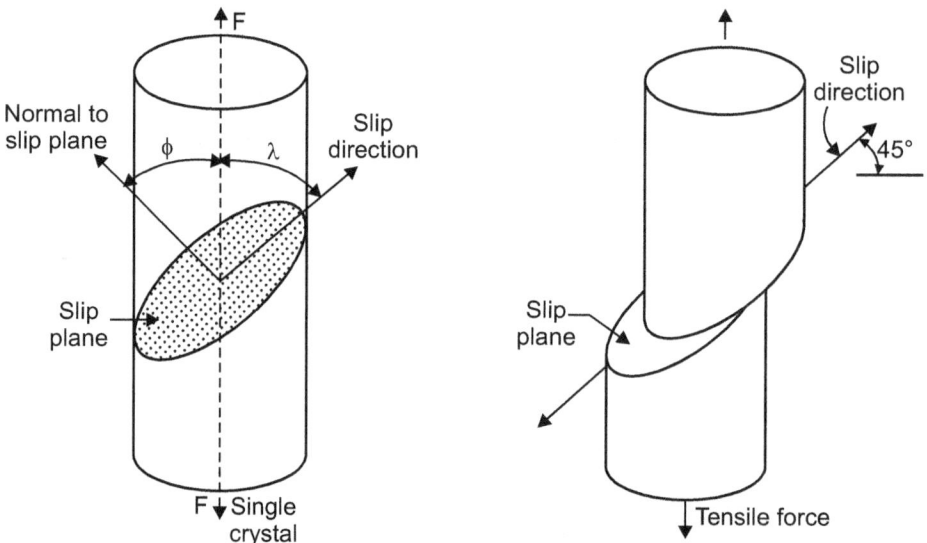

Fig. 2.9: Deformation of a single crystal by slip

From Fig. 2.9, it will be clear that ϕ is the angle between the direction for force and normal to the slip plane. λ is the angle between direction of force and the slip direction.

Since, the slip plane is inclined by an angle ϕ to the cross-section of the crystal, its area is given by

$$\text{Area of slip plane} = \frac{A}{\cos \phi}$$

where, A　-　cross-sectional area of the crystal.

The component of the axial load acting in the slip plane in the slip direction is F cos λ.

Critical resolved shear stress $(T_{cr}) = \dfrac{\text{Force}}{\text{Area}}$

$$T_{cr} = \frac{F \cos \lambda}{A/\cos \phi} = \frac{F}{A} \cos \phi \cos \lambda.$$

This is also referred as **Schmid's law**.

The shear stress will be maximum, when $\phi = 45°$.

The above relation is also expressed as -

$$T_{resolved} = \alpha_T \cos \phi \cos \lambda$$

If $\lambda = \phi = 45°$, T_{stress} is maximum and $T_{resolved}$ becomes equal to $\dfrac{\sigma_T}{2}$. Critical shear stress is constant for each material. It depends upon the type of bonding forces, temperature, rate of deformation etc.

SOLVED EXAMPLE

Example 2.1: A F.C.C. yields under a normal stress of 2.15 MPa applied in the $[\bar{1}\,2\,3]$ direction. The slip plane is $(1\,1\,1)$ and the slip direction is $[\bar{1}\,0\,1]$. Determine critical resolved shear stress for this crystal.

Solution: Using vector dot product, the values of $\cos \theta$ and $\cos \phi$ can be calculated.

Vector dot product: If two directions $[u\ v\ w]$ and $[u'\ v'\ w']$ are having angle of α then,

$$\cos \alpha = \frac{uu' + vv' + ww'}{(\sqrt{u^2 + v^2 + w^2}) \times (u'^2 + v'^2 + w'^2)}$$

Using the above formula,

$$\cos \theta = \frac{(\bar{1} \times \bar{1}) + (2 \times 0) + (3 \times 1)}{(\sqrt{1 + 4 + 9}) \times (\sqrt{1 + 0 + 1})}$$

$$= \frac{4}{(\sqrt{14}) \times (\sqrt{2})} = 0.756$$

and

$$\cos \phi = \frac{(\bar{1} \times 1) + (2 \times 1) + (3 \times 1)}{(\sqrt{1 + 4 + 9}) \times (\sqrt{1 + 1 + 1})}$$

$$= \frac{4}{(\sqrt{14})\,(\sqrt{3})} = 0.617$$

Let T_{cr} = CRSS, σ_{cr} = Critical normal stress.

Then, $T_{cr} = \sigma_{cr} \cos \theta \cos \phi$

                  $= 2.15 \times 0.756 \times 0.617 = \mathbf{1\ MPa}$

Table 2.3 gives critical shear stress values for some metals.

Table 2.3

Metal	Structure	Critical Stress (PSI)
Copper	F.C.C.	71
Aluminium	F.C.C.	114
Magnesium	H.C.P.	64
Cobalt	H.C.P.	960
Iron	B.C.C.	3980
Molybdenum	B.C.C.	10,400

It can be observed from the above table that F.C.C. metal requires low critical stress as they have higher slip systems. In other words, these metals possess higher ductility.

2.5 PLASTIC DEFORMATION OF POLYCRYSTALLINE METALS

(May 10)

- Commercially, metal exists in polycrystalline form and not in single crystal form. In polycrystalline metals, the crystal axes are randomly oriented.

- A polycrystalline metal contains a number of grains and grain boundaries. The grains are separated by grain boundaries. The slip movement is easy within grains. The grain boundaries offer more resistance to slip. These grain boundaries are the obstacles for movement of dislocations.

- During plastic deformation, the regeneration rate of dislocation increases at the grain boundaries. This increases dislocation density. The force required for plastic deformation depends upon density of dislocations. More the grain boundaries, more will be dislocation density and higher force will be required for plastic deformation.

- In fine grained structure, grain boundaries are more. Hence, fine grained metals require higher force for plastic deformation than a coarse grained metal.

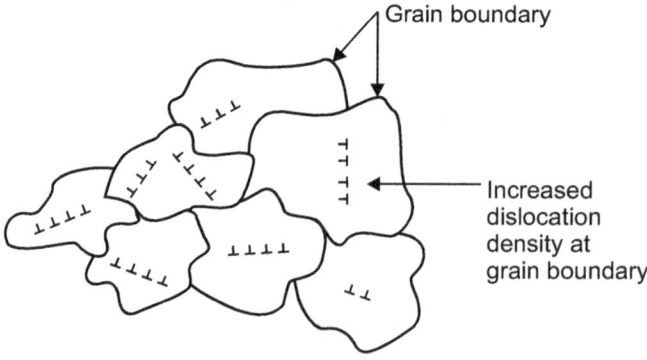

Fig. 2.10: Plastic deformation of polycrystalline material by slip

- During further plastic deformation, the dislocations pile up at the grain boundaries. As the dislocations cannot cross the grain boundary easily, plastic deformation becomes more difficult (Fig. 2.10).

2.6 WORK HARDENING   (May 10, 11, 12, 14, Dec. 11, 12, 13)

It is also called as **strain hardening**. It is defined as a phenomenon by which a ductile metal becomes hard and strong as it is plastically deformed.

For example, if a copper bar is bent (at the centre) at an angle, say 45° and again made straight and the process is repeated for a number of times, more and more force is required for next bending. The bar fails finally at the centre. This is due to increased hardness of bar due to continuous plastic deformation. Most metals strain harder at the room temperature.

The strain hardening can be explained by two theories viz. theory of slip and theory of dislocation.

(a) Theory of Slip

- During application of stress, plastic deformation occurs by slip. Within the initial degree of deformation, the slip planes get randomly oriented. This decreases the interplaner distance between two planes so the sliding of atomic plane becomes difficult. In other words, the movement of slip plane becomes difficult. Therefore, more stress is required for slip. This increases with increase in the degree of deformation. Thus, metal exhibits higher strength during deformation.

(b) Theory of Dislocation   (May 10, 11)

- Dislocation is a linear defect observed in crystal structure. Mismatching of atomic planes creates dislocation. The presence of an extra atomic plane or absence of an atomic plane results in the formation of dislocation. During plastic deformation, dislocation movement is observed. This results in slip.

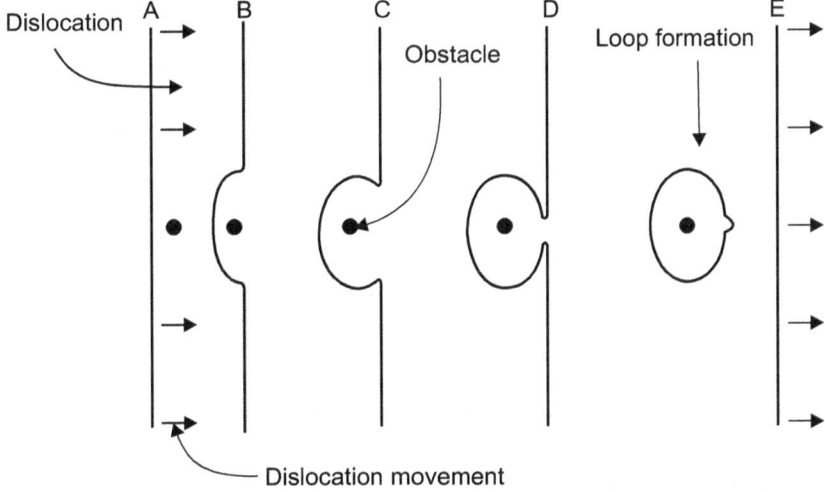

Fig. 2.11: Regeneration of dislocation during loop formation

- As the dislocations move, their density increases. If moving dislocations come across any obstacle as impurities, inclusion, precipitated phase etc., their movement is restricted requiring more stress for their movement. The dislocation forwards by leaving a loop around the obstacle (Fig. 2.11). If the dislocation is anchored at both the ends, it cannot easily bypass the obstacle. In this case, the dislocation bulges under the applied stress.

- The dislocation gets curved as shown in Fig. 2.12 in three steps a, b and c. Finally, in step d, the curved dislocation forms a loop that travels outwards to the grain boundary. As the loop disappears, the original dislocation is again created. This cycle repeats and dislocation density increases. This is called as 'Frank-Reed' source. Thus, the strength of metal increases, as it is work hardened/cold worked.

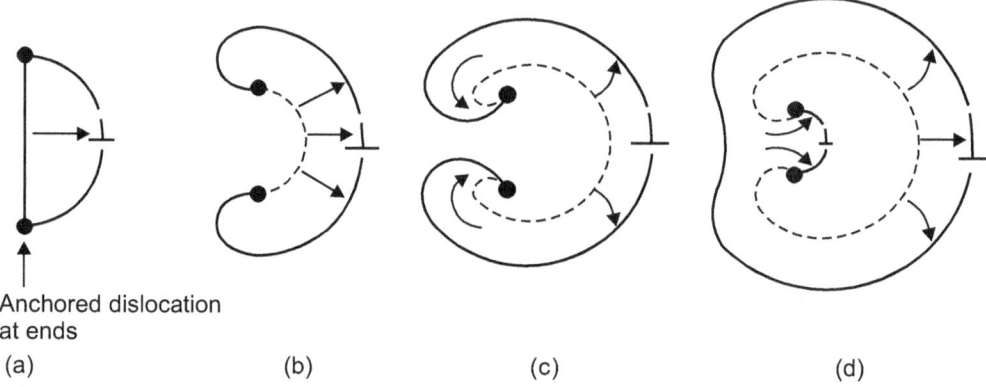

Anchored dislocation
at ends

(a)　　　　　(b)　　　　　(c)　　　　　(d)

Fig. 2.12: Regeneration of dislocation from an anchored dislocation

- The increase in strength by work hardening (i.e. cold working) is shown in Fig. 2.13.

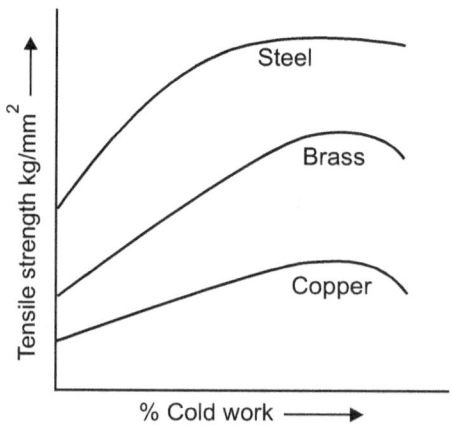

Fig. 2.13: Effect of cold working on strength of various metals

2.7 EFFECT OF COLD WORKING AND ANNEALING

(May 10, 11, 12, 13, 14, 17,Dec. 10, 11, 12, 13)

- If the metals are mechanically worked (i.e. deformed) below their recrystallization temperature, they are called as **cold worked**. The recrystallization temperature is given as

    Recrystallization Temperature = 0.5 × Melting temperature °K

- In cold worked metal, the grains are in distorted condition after deformation. The properties of metal depends upon the lattice structure.

- The properties such as strength, hardness, electrical conductivity etc. get affected due to cold working. The major properties such as tensile strength, yield strength and hardness increase, while per cent elongation decreases i.e. **cold working decreases ductility of metal** (Fig. 2.14).

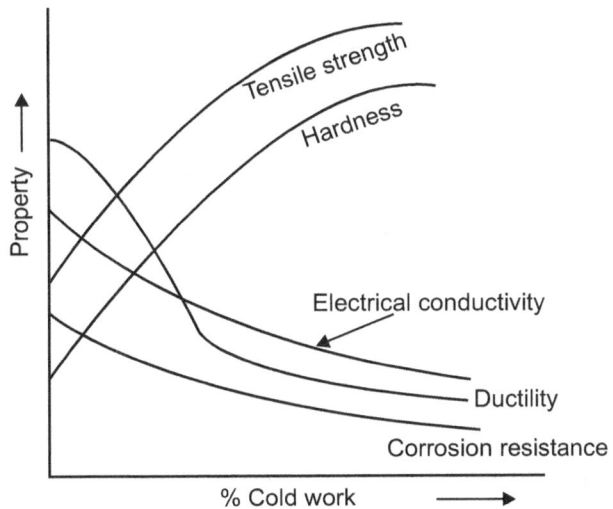

Fig. 2.14: Effect of cold working on properties of metals

- The distortion of the crystal structure restricts the passage of electrons. This results in decreasing electrical conductivity. The cold working increases the level of internal energy at grain boundaries. This results in decrease in intergranular corrosion resistance of metal in corrosive environments. The residual stresses also tend to make the metal more susceptible to stress-corrosion cracking.

- The cold working increases the hardness and results in brittleness of metal. Such hard and brittle metal cannot be further cold worked as it has tendency of cracking. Therefore, to improve the ductility of the metal for making further cold working possible, annealing is done.

- Annealing is a heat treatment in which a cold worked metal is heated at an elevated temperature for some time and then cooled at a very slow rate. The residual stresses developed during cold working are relaxed.

- This reduces lattice distortion, which improves ductility and other properties.The properties lost by cold working can be regained by annealing (Fig. 2.15). The structural changes occur in the following **stages during annealing.**

    (a) Recovery,

    (b) Recrystallization and

    (c) Grain growth.

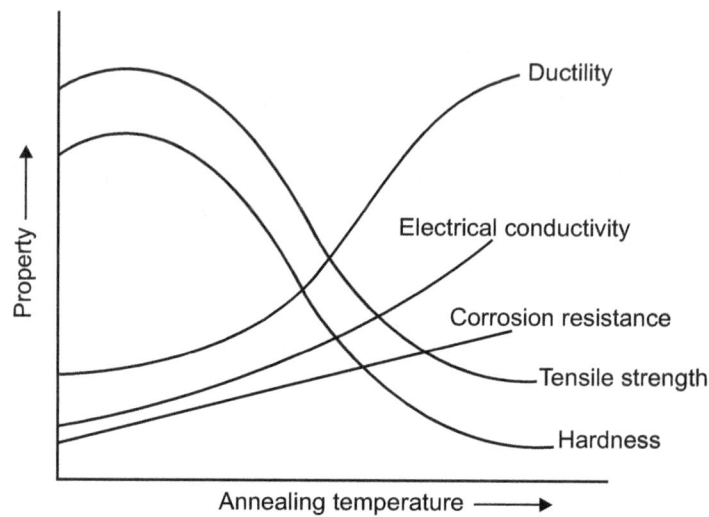

Fig. 2.15: Effect of annealing on properties of a cold worked metal

(a) Recovery

- This is a low temperature process. In this step, major changes in micro-structure are not observed.

- Due to thermal energy, the atoms show thermal oscillations, which result in reduction in elastic distortion. However, mechanically distorted grains remain as they are. The main effect of recovery is the relief of internal stresses due to the cold working. After recovery, the ductility of the metal improves slightly.

- Recovery eliminates some imperfections like vacancies. However, a majority of the dislocations and increased strain energy remain unchanged. Some dislocations rearrange themselves so that they are observed in a typical line arrangement. This is called as **polygonization**.

- Electrical conductivity is increased during recovery, while other mechanical properties remain unchanged. Recovery helps to minimize the tendency of cold worked metal towards intergranular or stress corrosion cracking. This low temperature treatment is also known as **stress relief annealing**.

(b) Recrystallization

- This is an important step in annealing. The process of formation of new equiaxed stress-free grains instead of initial deformed and distorted grains is called as recrystallization. This occurs at a temperature higher than the temperature of recovery. The newly formed crystals possess the same lattice structure as that of the original one.

- Recrystallization takes place by nucleation of stress-free grains, which grow at the cost of old deformed grains. In this stage, the dislocation density is reduced, which produces almost stress-free and strain-free grains.

- Micro-structural changes are observed after recrystallization. Therefore, recrystallization affects the mechanical properties of the metal to a large extent as follows

- **Mechanical Properties of Metal**
  - ➢ Hardness decreases.
  - ➢ Tensile strength reduces.
  - ➢ Internal stress level drops sharply.
  - ➢ Electrical conductivity increases.
  - ➢ Corrosion resistance increases sharply.
  - ➢ Ductility increases greatly.

- The temperature at which recrystallization occurs is called as recrystallization temperature. Usually, it is defined as the temperature at which 50 per cent of the cold worked metal is recrystallized in one hour. It is given as follows

$$T_r = K \times T_m$$

where, T_r　=　Recrystallization temperature in °K,

　　　　T_m　=　Melting point of the metal in °K,

　　　　K　　=　Multiplying factor depending on the material. It varies from 0.3 to 0.6; usually it is 0.5.

Recrystallization Temperature Depends upon Following Factors

- Degree of cold working
- Melting point of metal
- Initial grain size of metal
- Heating time
- Composition of metal

With increasing amount of cold work, lower temperature is required to start recrystallization.

A certain minimum amount of cold working is necessary for recrystallization. It is called as **critical degree** of cold work or simply **critical deformation**. This is usually 2 to 8 per cent. Higher the melting point, higher will be the recrystallization temperature. If the initial grain size of the metal is fine, the recrystallization temperature will be low because for equal amount of cold working, more strain hardening is introduced in fine grained metal than in coarse grained metal.

The recrystallization occurs at a lower temperature with increasing annealing time. Pure metals recrystallize at a lower temperature compared to impure metals and alloys.

Table 2.4 gives the recrystallization temperatures for some typical metals. From this table, it can be observed that recrystallization temperature of lead, tin and zinc is below the room temperature. Therefore, these metals cannot be cold worked at room temperature. Similarly, working of Tungsten at 1000°C is cold working as its recrystallization temperature is 1200°C.

Table 2.4: Approximate Recrystallization Temperatures of Some Metals

Metal	Melting Temperature, °C	Recrystallization Temperature, °C
Copper	1083	230
Aluminium	660	150
70 : 30 Brass	905	275
Zinc	420	25
Lead	327	27
Tin	232	– 20
Low Carbon Steel	1500	600
Tungsten	3410	1200
Nickel	1452	610
Gold	1063	200

(c) Grain Growth

- Coarse grained structure exhibits low free energy as they have less grain boundary area. This is the driving force for grain growth as the system tries to achieve its low energy level.
- As the temperature increases, the free energy of the metal decreases and the rate of grain growth increases. Grain coarsening also occurs if the metal is held at a high temperature for a long time. Grain growth is also referred to as **Secondary recrystallization**.
- Similar to recrystallization, the smaller grains merge to form coarser grains. In the grain growth process, the following changes in the properties are usually observed.

Properties

- The hardness decreases;
- Tensile strength decreases;
- Internal stresses are completely eliminated;
- Electrical conductivity increases to a smaller extent;
- Corrosion resistance is improved;
- Ductility increases.

2.8 HOT WORKING

* Hot working is defined as the mechanical working or plastic deformation of metals above their recrystallization temperature. Hot working is a combination of simultaneous cold working and annealing.

* A continuous crystallization takes place during hot working. Hot working completely eliminates the hardening effects due to plastic deformation. The dendritic structure of casting is destroyed due to hot working. The mechanical properties of a metal are anisotropic after hot working. They are higher along the fibres or hot working direction. Hot working eliminates casting defects such as porosity, blowholes etc.

* Mechanical properties such as ductility, toughness are improved due to the refinement of grains occurring during hot working.

* Cold working can be differentiated from hot working on the following points

Difference between Cold Working and Hard Working   **(Dec. 11, 12, May 13, 14)**

Cold Working	Hot Working
1. It is the working of metals below their recrystallization temperature.	1. It is the working of metals above their recrystallization temperature.
2. The metal tends to harden during cold working.	2. Work hardening does not occur in hot working.
3. Cold working involves only plastic deformation of metals.	3. Hot working involves plastic deformation as well as annealing.
4. With increase in the degree of cold working, further deformation becomes difficult.	4. Hot working is possible to any degree of plastic deformation.
5. Distortion of the micro-structure occurs in cold working.	5. The grain structure becomes equiaxed and refined.
6. Dislocation density is continuously increased.	6. Dislocation density does not increase.
7. Sometimes, cold worked materials require annealing heat treatment before use.	7. No post working treatment is required.
8. Cold working requires higher forces for deformation.	8. Comparatively, lower forces are required for deformation in hot working.
9. The cast metal is difficult to cold work.	9. Hot working destroys dendrites in casting and can be worked.

Cold Working	Hot Working
10. Cold worked metals are more prone to intergranular corrosion.	10. No such effect is observed.
11. Oxidation of metal is not observed.	11. Oxidation of metal is possible due to high temperatures.
12. Close dimensional tolerances can be achieved.	12. It is difficult to achieve fine dimensions.
13. Better surface finish is obtained.	13. Scale is deposited on surface, which makes it inferior.
14. Cold working do not require expensive tools.	14. It requires expensive tools.
15. Examples of cold working are cold rolling, cold forging, wire drawing, deep drawing etc.	15. Examples of hot working are hot rolling, hot forging, extrusion etc.

2.9 PREFERRED ORIENTATION

Preferred orientation is defined as a condition of polycrystalline metal in which crystal orientations are not random, but are in a typical direction.

It occurs, when certain lattice directions in the grains are aligned with the principle direction of metal flow. It is observed under severe deformation condition preferred orientation is usually in the direction of maximum strain. Typical examples of mechanical working, which develops preferred orientation are rolling and wire drawing.

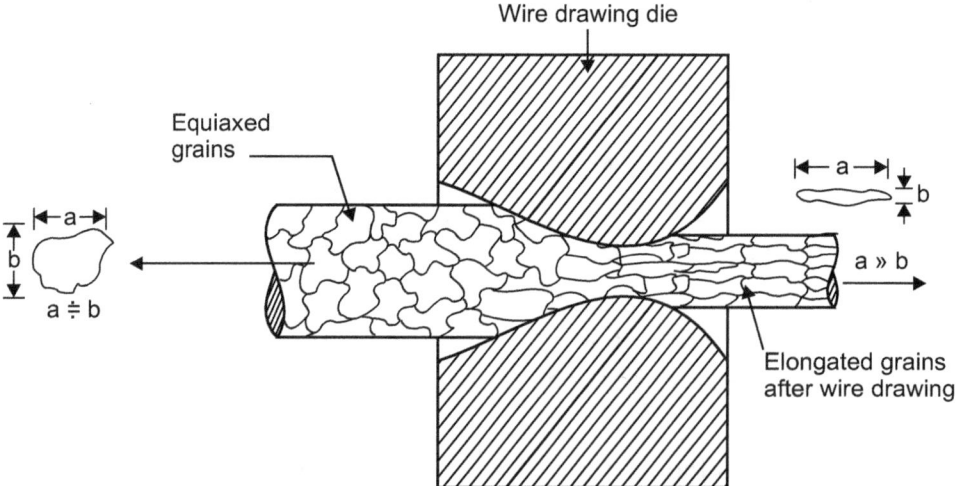

Fig. 2.16: Preferred orientation during wire drawing

Preferred orientation results in directional properties. Usually, better properties are observed in the direction of metal. In some cases, these properties are valuable. For example, increased magnetic permeability in the direction of flow is useful, if the metal is used for transformer laminations. However, the directional properties are harmful, if the working stress is perpendicular to the direction of metal flow. For example, cold working results in distortion of grains in one direction. So a typical fibrous structure is observed in preferred orientation (Fig. 2.16).

KEY NOTES

1. Some materials may be in form of one crystal or grain and are known as single crystals. Other consists of many crystals/grains and are known as polycrystalline materials. Regions between grains of a polycrystalline material are known as grain boundaries.

2. When plastic deformation is carried out below recrystallisation temperature, known as cold working.

3. The temperature at which reformation of the crystals take place is known as recrystallisation temperature.

4. Mechanical properties are almost unchanged after hot working. After cold working strength, hardness are increased and ductility, electrical conductivity are decreased.

5. To restore ductility after cold working in wire drawing industry, Annealing is done.

6. Mechanical properties are not recovered in the recovery stage of annealing, only stresses are relieved.

7. Point defects include vacancies, interstitial atoms, and substitutional atoms disturbing atomic arrangements. Surface defects include grain boundaries. Dislocations are line defects.

REVIEW QUESTIONS

1. Define the following terms
   - (a) Crystal.
   - (b) Unit cell.
   - (c) Space lattice.
   - (d) Lattice angles.

2. Explain the indexing method for planes and directions.

3. Calculate the average number of atoms for the following structures.
   - (a) S.C.,
   - (b) B.C.C.,
   - (c) H.C.P.,
   - (d) F.C.C.

4. What is atomic packing factor ? What is its importance ?

5. Show following planes and directions in a cubic cell (221), (632), [101], [0$\bar{1}$0].

6. What is a slip ? Why does plastic deformation occur by slip ?

7. Which properties get affected by cold working ? Why ?

8. "The properties lost by cold working can be regained by annealing." Explain the statement.

9. Define preferred orientation. Why does it occur ?

10. Represent following planes and directions $(1\bar{1}0)$, (212), $[112]$ $[221]$.

11. Explain property and microstructural changes during cold working and annealing of metals.

12. Define Burger vector.

13. What is point defect ? What are its effects ?

14. Explain work hardening.

15. Give typical slip planes and directions for F.C.C., B.C.C. and H.C.P. metals. Which type of metal shows more plastic deformation ? Why ?

16. Explain the structural and property changes during recovery, recrystallization and grain growth, stages of annealing.

17. What is cold working and hot working? In which respect the hot working is superior to cold working ?

18. What are dislocations ? What are the types of dislocations ? Explain their role in plastic deformations.

19. Represent following planes and directions within a cubic unit cell $(\bar{2}10)$, (113), $[1\bar{1}1]$, $[012]$.

20. Why strain hardening is more in fine grained material.

21. Distinguish between screw and edge dislocation. Also explain the effects of point defects on various properties of materials.

22. Is cold working always superior to hot working ? Explain.

23. Explain the following in brief

    (i)   Point defects   (ii) Polygonization

    (iii) Recrystallization   (iv) Dislocation

24. Calculate resolved shear stress of a single crystal if applied tensile stress is 30 kg/mm^2. The slip plane is oriented at 45° the tensile axis.

25. Explain the effect of the following crystalline defects on properties of materials.

    (i)   Point defects, (ii) Line defects.

26. What is recrystallization ? Define recrystallization temperature. Explain the factors affecting recrystallization process.

27. Derive the equation for critical resolve shear stress during slip in a single crystal.

28. How would a difference in grain size affect the change in mechanical properties on plastic deformation ?

29. Explain the phenomenon of strain hardening in detail.

30. Derive the equation for critical resolve shear stress during slip in a single crystal.

31. "Maximum shear stress is observed, if the slip plane is at 45° in a single crystal". Explain.

32. How plastic deformation in polycrystalline material is different from single ?

33. Why annealing is done after cold working ? Explain the changes in mechanism properties that take place during annealing with proper graphs.

34. Explain the basic characteristics required to produce good composites.

35. Give classification of crystal imperfections. Explain with neat sketches screw and edge dislocation.

36. Define slip planes and slip directions.

37. Define cold working. Draw microstructure of mild steel before and after cold working. Why cold worked materials are annealed ?

38. Give reasons:

    1. Find grained steels are more stronger than coarse grained steels.

    2. Dislocations play an important role during plastic deformation of metals.

39. Define recrystallization temperature and work hardening.

40. Obtain effective number of atoms per unit cell for cubic unit cell and state its significance.

41. What is work hardening ? How does it occur ?

42. Differentiate traditional and engineering ceramics.

UNIVERSITY QUESTIONS

DECEMBER 2013

1. Differentiate between slip and twinning.   **[4]**

2. Show the self explanatory diagram for point defects.   **[2]**

3. What is work hardening? Explain the property variation with proper graph before and after work hardening.   **[6]**

MAY 2014

1. Differentiate between cold working and hot working.   **[4]**

2. What is recrystallization? Explain the factors affecting recrystallization process. **[4]**

DECEMBER 2014

1. Differentiate between slip and twinning.   **[4]**

2. Explain any two Imperfection in Crystal (or Lattices) from the list given below:

   (i)   Edge Dislocation

   (ii)   Stacking fault

   (iii) Low angle boundary.   **[4]**

MAY 2015

1. Differentiate between cold working and hot working according to temperature, variation in mechanical properties, grain formation and areas of application.   **[4]**

2. Derive the expression for deformation of single crystal by slip. State the condition for geometrical hardening and geometrical softening.   **[4]**

NOVEMBER 2015

1. Explain work hardening on the basis of dislocations.   **[2]**

MAY 2016

1. What is plastic deformation in materials ? Differentiate between slip and twining. **[4]**

NOVEMBER 2016

1. Define the following :   **[4]**

   (i) Hot working

   [**Ans. :** Refer article 2.8]

2. Materials like Al shows more plastic deformation by the slip mechanism than twinning. Explain in detail.   **[4]**

   [**Ans. :** Refer article 2.3]

3. What do you understand by crystal imperfection ? Explain the Edge dislocation with a neat diagram.   **[6]**

   [**Ans. :** Refer articles 2.1,2.1.2(1)]

MAY 2017

1. What is strain hardening and how does it affect plastic deformation? Explain theory of dislocation on the basis of rotation of slip planes during plastic deformation. **[6]**

   [**Ans. :** Refer article 2.7]

2. What are different classifications of imperfections is crystal structure? Explain the point imperfection in detail.   **[6]**

   [**Ans. :** Refer article 2.1]

✠ ✠ ✠

Unit III

DESTRUCTIVE AND NON-DESTRUCTIVE TESTING

A. DESTRUCTIVE TESTING

3.1 INTRODUCTION

Mechanical testing of metals is carried out for the evaluation of their mechanical properties. The composition, processing and heat treatment influence the properties of metals. Important mechanical properties include strength, stiffness, elasticity, plasticity, ductility, brittleness, hardness etc.

Mechanical testing is required for the following purposes

- Routine testing of raw material.
- Testing after heat treatments and processing.
- Study of failure analysis.
- Research and Development.

The important mechanical tests include

- Tensile test
- Compression test
- Shear test
- Torsion test
- Bend test
- Cupping test
- Hardness test
- Impact test
- Fatigue test
- Creep test

This chapter describes principle, procedure, advantages, limitations and applications of above mentioned tests.

3.2 TENSILE TEST

This test is frequently used to evaluate certain properties of metals. This test has a great importance in many engineering applications.

Principle of Tensile Test

If a metallic specimen is subjected to a gradually increasing uniaxial tensile load, it gets plastically deformed and finally fails (breaks). During its plastic deformation, changes occur in cross-sectional area and length. Strength and ductility are the main properties, which are usually judged in this test.

Procedure

In tensile testing, the metallic specimen is gripped at the opposite end and is pulled apart. The test specimen elongates in the direction of applied load. A standard specimen is prepared as shown in Fig. 3.1. Usually, the specimen has a circular cross-section. The specimen may be having rectangular or square cross-section, if it is obtained from a plate or sheet form. At the end of specimen, the failure may occur due to stresses introduced by the gripping device. These stresses do not affect the central portion of the specimen. At this portion, the failure should occur due to applied force only. Therefore, the central portion is usually of a smaller cross-section than the end portion or shoulders.

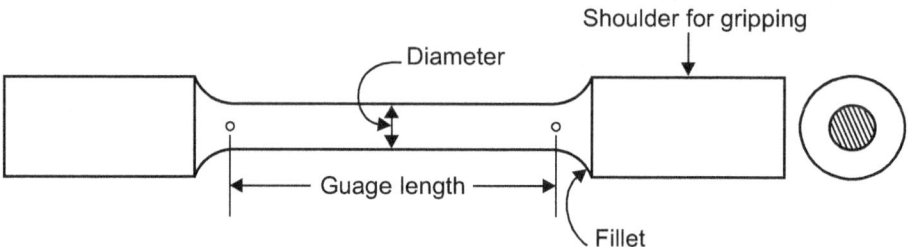

Fig. 3.1: A standard tensile test specimen

The ends of the specimen should be suitable (may be threaded) for proper gripping.

For brittle metals, the ends should be large and sufficient to avoid failure due to axial stresses and gripping stresses.

The joining area of the end portion and the central portion should have an adequate fillet (curve). This reduces the stress concentration resulting from abrupt change in the cross-section. The specimen should be symmetrical to avoid bending during loading.

3.3 IMPORTANCE OF GAUGE LENGTH

- Gauge length is the length of reduced central portion.

- The failure should occur in gauge length. It depends largely on material and its cross-section.

- Ductile metals show a large plastic deformation than the brittle metals. Therefore, they must be tested with more gauge length than brittle metal.

- As per ASTM (American Society for Testing Metals), the gauge length should be four times the diameter of specimen.

- The change in the length during testing is measured by an instrument called 'Extensometer'. It shows the extension of the specimen. It is attached to the specimen.

- For tension test, a Tensile Testing Machine (Fig. 3.2) or Universal Testing Machine or Tensometer is used. Tensometer is recommended mostly for tensile testing of wires and small rods. Usually, the tensile testing machines are hydraulically operated.

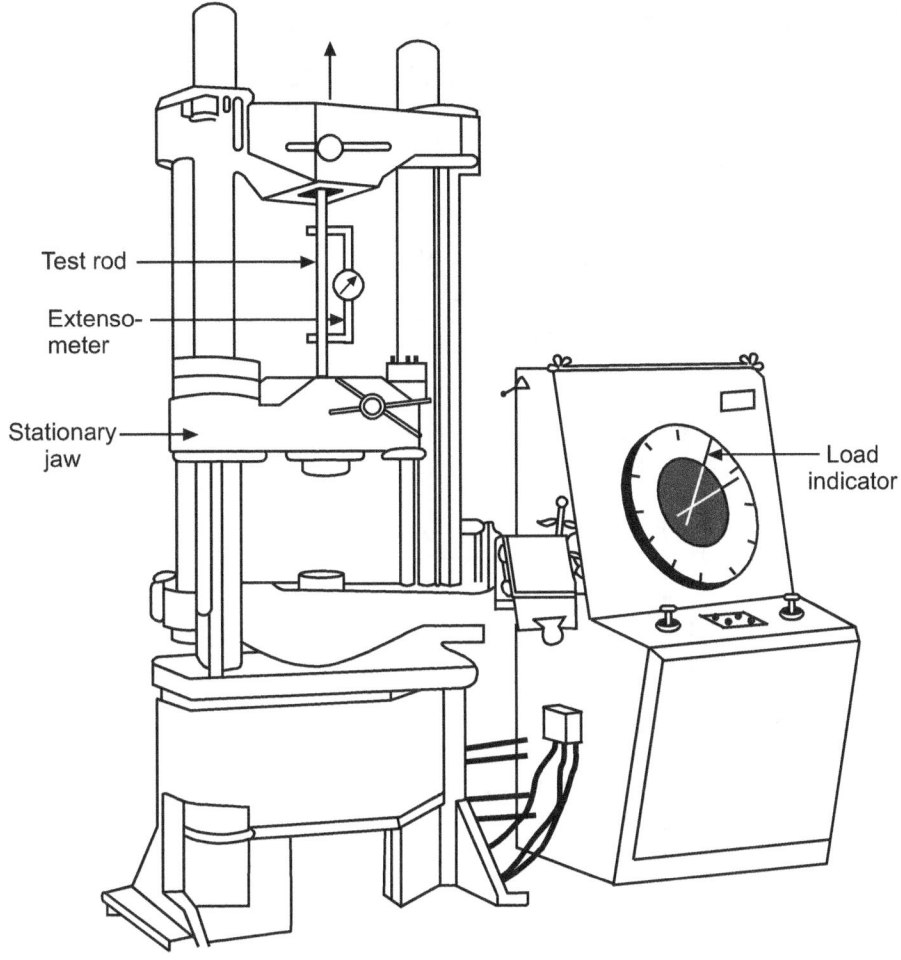

Fig. 3.2: Tensile testing machine

Scope of the Test

Tensile test has a useful scope in determining the following properties of a metal

- Elastic limit,
- Yield strength,
- Maximum stress,
- Breaking stress,
- Percentage elongation,
- Toughness,
- Resilience etc.

3.4 STRESS-STRAIN CURVES   (Dec. 10, May 12)

- The results of tensile tests are expressed in the graphical form called as stress-strain curve. Stress is defined as the **intensity of internally distributed forces that resist a change in shape of the metal**, whereas strain is defined as a **change per unit length in a linear dimension of the metal**. The results of tensile tests are also plotted as applied load (kgs) versus extension (mm). These are called as load extension diagrams.

• Stress-strain values are derived by load and extension values as follows

$$\text{Stress} = \frac{\text{Applied load}}{\text{Original cross-sectional area}}$$

$$\sigma = \frac{P}{A_O} \text{ kg/mm}^2 \qquad\qquad \text{... (3.1)}$$

$$\text{Strain} = \frac{\text{Change in length}}{\text{Original length}}$$

or $\qquad\qquad \text{Strain} = \dfrac{\text{Extension}}{\text{Original length}}$

$$e = \frac{dl}{l} \qquad\qquad \text{... (3.2)}$$

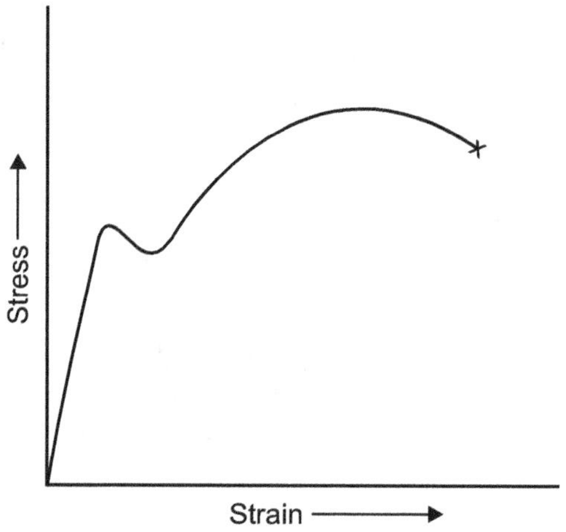

Fig. 3.3: A typical engineering stress-strain curve for low carbon steel

• There is no unit of expression for strain as both - extension and original length are in mm. A typical stress-strain curve is as shown in Fig. 3.3. The above discussion of stress and strain is based on the assumption that the dimensions of specimen do not change during testing (Actually, the length increases and diameter decreases). In this case, the stress and strain curves are called as engineering stress-strain curves as original cross-sectional area is used for computing all stress values.

3.5 TRUE STRESS-STRAIN CURVE   (Dec. 10; May 12)

• During tensile testing of a ductile metal, a considerable plastic deformation related to its change in dimensions is observed. Therefore, in true stress-strain calculations, the changing cross-sectional area is considered.

• True stress is obtained by dividing the applied load by actual instantaneous cross-sectional area and not by original cross-sectional area.

$$\text{True stress} = \frac{\text{Load}}{\text{Instantaneous cross-sectional area at that load}}$$

$$\sigma_{True} = \frac{P}{A_i} \qquad \qquad \dots (3.3)$$

- True strain, which is also called as 'Natural Strain', is the change in gauge length over the instantaneous gauge length. It is integration of engineering strains at all instants.

$$\in_{True} = \int_{L_o}^{L} \frac{dL}{L} = \ln \frac{L}{L_o}$$

$$\in_{True} = \ln \frac{L}{L_o} \qquad \qquad \dots (3.4)$$

3.6 RELATION BETWEEN ENGINEERING AND TRUE STRESS-STRAIN

(Dec. 10, May 12, 13)

We have Engineering strain (e) = $\frac{\Delta L}{L_o}$ ... (from equation 3.2)

Now, total length of a specimen is given as a sum of original length and extensions.

$$L = L_o + \Delta L$$

or $\qquad \Delta L = L - L_o$

Substituting the value of ΔL in equation (3.2), we get

$$e = \frac{L - L_o}{L_o}$$

$$= \frac{L}{L_o} - \frac{L_o}{L_o} = \left(\frac{L}{L_o} - 1 \right)$$

$$\frac{L}{L_o} = e + 1 \qquad \qquad \dots (3.5)$$

Substituting the value of $\frac{L}{L_o}$ in equation (3.4), we get,

$$\in_{True} = \ln (e + 1) \qquad \qquad \dots (3.6)$$

Similarly, we have

$$\sigma_T = \frac{P}{A_i} \quad \text{and} \quad \sigma_E = \frac{P}{A_o}$$

Taking ratio of these two

$$\frac{\sigma_T}{\sigma_E} = \frac{P}{A_i} \times \frac{A_o}{P} = \frac{A_o}{A_i}$$

Now, assuming that the volume of the same remains constant

$$V = A_O \times L_O = A_i \times L \qquad \qquad ... (3.7)$$

or $$\frac{A_O}{A_i} = \frac{L}{L_O} \qquad \qquad ... (3.8)$$

Substituting this value of $\dfrac{A_O}{A_i}$ in equation (3.7), we get

$$\frac{\sigma_T}{\sigma_E} = \frac{L}{L_O} = e + 1 \qquad \qquad ... \text{(from equation 3.5)}$$

$$\sigma_T = \sigma_E (e + 1) \qquad \qquad ... (3.9)$$

Finally, we have $\quad \sigma_T = \sigma_E (e + 1)$ and $\varepsilon_{True} = \ln (e + 1)$

In these equations, $\quad \sigma_T$ = True stress,

σ_E = Engineering stress,

$\in_{True}$ = True strain and

e = Engineering strain.

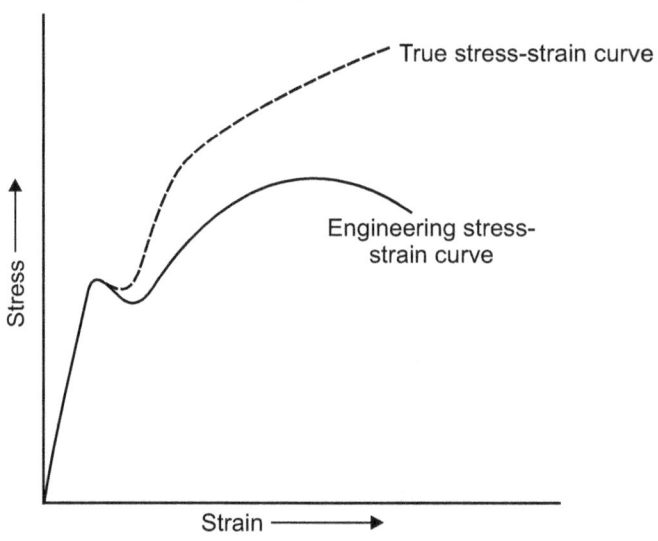

Fig. 3.4: A typical true stress - strain curve for mild steel superimposed on engineering stress-strain curve

Fig. 3.4 gives a typical true stress-strain curve for mild steel superimposed on engineering stress-strain curve. From this, it would be clear that, the true stress-strain curve is always to the left of the engineering curve upto maximum load.

3.7 NECKING

Necking is observed in the specimens during tensile testing. Usually, it occurs in the central portion of the specimen. When the metal specimen is pulled apart by application of load, it elongates. The length of the specimen increases, while its overall cross-sectional area decreases. After certain maximum load, the decrease in local cross-sectional area is observed. This is called as necking. The failure of metal occurs always at the area of necking. At the point, where the true stress value is equal to the slope of the true stress-strain curve, the necking occurs.

The inclined curve with decreasing stress indicates the beginning of necking.

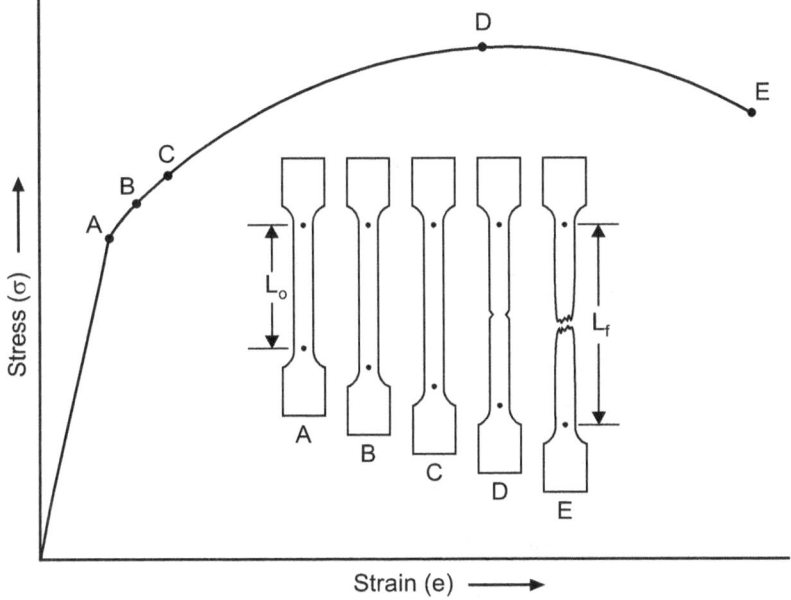

Fig. 3.5: Necking and failure of a specimen in tension test

$$L_o = \text{Initial length,}$$

$$L_f = \text{Final length}$$

Fig. 3.5 explains schematically the formation of necking and specimen failure.

3.8 EVALUATION OF PROPERTIES   (May 10; Dec. 11, 12, 13)

Tensile test evaluates the following properties of a metal

    (1) Elastic limit   (2) Yield stress

    (3) Proof stress   (4) Proportional stress

    (5) Ultimate tensile stress   (6) Breaking stress

    (7) Resilience   (8) Toughness.

The other properties, which are mentioned below are not indicated on the stress-strain curve. These properties are important in view of metal processing.

(a) Stiffness, (b) Ductility, (c) Malleability, (d) Plasticity.

All the above properties are defined and explained as below

(1) Elastic Limit

Within the elastic limit, the stress is proportional to strain. It is also defined as the **minimum stress value from which plastic deformation starts**. If the metal is stressed within the elastic limit and unloaded, it regains its original shape. In other words, the metal does not get deformed permanently.

In the elastic region, very less strain is observed for higher values of stress. This property is essential for the metals used for spring applications.

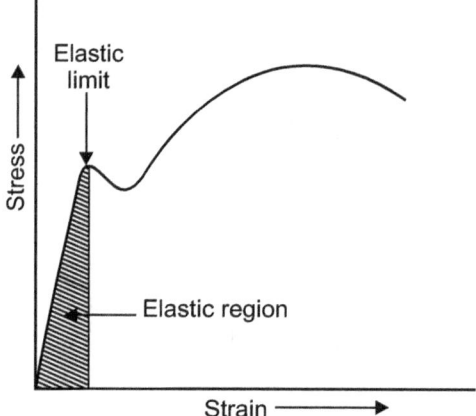

Fig. 3.6: Elastic limit and elastic region in a stress-strain curve of mild steel

Fig. 3.6 shows the elastic limit and elastic region in the stress-strain curve of mild steel.

(2) Yield Stress

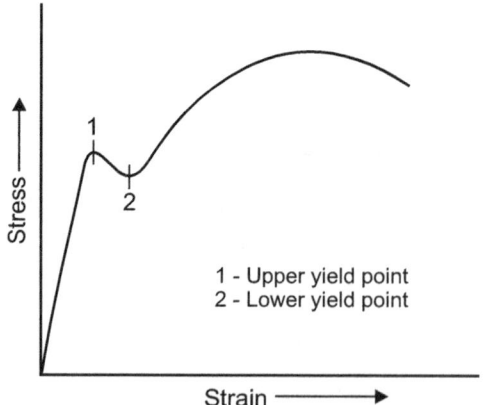

Fig. 3.7: A stress-strain curve for mild steel showing upper and lower yield point

This is the point on the stress-strain curve at which metal passes from elastic region to plastic region. **Yield stress is defined as the value of stress at which the metal starts yielding (or deforming plastically).** It is also called as yield point. In some of the materials, it is clearly indicated as a constant stress value, where strain occurs; while in some of the metals, a clear indication of yield point is not observed.

Two critical points are observed in yield region of mild steels. (a) Upper yield point and (b) Lower yield point. Fig. 3.7 shows a yield point in mild steel.

(3) Proof Stress

Proof stress is very similar to yield stress. It is expressed for metals, which do not exhibit yield point (Fig. 3.8).

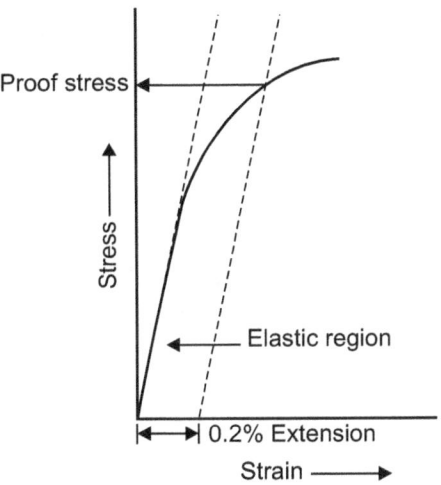

Fig. 3.8: Proof stress by Off-set method

It is defined on the lines similar to the way yield stress as defined, but with specific amount of plastic deformation. Proof stress is defined as the value of stress at which a specific plastic deformation occurs.

Proof stress value is calculated by a method called 'Offset method'. For a specified value on strain axis (usually 0.2%), a straight parallel line is drawn to the linear part of the stress-strain curve.

The stress corresponding to crossing point of these two lines is the proof stress for that metal (Fig. 3.8).

(4) Proportional Stress

It is defined as the stress at the limit of proportionality of stress and strain values.

It is also called as proportional limit. Fig. 3.9 shows the proportional stress.

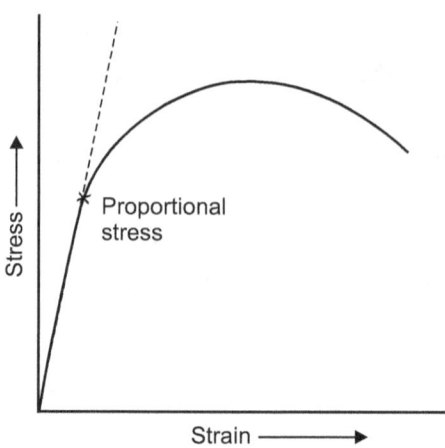

Fig. 3.9: A stress-strain curve showing proportional stress

(5) Ultimate Tensile Stress

Ultimate tensile stress is denoted as UTS and it is defined as the maximum value of stress in the plastic region, that the metal can sustain without failure.

The brittle metal fails or breaks, when stressed to the value of ultimate tensile stress. The ductile metal still continue to deform even after reaching UTS value. From the value of UTS, the stress decreases, while the strain increases. The stress-strain curve slants down from UTS point.

This is shown in Fig. 3.10.

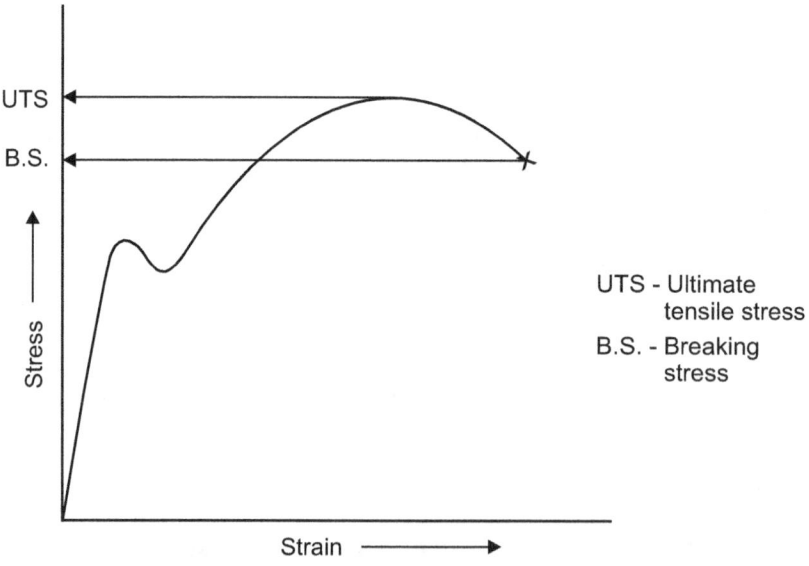

Fig. 3.10: A stress-strain curve of mild-steel showing UTS and BS

(6) Breaking Stress

It is also termed as failure stress or fracture stress. **It is defined as the value of stress at which the metal breaks.** This is the last value of stress shown by a stress-strain curve. Usually, it is the lowest value of stress in the plastic region for a ductile metal. A brittle metal may have close values of breaking and ultimate stress.

The breaking stress is shown in Fig. 3.10.

(7) Resilience

The stress-strain curve has two distinct regions viz. elastic region and plastic region.

Resilience is defined as a area under the stress-strain curve in the elastic region. It is also defined as the amount of energy absorbed by the metal without permanent deformation.

Higher values of resilience are important for typical applications. This includes shock absorbers, springs (laminated and coil) and diaphragms. The metals used for such applications include, brass (70% Cu, 30% Zn), copper 2, beryllium alloy and spring steels.

The modulus of resilience is the energy absorbed by per unit volume of a metal in the elastic region.

$$\text{Modulus of resilience} = \frac{\text{Energy absorbed}}{\text{Unit volume}}$$

The resilience can be represented as the region shown in Fig. 3.11.

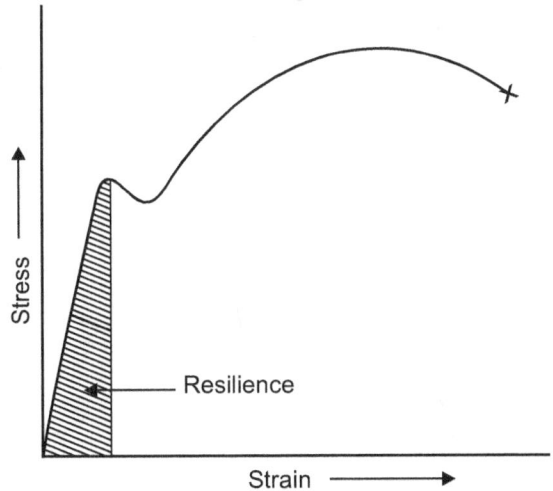

Fig. 3.11: A stress-strain curve showing resilience

(8) Toughness

The complete area covered by the stress-strain curve is referred as toughness. It is defined as the **amount of energy absorbed by the metal before its fracture**. Similar to resilience, toughness of metal is an important property from its engineering application point of view.

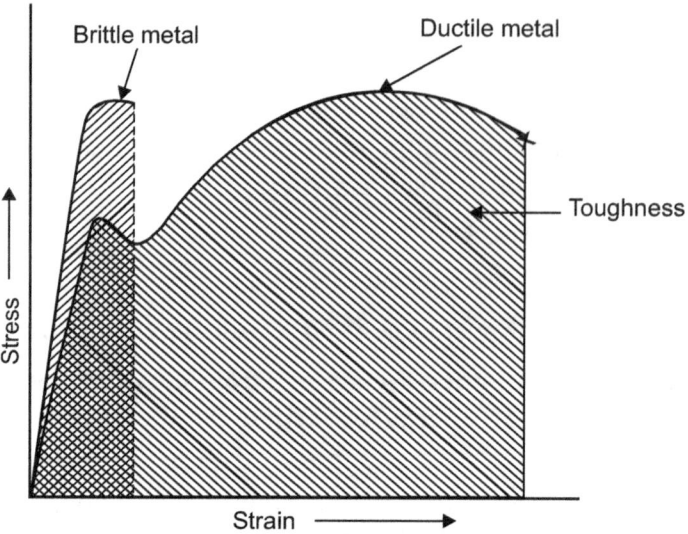

Fig. 3.12: A stress-strain diagram showing toughness

The modulus of toughness is the amount of energy absorbed per unit area by the metal in the elastic plus plastic region. The hardened and tempered steels have better toughness. The higher toughness is required for applications such as crankshafts, connecting rods etc.The brittle metals show very less values of toughness than ductile metals as shown in Fig. 3.12.

Other Properties Include

(1) Stiffness

It is defined as the **resistance offered by a metal for its elastic deformation**. It is also defined as the **slope on the linear portion of a stress-strain curve within the elastic limit**. It is measured by the rate of stress with respect to strain. The metal is stiff, if it requires greater stress to produce given strain.

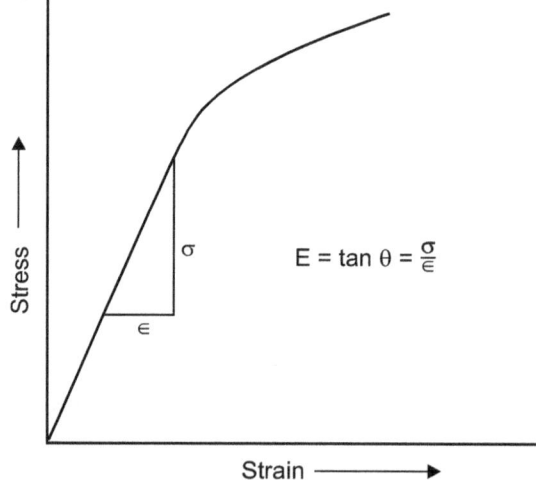

$$E = \tan \theta = \frac{\sigma}{\epsilon}$$

Fig. 3.13: A stress-strain curve showing Young's modulus or stiffness

Modulus of elasticity is the **ratio of stress to corresponding strain within the elastic limit** (Fig. 3.13). It is also called as Young's modulus. It is needed for computing deflection of beams. It is an important value to be considered in structural designing. It decreases with increase in temperature. Usually, metals and alloys show higher stiffness at room temperature.

(2) Ductility

It is defined as the **ability of a metal to undergo plastic deformation in tension without fracturing**. It is the property of a metal by which it can be drawn into wires. It is measured by

(a) Elongation or (b) Reduction in area.

$$\% \text{ Elongation} = \frac{\text{Change in length}}{\text{Original length}} \times 100$$

$$\% \text{ Reduction in area} = \frac{\text{Change in cross-sectional area}}{\text{Original cross-sectional area}} \times 100$$

Elongation is measured by the change in the gauge length, while reduction in area is measured by the difference between the original cross-section and final cross-section **areas**.

(3) Malleability

Malleability is defined as the **property of a metal to undergo plastic deformation in compression without fracturing**. It is the ability of a metal by which it can be rolled into sheets.

(4) Plasticity

Plasticity is the property of a metal by which it shows a large degree of plastic deformation.

(5) Strain Hardening Coefficient

Within the elastic limit, the stress is directly proportional to strain, but in plastic region it is not so. The true stress and strain may be related by the following relation in the plastic region

$$\boxed{\sigma_T = k \in^n}$$

In this expression, the constant n is called as **strain hardening coefficient** or exponent. It is a slope of log true stress – true strain curve. Usually, strain hardening coefficient is less than unity for most of the metals; e.g. for copper n = 0.54, 70/30 brass n = 0.49, steel n = 0.20. With different values of n, the stress-strain curve appears as shown in Fig. 3.14.

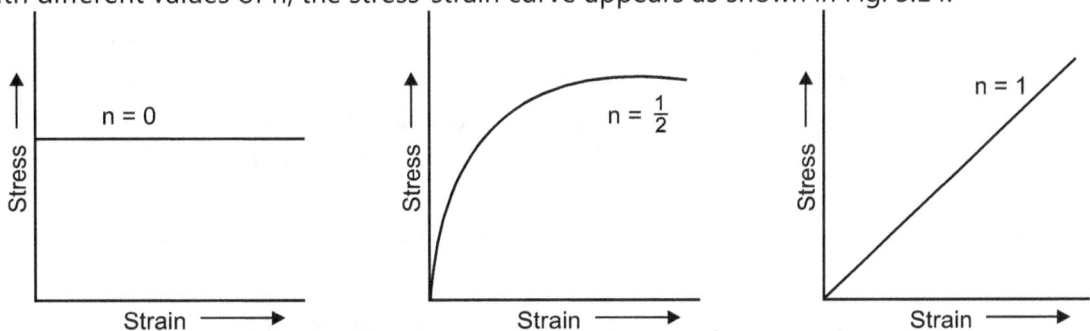

**Fig. 3.14: Effect of strain hardening coefficient (n)
on the appearance of stress-strain curve**

3.9 EFFECTS OF VARIOUS FACTORS ON TENSILE TEST

- Cold worked metals show less ductility than the hot worked metals because of strain hardening.

- With decreasing gauge length, percent elongation increases.

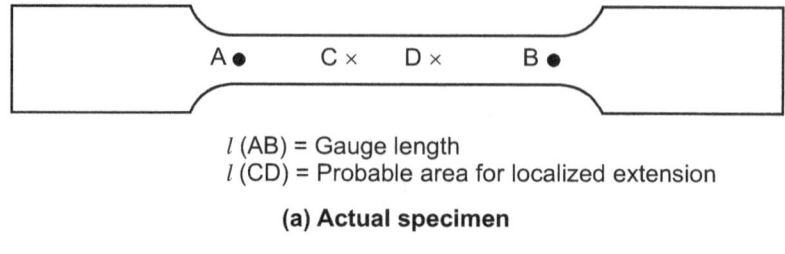

l (AB) = Gauge length
l (CD) = Probable area for localized extension

(a) Actual specimen

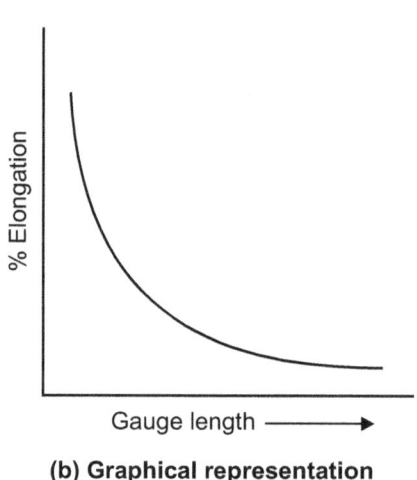

(b) Graphical representation

Fig. 3.15: Effect of gauge length on percent elongation

Explanation: Consider a specimen as shown in Fig. 3.15 [(a) and (b)] with gauge length equal to AB. The central portion is length CD, where localized extension is likely to occur during necking. During testing, the gauge length [l (AB)] and central portion [l (CD)] elongates equal. This is before necking. After necking, the localized extension occurs only at CD. So CD elongates, but l (AC) and l (DB) remains constant. This additional elongation is not directly calculated. If the gauge length is CD, more elongation is observed. Therefore, if the gauge length is reduced, more elongation is observed due to localized elongation.

- Geometrically, similar specimens respond equally in tension test for the same metal.

Explanation: With geometrically different specimens, varied results are observed. The specimens with different length to diameter ratio are shown in Fig. 3.16.

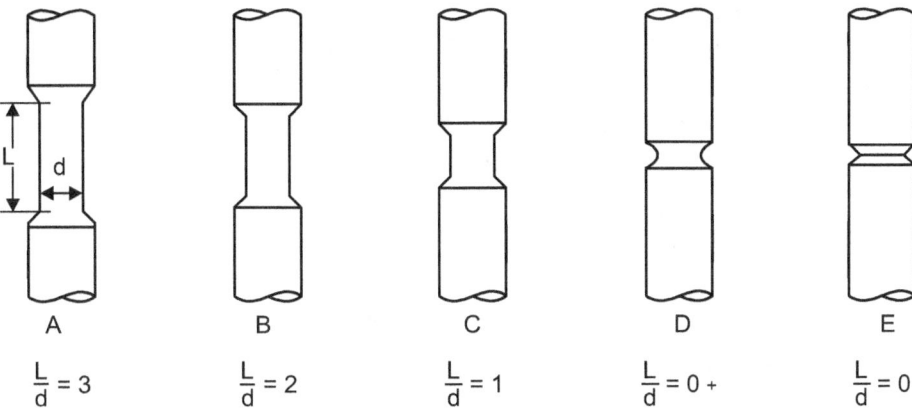

Fig. 3.16: Specimens with varying L/D ratios

If the diameter is constant and L/d ratio is increased from 0 to 3, the ductility increases. With 3 to 5 values of L/D, the elongation is constant. Then with further increase in L/D, the elongation decreases (Fig. 3.17).

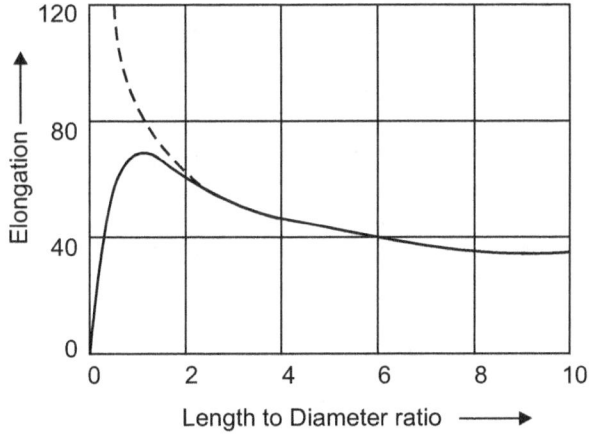

Fig. 3.17: Effect of gauge length (L) to diameter (D) ratio on elongation

• During tension test, the eccentric loading should be avoided.

   Explanation: Eccentric loading is produced due to faulty gripping devices and wrong procedure. This results in reduced proportional limit because of non-uniform stress distribution in the specimen (particularly in brittle metals). Due to this, certain part of the specimen reaches to proportional limit than does the other. This affects the elastic properties and results in wrong readings.

• With increase in rate of loading, the strength tends to increase and ductility tends to decrease.

SOLVED EXAMPLES

Example 3.1: A mild steel bar is subjected to tensile test. The gauge length was 80 mm, initial diameter was 12 mm. The load at yield point was 3750 kg, the maximum load observed 5500 kg and the breaking load was 3900 kg.

The final length at breaking point was 100 mm.

The diameter of sample was 8 mm at the fracture surface.

Calculate the following

(i)   Yield stress, UTS and breaking stress in mega pascals.

(ii) Ductility and percentage reduction in area.

Solution: L_o = 80 mm, d_o = 12 mm

$$A_o = \frac{\pi}{4} \times d_o^2 = 113.14 \text{ mm}^2 = 113.14 \times 10^{-6} \text{ m}^2$$

Now, load at,

$$\text{Y.P.} = 3750 \times 9.81 = 36{,}788 \text{ N}$$

$$\text{UTS} = 5500 \times 9.81 = 53{,}955 \text{ N}$$

$$\text{Breaking} = 3900 \times 9.81 = 38{,}259 \text{ N}$$

Hence,

$$\sigma_{\text{yield}} = \frac{36788}{113.14 \times 10^{-6}} = \textbf{325.15 MPa}$$

$$\sigma_{\text{UTS}} = \frac{53955}{113.14 \times 10^{-6}} = \textbf{476.89 Mpa}$$

$$\sigma_{\text{breaking}} = \frac{38259}{113.14 \times 10^{-6}} = \textbf{338.16 Mpa}$$

$$\text{Ductility} = \% \text{ elongation}$$

$$= \frac{\text{Change in length}}{\text{Original length}} \times 100$$

$$= \frac{100 - 80}{80} \times 100 = 25\%$$

$$\text{Reduction \% in area} = \frac{A_o - A_f}{A_o} \times 100$$

$$= \frac{113.14 - 50.28}{113.14} \times 100$$

$$= 0.556 \times 100$$

$$= \textbf{55.6\%}$$

Example 3.2: A tensile specimen of aluminum alloy rod having 5 cm length and 1.5 cm diameter is subjected to maximum load of 37,000 N. If diameter at fracture was 1.2 cm, calculate the following (i) Tensile strength (ii) True stress (iii) True strain

Solution: Given that l_o = 5 cm

d_o = 1.5 cm, d_f = 1.2 cm and P_{max} = 37,000 N

$$\text{Tensile strength} = \frac{P_m}{A_o} \qquad\qquad [A_o = \text{original C.S.A}]$$

$$= \frac{37000}{\frac{\pi}{4} d_0^2} = \frac{37000}{\frac{\pi}{4}(1.5)^2}$$

$$= \mathbf{209 \ MPa}$$

If volume remains constant than

$$V = A_o\, l_o = A_f\, l_f$$

(A_f = final area at fracture and l_f = final length)

So,

$$\frac{A_o}{A_f} = \frac{l_f}{l_o}$$

$$\frac{\frac{\pi}{4} d_0^2}{\frac{\pi}{4} d_f^2} = \frac{l_f}{5}$$

$$\frac{(1.5)^2}{(1.2)^2} = \frac{l_f}{5}$$

$$l_f = 7.8 \ cm$$

Now engineering strain $e = \dfrac{l_f - l_o}{l_o}$

So $\qquad\qquad e = \dfrac{7.8 - 5}{5} = 0.56$

We know that True stress = $(1 + e)$ engg. Stress

$$= (1 + 0.56) \times 209$$

[Tensile stress / tensile strength or engg. Stress is 209 MPa]

So   Due stress = **326 MPa**

Now   True strain = $l_n (1 + e) = l_n (1 + 0.56)$

$$= \mathbf{0.44}$$

Example 3.3: Determine true strain at fracture, if % R.C.A is 40. Also calculate the true stress at fracture in terms of Engineering Stress.

Solution: We know that

$$\% \ R.C.A = \frac{A_o - A_f}{A_o} \times 100$$

$$\frac{A_o - A_f}{A_o} \times 100 = 40$$

$$1 - \frac{A_f}{A_o} = 0.4$$

$$\frac{A_f}{A_o} = 0.6$$

Or $$\frac{A_o}{A_f} = 1.66$$

If volume remains constant then

$$A_o \, l_o = A_f \, l_f \, , \ \frac{A_o}{A_f} = \frac{l_f}{l_o} = \mathbf{1.66}$$

Now Engineering Strain $e = \dfrac{l_f - l_o}{l_o} = \dfrac{l_f}{l_o} - 1 = 1.66 - 1 = \mathbf{0.66}$

True strain $= ln \, (1 + e) = ln \, (1 + 0.66) = \mathbf{0.51}$

True stress $= (1 + e) \times$ engg. Stress

$= (1 + 0.66) \times$ engg. Stress

Thus true stress will be **1.66** times the engineering Stress.

3.10 FRACTURES

Following types of fractures are observed at the end of the tension test.

*   Basically, two types of fractures are observed.

    They are: (a) Ductile fractures; (b) Brittle fractures.

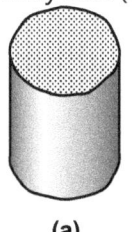 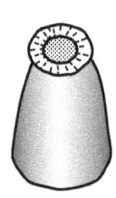 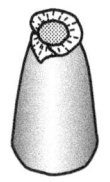 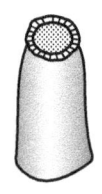  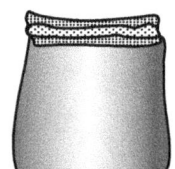

(a)	(b)	(c)	(d)	(e)	(f)
Flat, granular, cleavage	Cup-cone, silky	Partial cup-cone, silky	Star fracture	Irregular, fibrous	Cup-cone, silky (flat specimen)

Fig. 3.18: Typical tensile fractures of metals

*   A ductile fracture [Fig. 3.18 (b)] occurs in the metals showing more plastic deformation. The fracture appears as cup-cone shaped with silky texture. This is a typical fracture of mild steel specimen of cylindrical shape. Fig. 3.18 (a) shows a flat, rough surface and granular type of fracture. It has a little or no plastic deformation. It occurs in metals such as cast iron.

- Fig. 3.18 (e) shows a fibrous irregular fracture. It is a typical fracture of wrought iron. In this metal, slag is present, due to which fibrous fracture occurs.
- Fig. 3.18 (d) shows a star fracture. It occurs in a stressed metal due to cold working or heat treatment. In this fracture, the streaks radiate out from the centre.
- Fig. 3.18 (c) and (f) show a cup cone fracture in a flat specimen and a partial cup-cone fracture respectively.
- Some typical stress-strain curves for various metals, alloys and non-metals are shown in Fig. 3.19.

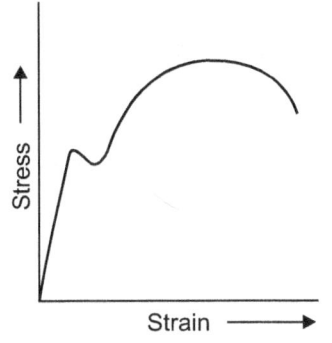

(1) Ductile metal with yield point

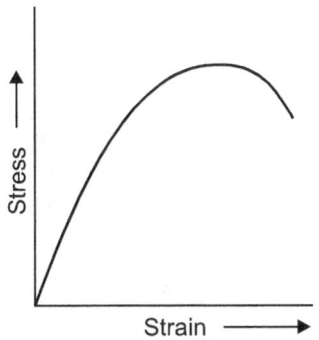

(2) Ductile metal without yield point

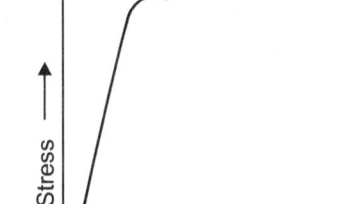

(3) A brittle metal

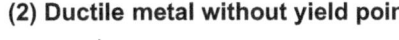

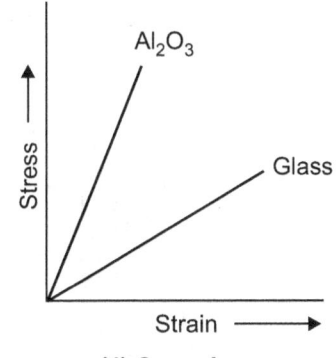

(4) Ceramics

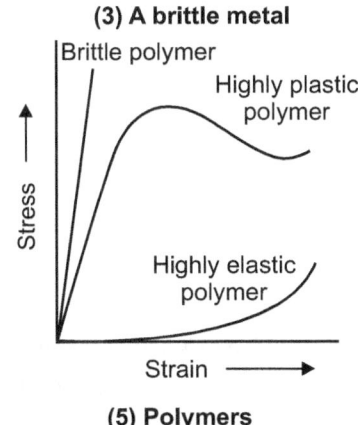

(5) Polymers

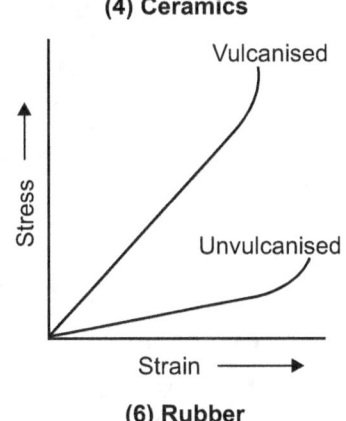

(6) Rubber

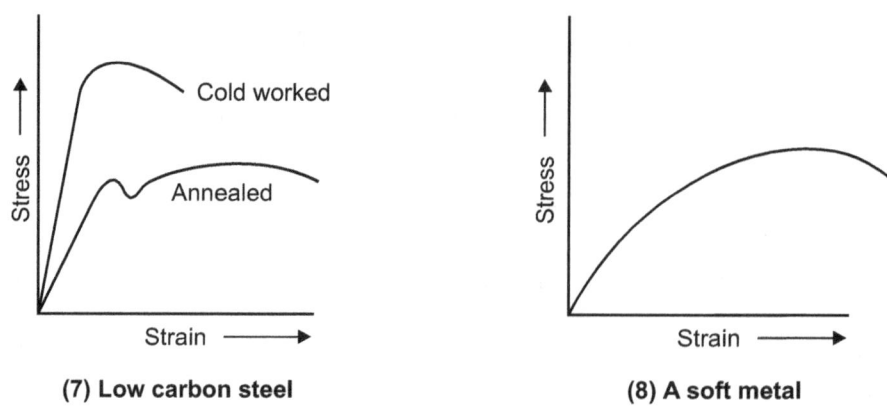

(7) Low carbon steel   (8) A soft metal

Fig. 3.19: Various stress-strain curves

3.11 COMPRESSION TEST   (May 10)

- This test is used for brittle metals as they have higher compressive strength.

- Compression test differs from the tensile test in the direction of loading. In the tensile test, the specimen is pulled apart, while in the compression test, the specimen is compressed (Fig. 3.20).

- During the application of load, in this test, the brittle metal breaks at a particular stress.

- Intermediate deformation is not observed similar to tension test. Therefore, only breaking stress is calculated and reported in terms of compressive strength.

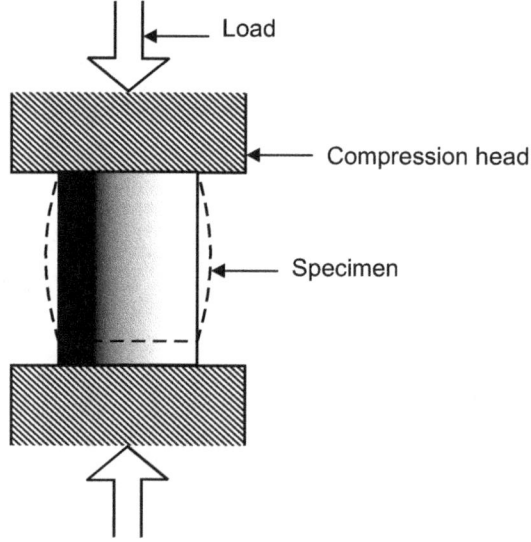

Fig. 3.20: Principle of compression test

Though this Test seems to be Simple, it Shows the Following Limitations

➢ The opposite faces of the specimen, on which the load is to be applied, should be perfectly parallel. Otherwise, an eccentric loading occurs resulting in wrong readings.

➢ The specimens having length equal to twice of its diameter are used. For such small specimens, the strain measurement becomes difficult.

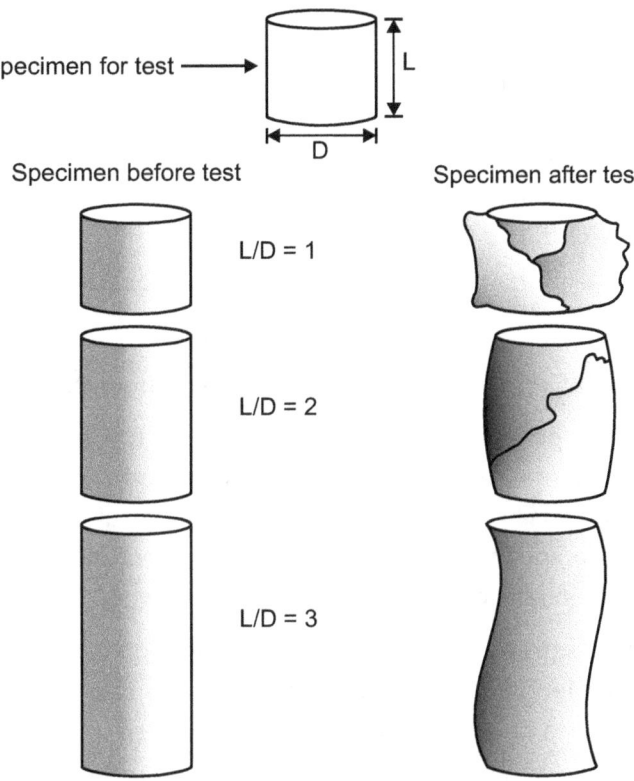

Fig. 3.21: Specimens in compression test

➢ Friction occurs at the contact area between the end surfaces of the specimen and the heads of the testing machine. This results in non-uniform stress distribution.

➢ A heavy testing machine (with higher capacity) cannot be used for a small sample. Similarly, a machine with less capacity may not be used for larger samples.

➢ A careful attention during loading is required for fracture observation. After fracture, loading should be stopped, otherwise the specimen gets crushed.

➢ Different length to diameter ratios of samples and their respective compressive strengths are used for plotting a curve. All samples should be taken from the same metal bar. Any heterogeneity in the sample may result in wrong readings (Fig. 3.21).

3.12 IMPORTANCE OF LENGTH TO DIAMETER RATIO OF SPECIMEN

• Usually, the specimens with circular cross-sections are used. A specimen with proper length and diameter should be selected (Fig. 3.22).

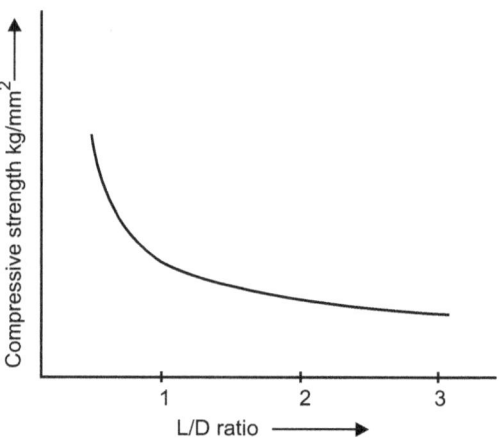

Fig. 3.22: Effect of L/D ratio on compressive strength of a metal

• As the length of the specimen increases, its tendency towards bending also increases. Also, as the length decreases, the friction between end surface of the specimen and heads of machine affects the stress distribution. This results in more expansion of the central portion of the specimen making it barrel shaped. In this case, more strength is observed and specimen fails by crushing.

• The lower limit for length to diameter ratio is 1.5 with upper limit 10, gives satisfactory results. However, the length to diameter ratio equal to two is preferred in most of the tests. With this sample, a perfect shear fracture is observed.

• These cases are shown in Fig. 3.22. The effect of L/D ratio on compressive strength is shown in Fig. 3.22. This indicates that lower L/D ratio shows higher compressive strength. It decreases with increasing L/D ratio and then remains constant.

Apparatus and Procedure

• Usually, the machine used for tension test can be used for compression test. The sample with flat and parallel opposite faces with proper L/D ratio is selected.

• A compressive load is applied. The load at fracture is observed and reported in terms of compressive strength.

$$\text{Compressive strength} = \frac{\text{Stress at failure}}{\text{Original cross-sectional area}}$$

3.13 FRACTURES IN COMPRESSION TEST

• If a ductile metal is tested for compression, it bulges at the centre making specimen barrel shaped. This occurs due to large plastic deformation of a ductile metal. Metals with comparatively low ductility and high hardness develop surface cracks. Brittle metals fail along a plane diagonal with the base plane. (Fig. 3.23).

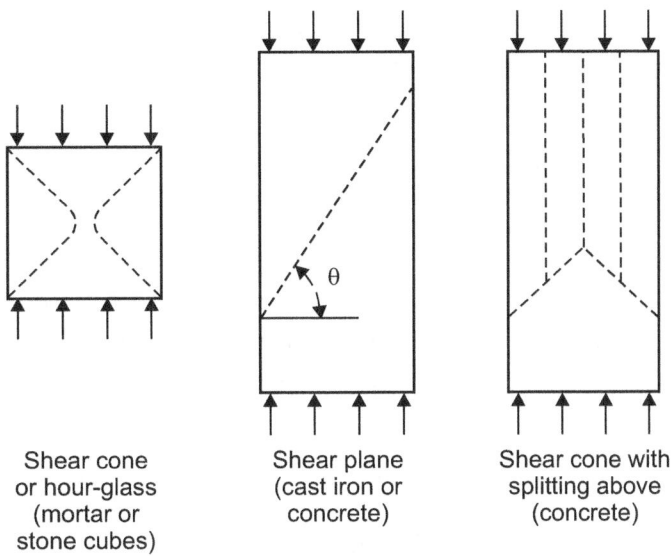

Fig. 3.23: Fractures in compression test

- Such metals also fail with a shear cone shaped fracture (called as hour glass fracture). Materials such as cast iron and concrete fails by a shear plane while stone fails by shear cone fracture. Specimens with higher L/D ratio do not fracture. They show buckling or bending. Too short specimens get crushed.

3.14 SHEAR TEST

- In a shear test, force tends to cause two parts of the same body to slide relative to each other in a direction parallel to their plane of contact. A shearing stress acts parallel to this plane, while tensile and compressive stresses act normal to the plane. Fig. 3.24 shows a shear stress and shearing strain.

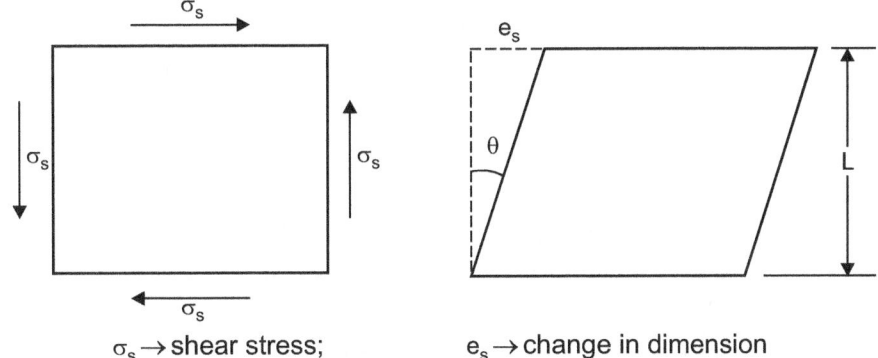

$\sigma_s \rightarrow$ shear stress; $e_s \rightarrow$ change in dimension

Fig. 3.24: Deformation during application of shear forces

- Shearing strain is the tangent of the angular distortion. It is expressed as,

$$\epsilon_s = \frac{e_s}{L}$$

- Usually, a direct shear or transverse shear test is carried out. In this test, a prism of the material is clamped and shearing load is applied. In this method, the stress required to shearing resistance is evaluated.

- This test is used in applications such as rivets, crankpins, wooden blocks etc. This test is not useful for the determination of elastic strength of a metal as the strain measurement is difficult.

- A punching shear test is applicable mostly for metals. The specimen is in the form of a plate. When a metal plate is punched, the punched area is removed by a slicing motion. The greater the clearance between the punch and the die, greater stresses are observed for shear.

  Fig. 3.25 (A) shows shear tests.

- A shear fracture differs from tension or compression fracture as it does not show localized elongation.

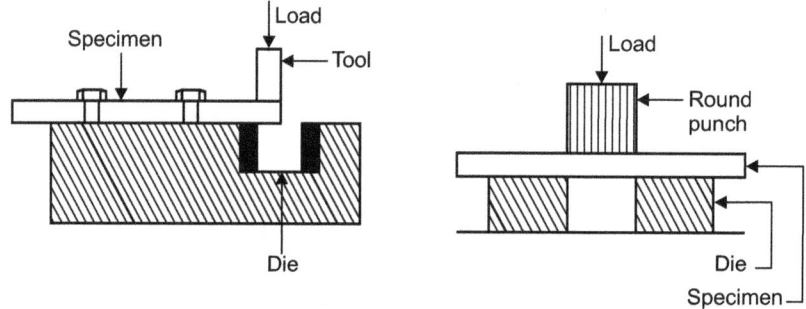

Fig. 3.25 (A): Shear test

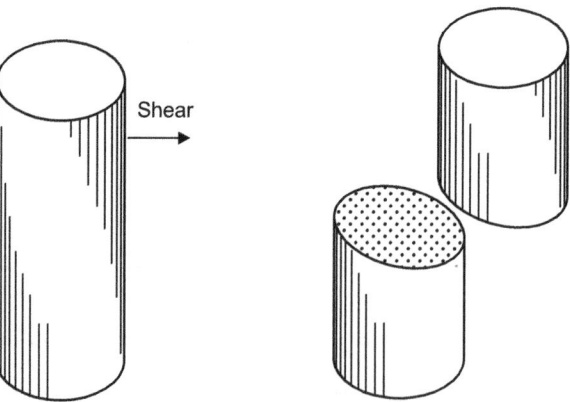

(a) Specimen before fracture (b) Specimen after fracture

Fig. 3.25 (B)

3.15 TORSION TEST

- Torsion is defined as a twisting action resulting in shear stresses and strains.
- In torsion, the applied forces are parallel and opposite, but do not lie in a plane of the longitudinal axis of the specimen. This results in a couple that produces a twist about longitudinal axis (Fig. 3.26).
- These torsional effects are termed as torque. Torsion is observed in rotating objects like shafts.

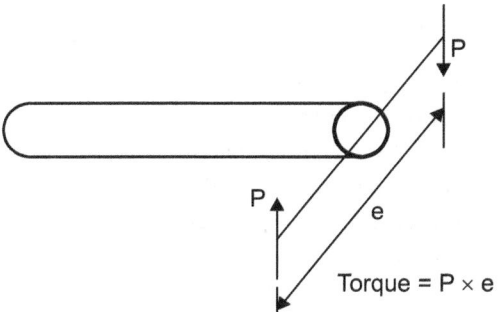

Fig. 3.26: Principle of torsion

- For torsion test, solid or hollow specimens of circular cross-section are used. A strainometer (called as troptometer) is used for strain measurement. It is useful to evaluate proportional limit, yield strength in shear, shearing resilience and stiffness. The strainometer is attached to a specimen having a suitable length. The specimen is carefully gripped in two twisting heads with proper centering.

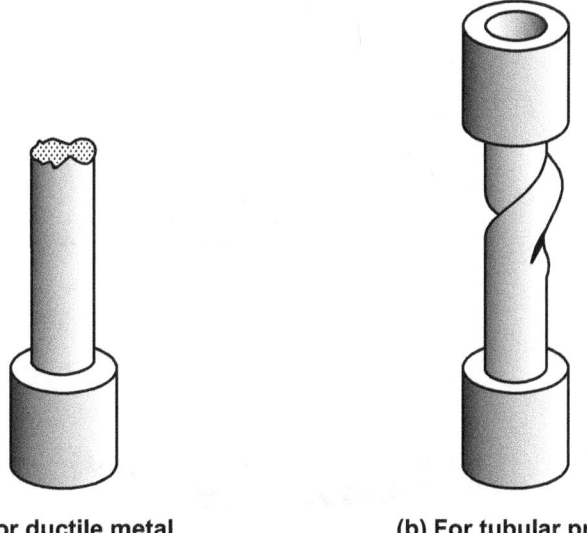

| (a) For ductile metal | (b) For tubular product |

Fig. 3.27: Torsion fractures

- One twisting head is attached to a power unit for rotation, while the other to a torque measuring system. A torque strain recorder is also used.

- The ductility of the specimen is determined from the amount of twist upto failure. Toughness is represented by the amount of twist.
- The stiffness is obtained from the angle of twist and the applied torque.
- Torsion test cannot be used to obtain the shearing strength of brittle material such as gray cast iron, because a brittle material fails in diagonal tension before the shearing strength value is reached.
- The torsional fractures for ductile metals are usually silky and slightly rough due to rubbing action. Brass or bronze specimen brakes into fibres like a rope. Tubular sections usually fail by buckling (Fig. 3.27).

3.16 BEND TEST

- This is also called as a **formability test**. It is used to determine the ductility of a metal. In bending, the applied forces induce compressive stresses over one part of a cross-section of metal and tensile stresses over the remaining part. Bending action in beams is often referred as flexure. In a cross-section of a beam, the axis along which bending stresses are zero; is termed as the neutral axis.
- Following are the various bend tests used for determining forming properties.

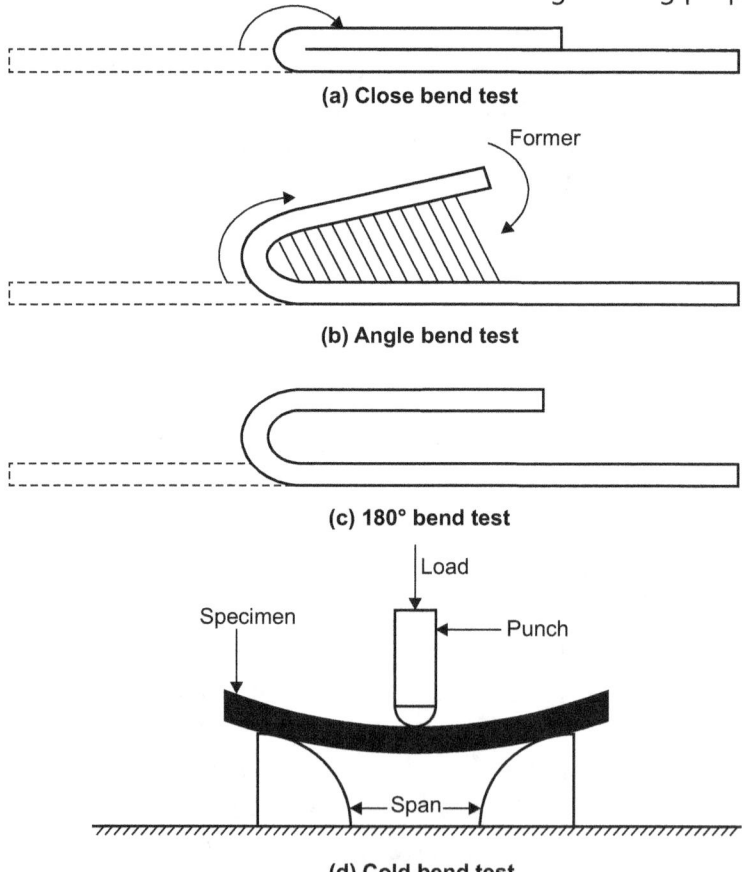

(a) Close bend test

(b) Angle bend test

(c) 180° bend test

(d) Cold bend test
Fig. 3.28: Typical bend tests

➢ **Close Bend Test:** In this test, a part of the specimen is bent over the remaining part and flattened [Fig. 3.28 (a)]. The specimen should not show spring back. If the specimen can bend complete without cracking, it is said to be acceptable.

➢ **Angle Bend Test:** In this test, a former with a standard nose angle and radius is used. The specimen is bent over this former. Here also, the specimen should not show spring back. This test is modified and called as defined angle bend test. In this test, the specimen is bent over a former of 180° bending radius [Fig. 3.28 (b) and (c)].

➢ **Reverse Bend Test:** In this test, the specimen is bent round a former of the nose angle 90° or 180°. The test is repeated for a number of times till the crack is observed. This test is used for very ductile metals.

➢ **Cold Bend Test:** In this test, the specimen is supported at two points and load is applied at the centre. The diameter of the punch, used for load application, is decided as per the thickness and width of the specimen as well as the distance between the two supporting points [Fig. 3.28 (d)].

3.17 ERICHSON CUPPING TEST

• It is already discussed in the tension test section, that per cent elongation is a measure of ductility. However, ductility can also be expressed by 'Erichson cupping test'. This test is widely used to measure the ability of a sheet metal for deep drawing. This is one of the important processes used in press-shop. In this test, a sheet sample is deep drawn and its depth is measured.

• Erichson cupping test machine (Fig. 3.29) consists of
   ➢ Spherically ended punch,
   ➢ Die,
   ➢ Micrometer dial and
   ➢ Mirror for cup observation.

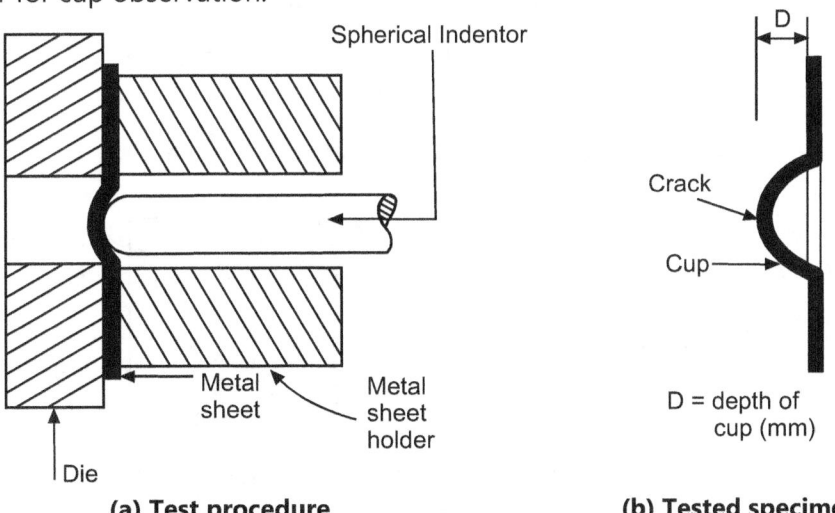

(a) Test procedure   (b) Tested specimen

Fig. 3.29: Principle of Erichson cupping test

The procedure of this test is very simple. The specimen in this test is in a sheet form (0.2 to 2 mm thick). It is a circular or square blank. It is gripped between the pressure ring and die. The spherically ended punch is then pressed manually into the sample blank. The sample gets deep drawn into the die. The pressing of the punch is then continued till the crack is observed on the drawn cup. The depth of the cup is measured on a micrometer dial. This is the measure of drawing ability of the sample.

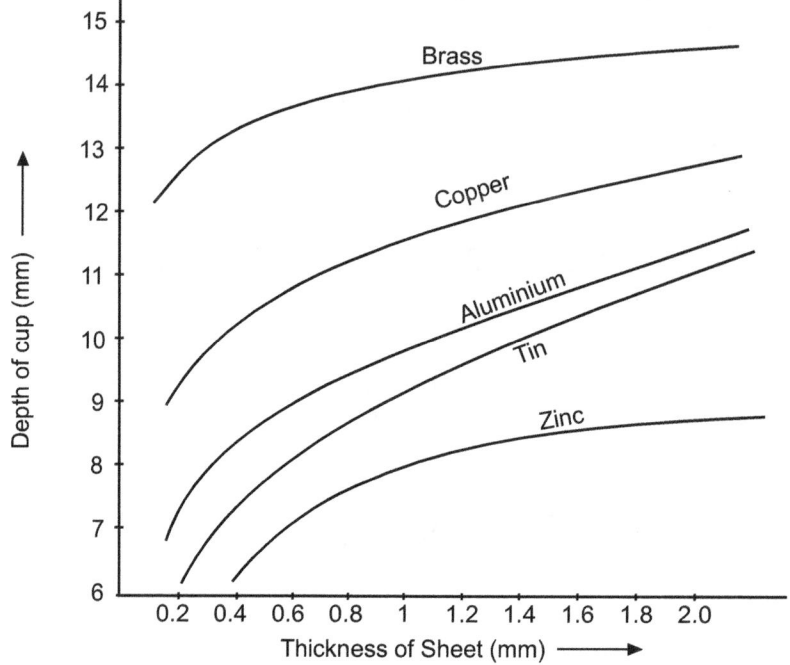

Fig. 3.30: Erichson standard chart

Erichson standard curves shows (Fig. 3.30) typical values of depth of cup expected for various thicknesses of metals.

Two types of cracks (Fig. 3.31) are observed: (1) Radial and (2) Circular.

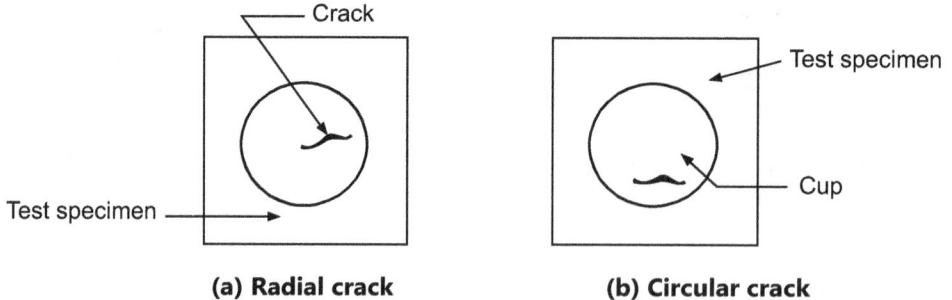

(a) Radial crack   **(b) Circular crack**

Fig. 3.31: Types of cracks observed in cupping test

The metal, which fails with radial crack, is said to have poor drawing ability.

When the radial crack is parallel to the rolling direction, it indicates that sheet metal shows poor formability. The most probable reason for this may be the anisotropy developed during the rolling operation.

Table 3.1: Some of the Typical Values of Cup Depth, Nature of Crack and Remark

Metal	Thickness (mm)	Cup Depth (mm)	Nature of Crack	Remark
Brass	0.49	7.65	Circular	Good
Copper	0.91	6.2	Radial	Not Good
Aluminium	1.41	8.5	Circular	Good
Mild steel	0.49	7.65	Circular	Good

3.18 HARDNESS TEST   (May 10)

Broadly speaking, the hardness of a metal is defined as its resistance to plastic deformation, mostly by indentation. Hardness is not a fundamental property of a metal as it gets easily changed by various heat treatments and cold working. Hardness is defined in a number of ways.

Elastic Hardness: It is defined as the amount of energy absorbed under impact loads. It is also called as rebound hardness.

Indentation Hardness: It is defined as the resistance offered by a metal to permanent indentation during application of static (gradual) or dynamic (impact) loads.

Scratch Hardness: It is defined as the resistance of a metal to scratching.

Machining Hardness: It is defined as the resistance of a metal to various machining operations such as cutting, drilling etc.

Wear or Abrasion Hardness: It is defined as the resistance of a metal to wear or abrasion.

3.19 CLASSIFICATION OF HARDNESS TESTS

There are several hardness tests carried out in the engineering industries. These different hardness tests are classified as follows

- Brinell Hardness Test
- Vicker's Hardness Test
- Rockwel Hardness Test
- Micro-Hardness Test
- Superficial Hardness Test
- Poldi Hardness Test
- Shore Scleroscope Hardness Test
- Durometers
- Moh's Hardness Test.

3.20 BRINELL HARDNESS TEST   (Nov. 16)

Brinell hardness testing machine is a simple hydraulic press. Usually, it is operated manually. In this test, an indentation is made by load applied on a hardened steel ball or a tungsten carbide ball. This is followed by measuring the diameter of indentation. The Brinell hardness number is found by using standard charts or by using the following formula

$$B.H.N. = \frac{Load}{Area\ of\ indentation}$$

$$B.H.N. = \frac{2P}{\pi D\ (D - \sqrt{D^2 - d^2})}$$

where, P = Load applied in kgs,

D = Diameter of indentor in mm,

d = Diameter of indentation in mm,

and B.H.N. = Brinell hardness number.

ASTM has specified following loads for ferrous and non-ferrous metals.

Metals	Ball diameter	Load	Loading time
Ferrous	10 mm	3000 kg	10 sec
Non-ferrous	10 mm	500 kg	30 sec
Very soft metals	10 mm	100 kg	60 sec

The indentation diameter is measured by a graduated microscope called as Brinell microscope. This microscope is mounted on a testing machine or may be used separately.

A large indentation diameter indicates less hardness number (BHN) of that metal.

Specimen Variables

- Very small specimens (such as pins, small watch-gears) or very thin specimen (such as razor blade) cannot be tested by this method, because the indentations may be greater than the thickness of the specimen.

- The thickness of the specimen should be atleast 10 times the depth of the indentation.

- Similarly, during measurement of hardness of case hardened steel, the penetration depth may be more than the case depth.

- So instead of case, the hardness of soft core metal gets measured.

- Extremely hard metals may deform the ball indentor. This increases diameter of indentation and results in lower readings. Hence, this test should not be used for the metals having hardness greater than 600 B.H.N.

- Brinell hardness test is not suitable for measuring hardness of plating. Usually, plating thickness is in microns.

- The depth of indentation is more than the plating thickness. So, instead of plating, the hardness of base metal gets measured.

- The surface of the specimen should be perfectly flat and well polished. It should be free from rust, oil, grease etc. This is because, the indentation is measured by a microscope, which requires a polished surface for better reflection.
- Very soft metals may not be able to achieve a polished surface. In such cases, the indentation clarity can be increased by using a pigment on the ball.
- Soft metals such as aluminium show encircling ridges [Fig. 3.32 (a)], while manganese steel being a hard metal shows encircling depressions [Fig. 3.32 (b)]. Both result in wrong measurement of indentation and hence, the wrong measurement of hardness.

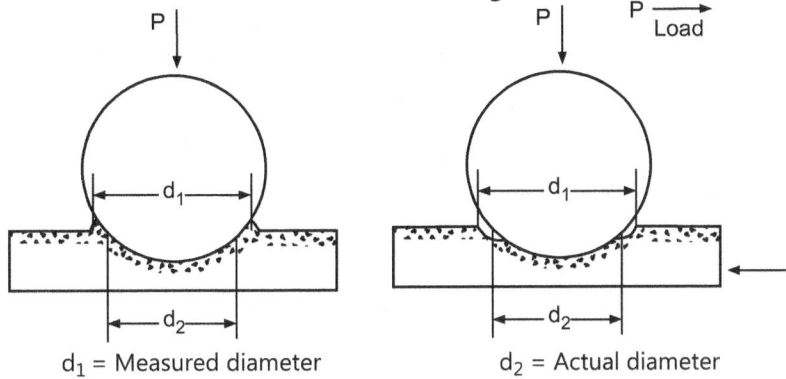

d_1 = Measured diameter　　　d_2 = Actual diameter

(a) Encircling ridge (b) Encircling depression
Fig. 3.32: Indentations in Brinell test

If the indentation is made too close to the edge of specimen, it results in large and unsymmetrical indentation. The lack of sufficient support of metal to resist the indentation creates such a case.

- However, Brinell hardness testing becomes more useful in the case of heterogeneous materials, as the indentation covers a comparatively large surface area of the metal.

Table 3.2 gives the Brinell hardness numbers for the various metals and alloys.

Table 3.2

Metal or Alloy	B.H.N.
Low Carbon Steel	100 - 150
Medium Carbon Steel	200 - 250
High Carbon Steel	275 - 330
Stainless Steel	180 - 250
White Cast Iron	375 - 550
Malleable Cast Iron	135 - 260
Gray Cast Iron	150 - 300
Nodular Cast iron	150 - 300
70: 30 Brass	50 - 70 (with 500 kg load)
Bronze	60 - 100 (with 500 kg load)
Cupronickel	100 - 125 (with 500 kg load)
Duralumin	50 - 70 (with 500 kg load)
Babbit	12 - 30

3.21 NON-STANDARD BRINELL HARDNESS TEST

- The Brinell hardness test carried out by using a steel ball indentor of 10 mm diameter under 3000 kg load is called as a standard test. However, in commercial practice, lower loads with reduced ball diameter can be used. This is called as a non-standard Brinell hardness test. The Brinell hardness testing machine (Fig. 3.33) is having a facility to adopt various ball indentors and various loads. Brinell hardness number is a load dependent. During indentation, the ball does not make a constant angle with the metal surface. As shown in Fig. 3.34 (a), the ball makes a large contact angle with smaller loads resulting in a small impression. This gives less hardness. Similarly, as shown in Fig. 3.34 (b), the ball makes a less contact angle with higher loads resulting in larger impression.

- This gives more hardness for the same metal.

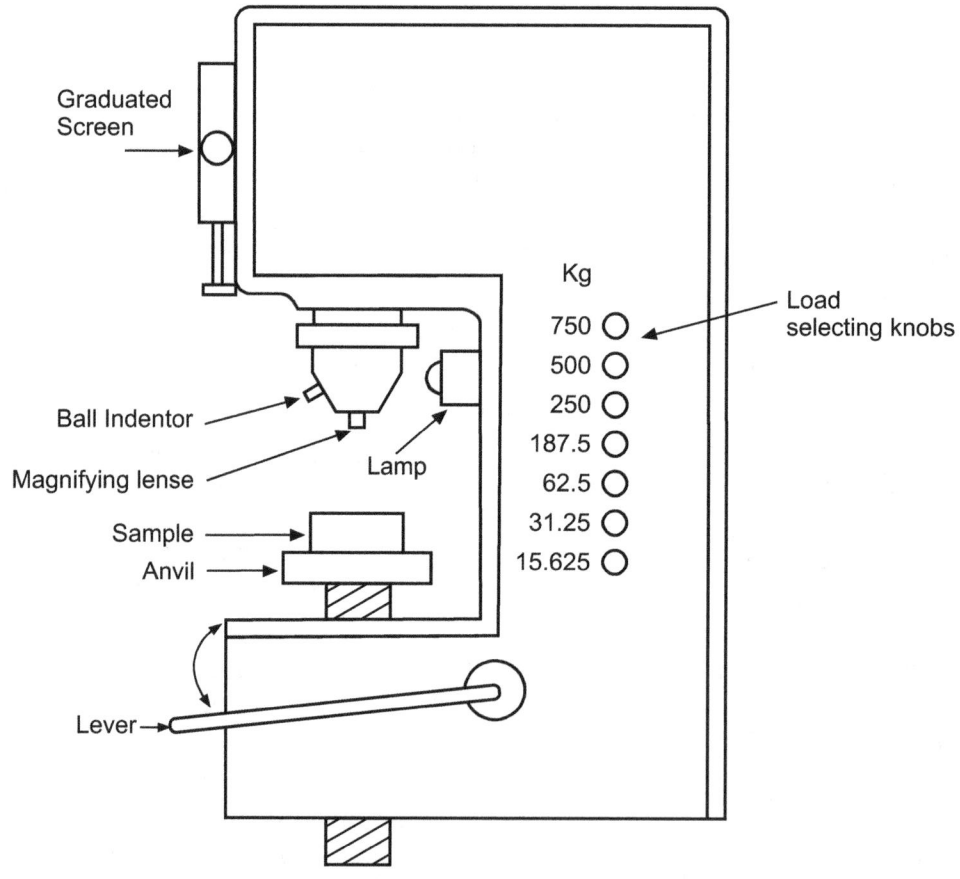

Fig. 3.33: Brinell hardness testing machine

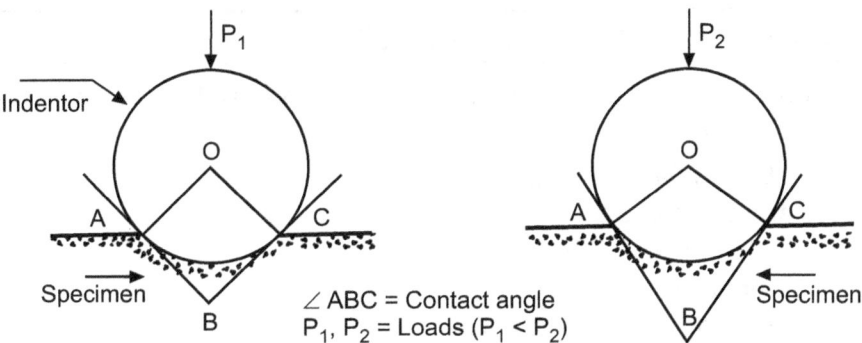

$\angle$ ABC = Contact angle
P_1, P_2 = Loads ($P_1 < P_2$)

(a) Larger contact angle with small load　　(b) Smaller contact angle with large load

Fig. 3.34: Effect of load on indentation in Brinell hardness test

- Moreover, a linear relationship is not observed between the contact angle and indentation diameter. Hence, the Brinell hardness number is said to be load dependent.

As shown in Fig. 3.35, it is observed that $d = D \sin \phi$.

We have,

$$\text{B.H.N.} = \frac{2P}{(\pi D)\,(D - \sqrt{D^2 - d^2})}$$

Substituting　　　　$d = D \sin \phi$ in the above expression

$$\text{B.H.N.} = \frac{2P}{(\pi)\,D^2\,(1 - \cos \phi)}$$

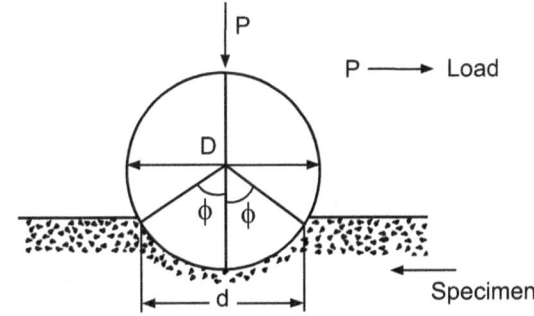

Fig. 3.35: Principle of a non-standard Brinell hardness test

- The same value of B.H.N. as in the standard test, can be obtained by using non-standard load or ball diameter, if the angle 2ϕ is constant. Then, for obtaining the constant value of BHN and angle ϕ, the ratio of load and ball diameter must satisfy the equation

$$\frac{P_1}{D_1^2} = \frac{P_2}{D_2^2} = \frac{P_3}{D_3^2}$$

3.22 B.H.N. AND UTS RELATIONSHIP

A relation exists between B.H.N. and strength of metals. This can be given as follows

- For annealed plain carbon steels

  UTS (MPa) = B.H.N. × 3.55

- For hardened and tempered plain carbon steels

  UTS (MPa) = B.H.N. × 3.20

- For ductile copper alloys

  UTS (MPa) = B.H.N. × 5.5

- For aluminium alloys

  UTS (MPa) = B.H.N. × 4.25

3.23 POLDI HARDNESS TEST   (May 14)

- Poldi hardness test is very similar to Brinell hardness test, but it is more simple to perform. Poldi hardness tester is a small and portable instrument consisting of a ball indentor at the bottom and striking head at the top. The steel ball indentor is of 10 mm diameter. A standard bar is inserted in a slot above the ball. The hardness of the standard bar is known and is usually engraved on it. The tester with standard bar is held vertically on the surface of the specimen. A hammer blow is given on the striking head. This results in an impression on the specimen as well as on the standard bar.

  The diameter of both the indentations are measured by using a magnifiscope (Fig. 3.36).

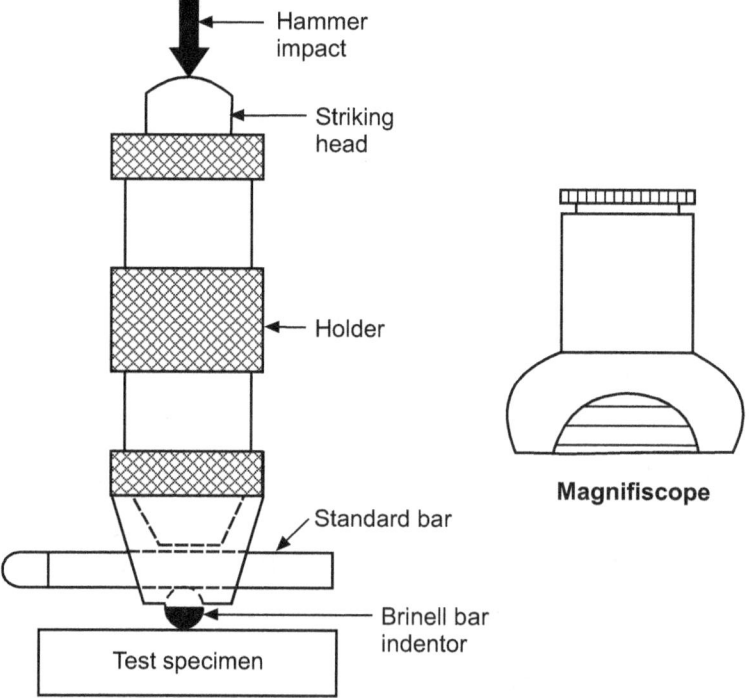

Fig. 3.36: Poldi hardness tester

- The hardness number of the specimen can be found out

  (a) By using standard charts or

  (b) By using the formula obtained by equating the loads. As the load is applied in a single stroke for making an indentation on both standard bar and test specimen,

$$\text{B.H.N.} = \frac{D - \sqrt{D^2 - d_1^2}}{D - \sqrt{D^2 - d_2^2}} \times \text{B.H.N. of standard bar}$$

  where, D = Diameter of a steel ball indentor,

  d_1 = Diameter of the indentation on standard bar

  and d_2 = Diameter of the indentation on specimen.

- The Poldi hardness tester is more advantageous than the Brinell hardness tester; as it is portable and requires less time. A particular load selection is not required; as the hammer blow makes an impression both on the standard bar as well as on the specimen.

- A hammer blow should not be either too heavy or too light. A heavy blow deforms the steel ball, while light hammer blow may produce a very small indentation; which may be difficult to measure. The test may produce faulty results, if the tester is not perpendicular to the surface of the specimen.

- Compared to Brinell hardness test, the results produced in this test are not so accurate. The standard bar gets consumed during use and it may be one of the costly factors to be considered.

- This test is useful, mostly for large sized forgings and castings, which cannot be kept on the anvil of the Brinell hardness test machine.

3.24 VICKER'S HARDNESS TEST   (May 10)

- Similar to Brinell hardness test, the Vicker's hardness test consists of making an impression on the specimen. The hardness number is expressed by measuring the dimensions of the impression and using a ratio of load and area.

- In this test, a square based diamond pyramid indentor is used instead of a ball indentor. The pyramid indentor has an included angle of 136° between the opposite faces (Fig. 3.37). The loads are usually in the range of 1 to 120 kgs.

- During testing, the specimen is placed on the anvil and raised until it is close to the indentor. The load is slowly applied and then released. The anvil is lowered and a microscope is focussed over the impression. In this test, a square impression results. The diagonals of the impression are measured.

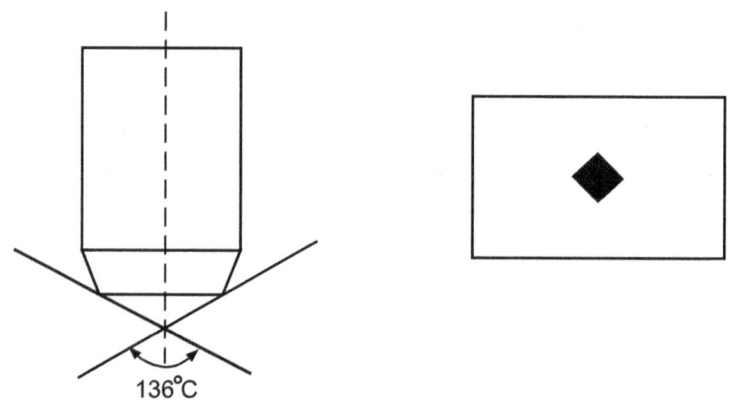

(a) Vicker's pyramid indentor (b) Square indentation on a specimen

Fig. 3.37

- The Vicker's hardness number is expressed as

Vicker's hardness number (VHN) = $\dfrac{\text{Load}}{\text{Area}}$ = $\dfrac{1.8544\ P}{d^2}$

where, d = average diagonal of the square impression.

(VHN is also written as VPN - Vicker's pyramid number or HV-Vicker's hardness). Standard charts are used to convert the measured diagonals to hardness numbers. This test is not load dependent as the angle between opposite faces of the pyramid indentor is constant i.e. 136°. Therefore, increasing load does not change the contact angle as in case of Brinell hardness test.

Advantages

- More accurate readings can be taken from the square impressions than circular impressions.
- The test is suitable for finished components as very small impressions are produced.
- The indentor's life is more.
- This test is suitable even for very thin specimens (0.15 mm thick).
- The test can be used for very hard specimens. It gives the hardness as high as 1300 VPN, which is equivalent to 850 BHN. This is because diamond indentor is very hard and does not deform itself during testing.

Limitations

- Heterogeneous materials cannot be tested as the impression is very small.
- Good surface polish is required.
- Very large sized forgings or casting cannot be tested because of the small size of the anvil.
- The Vicker's hardness test is used for the components where more accurate results are required. It is also used for thin case hardened parts (as nitrided surface) plated components and thin tubings.

3.25 ROCKWELL HARDNESS TEST   (Dec. 10, 13)

- This test is similar to Brinell hardness test in which the resistance of metal to indentation is expressed as the hardness. In Rockwell test, the depth of indentation is measured instead of its diameter. The hardness value is expressed directly on the indicator dial.

- Rockwell hardness tester works on the principle of differential depth measurement. The depth of indentation will be more for soft metals and less for hard metals. In other words, the depth of indentation is inversely proportional to the hardness of the metal.

- The specimen surface should be flat. It should be cleaned to remove any dirt, grease, oil or scale from surface. However, similar to Brinell or Vicker's hardness test, a polished surface is not necessary. The specimen should be sufficiently thick. The indentation should not produce any marking on the surface opposite to the test surface. The specimen as thin as 0.25 mm can be used for hardened steels.

- While testing the hardness of a bar, axle, a small test area should be filed and flattened. Otherwise, the curved surface would result in error.

- In Rockwell hardness tester, the loads are applied by systems of weights and lever (Fig. 3.38). Two types of loads are used,

  (a) Minor load of 10 kg.   (b) Major loads as 60 kg, 100 kg or 150 kg.

- The minor load is necessary to break surface film on the specimen as well as to hold the specimen in position. This confirms that the applied major load gives a true indentation on the specimen. The specimen is kept on the anvil and raised to touch the indentor.

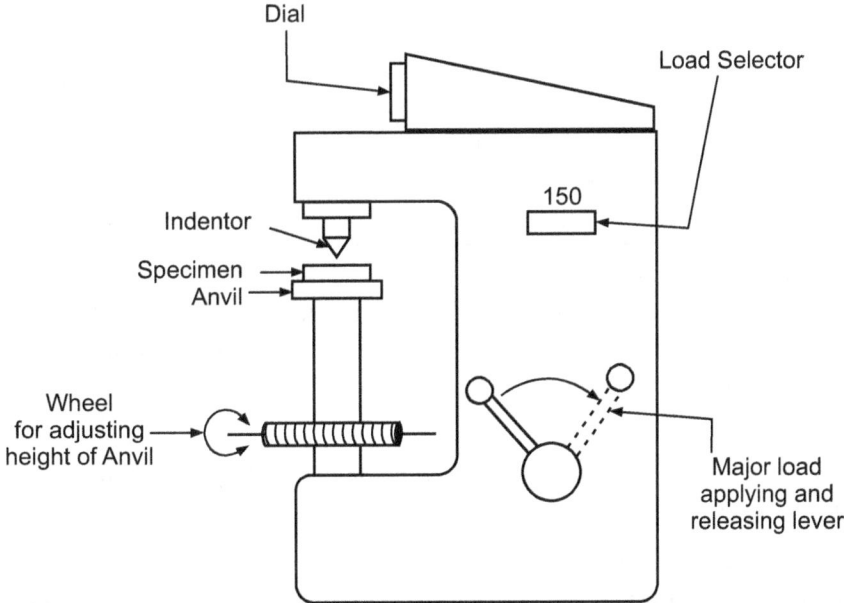

Fig. 3.38: Rockwell hardness testing machine

The Indentors are of Two Types

(a) Steel ball indentors   (b) Diamond cone with rounded tip.

The anvil is raised until the minor load is applied. This is indicated by a pointer on the dial. This is followed by application of appropriate load for sometime and then released. The hardness number is indicated directly on the dial having scales of two colours - black and red. These differ by 30 hardness number. The dial scale is inversely calibrated to the depth of indentation. Three scales as A, B and C are used with combinations of loads and indentors (Table 3.3). Use of these scales avoids the negative hardness numbers on the soft metals.

Table 3.3

Indentor	Major Load, (kg)		
	60	**100**	**150**
Ball	–	B	–
Cone	A	–	C

Other scales such as D, E, F, ... etc. are also used by varying the diameter of ball indentor. These are listed in Table 3.4.

Table 3.4

Scale	Indentor	Major Load	Dial	Use
B	1/16" ball	100	Red	Copper alloys and Annealed steels
C	Cone	150	Black	Hard steels and cast irons
A	Cone	60	Black	Case hardened steels
D	Cone	100	Black	Thin and less hard steels
E	1/8" ball	100	Red	Cast iron and bearing metals
F	1/16" ball	60	Red	Soft copper alloys
G	1/16" ball	150	Red	Bronzes
H	1/8" ball	60	Red	Aluminium, zinc

Other scales as K, L, M etc. are used for plastics.

The hardness number is expressed as RC 30. It means that the metal has hardness of 30 on C scale. A metal having hardness of say RB 70 is more soft than a metal having hardness of RC 30 as the C scale is recommended for hard metals.

Advantages

- A range of metals from soft to hard can be tested, which are difficult to test in Brinell or Vicker's hardness test.
- A polished surface is not required.
- Calculations are not involved as the hardness is indicated directly on the dial.
- Very thin and case hardened steels can be tested.

Limitations

- The choice of wrong scales and loads may result in faulty readings.
- The steel ball gets deformed, if used for hard metals.
- Test is not useful for some materials such as porous bearings and heterogeneous materials.
- Periodic calibration is necessary.
- Only hardness number is not sufficient. The scale should also be reported with the hardness number.
- Rockwell hardness test is used for finished parts such as bearings, nuts bolts, pins, cutting tools, scissors, electrical contacts, cemented carbide etc.

3.26 ROCKWELL SUPERFICIAL HARDNESS TEST

- This is a special purpose test. This test is used for specimens, which require very small and shallow indentation close to the surface. In this test, very small loads are used (3 kg - 45 kg). This test is used to measure hardness of nitrified steel, razor blade, lightly carburised steel, non-ferrous alloys and steel sheets.

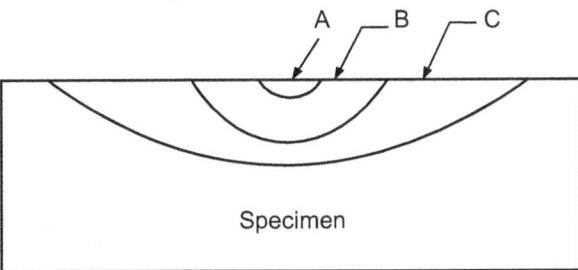

Fig. 3.39: Comparison of indentations obtained in

(A) Rockwell superficial test, (B) Rockwell test, (C) Brinell test

- Fig. 3.39 shows comparison of indentations obtained in Brinell, Rockwell and Rockwell superficial.

3.27 SCLEROSCOPE HARDNESS TEST

- In this test, a dynamic or impact load is used. This test uses the rebound energy for the measurement of hardness. Two types of Scleroscopes are used
  - Direct reading or visual type and
  - Dial recording type.
- In this test, a diamond tipped hammer is used. The hammer is dropped from certain height on the surface of the specimen (Fig. 3.40). When this hammer falls on the specimen surface, a part of its energy is absorbed by the specimen. With the remaining energy, the hammer gets rebounded. This height of rebound is measured. The hammer

makes an impression on the specimen surface. Larger impression is observed on soft metals. This results in lower rebound height.

- Similarly, hard metals show smaller impression resulting more rebound height. Therefore, the height of rebound is directly proportional to the hardness of metal.

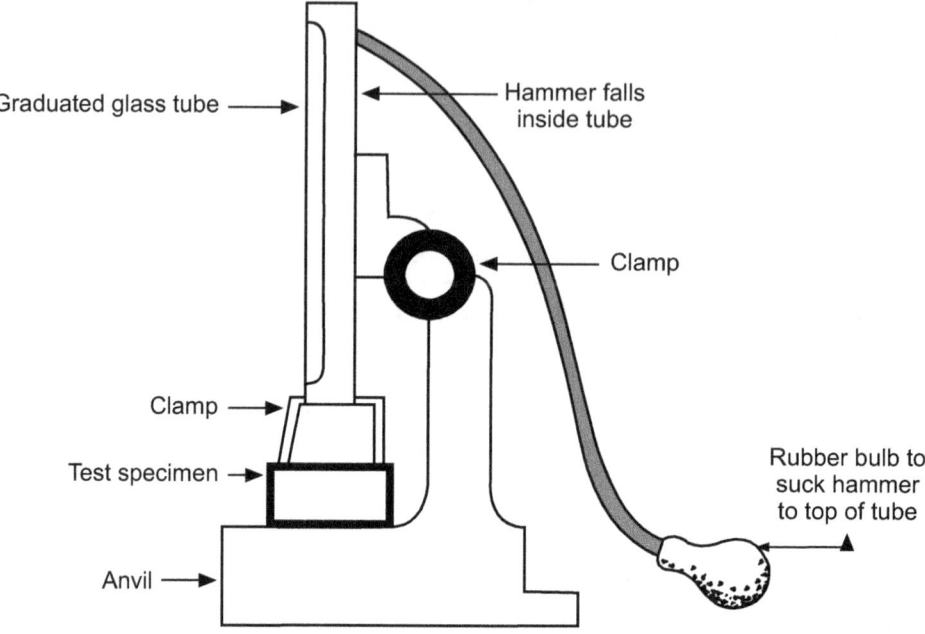

Fig. 3.40: Direct reading type scleroscope

- In a direct-reading or visual type Scleroscope, the height of rebound should be visually noted. In a dial recording instrument, the indicator shows the height of rebound.

- The diamond point of the hammer should be frequently checked as cracking or chipping of the diamond may occur during use. The scale of the scleroscope is divided into 140 divisions.

- A high carbon steel in a hardened condition shows a rebound of 100 divisions.

Advantages

- It is a portable instrument.
- It can be used for finished components as the impressions are very small.
- Hard and thin components can be tested.
- Very fast results are obtained as the calculations are not involved.

Limitations

- The glass tube, through which the hammer falls, should be perfectly vertical to avoid rubbing of the hammer which may give wrong readings.
- The inertial effects of the specimen give faulty readings, if test piece is not clamped on anvil.

- The test may result in strain hardening of the tested surface.

- The diamond point may get cracked in use.

Applications

- This test is used for thin components like razor blades or case hardened parts. This is also suitable for cold rolled ferrous and non-ferrous metal sheets.

3.28 DUROMETERS   (May 14)

- Durometers are different from the usual hardness measuring instruments. They appear like a table clock. Durometers are very small and portable, when compared to the other hardness measuring instruments. They are used mainly for measuring the hardness of rubber and plastics. When the durometer is pressed on a specimen surface, it indicates the hardness number directly (Fig. 3.41).

- It measures the depth of indentation. The load applied on the indentor is inversely proportional to the depth of penetration. The load is maximum for zero penetration, while it is almost zero for maximum penetration. External weights can also be used for application of constant loads. The hardness values are from 0 to 100.

- For a hard material, the zero indentation corresponds to the hardness value of 100. For extremely soft material, the indentation is 3.54 mm corresponding to the hardness value as zero.

- The materials, which produce an indentation greater than 3.54 mm cannot be tested by durometers. So the material thickness should be more than 3 mm.

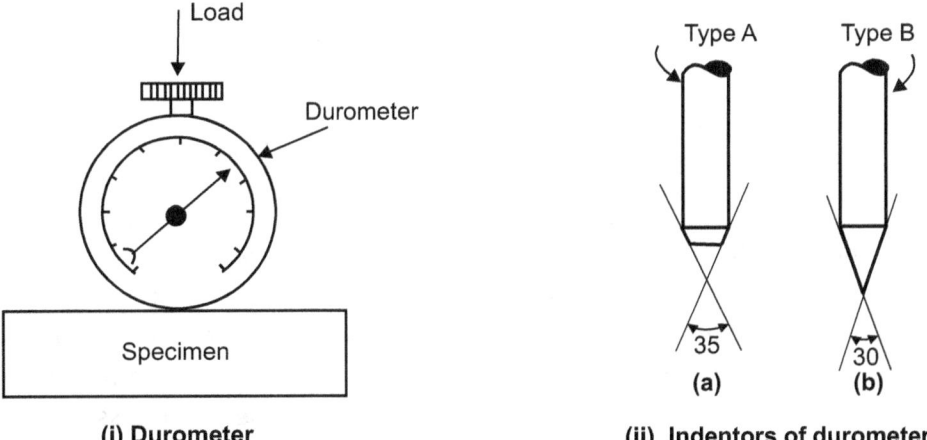

(i) Durometer   (ii) Indentors of durometer

Fig. 3.41: Durometer and indentors

- Two types of Durometers are used in practice.
  (1) A type durometer: For soft rubber and non-rigid plastics.
  (2) D type durometer: For hard rubber and plastics.

- Durometer differs in the sharpness of the point of the conical steel indentor. The type D Durometer is sharp and most heavily loaded indentor.

3.29 MOH'S HARDNESS TEST

- This test is also called as scratch hardness test or mineralogical test.

- This test is based on comparative hardness method and does not give direct readings. The test is based on the principle that a metal gets scratched by a material; which is more hard. The test uses a scale in which 10 minerals are arranged in a typical order. The scale consists of soft mineral at the top having least hardness number, while a hard mineral at the bottom having more hardness number.

- The lowest hardness number is of talc while the highest hardness number is of diamond. Some of the other minerals are intermediate between these two.

- Moh's scale is as follows

Hardness No.	Reference Mineral
1	Talc
2	Gypsum
3	Calcite
4	Fluorite
5	Apatite
6	Feldspar (or Orthoclase)
7	Quartz
8	Topaz
9	Corundum (or sapphire)
10	Diamond

- In this method, the metallic specimen is scratched initially with talc. If talc does not produce any scratch then next mineral is used, e.g. if a steel piece gets scratched by quartz and not by minerals upto feldspar then its hardness number on Moh's scale is 7. This scratch test is very fast and simple. It is applied to check the hardness very roughly. It is also useful to segregate mixed up components as per their hardness values.

3.30 MICRO-HARDNESS TEST   (May 10)

- This test may be referred as a modified form of Vicker's hardness test, which uses small loads. Micro-hardness test is effectively used for very small and thin components. This is because of very small impressions produced by less loads. Test loads are between 1 and 1000 gms. In this test, two types of indentors are used.

They are

> ➤ 136° square-based Vicker's diamond pyramid indentor

> ➤ Elongated knoop diamond indentor.

- The knoop indentor is made of diamond and ground to pyramidal form, so that it produces a diamond shaped indentation. The ratio of the long diagonal to the short is about 7: 1. The knoop indentor has included longitudinal angles of 172° 30' and transverse angles of 130° (Fig. 3.42). The depth of indentation is about 1/30 of its length.

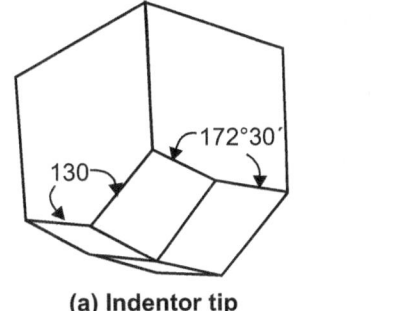

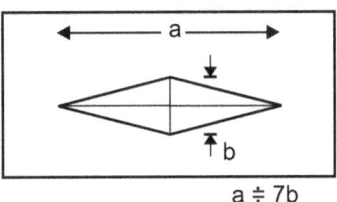

(a) Indentor tip   **(b) Indentation on component**

Fig. 3.42: Micro-hardness test

- If the Vicker's indentor is used, the hardness number is expressed by the following formula

$$\text{V.P.N.} = 1.8544 \times \frac{P}{d^2}$$

where, P = applied load (kg),

        d = diagonal of the impression.

- The Knoop hardness number (HK) is calculated as follows

$$HK = \frac{14.229\ P}{d^2}$$

where, P = load (kg),

        d = length of the long diagonal.

- The Tukon tester with Knoop indentor is a fully automatic machine with attached microscope.

- Micro-hardness test is used for testing the hardness of very small parts like watch gears, wires, springs, tips of cutting tools, micro-structural phases, plated surface, coatings, thin foils, very brittle and fragile materials etc.

3.31 HARDNESS CONVERSION

Various hardness scales can be converted into each other as follows

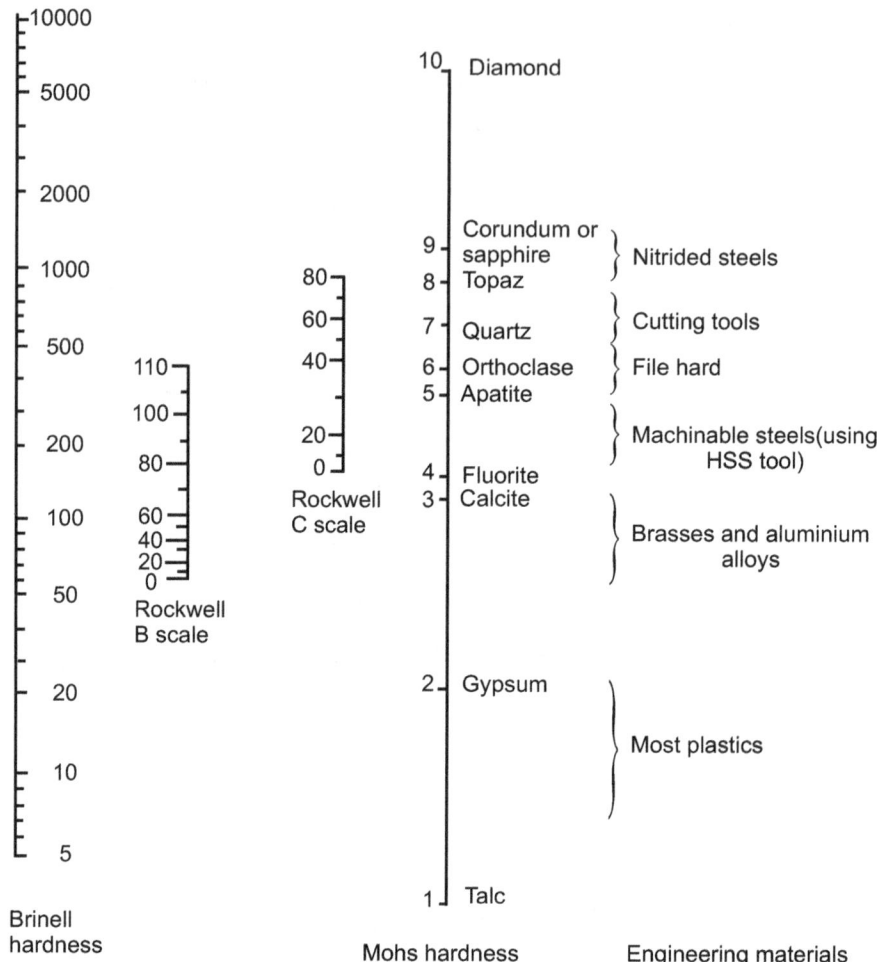

3.32 IMPACT TEST   (May 10, 11, 12,17)

- It is already discussed under heading of tension test that the toughness of a metal can be judged by the area under the stress-strain curve. However, in practice, toughness is an important property for the components working under impact or shock loads such as rails, axles etc. For this purpose, an impact test is used.

- Impact test is also called as dynamic test. In this test (Fig. 3.43), a specially designed specimen is struck and broken by a single blow of a hammer. The energy absorbed in breaking the specimen is measured, which expresses its toughness. Due to the impact or sudden loading, a ductile metal shows a brittle fracture. This occurs due to a triaxial stresses developed at the tip of the defect present in the metal.

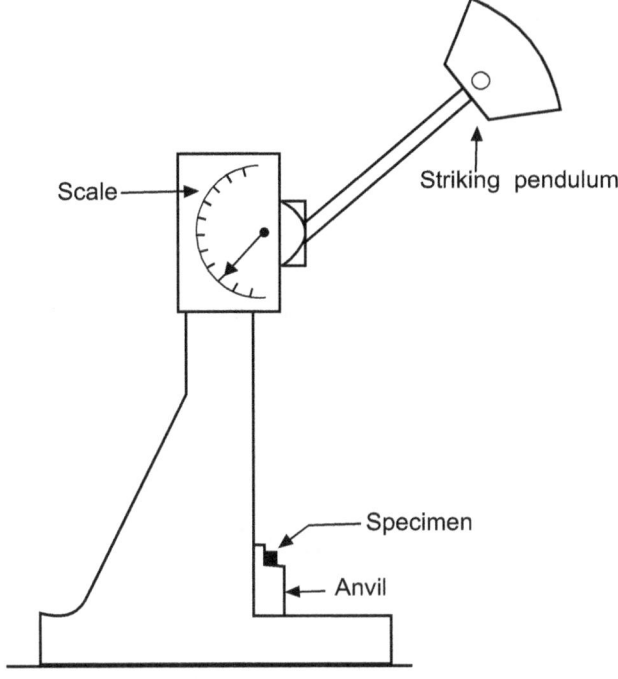

Fig. 3.43: An impact testing machine

Therefore, the specimens used in the impact test are notched.

- A notch gives rise to triaxial stress condition. The tendency of a ductile metal to fail as a brittle metal, when it is notched, is called as 'notch sensitivity'. Cast iron is not a notch sensitive metal like steel. The graphite flakes present in the cast iron gives a notch like effect. This effect cannot be increased by additional effect of the external notch. Therefore, cast iron is not often used, where high shock resistance is required.

3.33 TYPES OF IMPACT TESTS   (May 10, 11, 12)

Two types of impact tests used are

   (a) Charpy impact test

   (b) Izod impact test.

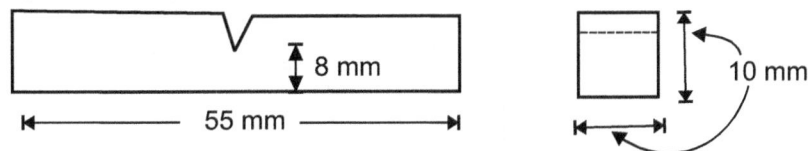

Fig. 3.44: A Charpy specimen with V notch

(a) Charpy Impact Test

- In the Charpy impact test, a standard specimen of the size $10 \times 10 \times 55$ mm (Fig. 3.44) is used. The specimen has a notch at the centre.

Following notches are used

1. U-notch [Fig. 3.45 (a)]

2. Keyhole notch [Fig. 3.45 (b)]

3. V-notch [Fig. 3.45 (c)]

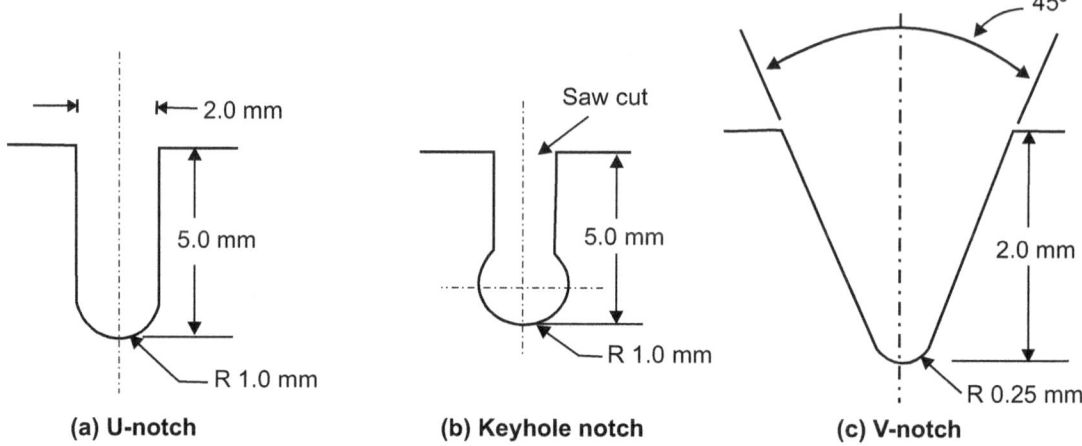

(a) U-notch   **(b) Keyhole notch**   **(c) V-notch**

Fig. 3.45: Standard notches in a Charpy specimen

- Charpy specimen is kept on the anvil as a simply supported beam with a notch on the opposite side of the striking hammer (Fig. 3.46).

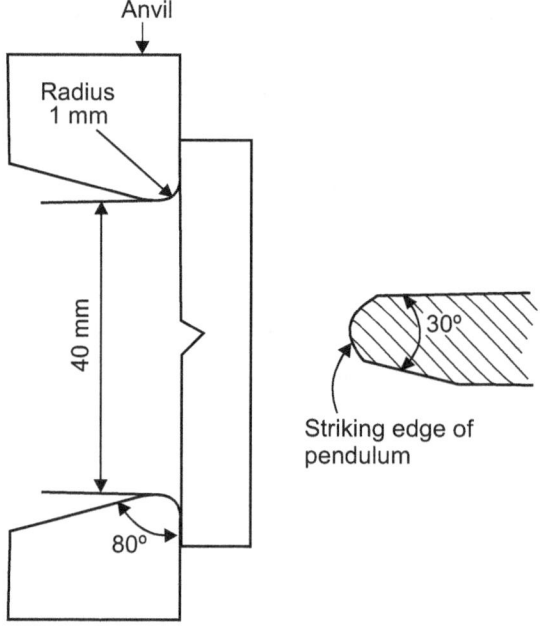

Fig. 3.46: Charpy test

(b) Izod Impact Test

- In Izod impact test, a standard specimen of the size $10 \times 10 \times 75$ mm (Fig. 3.47) is used.

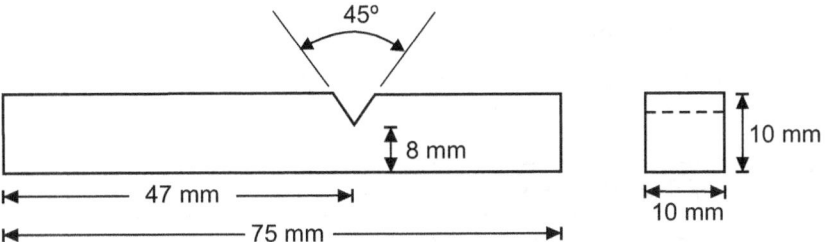

Fig. 3.47: An Izod specimen with V notch

- The specimen has a V notch at 28 mm from one end. It is held vertically in a vice as a vertical cantilever with the notch on the same side of striking hammer.

- A typical impact testing machine consists of a hammer, which is suspended like a pendulum. The dial of one machine usually indicates the energy absorbed in joules (J). The dial indicates zero energy absorption, if maximum overswing of the hammer occurs as the specimen is not placed on the anvil. Similarly, maximum energy absorption is indicated on the dial if the hammer is stopped by the specimen with no overswing. Intermediate values are the impact values of the metals being tested (Fig. 3.48).

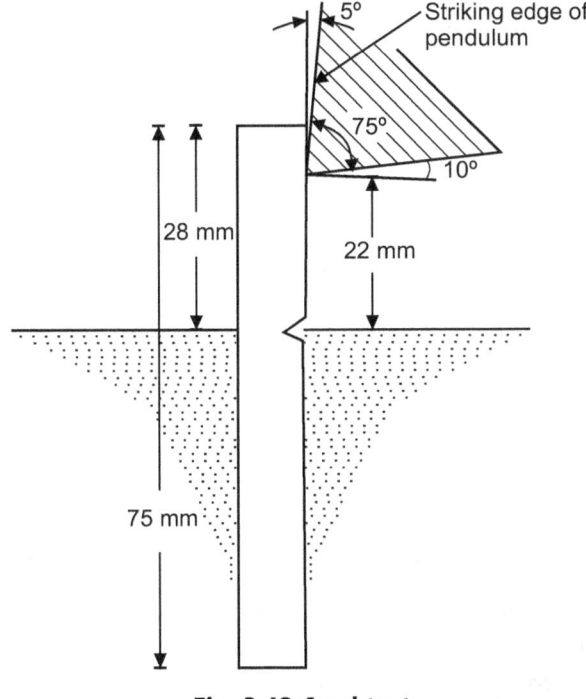

Fig. 3.48: Izod test

- Toughness is also calculated by using the following formula

$$\text{Toughness} = W \quad (h_1 - h_2)$$

$$\text{(kg-m)}$$

where, W = Weight of the pendulum or hammer (kg),

h_1 = Original height of the pendulum (m)

and h_2 = Swing height of the pendulum (m).

3.34 EFFECT OF VARIABLES

Impact test results are affected by following factors

Velocity: This is the velocity of the striking hammer. The velocity of 3 to 5 m/s does not affect the results. Above some critical velocity, impact resistance decreases remarkably. Therefore, practical velocities are usually kept below the critical velocity.

Specimen: The energy absorption of the specimen decreases with decreasing either its width or its thickness. This is due to decrease in the volume of the specimen.

The angle of the notch does not appreciably affect results until it exceeds 60°. However, the sharpness of the notch influences the test results. The energy required to failure, decreases as the sharpness of the notch increases. This is due to increase in the stress concentration.

Temperature: Fig. 3.49 shows the effect of temperature on the energy to failure. Below certain temperature, metals fail as brittle showing less energy to failure.

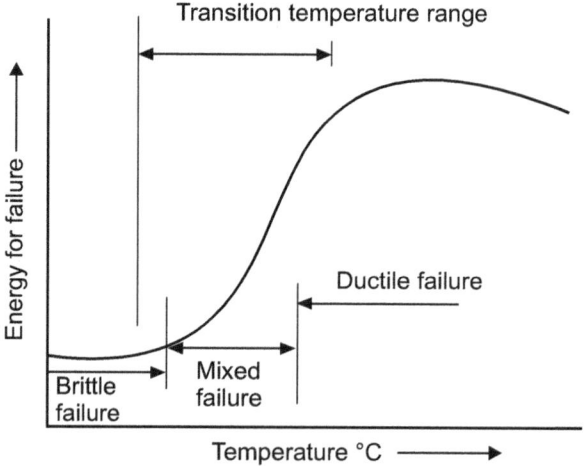

Fig. 3.49: Effect of temperature on energy required to failure in impact test

- Similarly, above certain temperature, a ductile failure is observed, which requires more energy to failure. This intermediate temperature range, where a mixed failure is observed is called as **Transition temperature range**.   **(May 11)**

- Coarse grain size and work hardening tend to raise the transition temperature range. Steels having a fine grained structure show superior impact values at a low temperature.

Impact Fractures

Three main fractures are observed in the impact test.

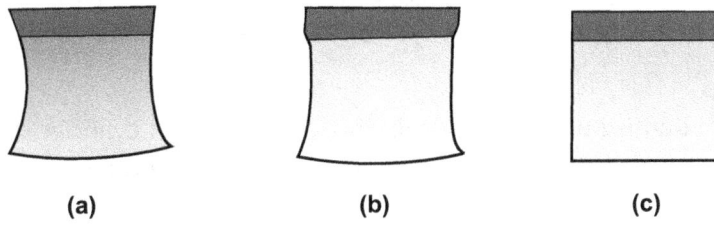

(a)   **(b)**   **(c)**

Fig. 3.50: Impact fractures

- Fig. 3.50 (a) shows a dull gray and fibrous fracture surface. The plastic deformation is indicated by curved edges. The fracture mode is shear.

- Fig. 3.50 (b) shows the fractured surface both-shiny and dull with a little plastic deformation at edges. The fracture mode is mixed-shear and cleavage.

- Fig. 3.50 (c) shows the bright and shiny fractured surface with straight edges. This indicates the absence of plastic deformation. The fracture mode is cleavage.

Table 3.5: Typical Impact Test Values of Metals

Metal	Condition	Charpy (J)
Low carbon steel	Hot rolled	50
Stainless steel	Annealed	200
Medium carbon steel	Hardened and Tempered	60
Cartridge brass	Annealed	88
	Hard	20
Gray cast iron	As Cast	2.5
Aluminium bronze	Annealed	100
	Hard	30

3.35 FATIGUE TEST   (May 11, 12, 14; Dec. 14)

- Some of the structural components are subjected to fluctuating stresses in practice. Usually, this is observed in rotating parts. Though the fluctuating stress is less than the strength of the metal, it may cause the failure of metal. Such failure is often termed as fatigue failure.

- Fatigue failures are the most common type of fractures constituting of about 75 per cent of all fractures.

Fatigue Stresses are Observed in Three Types of Load Cycles.

Reverse Loading: This is observed in a rotating shaft under a bending load. In such cases, tension and compressive stresses act alternately [Fig. 3.51 (a)].

Unidirectional Loading: This is observed in a progressive increasing load from zero to maximum [Fig. 3.51 (b)] and zero. A typical example is of a punch used during powder compaction.

Unidirectional Loading with a Preload: This is observed in cylinder head bolts in which the stress varies from minimum to maximum without reaching zero [Fig. 3.51 (c)].

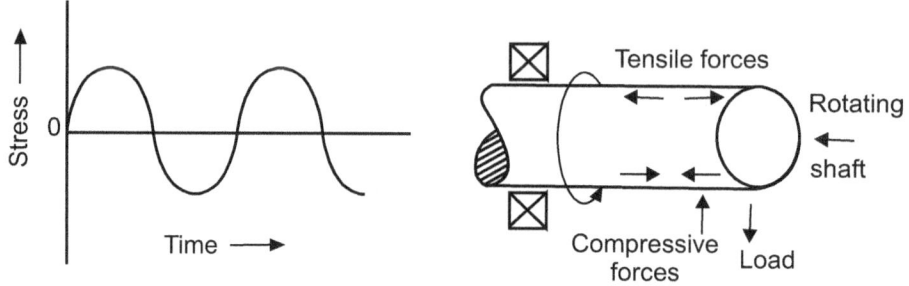

(a) Reverse loading in rotating shaft

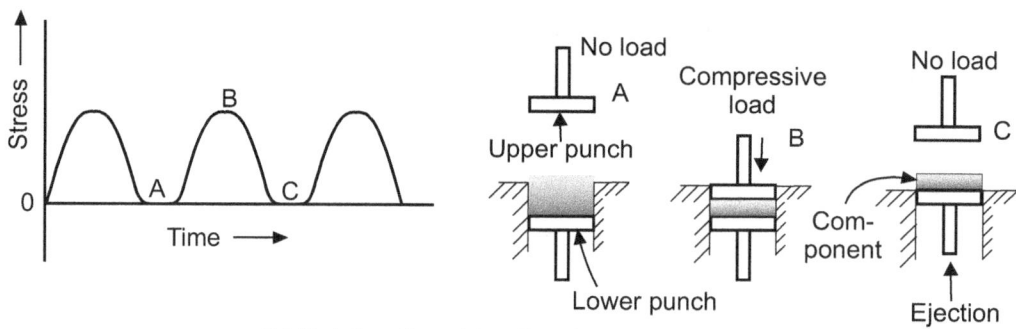

(b) Unidirectional loading in press punch

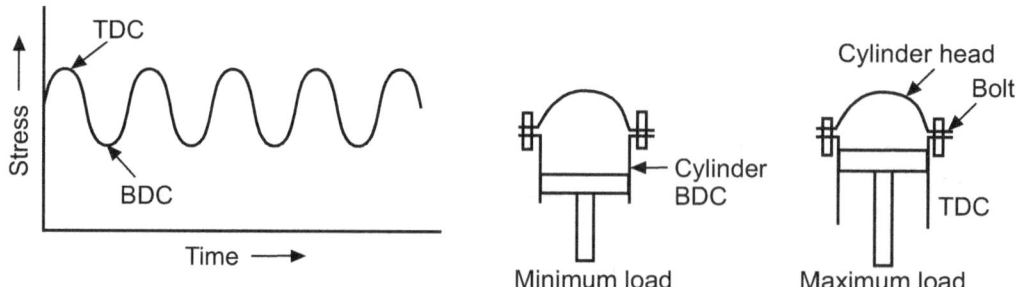

(c) Unidirectional loading with preload in tightened bolts holding cylinder and cylinder head of compressor

Fig. 3.51: Types of loading in Fatigue

Fatigue Strength: It is defined as the **stress value at which a metal fails by fatigue after a certain number of cycles**.

Endurance Limit or Fatigue Limit: It is defined as the **value of limiting stress below which a load may be applied repeatedly for an indefinitely large number of times**.

- The fatigue testing machine consists of a motor for rotating the specimen and a counter to measure the number of load cycles for failure (Fig. 3.52). This is a rotating beam type flexural testing machine. A specimen is held at its ends in special holders and loaded through two bearings equidistant from the centre of the specimen.

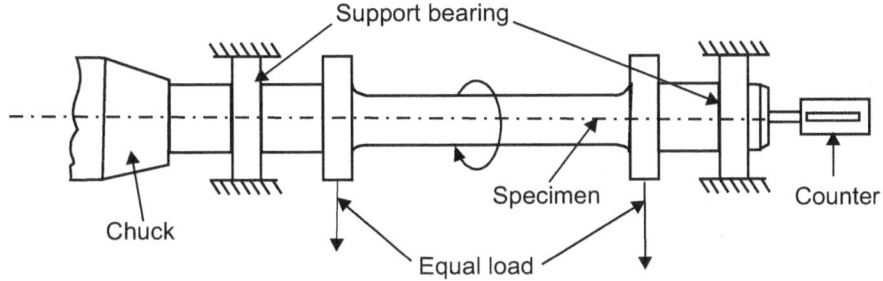

Fig. 3.52: Fatigue testing machine

- Equal loads are applied by means of dead weights on these bearings. The specimen is rotated by a motor. The upper fibres of the rotating specimen are always in compression, while the lower fibres are in tension. Therefore, all fibres undergo alternating tensile and compressive stresses during rotation. The test is carried out till the component fails. The test is repeated for various loads with different test pieces.

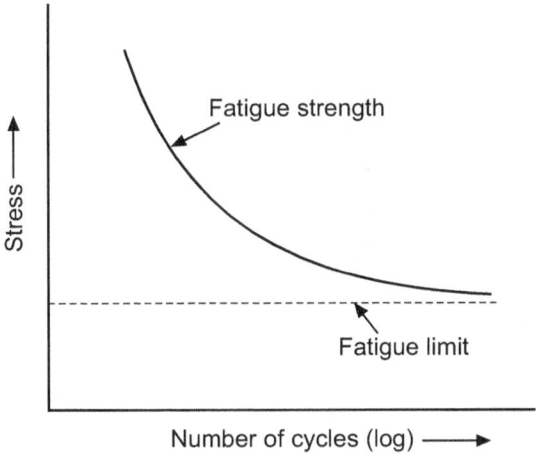

Fig. 3.53: A typical S-N curve

- The results of fatigue tests are expressed in terms of stress and number of cycles required for failure. These are called as S-N curves (Fig. 3.53). In these curves, the number of cycles are expressed in log scale. Typical S - N curves for different metals are shown in Fig. 3.54.

From these curves, it is concluded that

➢ First three curves (i.e. for ferrous metals) show that the metal fails at a higher stress and with less number of cycles. At the low stress, these metals do not fail for indefinite number of cycles. This is because the ferrous metals have a definite fatigue limit.

➢ For non-ferrous metals (curves 4 and 5) as the stress is decreased, the number of cycles for failure goes on increasing. These metals do not have any well defined fatigue limit. Therefore, fatigue strength is reported instead of fatigue limit. This is because of soft and highly ductile nature of many of the non-ferrous metals.

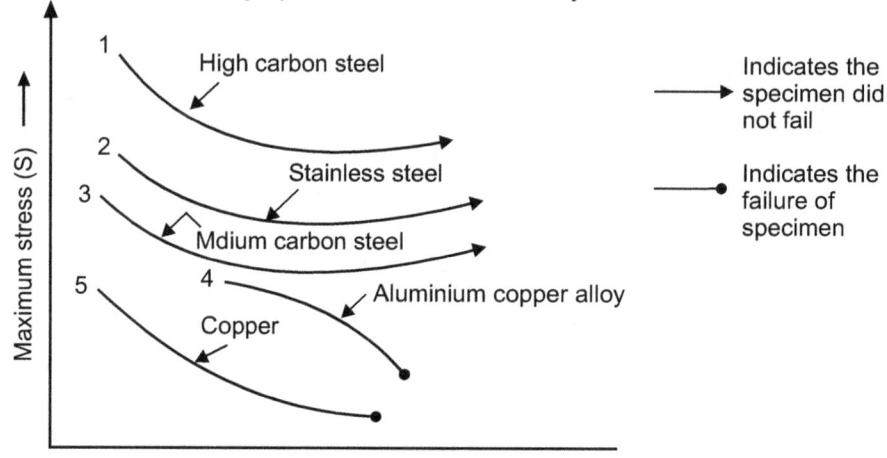

Fig. 3.54: S-N curves for various alloys

3.36 BAUSCHINGER'S EFFECT

• When the plastic deformation of a metal in one direction is followed by the deformation in the opposite direction, then the yield stress gets lowered.

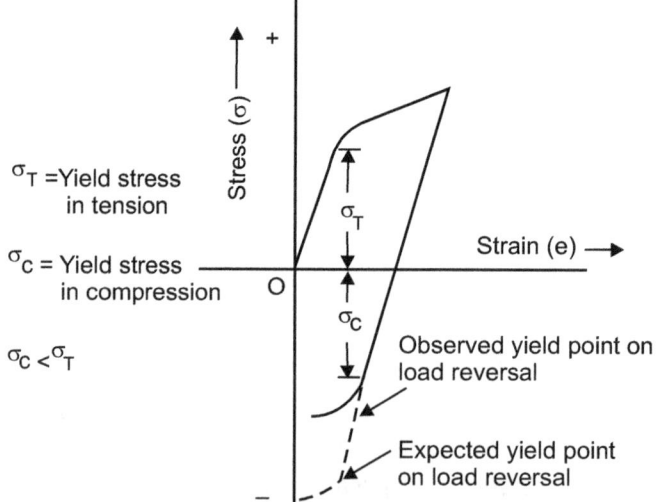

Fig. 3.55: Bauschinger's effect

- This is called as a **'Bauschinger's effect'**. Bauschinger's effect is observed due to residual stresses left in the material during previous plastic deformation.

- For example, the specimen is deformed plastically above the yield stress in one direction (i.e. tension) and then unloaded. This is followed by reloading in the opposite direction (i.e. compression).

- The yield stress for compression is less than the yield stress required previously for tension (Fig. 3.55).

3.37 FATIGUE FRACTURE   (Dec. 13; May 11, 14)

Fatigue fracture starts at any surface defect such as crack or at keyhole or the sharp corner. This is because stress concentration occurs at such areas. The crack is formed by a mechanism of slip and work hardening. Once a crack is formed, it grows. Its rate of growth depends upon

- Stress magnitude,
- Stress gradient,
- Endurance limit of the metal,
- Notch sensitivity,
- Presence of structural defects.

The crack does not propagate further, if the stress is reduced to a value which is required to initiate the crack. If the stress is large enough then the crack grows perpendicular to the direction of maximum tensile stress. As the metal section gradually weakens the crack, growth is faster, finally, leading to the component failure. A typical fatigue fracture is shown in Fig. 3.56.

Fig. 3.56: A typical fatigue fracture

This figure indicates the following points

- Initiation of a crack.
- The rough surface is initially fractured area due to sudden opening of the crack.
- The shiny region shows the rubbing action of the surfaces.
- Variation in cyclic load causes small beach marks to develop on the fracture surface.

- The fracture is transgranular. In such a fracture, the crack moves across the grains and not along the grain boundary (Fig. 3.57).

 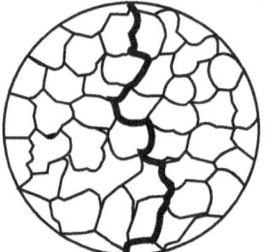

(a) Transgranular fracture   (b) Intergranular fracture

Fig. 3.57: Types of fractures

3.38 EFFECT OF VARIABLES

The fatigue life of a metal is affected by the following factors

- Alloying elements increase the fatigue strength of steel.
- Proper heat-treatment tends to increase the fatigue life of steel.
- Specimens refrigerated before tempering have a higher fatigue limit than unrefrigerated specimens, as refrigeration tends to decrease the amount of retained austenite in the hardened steel.
- Cold working of a ductile metal increases its fatigue limit.
- Rough surface finish reduces the fatigue limit of the metal.
- Abrupt changes in the cross-section of a component reduce its fatigue life. This is because of high stress concentration that occurs at such transition.
- Smaller the range of reversal stress, higher is the fatigue limit.
- Fatigue strength increases with increasing rate of loading.
- Corrosive atmospheres reduce fatigue life (corrosion fatigue).

3.39 METHODS FOR INCREASING FATIGUE LIFE   (May 11; Dec. 12)

Shot-Pinning: In this method, hard steel balls are made to impact on the surface of a component. These shots introduce high compressive residual stresses at the surface due to plastic deformation.

Heat Treatment: Case hardening treatments such as carburising and nitriding improve fatigue limit. Carburising followed by hardening introduces compressive residual stresses at ease because of high carbon martensitic transformation. While alloy nitride formation occurs in nitriding. Due to increase in volume, compressive stresses are introduced in such heat treatments.

Grain Size: Fine grain size of metal, improves fatigue life, because fine grained material is stronger than coarse grained material. Secondly, the tendency of transgranular fracture is less in fine grained material.

Surface Finish: Highly polished surface has better fatigue strength. The polishing reduces stress raising points, such as machining marks, grinding marks etc.

Inclusions: Matrix discontinuties, such as slag inclusions, oxide inclusions and sulphur inclusions reduce fatigue life, if they are present near the surface of the component. Use of killed and clean steel, therefore, increases the fatigue life of the component.

3.40 CREEP TEST   (May 10, 17; Dec. 10, 13)

Creep is a high temperature phenomenon. It is defined as a time dependent strain which occurs under stress at elevated temperature. Due to creep, metals show a very slow and progressive plastic deformation. Most of the metals show creep at a temperature above 40 percent of their melting point (in °K). Metals having low melting point show creep at room temperature. The study of creep is important for metals used at high temperature applications such as heat exchangers, furnace linings, boiler baffles, jet engine burner liners, exhaust systems in gas turbine, manifolds, power plants, steam turbines, nuclear applications etc.

Creep Strength: It is defined as the constant nominal stress that causes a specified amount of deformation in a given time at a constant temperature.

Creep Rupture Strength: This is the highest value of the stress that a metal can sustain for a given time without failure (or rupture).

3.41 PROCEDURE   (Dec. 10)

* Creep test is simply a tensile test performed at high temperature. For creep test, three major equipments are necessary.
* They are: (a) Electric furnace with suitable temperature control; (b) Extensometer and (c) A loading device.

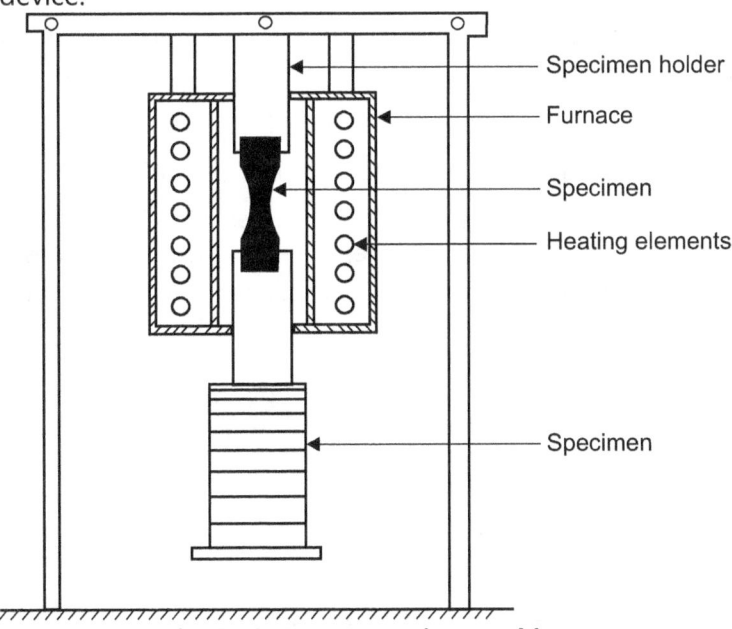

Fig. 3.58: A creep testing machine

Fig. 3.58 shows a typical creep testing machine. The ends of the furnace should be closed to avoid oxidation. The load is applied to a specimen by using direct weights. The total creep or percentage elongation is plotted against time (Fig. 3.59). This curve is called as creep curve. It shows various stages.   **(May 11)**

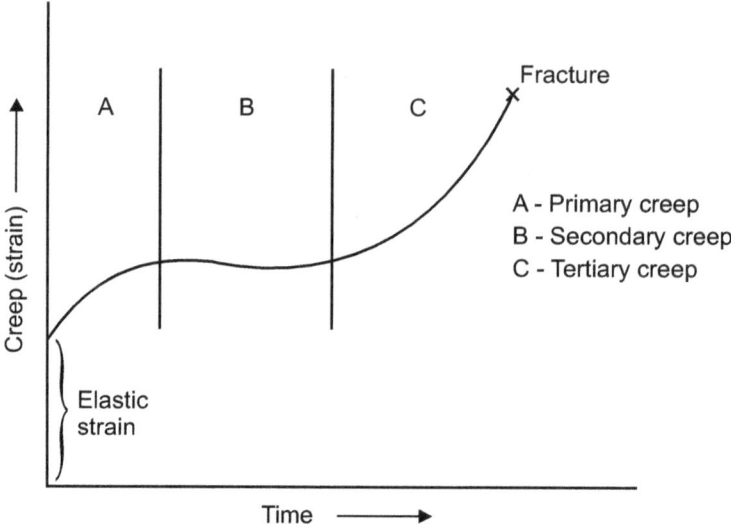

Fig. 3.59: A typical creep curve   **(May 10, 11)**

Elastic Strain Stage: This stage is observed initially. With application of load, an instantaneous elastic elongation occurs. This strain is regardless of the duration of load applied.

Primary Creep: Primary creep curve shows a rapid strain rate initially, but it slows down due to strain hardening. The slip and strain hardening takes place in most favourable oriented grains.

Secondary Creep: In this stage, the deformation continues at a constant rate. During this stage, the rate of work hardening and rate of softening gets balanced. This occurs due to recovery and recrystallization in metal. The creep rate is constant and may decrease at a very slow rate. This results in continuation of the second stage for a very long time.

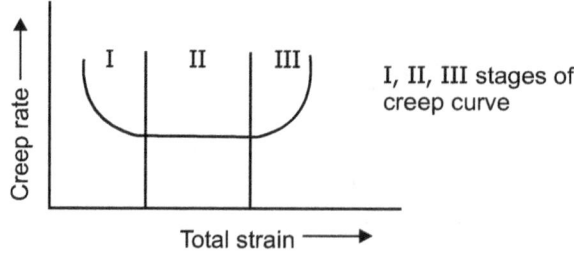

Fig. 3.60: Effect of creep rate on creep curve

Tertiary Creep: This stage occurs, if the stress is sufficiently high. In this stage, the strain rate rapidly increases. This results in necking and finally failure of metal. If this stage occurs after a long time, grain coarsening occurs in metals. Creep rate values can be obtained by drawing a tangent to the creep curve or by using the following formula

$$\text{Creep rate} = \frac{de}{dt}$$

where, e is creep strain and t is time.

Creep rate gives an idea about the amount of creep occurring in a unit time. This shows a higher value, when the load is initially applied. The steeper the creep curve, greater is the creep rate (Fig. 3.60).

3.42 CREEP FRACTURE   (May 11, Dec. 13)

At high temperature, grains show more strength than the grain boundaries (Fig. 3.61).

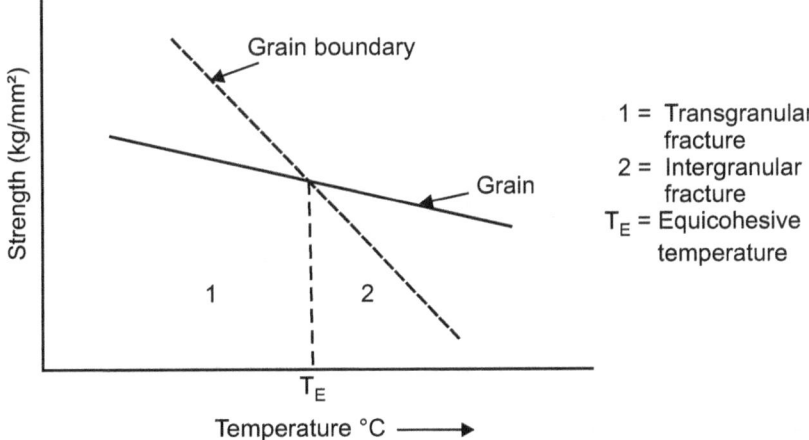

Fig. 3.61: Effect of temperature on the strength of grains and grain boundary

At equicohesive temperature, the strength of grain and grain boundary is equal. Crack always initiates and propagates through weak portion i.e. along grain boundaries. Therefore, creep fractures are always intergranular (Fig. 3.62). These fractures are usually similar to typical ductile fractures with a considerable amount of plastic deformation.

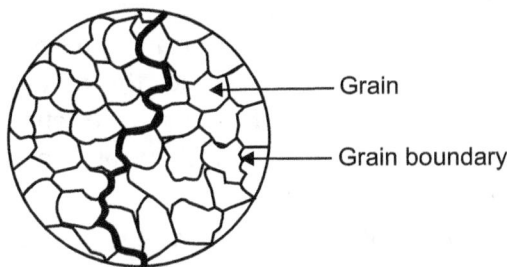

Fig. 3.62: Intergranular creep fracture

3.43 EFFECT OF VARIABLES   (May 13, 17)

Following factors influence the creep property of a metal

- Higher creep resistance is observed with the metals having a high melting point.
- A coarse grained metal has higher creep resistance than a fine grained metal.
- Refractory metal additions improve creep resistance of steels.
- Metals having higher oxidation and scaling resistance possess more creep strength.
- For steels, increase in carbon content increases creep resistance.
- Aluminium is added to steels for its deoxidation, which makes the steel fine grained. This results in low creep strength.
- Plated components exhibit more creep strength.
- For constant temperature, creep strain increases with increasing stress [Fig. 3.63 (a)].
- For constant stress, creep strain increases with increasing temperature [Fig. 3.63 (b)].

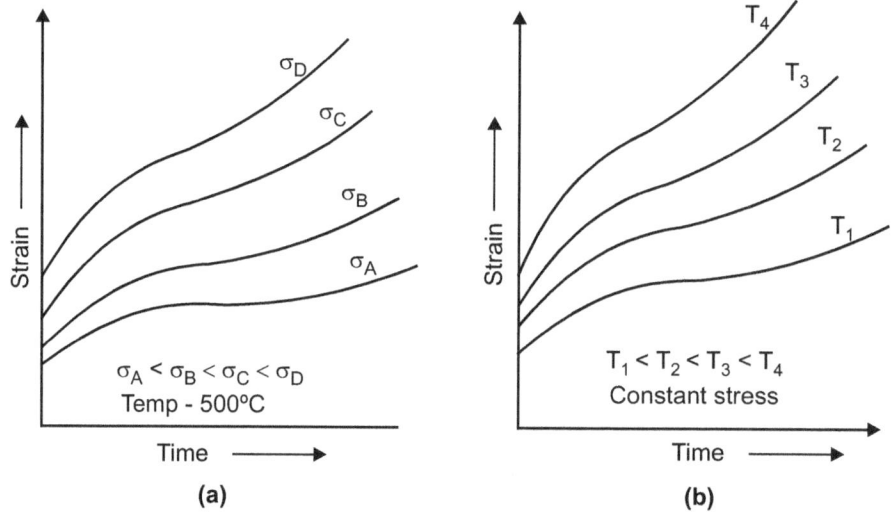

Fig. 3.63: Effect of (a) Strain and (b) Temperature on creep curve

B. NON-DESTRUCTIVE TESTING

3.44 INTRODUCTION   (May 17)

Non-destructive testing (NDT) is one of the important methods used for evaluation and quality control of metal components. During testing, the metal component does not get damaged. Therefore, these methods are called as non-destructive testing methods. Though NDT methods do not directly evaluate any mechanical property, these are becoming popular because of the following advantages

- Rapid inspection of each and every component is possible. Hence, 100 percent production can be inspected.
- NDT methods can be automated to lower their cost.

- Testing on shop floor is possible because portable equipments are used. This controls the quality of further production.

- The same component can be used for various tests as it does not get damaged.

- Permanent records of testings can be made during testing.

- The defective parts can be segregated in the early stages of manufacturing. This saves time and production cost.

- Higher accuracy, reliability and repeatability in test results can be obtained.

However, in certain cases, NDT methods has limitations such as the operator's skill and standardization of process, which plays an important role in testing. This chapter deals with the principle of working, advantages, limitations and applications of the various NDT methods.

General Applications of NDT

The following are the various applications of NDT methods

- For detection of defect,

- For determination of type, size and location of defect,

- Measurement of physical and chemical properties such as electrical conductivity, density, chemical composition etc.,

- Sorting of mixed materials on the basis of chemical composition, hardness, heat treatment etc.,

- Measurement of component thickness,

- Measurement of coating and plating thickness.

Non-Destructive Testing Methods

Following are some of the important non-destructive testing methods

- Visual testing,

- Magnetic particle testing,

- Liquid penetrant or dye penetrant testing,

- Eddy current testing,

- Ultrasonic testing and

- Radiographic testing.

Other methods such as spectroscopic testing, acoustic emission testing, leak testing etc. are also in use. However, in this chapter, the above six methods are discussed.

3.45 VISUAL TESTING

This is one of the simple and oldest methods of testing. For each NDT method, visual testing is a final step. Visual testing is carried out usually with unaided eyes. Following instruments are also available for this testing.

(a) **Magnifying Lenses:** These are used to observe the surface area under study in the enlarged form. Various lenses with different magnifications are used. The choice of a lens depends upon the study. These lenses are used for inspection of machined parts to evaluate surface finish, surface shapes, profiles and surface macro-structures.

(b) **Borescopes:** This instrument is used to observe internal or closed area of a component. This is a long tubular optical device (Fig. 3.64) that illuminates and allows the inspection of inner surfaces. Rigid and flexible borescopes are available. These are used for inspection of pipes, tanks, ducts etc.

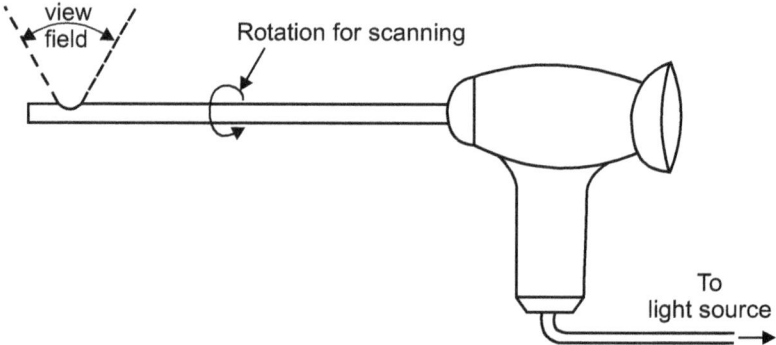

Fig. 3.64: Principle of a borescope

The defects which can be detected by visual examination are shrinkage cavity, porosity, pitting, scaling, corrosion deposits, orange peel in brass, short run in casting, mismatch, seams in rolling, surface open cracks etc.

3.46 MAGNETIC PARTICLE TESTING (MAGNAFLUX)

(Dec. 10, 13; May 11, 13)

This is one of the important NDT methods used for detection of surface and sub-surface defects in magnetic materials.

Principle

This works on the theory of induced magnetism. When a metallic part is magnetized, magnetic flux flows in it. This flux gets disturbed due to presence of a defect such as a crack. The flux leaks out at the crack. This leakage can be detected by spraying fine iron powder on the surface as iron powder gets accumulated at the leakage flux. A magnetic probe can also be used to sense the flux leakage.

Methods of Magnetization

Two types of magnetic fields are produced using an electric current:

(a) Circular magnetization   (b) Longitudinal magnetization.

(a) Circular Magnetization: When an electric current passes through a straight conductor, a circular magnetic field forms around it (Fig. 3.65). In this type, the magnetic lines are at right angles to the direction of the current. This type of magnetization detects the defects, which are perpendicular to magnetic field i.e. the defects in longitudinal direction.

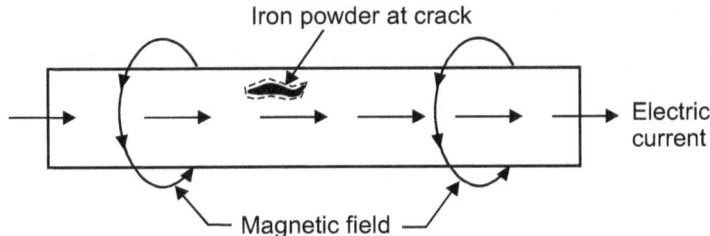

Fig. 3.65: Principle of circular magnetization

(b) Longitudinal Magnetization: In this method, the conductor is wound to produce a coil and an electric current is passed through it. This produces magnetic field in the longitudinal direction (Fig. 3.66). This type of magnetization detects cracks, which are in a circular direction.

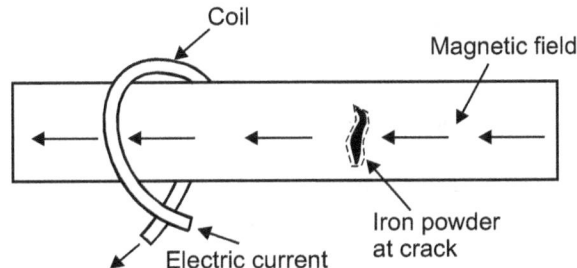

Fig. 3.66: Principle of longitudinal magnetization

Testing Units: Three types of testing units are used in magnetic particle test method. They are

Portable Units: These units are small in size and are used with currents upto 2000 Amps. These units are used with prods or yokes (Fig. 3.67) on a small area for testing cracks.

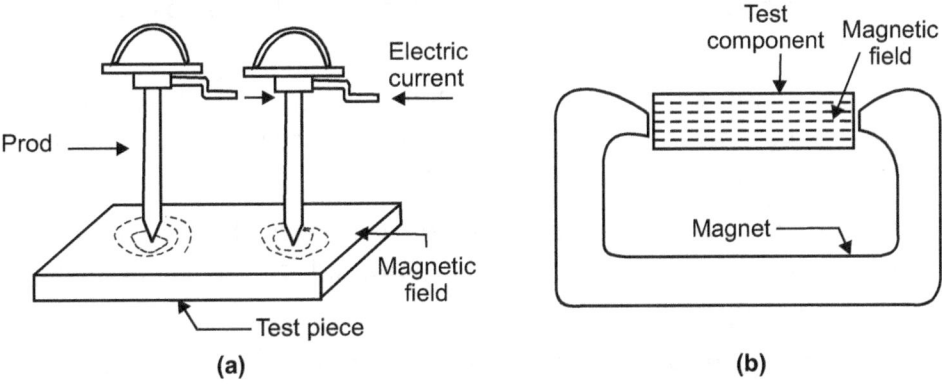

Fig. 3.67: Test unit with (a) Prod and (b) Yoke for magnetization

Mobile Units: These units are mounted on a trolley. Mobile units are used upto 5000 Amps current. These are mainly used for crack testing of castings and forgings.

Stationary Units: These are heavy and big machines. These can be operated upto 10,000 Amps. Stationary units are used for detecting cracks on bars, pipes, shafts etc.

Types of Magnetizing Current

Alternating Current: Alternating currents flow on surface (skin effect). Hence, they are sensitive to fine surface defects. By stepping down the voltage, currents of several thousand amperes can be obtained.

Direct Current: These can be obtained by rectification of alternating currents. Direct currents penetrate deeply in metals and hence, the cracks upto 6 mm deep can be detected.

Half wave Direct Current: These are half wave rectified alternating currents. These are used for surface as well as sub-surface crack detection.

Permanent Magnet: This magnet gives weak magnetization. It is more useful for detection of cracks in thin foils or sheets. Usually, it is available in a U shape.

For example: For the detection of cracks in a 100 mm diameter rod, the following currents are recommended

$$D.C. \text{ source} = 2800 \text{ Amp}$$

$$A.C. \text{ source} = 2000 \text{ Amp}$$

$$\text{Full wave rectified} = 1800 \text{ Amp}$$

$$\text{Half wave rectified} = 900 \text{ Amp}$$

Inspection Medium

Inspection medium consists of finely divided ferromagnetic particles. In dry method, only dry powder is used, while in wet method, powder is suspended in a suitable liquid medium. The colour of the magnetic particles should have some contrast to the colour of the metal, for easy detection.

Dry powder is more sensitive than wet powder. But, it may not be able to detect fine cracks. The dry powder method is used for testing of large parts as large castings or forgings. The wet powder method is more suitable for small parts.

In dry powder method, the powder is sprinkled over the surface, while in wet powder method, the inspection medium is sprayed or brushed on the surface. Immersion of components in medium is also allowed in wet method.

Wet method also uses fluorescent magnetic particles. These particles glow, when exposed to ultraviolet light. This helps in detecting the hairline cracks.

Test Procedure

Magnetic particle testing procedure consists of

- Preparation of test surface.
- Magnetization of test piece.
- Application of magnetic powder.
- Observation.
- Demagnetization of test piece.

The surface to be tested should be clean enough and free from rust, grease or scale. Any plating or coating on the surface should be removed. A suitable magnetization method is used. A careful observation should be done after application of magnetic particles. After observation, the component may be photographed for preservation of results.

Demagnetization

- This is one of the important steps in magnetic particle testing. It is carried out at the end of the test. The metal component remains magnetized for a considerably long time. This creates troubles, if the component is to be assembled with sensitive electrical instruments. The local N and S poles formed at the end attract ferrous particles. This causes excessive wear due to abrasive effect. For example, in the aircraft construction, the steel parts in the proximity of the aeroplane compass should be demagnetized. The axles and shaft of an automobile should be demagnetized after testing. Otherwise, they may not be able to rotate.

- Demagnetization takes place automatically, if the specimen is heated above its curie temperature.

- Demagnetization is also achieved by subjecting the specimen to a magnetizing force that is continuously reversing in direction and decreasing in strength.

- If the piece is inserted in the field of alternating current coil, it can be demagnetized.

Advantages

- This is a sensitive method for locating small and shallow surface cracks.
- Sub-surface cracks (i.e. cracks just below the surface) can be detected.
- No electronic display or read out is required. The cracks are indicated directly on the surface.
- There is almost no limitation for the size or shape of the component.
- Instruments are portable and easy to handle.

Limitations

- Surface plating or thin paint coating affects the sensitivity of the test.
- This method can be used only on ferromagnetic materials.

- For better results, magnetic field should be induced in the circular and longitudinal direction. This is because, horizontal cracks are detected by circular magnetization, while circular cracks are detected by longitudinal magnetization.
- After testing, demagnetization is a must.
- Local heating and sparking is possible, if care is not taken in product testing.

Applications

Magnetic particle test is used for inspection of

- Rods, bars, forging blanks and rough castings.
- Parts in transportation industries as rail road, aircraft, automobiles etc.
- Critical parts as crankshaft, frames, flywheels, crane hooks, steam turbine blades, welded parts etc.

3.47 LIQUID PENETRANT TESTING   (Dec. 13, Nov. 16)

This test is also called as dye penetrant testing. This is a universal testing method applicable for almost all engineering materials.

Principle

When a liquid penetrant is applied to a metal surface, it enters into surface defects such as cracks. The excess penetrant is removed and a developer is applied. Due to blotting action, this developer draws out penetrant from the defect. As the penetrant is coloured (usually red) and the developer is white, a clear indication of crack is possible.

Liquid Penetrants

A penetrant is a suitable liquid having good wettability with the material. Various types of penetrants are used. Following are some of the penetrants used practically

Water Soluble Penetrants: They are also called as water washable penetrants. They can be used quickly and efficiently for testing of rough surfaces and large quantities of small size parts.

Post Emulsifiable Penetrants: They are used for the detection of minute cracks. The penetrants are not directly water washable.

Solvent Removable Penetrants: They are used, when it is necessary to inspect only a localized area of the work.

Fluorescent Penetrants: Fluorescent penetrants are usually green in colour and glow brightly, when exposed to ultraviolet light. These are more sensitive than the visible penetrants. Zyglo, dyglow and quickglow are some of the trade penetrants available in the market.

Developers

The purpose of developer is to make the penetrant in the crack visible. The blotting action of developer draws out penetrant from the crack and spreads over the surface. Following types of developers are used

Dry Developers: These are used mainly with fluorescent penetrants. They should be used carefully as like other dust particles, they can dry and irritate the skin. They are usually recommended for rough surfaces.

Water Soluble Developers: These can be used for both fluorescent and visible penetrant. This developer is very convenient due to ease of application and removal.

Water Suspendible Developers: These are also suitable for fluorescent and visible penetrants. The water suspension of these developers should be made carefully. Too much or very little amount of developer in water affects it's sensitivity.

Non-Aqueous Solvent Suspendible Developers: These are also recommended for fluorescent and visible penetrants. This form of developer produces a white coating on the surface of the part. This coating gives maximum white colour contrast with red penetrants. Hence, very fine and deep cracks can be detected by this developer.

Test Procedure

Liquid or dye penetrant testing procedure (Fig. 3.68) involves the following steps

- Surface preparation,
- Application of penetrant,
- Removal of excess penetrant,
- Application of developer,
- Inspection and
- Post cleaning.

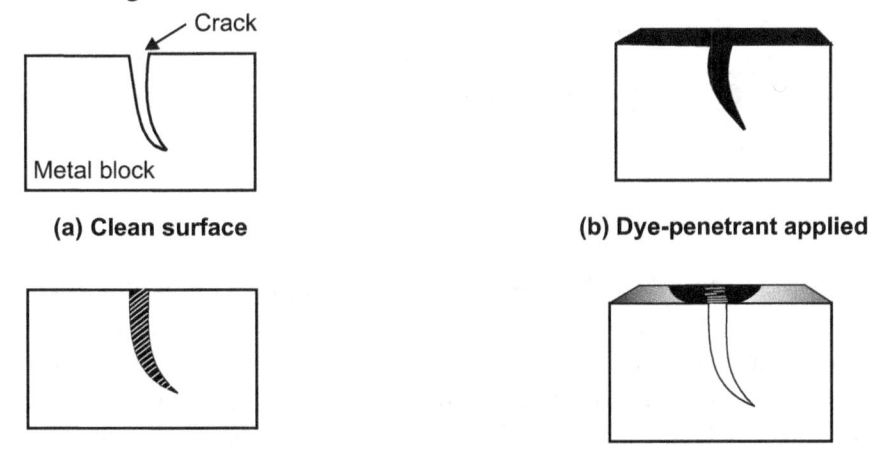

(a) **Clean surface**   (b) **Dye-penetrant applied**

(c) **Excess penetrant removed**   (d) **Developer applied and crack is observed**

Fig. 3.68: Principle of dye penetrant test

After application of penetrant, sufficient time should be allowed for proper penetration. The penetrant enters in crack by capillary action. After this, the excess penetrant is removed from surface lightly. This ensures the existence of the penetrant only in the crack. This is followed by application of developer. Usually, developer dries quickly. It forms a white coat on the surface. Due to blotting action of the developer, the penetrant from the crack comes out and gives an indication. Due to red colour of the penetrant on white background of developer, a crack becomes visible.

Advantages

- This test is not restricted to type of material e.g. magnetic, non-magnetic etc.
- It is very simple to utilize and control.
- It does not require any machine or instrument.
- Its sensitivity is greater than that of magnetic particle testing.
- Fast interpretation of results is possible.
- The results do not require any electronic display or calculations.
- The cost is relatively very less.

Limitations

- Surface films and coatings, may confuse the results.
- Cleaning is must before and after the test to avoid rusting.
- Only surface defects can be detected.
- It should not be used for powder metallurgical part as their inherent porosity makes difficulty in interpretation.

Applications

- For surface detection of forgings, castings, weldments etc.

3.48 EDDY CURRENT TESTING (ECT)   (Dec. 10, 14; May 13)

Eddy current testing is one of the most important methods as it is used for several purposes, other than crack detection.

Principle

This method of testing is based on the theory of electromagnetic induction of Eddy currents. In Eddy current testing, an alternating current is passed through a coil and the metal component to be tested is exposed to changing electromagnetic field of the coil. Due to this, Eddy current is generated in the metal component. An electromagnetic field created by Eddy current opposes the field of the coil. The electromagnetic field is sensed and evaluated.

The response of Eddy current depends on the following metal variables

- Electrical conductivity,
- Physical dimensions,
- Structural defects,

- Magnetic permeability,
- Hardness and
- Chemical composition of metal.

In fact, all the above variables are inter-related. Therefore, by keeping, the remaining factors constant, any one factor can be evaluated. For example, keeping chemical conditions constant, structural defects can be evaluated. Non-ferrous metals do not have magnetic permeability. Therefore, Eddy current response greatly depends upon electrical conductivity of non-ferrous metals.

Eddy current test methods are also called as Indirect testing methods, because the method does not give direct measure of properties. Eddy current methods are based on a comparison technique. For example, by using known standard samples, the instrument is calibrated and then unknown samples are tested.

Eddy Current Test Instrument

Eddy current test instrument consists of

- A probe or encircling coil, which generates and sense Eddy currents (Fig. 3.69).
- Electronic units for frequency generation.
- Display units like CRT, recorders etc.

The encircling coil differs from a probe. The samples are inserted in coils, whereas a probe is kept on the surface of specimen. A probe is recommended for spot testing. A solid ferrite rod is used in probe, while a ferrite core is used in an encircling coil.

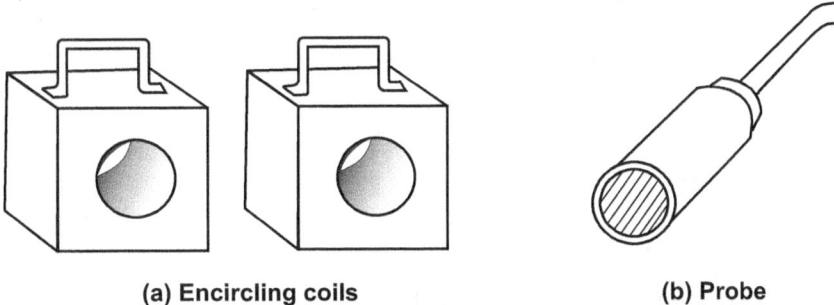

(a) Encircling coils   **(b) Probe**

Fig. 3.69: Eddy current test units

Single frequency, variable frequency and multi-frequency units are available. They are used as per the job requirements.

Test Procedure

1. **By using encircling coils:** In this test, as shown in Fig. 3.70, two encircling coils are used. Suppose, two identical components, e.g. En 24 (En 24 is a British specification used to express one of the standard composition of steel) are placed in two encircling coils. Then the display is balanced for a certain shape of waveform. Now, one En 24 component is withdrawn and any unknown component is inserted in the coil. If it is identical then a waveform similar to the previous one would be displayed. A different waveform display indicates that the component is not identical to the standard.

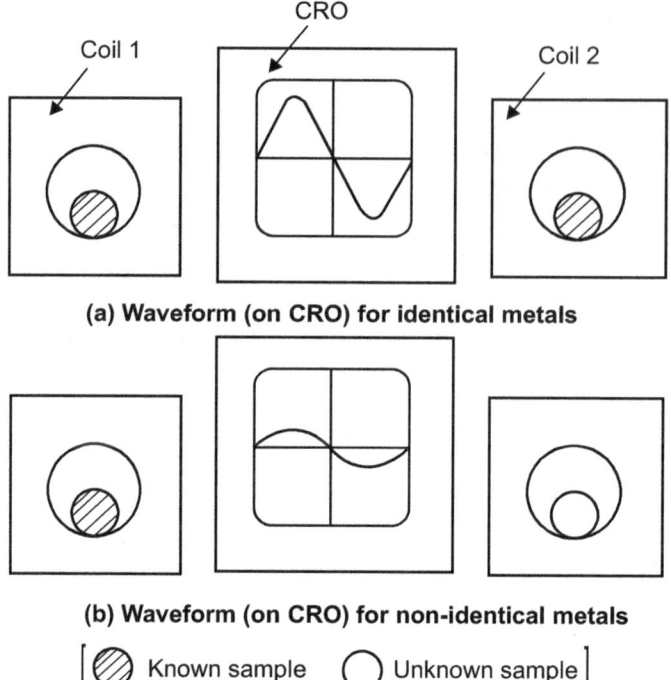

(a) Waveform (on CRO) for identical metals

(b) Waveform (on CRO) for non-identical metals

[⊘ Known sample   ◯ Unknown sample]

Fig. 3.70: Principle of Eddy current test using encircling coils

2. **By using probe:** In this test, as shown in Fig. 3.71, the probe is moved over the surface for scanning. Initially, a known standard sample is used to set the display. Then the unknown sample is scanned by the probe. The variation in the display may be calibrated for results.

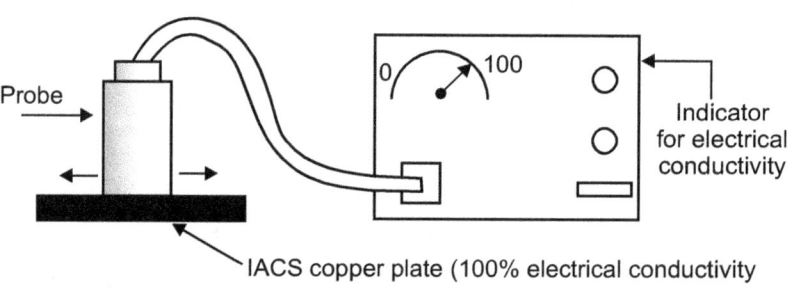

IACS copper plate (100% electrical conductivity

(a) Calibration using a standard copper plate

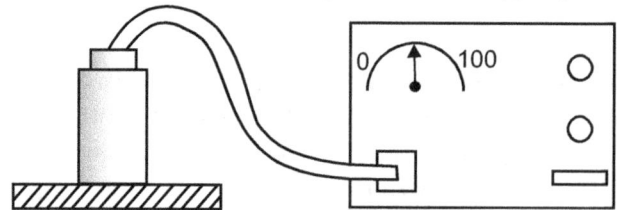

(b) Unknown sample showing 50% IACS electrical conductivity

Fig. 3.71: Principle of Eddy current test using probes

Usually, encircling coils are used for metal segregation, depending upon chemical composition, heat treatment, dimensions etc. The probe is recommended for thickness measurement, crack detection and electrical conductivity measurement.

Advantages

- It is a versatile test method used for various applications.
- It shows higher sensitivity towards material property.
- It is a rapid method and can be easily automated.
- Permanent record of test results can be available.

Limitations

- Some variables within the material that are not important in terms of material serviceability may interfere.
- The instrument standardization and calibration is necessary.
- It is limited to size and shape of component. Very big castings, forgings cannot be inserted in the encircling coils. Even this testing becomes impracticable with probe.
- Instruments and display units are costly.

Applications

Compared to other NDT methods, ECT method is very useful for the following applications

- Detection and estimation of size or depth of surface defects in various products.
- For measurement of electrical conductivity.
- For segregation or sorting of metal parts as per
  - (a) Chemical composition
  - (b) Hardness variation
  - (c) Grain size variation
  - (d) Heat treatment condition
  - (e) Dimensional variation
- Thickness measurement: ECT methods are used for
  - (a) Measurement of material thickness,
  - (b) Measurement of coating thickness i.e. non-magnetic coating on magnetic material or non-conducting coating on conducting material,
  - (c) Measurement of plating thickness.

3.49 ULTRASONIC TESTING   (May 10, 11, 17; Dec. 10, 11, 13, Nov. 16)

- The detection of defects by using sound waves is a very old method. If a metal piece is struck by a hammer, it radiates audible sound. Due to presence of internal defects, the pitch and damping of sound gets affected. Ultrasonic testing is a more refined method which uses sound waves.

Principle

- Ultrasonic waves travel through any solid body from one end to another. In the presence of any internal defect, the waves are reflected; which can be measured by suitable means (Fig. 3.72).

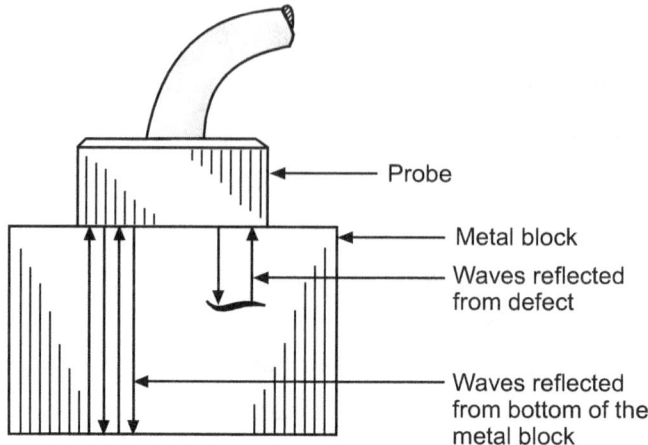

Fig. 3.72: Principle of ultrasonic test

- Ultrasonic waves are sound waves above the audible range with a frequency of 1 to 5 million Hz (Hz - cycles per second).
- Compared to X-rays, which are electromagnetic waves, ultrasonic waves are mechanical waves that consist of oscillations or vibrations of the atomic or molecular particles in the metal piece about their equilibrium position.

Generation of Ultrasonic Waves

- Ultrasonic waves for non-destructive testing are generated by using piezoelectric materials. These materials show a change in the physical dimensions, if subjected to electric field. They convert electrical energy into mechanical energy by a property called as piezoelectric effect. When alternating current is applied to a piezoelectric crystal, it expands during the first half of the cycle and contracts during the next half of cycle. This mechanical vibration (i.e. sound waves) can be varied by varying frequency of alternating current. Such type of crystal is called as transducer, which converts one form of energy into another.

3.49.1 Ultrasonic Test Methods   (May 11; Dec. 12, 13)

Following types of ultrasonic testings are used

(a) Through transmission method,   (b) Pulse-echo method.

(a) Through Transmission Method: In this method, two ultrasonic transducers are used. They are placed on each side of the component to be tested. One transducer will work as transmitting transducer while another will be a receiving transducer. If an electrical signal of desired frequency is applied to transmitting crystal, the ultrasonic waves are produced and they travel through the metal component to the other side. The receiving transducer receives vibrations and converts them into electric signal. This signals is observed on cathode ray tube of an oscilloscope or on an intensity meter. The received signal are of high intensity in case of defect free component. The component with an internal defect reflects some of the ultrasonic waves and thus, reduces the intensity of outcoming signal (Fig. 3.73).

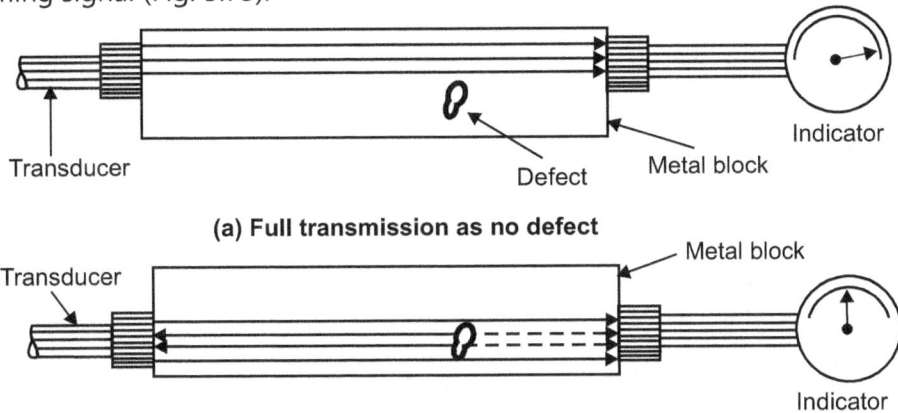

(a) Full transmission as no defect

(b) Less transmission due to defect

Fig. 3.73: Principle of through transmission method

(b) Pulse-Echo Method: This method is more suitable than through transmission method. This method uses only one transducer. It serves as transmitter as well as receiver. When an electric signal of desired frequency is given to the transducer, it produces ultrasonic waves. When these waves enter in a metal component, one signal is observed on CRT.

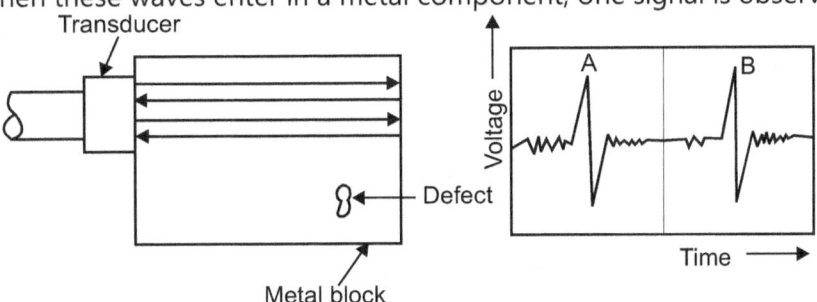

A : Initial signal at test surface

B : Final signal of reflected waves

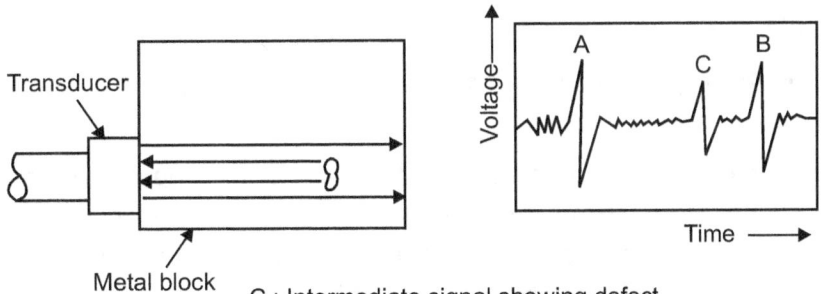

C : Intermediate signal showing defect

Fig. 3.74: Principle of pulse-echo method

The waves travel through component and reach the opposite surface. From this surface, waves are reflected back giving another signal on CRT. If the component is defect free, only two signals are observed. The distance between these two signals is directly proportional to the testing thickness of the component. If this component has an internal crack, some of the ultrasonic waves are reflected from the crack while the remaining from opposite surface. This creates one more signal between the two signals. The intermediate signal is an indication of a defect (Fig. 3.74).

In both methods, oil is used in between transducer and metal surface as a couplant. This ensures better contact.

Advantages   **(May 10; Dec. 11)**

- Ultrasonic waves have a superior penetrating power. This allows better detection of flaws situated deep in the metal.

- Due to its high sensitivity, fine flaws can be detected.

- Better accuracy and reliability.

- The equipment is portable and easy to handle.

- The output can be processed by a computer, which improves result reliability.

Limitations   **(May 10, Dec. 11)**

- As it is operated manually, a careful attention is required.

- For setting up the procedure and to standardize the equipment, highly skilled operators are required.

- Irregular shaped and rough parts are very difficult to examine.

- Sub-surface discontinuities are not easy to detect.

- Couplants are needed.

Applications: Ultrasonic test methods are used for   **(May 10; Dec. 11)**

- Defect detection and   • Thickness measurement.

3.50 RADIOGRAPHIC TESTING   (Dec. 10, 11, 14; May 13)

Two types of radiographic testings are used

(a) X-ray radiography and   (b) Gamma-ray radiography.

Principle

- In this test method, the metal component to be tested is exposed to radiations, such as X-rays or gamma rays. These radiations penetrate through the component and are absorbed by it. More absorption of radiation occurs by thick or dense section. The transmitted radiations are made incident on a photographic film. This gives a permanent record.

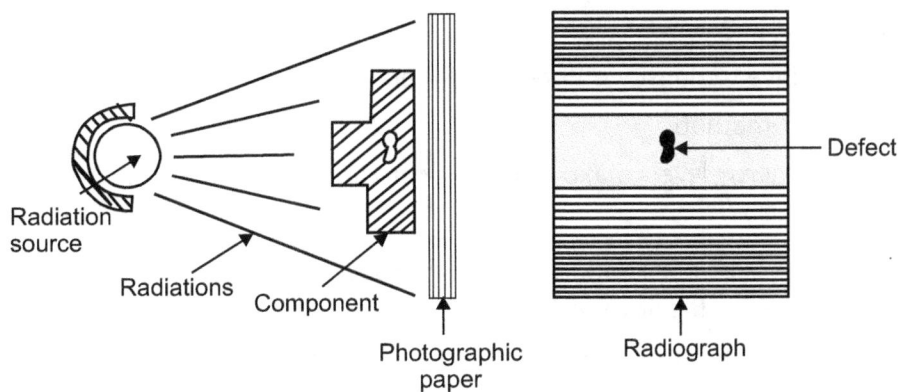

Fig. 3.75: Principle of radiography and a radiograph

Radiograph

• A radiograph is a sort of photograph of the component produced by radiation. The radiographic film is similar to photographic film. The film turns black due to radiation. The lower density region of the component absorbs less radiation and transmits more radiation, making that part of the film dark. The higher density or more thick regions of components absorb more radiation and transmit less radiation making that part of the film less dark. Therefore, a hole or crack appears as a dark area, while inclusions as light area (Fig. 3.75).

(A) X-ray Radiography: X-rays are produced, when high velocity moving electrons collide with atoms of a solid. X-ray generator unit consists of anode and cathode placed in a vacuum tube. The heating element inside the cathode emits electrons. These electrons are focussed and accelerated towards a metal target in anode assembly. The metal target is made of a heavy metal such as tungsten. Due to impact of electrons on the target, a part of their kinetic energy is converted into radiation energy i.e. X-ray (Fig. 3.76). The voltage difference between anode and cathode regulates the velocity of electrons and thus wavelength of X-rays.

Portable and stationary equipments are used for X-ray radiography.

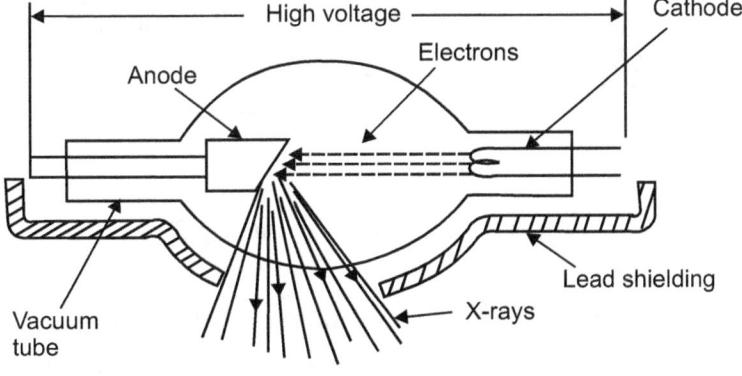

Fig. 3.76: X-ray generation

Advantages

- Highly sensitive to density difference of metal.
- Very fast test method.
- Adjustable energy levels make it suitable for various applications.

Limitations

- X-rays have less penetration power because of longer wavelength. So, thick components are difficult to test.
- Because of scattering nature, X-rays are not suitable for testing of components with more thickness variations.
- Only one component can be tested at a time.
- Involves high initial cost.
- Radiation is hazardous to living organisms.

Applications

- For detection of internal defects.
- For detection of porosity, cracks, lack of fusion in weldment, castings etc.
- For measurement of geometry variation in components.
- For thickness, measurement of rolled or extruded parts.

(B) Gamma-Ray Radiography: In this type of radiography, a radioactive source of gamma ray is used. Cobalt[60], Cesium[137] and Iridium[192] are typical gamma ray sources. This radioactive material is kept in a lead shielded box called as camera. This camera has a number of windows through which gamma rays are radiated (Fig. 3.77). Similar to X-ray technique, the samples are kept between the camera and the photographic film. The radiograph has the same results as that of X-ray radiograph.

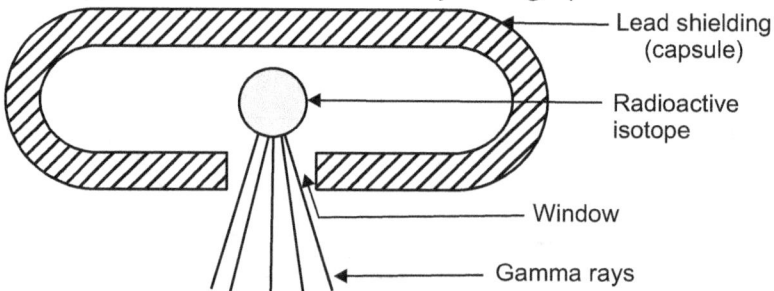

Fig. 3.77: Gamma ray generation

Advantages

- Due to shorter wavelengths, γ-rays show more penetrating power.
- The scattering of γ-rays being less, components with non-uniform thickness can also be tested.

- This technique can be used to inspect a number of components at a time as γ-rays radiate in all directions.
- The results can be recorded permanently.

Limitations

- The intensity of gamma-rays cannot be controlled as the radiations are natural. They can not be accelerated.
- After some period, radioactive decay is observed.
- Involves radiation hazards.
- Trained operators are required.

Application

- This is used for the same applications as that of X-ray radiography.
- Concluding the NDT, the following Table 3.6 gives a broad guideline for the selection of NDT method for any typical use.

Table 3.6: NDT Methods for Typical Applications

Application	NDT Method
Surface defects detection	Visual testing, Magnetic particle test, Liquid penetrant test, Eddy current test
Internal defects detection	Ultrasonic test, Radiography,
Segregation as per Chemical composition	Eddy current test
Conductivity measurement	Eddy current test
Crack depth measurement	Eddy current test, Ultrasonic test
Thickness gauging	Eddy current test, Ultrasonic test. Radiography test.

KEY NOTES

1. Mechanical tests are conducted to evaluate the mechanical Properties of the materials to easily select proper material for proper application. These are also known as destructive tests because after performing the test permanent deformation or destruction essentially occurs and material cannot be reused that so why these tests are not performed on the finished components.

2. Brinell test is suitable to measure hardness of heterogeneous components as it covers larger area. Vicker is suitable for thin and hard components. Rockwell is suitable for any kind of metal/alloy.

3. VHN is independent of applied load because the contact angle remains same and the geometry of the impression also remains same.

4. Nominal Engineering stress is the ratio of load to original area of cross section. True stress is the ratio of load to corresponding (actual) area of cross section. As the area continuously decreases during plastic deformation in tensile test so the true stress is always higher than engineering stress.

5. Tensile test is conducted under static condition of loading (load is slowly increased) while Impact test is conducted under dynamic loading and fatigue test under cyclic loading.

6. Impact test is conducted to determine the tendency of a material to fracture in brittle manners. Due to great difficulty or even impossibility of stress calculation at the tip of the notch the results of impact test is not represented in form of stress. The amount of energy absorbed by the material in a single blow before failure is taken as the measurement of impact strength.

7. Triaxial state of stress is generated at the tip if the notch (condition similar to the presence of a defect in the component), so notched specimens are used. This aspect has not been taken into account in any other mechanical test. Transition temperature is the temperature at which change in behavior of the material is observed from ductile to brittle.

8. For ferrous metals true fatigue limit (value of stress at and below which material does not get failed despite repeating infinite number of cycles) is obtained while for non- ferrous S-N curve does not become horizontal at any stage of the test because most of the non-ferrous metals like Al, Cu are soft and ductile and their atomic planes are not enough rigid to prevent permanent deformation even at lower stresses.

9. For ferrous metals like steel the fatigue strength is generally half of the UTS. For non ferrous it is reported in terms of number of cycles for failure at the given value of stress.

10. Wherever there is a rotating part it is likely to be subjected to fatigue failure that so why fatigue failure is most common in the industries. Fatigue failure begins at the surface/sub-surface that so why parts requiring to have good fatigue life must have very nice surface finishing.

11. Creep test is useful to predict the behavior of the material at high temperature under constant load e.g. rocket engines, gas turbines, ballistic missiles etc.

12. Most of the life of the component depends upon the secondary stage of creep curve as here deformation is almost constant or minimum creep rate is observed in this stage.

13. Creep strength is superior for coarse grained (less number of grains) materials while tensile, fatigue and impact strengths are superior for fine grained (more number of grains) materials.

14. Non-destructive tests, as their name indicates do not cause any damage to the material under test. These tests are always conducted on the finished components to find out the presence of any defect (surface, subsurface up to the depth of 5 mm and internal lying below 5 mm).

15. In the presence of any defect the mechanical behaviour gets deteriorated (due to stress concentration under application of load) thus timely detection of defect is necessary to avoid any premature failure of the component.

16. Dye penetrant for detection of surface, magna flux for detection of surface and sub-surface in ferrous parts, Eddy current for detection of surface and sub-surface in ferrous as well as non-ferrous parts and ultrasonic/radiography for detection of internal defects may be used.

17. Demagnetisation is essential after performing the magna flux test as the part made out of ferrous material when comes in contact with other ferrous parts of the machine assembly e.g. nuts, bolts, gears, connecting rods, etc. it may cause wear because the part is in magnetised state.

18. Demagnetisation may be done either by flowing current in reverse direction to cancel out the magnetic flux or by heating the part upto the curie temperature i.e. 768°C.

19. Torsion is defined as a twisting action resulting in shear stresses &strains. The test has not been standardised and the torsion test is not so widely used as tensile test. For steels the torsional strength may be 0.75 times their tensile strength.

REVIEW QUESTIONS

DESTRUCTIVE TESTING

1. State whether true or false and justify
   (a) A tensile test specimen has a constant cross-section over its entire length.
   (b) A tensile test specimen usually fails in its gauge length.
   (c) A true stress-strain curve differs in nature from an engineering stress-strain curve.
   (d) A brittle material usually shows the same values of ultimate stress and breaking stress.
   (e) Geometrically similar specimens respond equally in tension test for the same metal.
   (f) Too small or very thin specimens are not suitable for Brinell hardness test.
   (g) Brinell hardness numbers are load dependent.
   (h) Poldi hardness test is recommended for large and heavy castings or forgings.
   (i) Rockwell hardness test is used for surface hardened steels.
   (j) Minor load is applied in Rockwell hardness test.

(k)   Rockwell superficial test can be used for porous components.

(l)   Vicker's hardness test is load dependent.

(m) Vicker's hardness test gives more accurate results than does Brinell hardness test.

(n)   Micro-hardness test is used for measuring hardness of chrome plated steels.

(o)   Shores scleroscope test may give faulty readings, if the specimen is not clamped on the anvil.

(p)   Durometers should be used for rubber and plastics.

(q)   Moh's hardness test is also called as scratch hardness test.

(r)   Compression test measures the breaking stress only.

(s)   Compression test results are test piece dimension dependent.

(t)   A notch is necessary in impact test specimens.

(u)   The temperature of specimen in impact test affects the results.

(v)   Bauschinger's effect should be considered during study of fatigue loading.

(w) Fine grained metals exhibit higher fatigue properties, while coarse grained metals exhibit higher creep properties.

(x)   A high temperature tensile test is creep test.

(y)   A creep curve shows three distinct regions.

(z)   Higher melting point metals show a high creep resistance.

Ans.

(a) False	(b) True	(c) True	(d) True	(e) True	(f) True
(g) True	(h) True	(i) True	(j) True	(k) False	(l) False
(m) True	(n) True	(o) True	(p) True	(q) True	(r) True
(s) True	(t) True	(u) True	(v) True	(w) True	(x) True
(y) True	(z) True				

2.   What is meant by mechanical testing of a metal ? Why is it necessary ? What are various mechanical test methods ?

3.   Which are the properties evaluated in tension test ? Explain the importance of gauge length.

4.   Draw a typical engineering and true stress-strain curve for mild steel. Comment on the nature of the curve.

5.   Discuss various factors that affect tensile test results.

6.   What are the factors affecting the compression test ?

7.   Discuss the nature of fracture in tensile and compression test.

8.   Give various definitions of hardness.

9.   Classify various hardness tests.

10. What is the principle of Brinell Hardness Test ? What are the factors affecting the test results ?

11. What is non-standard Brinell Hardness Test ?

12. What is the working principle of Poldi hardness test ? What are its limitations ?

13. Why does Vicker's hardness test measures accurate hardness ? Give typical applications of Vicker's hardness test.

14. What is micro-hardness test ? How does it differ from Vicker's hardness test ?

15. What is the principle used in the Rockwell hardness test ? What is Superficial Rockwell hardness test ?

16. Sketch the typical impressions obtained in the various hardness tests.

17. Discuss the factors that affect Impact test.

18. Comment on the nature of fracture in fatigue and creep test.

19. Write short notes on

    (a)   Shear test,   (b)   Bend test,

    (c)   Torsion test,   (d)   Moh's Hardness Scale,

    (e)   Durometer,   (f)   Scleroscope,

    (g)   Notch sensitivity in impact test,

    (h)   Types of loading cycles in fatigue,

    (i)   Typical fractures in compression test;

20. What is Barba's law ? What is its significance ? Derive the relation between engineering stress and true stress.

21. Write short note on: S-N curve for ferrous and non-ferrous metals.

22. Draw a typical fatigue fracture. Suggest way to improve fatigue life at a component.

23. Draw a typical stress-strain curve for the following:

    (a) Mild steel,   (b) Cast Iron,   (c) Ceramic,   (d) Polymer.

24. With neat sketch explain procedure for Rockwell hardness test.

25. Give reason why – Specimens are notched in impact test.

26. Define engineering and true stress. Obtain a relationship between them.

27. Draw a neat sketch of creep testing machine and explain the procedure.

28. Differentiate between Brinell, Vicker's and Rockwell hardness tests in view of their advantages, limitations and applications.

29. Explain the Impact test. What are the different types of notches ? Differentiate between Charpy and Izod impact tests.

30. What is fatigue ? Define fatigue strength and fatigue limit.

31. What is Creep ? In which application it should be considered ? How is the creep resistance improved ? Draw typical creep curve.

32. What is endurance limit?

33. Why mechanical tests are also known as the destructive tests ?

NON-DESTRUCTIVE TESTING

1. State whether true or false and justify

    (a) For detection of longitudinal cracks, circular magnetization should be used in magnetic particle testing method.

    (b) Demagnetization is necessary after magnetic particle test.

    (c) Powder metallurgical parts cannot be tested by dye penetrant test.

    (d) Internal cracks can be detected by dye penetrant test.

    (e) Eddy current testing can be used for estimation of chemical composition.

    (f) Gamma-ray radiography is used for finding out surface defects.

    Ans.: (a) True (b) True (c) True (d) False (e) False (f) False.

2. Distinguish between the following

    (a) Ultrasonic and Eddy current test.

    (b) X-ray and Gamma-ray radiography.

3. What are the applications of the Eddy current test other than flaw detection ?

4. Suggest suitable NDT methods for the following

    (a) Detection of sub-surface cracks in Aluminium casting.

    (b) Detection of surface cracks for a non-magnetic material.

    (c) Measurement of wire diameter during continuous wire drawing.

    (d) Segregation of copper plated steel bars and pure copper bars.

    (e) Detection of scale deposition on inner surface of boiler tube.

    (f) Detection of hairline cracks on surface of heat treated steel.

    (g) Measurement of electrical conductivity of silver plated electrical contacts.

    (h) Detection of dezincification in brass components.

5. Compare and contrast the advantages and limitations of all NDT methods.

6. Suggest suitable hardness test for:

    (i) Gray iron casting, (ii) Cemented carbide tool, (iii) Gold plated article, (iv) Glass.

    Justify your answer.

7. Which NDT method do you suggest to sort out steel bars of same shape and size but different chemical composition ? Explain only principle of that test.

8. Distinguish between the following: Dye penetrate and magnetic particle test.

9. Suggest suitable nondestructive test for:

    (i) Sorting of steel components of identical shape and size from mixed lot.

    (ii) Subsurface cracks in steel bars.

    (iii) Surface crack in 8 cylinder crankshaft.

    (iv) Slag inclusions in welded joint.

10. Explain magnetic particle test.

11. Give reasons:
    (i)   Ultrasonic flow inspection is not suitable to detect the defects in thin materials.
    (ii)   Magnaflux test is used to detect surface and subsurface defects.
    (iii) Radiography is used to detect the defects in welded joints of boilers.
    (iv)   Eddy current test can be used for sorting the steels.
12. With a neat sketch explain the procedure for Rockwell hardness test. State two main differences between Brineel and Rockwell hardness test.
13. Give reasons (i) specimens are notched in impact test.
    (ii) Eddy current can be used for sorting of steels.
14. Explain principle of ultrasonic testing.
15. Explain principle and procedure of magnetic particle testing. Why demagnetization is necessary after the test is over.

UNIVERSITY QUESTIONS

DECEMBER 2013

1. With a neat diagram explain fatigue fracture in detail.   **[4]**
2. Define toughness, Notch sensitivity.   **[2]**
3. What is mint by transducer, explain the respective NDT method makes the use of sound waves.   **[4]**
4. What are the advantages of Dye Penetrant test over the other NDT methods?   **[2]**
5. In a brass component subsurface defect can be easily determined by magnetic particle test.
6. Write true or false and justify your answer.   **[12]**
    (a)   Creep fracture is a transgranular fracture.
    (b)   Erichson cupping test is used for sheet metals only.
    (c)   For checking the hardness of phases in metals, Rockwell C scale is used.
    (d)   In a brass component subsurface defect can be easily determined by magnetic particle test.
7. What is spring back?   **[1]**

MAY 2014

1. Explain the strain hardening with curve.   **[4]**
2. What is endurance limit ? Explain fatigue fracture with suitable figure. Also state the applications where fatigue strength is necessary.   **[6]**
3. Write short notes on :   **[7]**
    (1) Poldi hardness test   (2) Compression test.
4. Which type of test is carried out at high temperature of metal sample under test? Also explain the related curve obtained. (Draw suitable figure).   **[7]**
5. Write short notes on :
    (1) Erichson cupping test   (2) Durometers.

DECEMBER 2014

1. The following observations are made during tension test carried out on a 15 mm diameter plain carbon steel rod

   Yield load = 68 kN

   Ultimate tensile load = 105 kN.

   Find the yield strength and ultimate tensile strength of the steel rod.   **[4]**

2. Which non-destructive test is suitable for the following situations ?   **[4]**

   (i)   For detection of surface cracks on brass components.

   (ii) For detection of slag inclusion of welded joint.

3. What are the non-destructive applications of Eddy current testing ?   **[4]**

4. Explain fatigue test.   **[4]**

5. Explain piling up and sinking effects on surface of test piece found when conducting Brinell Hardness test.   **[4]**

6. Explain the principle advantages and limitations of Radiographic test.   **[4]**

MAY 2015

1. What is the concept of True stress and True strain ? Derive the relations between them also find out the condition for necking.   **[5]**

2. What do you mean by the term 'Hardness of the material' ? Explain any four testing methods for checking the hardness of the material.   **[4]**

3. What do you mean by 'non-destructive testing'? Explain ultrasonic method of testing with working principle, advantages and drawbacks.   **[4]**

4. Identify the methods of NDT in the following cases :   **[5]**

   (i)   Cavities, cracks or region of variable density for the metal/ non-metallic components manufactured by casting, welding and forging etc.

   (ii) To sort out dissimilar metals and detect differences in their composition, microstructure etc.

   (iii) Detecting internal defects such as cracks, porosity and laminations in Metallic and non-metallic components during or after production.

   (iv) Various kinds of flows in ferromagnetic components made from various welding, castings and forging etc.

   (v)   Invisible cracks, porosity and other similar defects on the surface of components made up of metal, non-metal, plastic, glass etc.

5. Explain with working principle the material test for the component which shows a plastic deformation under constant stresses for a longer time at high temperatures. Draw the type of possible microstructure during this test.   **[4]**

6. What is the purpose of 'Impact Test' ? Explain with and the factors affecting the impact values of the component.   **[4]**

NOVEMBER 2015

1. A cylindrical specimen of steel having an original diameter 12.8 mm is tensile tested to fracture and found to have an engineering fracture strength of 460 MPa if its cross-sectional diameter of fracture is 10.7 mm, determine :
   (i)   Ductility in terms of percent reduction in area.
   (ii) True stress at fracture.   **[6]**
2. What is fatigue ? Draw S-N curve for Mild Steel and Aluminum and explain Endurance limit.   **[6]**
3. Explain the methods of magnetization and demagnetization of component during magnetic particle inspection. Why the demagnetization is necessary after testing? **[6]**
4. Differentiate between dye penetrant inspection and fluorescent penetrant inspection.   **[4]**
5. Explain Moh's hardness scale.   **[2]**

MAY 2016

1. What do you mean by "True stress and True Strain in materials" ? Derive the relationship between both of it.   **[4]**
2. What is the difference between Hardness and Toughness of the material ? Explain any two testing methods for checking the hardness of the material with their principal of working and mathematical formula for calculation ?   **[5]**
3. What is Notch toughness in Impact Test ? List out the factors by which the Impact values of materials get affected.   **[4]**
4. What do you mean by 'Non Destructive Testing ? Explain Radiography method of testing with working principal, advantages and applications ?   **[4]**
5. Identify the methods of material testing in the following cases :   **[5]**
   (i)   To measure hardness of cast components, heterogeneous materials like cast irons and porous powder metallurgy components.
   (ii) To measure the properties like electrical conductivity, magnetic permeability, grain size, heat treatment conditions, hardness and physical dimensions.
   (iii) To test large sized, uniform thickness and one/many components at the same time.
   (iv) In quality control test for detecting internal defects such as cracks, porosity, and laminations in metallic and non-metallic components during or after the production.
   (v)   Materials working for a continous high temperature service under stressed conditions such as jet engine components, gas and steam turbines, nuclear reactors and tungsten filaments for electric bulbs.

6. Explain the working principle of fatigue test machine ? What are the different protection methods of fatigue life ? **[4]**

7. What do you mean by the term 'creep fracture' ? What are the requirements for creep resistant materials ? **[4]**

NOVEMBER 2016

1. Compare and contrast between. **[6]**

   (i) Dye penetrant test and ultrasonic test

   (ii) Brinell harness tester and Rockwall hardness tester.

   [**Ans. :** (i) Refer articles 3.4.7, 3.49 (ii) Refer articles 3.20, 3.25]

2. Draw the self-explanatory diagram for the following: **[4]**

   (i) Stress-strain diagram for Cast Iron.

   (ii) S-N diagram for Cu.

   [**Ans. :** (i) Refer articles 3.10, Fig. 3.19 (3) (ii) Refer article 3.35, fig. 3.54]

3. For checking internal defects in brass component which NDT methods are used, justify your answer. **[3]**

   [**Ans. :** Refer articles 3.50(A)]

MAY 2017

1. What is the basic difference between destructive and non-destructive testing? Explain the purpose of the following testing methods:

   (1) Tensile test

   (2) Ultrasonic

   (3) Creep test. **[7]**

   [**Ans. :** (1) Refer article 3.44]

   [**Ans. :** (2) Refer article 3.2]

   [**Ans. :** (3) Refer article 3.40]

2. What is the basic difference between hardness and toughness of the material? Explain the method to determine the toughness. **[6]**

   [**Ans. :** Refer article 3.32]

✠ ✠ ✠

METALS CORROSION AND ITS PREVENTION

4.1 INTRODUCTION

Metallic materials were much frequently used for various engineering and technological applications. All the metals and their alloys except noble metals occur in nature as a chemical compound viz. oxides, sulphates, halides, etc. Pure elemental metals are obtained from naturally available minerals and then metal can be used for various applications. When a metallic material is exposed to the environment enriched with moisture and gases or immersed in liquid like acids or alkalies, it will undergo disintegration and lead to the formation of its chemical compound. This process will reduce the service life period of the metallic component or damage the equipment.

Now-a-days, it is a very severe problem and the destruction of metals due to environment has lead to form a separate study matter under the name, 'corrosion science.'

Definition

*   Corrosion is defined as unintentional destruction of solid body due to direct chemical or electro-chemical reactions starting from the surface.

*   "Corrosion is defined as destruction or deterioration and consequent loss of a solid metallic materials, starting at its surface, due to an unintentional chemical or electro-chemical attack, by their environment."

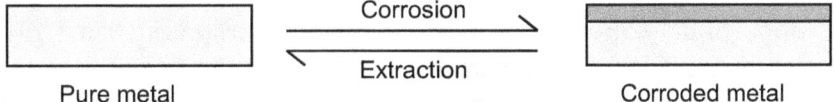

Fig. 4.1: Corrosion versus extraction

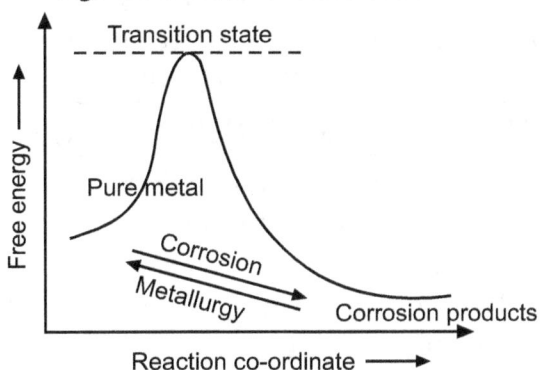

Fig 4.2: Free energy change during corrosion

- Thermodynamically, the compounds of metals are more stable (hence less energetic) as compared to the pure metals. i.e. if a pure metal is obtained after metallurgy, then slowly they get converted to their combined form (or compounds) naturally.

4.2 CAUSE OF CORROSION

- Except noble metals (gold, silver, etc) all other metals exist in nature in the combined forms such as oxides, hydroxides, carbonates, sulphides, sulphates, etc. The extraction of metals from their ores requires a considerable energy to be supplied to the process.

- Therefore, the isolated pure metals can be considered as being in a much higher energy state than in the corresponding ores and hence, they exhibit a natural tendency to return back to their lower energy state (i.e. combined state or compound form). Thus corrosion can be regarded as the tendency of the metals to revert back to their more stable chemical forms such as oxides, sulphide, etc. in which they occur in nature.

4.3 ECONOMIC IMPORTANCE

- Everyday corrosion of many metallic items of common use is taking place all around. Corrosion is a serious problem because the life of the plant or equipment is very much reduced due to corrosion. An engineer whether dealing with design or process operation, or may be a mechanical, chemical or civil engineer has to face this serious problem of corrosion. For example, chemical industries face many corrosion problems, some of which are so serious as to cause shut down of plants and collapse of structures involving hazards to human life. It is very difficult to assess the exact loss caused due to corrosion. This changes from process to process and from locality to locality.

- In tropical countries, like India, the corrosion problem is more serious than in cold countries. In India the direct loss due to corrosion per annum is estimated to about Rs. 200 crores and annual expenditure in controlling corrosion is to the order of Rs. 50 crores. Thus corrosion is a matter of grave concern due to the enormous cost involved in the replacement and maintenance of metallic parts in all kinds of applications.

- However, in order to be able to make rational decisions regarding (i) avoiding severely corrosive conditions or (ii) providing efficient protection against corrosion, it is necessary to have a basic understanding of corrosion behaviour.

4.4 CLASSIFICATION (TYPES OF CORROSION)

- The corrosion of metals and alloys is due to either chemical or electro-chemical reactions between a metal surface and the medium or environment.

- Although corrosion occurs in many ways depending upon the corrosive environment, these may be broadly classified into (i) Dry corrosion or Direct chemical corrosion and (ii) Wet corrosion or Electro-chemical or immersed corrosion.

- Dry corrosion occurs at a gas-metal interface and the reaction is a chemical combination between the metal and an oxidising component of its environment.

- The wet corrosion occurs at solution - metal interface and is the result of electro-chemical reaction between a metal and its surroundings.

- In both cases, the reactions take place at the interfaces of metal and surrounding; and the rate of reaction is modified by the properties of the corrosion products i.e. metallic compounds that are formed as a result of corrosion. The formation, destruction or removal and reformation of naturally occurring film on the surface of metals at the site of corrosion reaction largely affects the rate of corrosion and corrosion control.

4.5 DRY OR DIRECT CHEMICAL CORROSION

- In this type of corrosion, the metal is surrounded by gases such as oxygen, halogen, sulphur dioxide, hydrogen sulphide, etc. in the surrounding environment and as a result, corrosion occurs mainly through the direct chemical action of environment or atmospheric gases with the metal surfaces in immediate proximity.

- "Dry corrosion is a phenomenon involving direct chemical reactions between metal and a gas or liquid, which is not an electrolyte."

- This type of corrosion produces two important effects on the metal (a) metal is consumed and (b) the properties of the metal are changed.

- The extent of dry corrosion depends upon the following factors

  ➢ Chemical affinity between the corrosive environment and solid metals.

  ➢ Capacity or ability of reaction products to form a protective film on the metal surface.

There are three types of dry corrosions depending on the corrosive environment.

(a) Oxidation corrosion, (b) Corrosion by other gases and (c) High temperature corrosion.

4.6 OXIDATION CORROSION

It is brought about by the direct action of oxygen at allow or high temperatures on metals, usually, in the **absence of moisture**. At ordinary temperatures metals, in general, are very slightly attacked. However, alkali metals (Li, Na, K etc.) and alkaline earths (Be, Mg, Ca, Sr etc.) are even rapidly oxidised at low temperatures. At high temperatures, almost all metals (except noble metals viz. Ag, Pt, Au) are oxidised.

Mechanism of Oxidation

The reactions in the oxidation corrosion are

$$2\,M \longrightarrow 2\,M^{n+} + 2\,ne^- \qquad \text{[Oxidation or loss of electron]}$$
$$\text{(Metal ion)}$$

$$2\,ne^- + O_2 \longrightarrow nO^{2-} \qquad \text{[Reduction or gain of electron]}$$
$$\text{Oxide ion}$$

Overall: $2\,M + O_2 \longrightarrow 2\,M^{n+} + nO^{2-}$
$$\text{[Metal oxide]}$$

- The oxidation occurs first at the surface of the metal and the resulting metal oxide layer forms a barrier that tends to restrict further oxidation. The gas molecules are adsorbed rapidly by the surface of the metal as molecules, atoms or ions and then diffusion of gas in metal takes place. The gas molecules are held by the molecules of the metal through the residual valency of surface molecules. This layer of adsorbed gas is only one molecule thick.

- When the temperature rises, the adsorption, which is a purely physical phenomenon, turns into chemisorption and the gas molecules dissociate into atoms and a solid or liquid reaction product is formed on the surface. The reaction continues as these freshly formed atoms or ions diffuse into the metal lattice at isolated points and form oxide lattice. In the case of oxygen, oxide film is formed, in the case of H_2S, sulphide is formed.

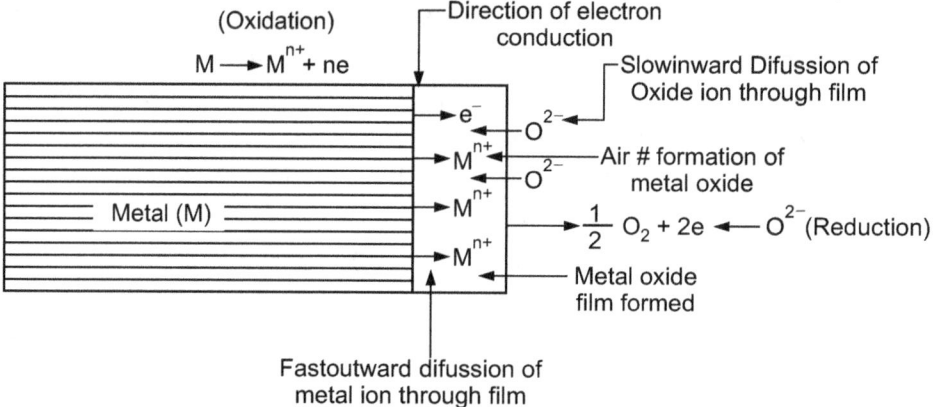

Fig. 4.3: Mechanism of oxidation

- For oxidation to continue, either the metal must diffuse outwards through the film to the surface or the oxygen must diffuse inwards through the film to the underlying metal. The metal cations are appreciably smaller than the oxygen ions (anions) and therefore, cations have much higher mobility. Thus the outward diffusion of metal is generally much more rapid than the inward diffusion of oxygen.

- The nature of the oxide formed plays an important role in oxidation corrosion process

    Metal + Oxygen $\longrightarrow$ Metal oxide (corrosion product)

- When oxidation starts, a thin layer of oxide is formed on the metal surface, and the nature of this layer of film decides the further action. (A layer is called film, when its thickness is less than 300 A^{∞} and it is called scale, if its thickness exceeds 300 A). $(1\ A^{\infty} = 10^{-8}\ cm)$

4.7 NATURE OF FILMS

The film formed may be unstable, volatile or stable.

Unstable: The oxide film may be unstable, which decomposes back into the metal and oxygen.

Metal oxide $\rightleftharpoons$ Metal + Oxygen

Therefore, oxidation corrosion is not possible in such cases. e.g. silver, platinum, gold etc. do not undergo oxidation corrosion. In the case of noble metals, e.g. platinum oxide formed is unstable and so there will be no corrosion.

Volatile: The oxide film volatilizes as soon as it is formed; thereby leaving the underlying metallic surface exposed for further attack. This causes rapid and continuous corrosion, leading to excessive corrosion. e.g. molybdenum oxide (MoO_3) is volatile.

Stable: A stable layer, fine grained in structure which can get adhered tightly to the metal surface. Such type of layer or film may cut off the penetration or diffusion of oxygen into the underlying metal and seals the metal surface from any further attack of atmospheric oxygen. Such a protective film act as a shield for metal surface and prevents futher oxidation corrosion. The oxide films formed on the surface of most of the metals like Al, Pb, Cu, Sn etc., are stable and protective, adhering and impervious in nature and consequently prevent further oxidation corrosion.

The stable films formed on metallic surfaces may be further divided into three types

(a) **Stable but porous, (b) Stable, non-porous and tenacious, (c) Stable, non-porous but brittle.**

(a) **Stable but Porous:** The film of the product formed, which cannot completely cover the metallic surface forms a porous film. Therefore, the atmospheric oxygen has an access through the pores to diffuse into the underlying surface of metal. This causes serious corrosion.

According to Pilling-bedworth rule, "an oxide is protective or non-porous, if the volume of the product (oxide in this case) is at least equal in volume to that of the metal from which it is formed." On the other hand, "If the volume of the product is less than the volume of the metal from which it is formed then the layer or film formed is porous (i.e. non-continuous) and hence non-protective; because it cannot prevent the access of oxidising substance (oxygen in this case) to the fresh metallic surface below."

$$\text{Pilling-Bedworth ratio} = \frac{\text{Volume of oxide}}{\text{Volume of metal forming the oxide}}$$

$$= \frac{\text{Mole weight of oxide/density of oxide}}{\text{Mole weight of metal/density of metal}}$$

If P.B. ratio > 1, film is stable and protective

If P.B. ratio > 1, film is unstable and non-protective

If P.B. ratio > 2, again unstable due to compressive stresses.

Alkali metals (such as Li, Na, K etc.) and alkaline earth metals (such as Be, Mg, Ca etc.) form oxides which have smaller volumes than the metals from which they are formed. Hence the oxide formed on the surface is porous in nature and this porosity of oxide films does not offer any resistance to oxygen of the surroundings and easily allows the oxygen to diffuse into the metal. In general, oxides which are porous in nature and occupy less volume than the metal itself offer no protection to the surface of the metal and the metal is, therefore, easily corroded even at low temperatures.

(b) Stable, Non-Porous and Tenacious: The film of the product may be non-porous and tenacious which built upto certain thickness. In such cases, the rate of corrosion decreases with time. This type of corrosion is common in most of the metals.

Metals like aluminium forms oxide whose volume is greater than the volume of metal (Al) and an extremely tightly-adhering non-porous layer is formed. Due to the absence of any pores or cracks in the oxide film, it forms a barrier for further action and hence, the rate of oxidation is rapidly decreased to zero.

(c) Stable, Non-Porous but Brittle: In some cases, non-porous product i.e. film may be brittle and may crack after sometime. Hence deeper corrosion may take place in such cases.

Heavy metals form an oxide film which is continuous and does not allow the atmospheric oxygen to diffuse into the metal so easily. These oxide films, therefore, offer resistance to process of oxidation and protect the metal from corrosion. The rate of thickening of these oxide films follows a decreasing parabolic growth law, but the film of oxide is under great lateral compression, as a result of which these oxide films have a tendency to crack. This tendency of cracking increases with increase in thickness, especially at high temperatures. Hence when there are fluctuations in temperature, the film may crack and the oxidation which has stopped because of thickness of oxide layer, may once again increase. This goes on intermittently.

If the temperature is very high, the oxygen diffuses into the metal through the intervening layer of oxide and the metal also diffuses outwards through the oxide film. Thus diffusion occurs both ways. The composition of the scale varies in composition from layer to layer. Iron and iron-rich alloys provides example of this type.

4.8 CORROSION BY OTHER GASES

- Whether corrosion of a metallic surface by other gases such as SO_2, CO_2, Cl_2 etc. will take place or not, depends on their chemical affinity for the metal under consideration and the intensity of attack depends on the nature of the film formed on the metallic surface, i.e. protective or non-protective. e.g. AgCl film formed due to the attack of chlorine on silver is protective i.e. non-porous which decreases the intensity of attack. While when chlorine acts on tin surface the $SnCl_4$ formed being volatile leaves and the metal surface is exposed for further attack. This results in gradual but complete destruction of the tin metal.

- **Hydrogen embrittlement** is the action of atomic hydrogen formed as a result of chemical or electrolytic action, occurring at metal surfaces under specific environments. For example, in petroleum industry, the presence of aqueous solutions of H_2S in the system causes evolution of atomic hydrogen at the steel surface and forming a troublesome FeS scale at ordinary temperature.

$$Fe + H_2S \longrightarrow FeS + 2H$$

- The evolved atomic hydrogen readily diffuses and collects in the voids or larger faults in the metal. In these voids, the atomic hydrogen recombines to form entrapped molecular hydrogen.

$$H + H \longrightarrow H_2$$

- As this diffusion and accumulation of molecular hydrogen continues, a high pressure is built up. If this pressure exceeds the yield strength of the metal then blistering and fissures occur which results in lowering the strength and ductility of the metal. At times, this may result in embitterment of the metal.

- At high temperatures, the atomic hydrogen is formed by the thermal dissociation of molecular hydrogen. This atomic hydrogen which is chemically very active at high temperature readily combines with C, S, O and N (which are normally present in small quantity in metals). When it reacts with carbon of steel, methane (CH_4) gas is formed which develops intergranular cracking, blistering etc. This is called 'decarburization.' Decarburization causes brittleness and reduction in strength of the steel.

4.9 HIGH TEMPERATURE CORROSION

- The scaling of metals which takes place at elevated temperatures under dry conditions is known as high temperature corrosion.

- At ordinary temperatures, the stable state of most metals is in the form of an oxide. This can be seen from Table 4.1, which lists the free energy of formation of one mole of different oxides at 25° C.

Table 4.1: Free Energy of Formation of Metal Oxides (kJ mol^{-1})

Metal Oxide	Free Energy of Formation	Metal Oxide	Free Energy of Formation
Al_2O_3	− 1576	NiO	− 217
Cr_2O_3	− 1045	Cu_2O	− 145
TiO_2	− 853	Ag_2O	− 13
Fe_2O_3	− 740	Au_2O_3	+ 163

- Except in the case of gold, the free energy change is negative, indicating that the stable form is the oxide. Only gold occurs in the metallic form in nature. All other metals are to be reduced to the metallic state by an extraction process. While using most metals in the metastable state, we depend on the fact that the thermal energy at the service temperature will be small enough to keep the oxidation rate within the desired limits. As the service temperature increases, the oxidation becomes a serious problem.

- The rate of oxidation of a metal at an elevated temperature depends on the nature of the oxide layer that forms on the metal surface. For good oxidation resistance the oxide layer should be adherent to the surface. The adherence of an oxide film is dependent on the ratio of the volume of oxide formed to that of metal consumed during oxidation. This ratio is known as the Pilling - Bedworth ratio. If the ratio is less than unity, tensile stresses will be set up in the oxide layer. The oxide being brittle cannot withstand tensile stresses, therefore, it cracks and does not remain protective against further oxidation. While if the ratio is more than unity, the oxide layer will be in compression and will cover the metal surface uniformly and becomes protective. If the ratio is much greater than unity, there is a risk of too much compressive stresses being set up and again cracking the layer.

Table 4.2: Pilling - Bedworth Ratio for Some Oxides

Metal Oxide	Ratio	Metal Oxide	Ratio
Fe_2O_3	2.16	Al_2O_3	1.38
Cr_2O_3	2.03	MgO	0.79
Cu_2O	1.71	Na_2O	0.58
NiO	1.60	K_2O	0.41

- When a metal is subjected to alternate heating and cooling cycles in service, the relative thermal expansion of the oxide and the metal also determines the stability of the protective layer. Thermal shock caused by rapid heating or cooling may cause the layer to crack. If the oxide layer is volatile as is the case with molybdenum and tungsten oxides at high temperatures, there can be no protection.

- When the oxide layer is adherent to the metal surface, further oxidation can take place only by means of diffusion through the oxide layer of the oxygen anions or the metal cations. When the diffusion of the oxygen anions controls the oxidation rate then oxidation takes place at the metal-oxide interface. If the metal cations diffuse through the oxide layer in the opposite direction then oxidation takes place at the oxide-oxygen interface. As the oxide layer increases in thickness, the diffusion distance through the layer also increases.

- The thickness of the layer increases as the square root of time at constant temperature.

$$x = \sqrt{Dt}$$

where x = increase in thickness

   D = Diffusion coefficient

   t = time

- This is called the parabolic law of oxidation. Many metals obey the parabolic law at some temperature range of oxidation. The square of the layer thickness is proportional to the diffusion coefficient. The diffusion coefficient increases with temperature in an exponential manner. Correspondingly, the oxidation rate also increases exponentially with temperature. According to Arrhenius equation as -

$$k = A e^{-(E/RT)}$$

where k = rate of corrosion, A = frequency factor

E = activation energy, R = gas constant

T = absolute temperature.

- Hence as the temperature increases, problem of metal protection also aggravates rapidly. The activation energy for oxidation is the same as the activation energy for diffusion through the oxide layer.

- If the Pilling - Bedworth ratio is much greater than unity, the oxide layer tends to crack on reaching a critical thickness. This mainly happens when the oxidation process occurs at the metal - oxide interface, where the expansion cannot be accommodated as easily as at the oxide - gas interface. When the excess layer beyond the critical thickness peels off, the oxidation rate becomes constant indicating a constant critical oxide thickness at the metal surface.

- The oxidation resistance of a metal can be improved by the addition of suitable alloying elements to the base metal. The alloying element must be present in sufficient concentration to produce the desired oxide layer. The most common alloying elements added to iron for this purpose are Cr, Al and Ni. The oxidation rate of iron as a function of chromium content is shown in Fig. 4.4. The rate decreases with increasing chromium content. The addition of chromium enables the formation of a thin protective layer of Cr_2O_3 on the surface of iron.

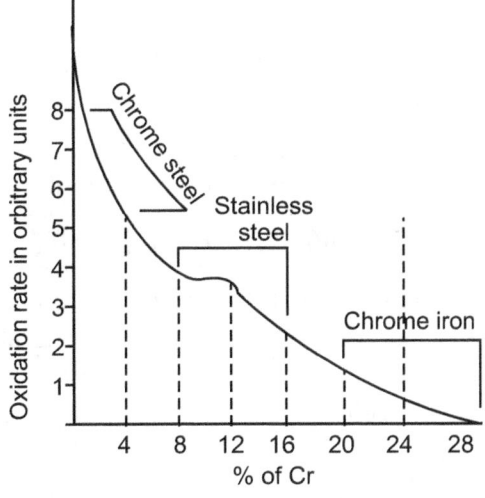

Fig. 4.4: Oxidation rate of Fe as a function of % Cr

- For oil refinery components upto 10 % Cr is alloyed with iron. Alloys with greater than 12 % Cr are called stainless steels which are used for turbine blades, furnace parts and valves of I.C. engines 12% Cr in steel gives excellent corrosion resistance upto 1000°C; while for resistance above 1000°C, 17 % Cr is used, 18 - 8 stainless steel containing 18 % Cr and 8 % Ni is best commercially available oxidation - resistant alloys. Kanthal with 24 % Cr; 5.5 % Al and 2 % Co added to Iron is used for furnace windings upto 1300° C. Inconel with 76 % Ni; 16 % Cr and 7 % Fe has excellent oxidation resistance and good mechanical properties Chromel, (10 % Cr alloyed with Ni) and alumel, (2 % Al; 2 % Mn; 1 % Si alloyed with Ni) are used upto 1100°C as heat resistant thermocouple wires.

- Another form of high-temperature corrosion occurs when liquid metals flow past other metals. This type of corrosion occurs in soaking pits for molten metals, reheating furnaces and heat-exchangers carrying liquid metal coolants used in nuclear power systems. The corrosion reaction in this case is essentially a process of mass transfer and is not dependent upon local cell potentials for its driving force. Actually, the corrosion is due to the tendency of the solid to dissolve in the liquid metal upto the solubility limit at the given temperature.

- The liquid - metal attack may either form a simple solution of the solid metal, a chemical compound or be the selective extraction of one of the component metals in a solid alloy. This occurs when there is a temperature or concentration gradient within the solid - liquid system. Serious damage by liquid-metal attack is observed in heat exchangers carrying (Bi and Na) liquid coolants. As the solid container usually copper tubing, approaches equilibrium with the liquid - metal coolant in the hot zone of the heat exchanger, a portion of solid container dissolves in liquid-metal coolant. When this coolant liquid-metal moves towards the cooler parts of the heat-exchanger, the solubility limit decreases and therefore, some of the dissolved solid metal is thrown out, which deposites on the inner walls at cooler end. Thus because of temperature gradient within the solid-liquid system, the exchanger tube at the hot zone gets corroded and the cold end gets plugged with the corrosion product. This may result in shut down of liquid-metal heat-exchangers if proper precaution is not taken.

- The life of heat exchangers can be prolonged by the addition of certain inhibitors to the liquid alloy coolant to form protective films to prevent high temperature corrosion.

4.10 WET OR ELECTRO-CHEMICAL CORROSION

- Though electro-chemical mechanism is followed during corrosion still it is customary to classify the different corrosion reactions into a few general types depending on the special situations in which these occur. e.g. (1) Immersed corrosion, (2) Galvanic corrosion, (3) Concentration cell corrosion, (4) Pitting corrosion, (5) Intergranular corrosion, (6) Water line corrosion, (7) Stress corrosion, (8) Soil corrosion etc.

- In all these cases to follow the electro-chemical mechanism, the following factors are essential

  ➤ Formation of anodic and cathodic areas separated by finite distance.

> ➤ A conducting medium called electrolyte to maintain good electrical contact between anodic and cathodic areas.

> ➤ A potential difference between anodic and cathodic areas (These may be two dissimilar metals or two different areas on the surface of the same metal or alloy) to maintain a constant flow of electric current.

- Anodic and cathodic areas are developed on the metal surfaces due to the structural and chemical in homogeneity existing in metals and environments.

- Anode or anodic area is that portion of the metal surface which is corroded (i.e. oxidised or loses electrons) and dissolves as ions. From anode current (electrons) leaves the metal and enters the electrolyte.

- Cathode or cathodic area is that portion of the metal surface from where the electron current leaves the electrolyte and enters or returns to the metal. Here the metal is not affected as reduction takes place.

- As both anodic and cathodic areas are immersed in the electrolyte hence electrical balance of the system is restored by the reaction between electrons and the positive ions in the electrolyte.

- On prolonged corrosion, the metal would deteriorate over the complete surface as the anodic and cathodic areas interchange during the actual corrosion.

4.10.1 Basic Principles

(a) Electrochemical Cells

An electrochemical cells is one in which channel reactions generate electricity. The essential components of an electro-chemical cell are electrolyte (ionic conductor), anode, cathode and external circuit (electronic conductor). In electro-chemical cells at cathode reduction reaction occurs while oxidation reaction occurs at anode.

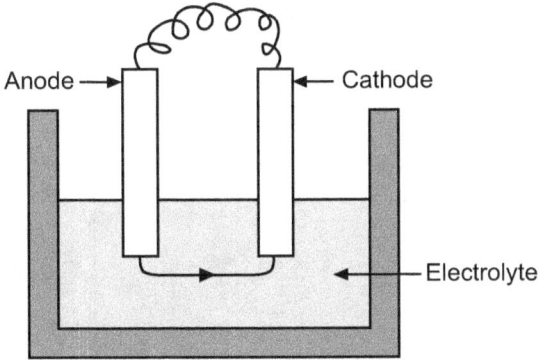

Fig. 4.5: Electro-chemical cell

(b) Electrode Potential

If an electrode is immersed in an electrolyte contained its own ions, two types of reactions (1) oxidation i.e., dissolution of metal electrode ($M \rightarrow M^{n+} + ne$) and (2) reduction i.e., deposition of metal ion at the electrode ($M^{n+} + ne \rightarrow M$) occur. Due to these reactions the electrodes acquires a charge i.e., it will acquire a negative charge (anode) when metal dissolution reaction occurs at its surface and acquire a positive charge (cathode) when metal deposition reaction occurs. These reactions continue till equilibrium is established between the electrode surface and electrolyte. This difference of electrical potential between electrode and electrolyte is termed as single electrode potential or half cell potential.

To measure a single electrode potential, it is connected by another half cell, so that potential difference between the two electrodes can be measured. Thus, relative value of single electrode potential with respect to another electrode which is called reference electrode can be measured. This reference electrode is a standard hydrogen electrode whose potential is taken to be zero.

The standard electrode potentials at 25°C for various metals with reference to hydrogen are listed in Table 4.3.

Table 4.3: The e.m.f. or Galvanic Series

Elements	Electrode Potential at 25°C (Volts) Anode	
Li	+ 3.02	Anode
K	+ 2.92	(Active)
Na	+ 2.72	
Mg	+ 2.34	
Al	+ 1.67	↑
Zn	+ 0.76	Chemical
Cr	+ 0.56	activity
Fe	+ 0.44	increases
Pb	+ 0.12	
H_2	0.00 (Reference)	
Cu	− 0.34	
Ag	0.80	Cathode
Au	− 1.70	(noble)

Gold is the most noble metal and will not dissolve easily and hence has outstanding corrosion resistance. Lithium at the top of the list is the most active metal and hence exhibit poor corrosion resistance.

If two different metals are coupled together in the same electrolyte, the metal with the more positive potential will suffer corrosion.

(c) Galvanic Cells

A galvanic cells is formed. When two dissimilar metals are in electrical contact with each other and are dipped in an electrolyte. Fig. 4.6 shows a galvanic cell in which zinc and iron electrodes are dipped in an electrolyte solution ($FeCl_2$) and are electrically connected.

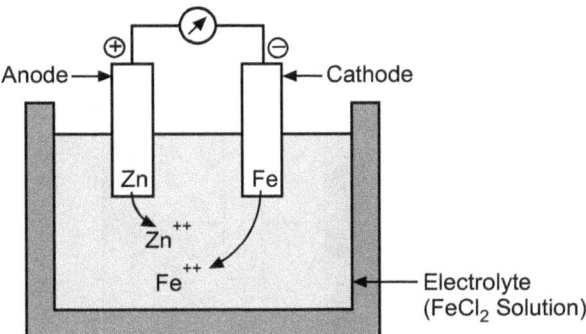

Fig. 4.6: Galvanic cell

When two dissimilar metals are electrically connected, the metal higher in the electromotive series (Table 4.3) corrodes and becomes anode. The metal which is lower in the series becomes cathode. In this case zinc electrode, acts as anode and iron electrode acts as cathode. The dissolution of zinc (anode) takes place as per the reaction

$$Zn \rightarrow Zn^{++} + 2e$$

These electrons move through the electrolyte to the iron electrode (cathode). Hence, zinc dissolves and iron is protected.

The potential difference between the electrodes and the ratio of the areas of cathode to the anode controls the rate of galvanic corrosion. Corrosion rate will be very high if the difference in potential and/or the ratio of cathode to anode areas, is more.

Types of Galvanic Cells

There are three types of galvanic cells

    (i)   Composition cells.

    (ii) Concentration cells.

    (iii) Stress cells.

(i) Composition Cells

The best examples of composition cell is galvanized steel i.e. coating of zinc on steel. The zinc coating which is less noble than iron serves as anode and iron serves as cathode. Hence, iron is protected even if it is exposed to atmosphere whereas the zinc coating is peeled off.

Other examples of composition cells are

    ➢ Steel screws in brass.

    ➢ Steel shaft in bronze bearings.

    ➢ Lead-tin solder around the wire.

(ii) Concentration Cells

When two electrodes of same metal are immersed in the same electrolyte with different concentrations, a concentration cell is formed. The electrode in the dilute solution is anodic with respect to the electrode in the concentrated solution since the electrode potential depends upon the concentration of the electrolyte.

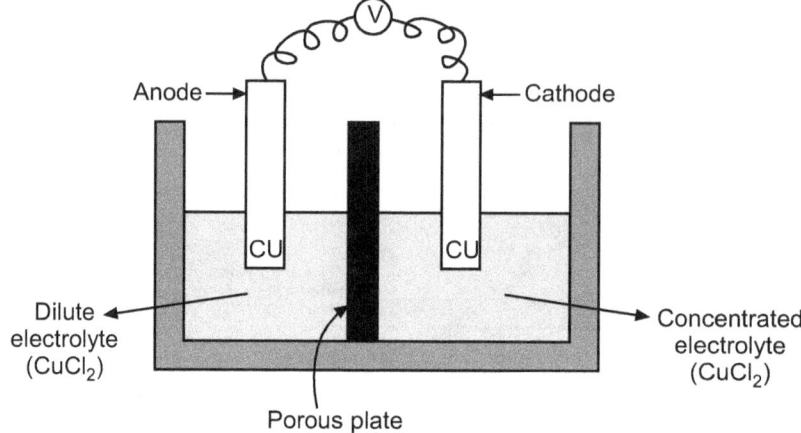

Fig. 4.7: Concentration cell

(iii) Stress Cells

Stress cells are formed due to residual stresses which are induced during cold working of metals. The over-stressed region is more active and becomes anode with respect to a stress free region.

In polycrystalline materials, stress cells are also formed because the atoms at the grain boundaries will have a different electrode potential than the interior atoms. Usually the grain boundaries are anodic to the interior of the grains.

4.11 MECHANISM OF WET OR ELECTRO-CHEMICAL CORROSION

- Corrosion of metallic surfaces in aqueous solutions or moist conditions is electro-chemical phenomenon associated with electron flow (electric current) between anodic and cathodic areas. Reaction at anode is the dissolution of metal and formation of corresponding ions, while at cathode either hydrogen gas is evolved or oxygen is absorbed depending on the nature of corrosive environment.

- Depending on the nature of metallic component and the surrounding medium, the wet corrosion takes place by either of the following two ways
  1. By Hydrogen evolution mechanism or
  2. By Oxygen absorption mechanism.

4.11.1 Hydrogen Evolution Mechanism

- Corrosion by hydrogen evolution mechanism takes place in acidic environments (pH ≤ 4) such as acid industrial waters, solutions of non-oxidising acids (HCl), and where the concentration of dissolved oxygen is low.

- Here, simply the displacement of hydrogen ions from the solution by metal ions takes place. Therefore, all metals which are above hydrogen in the electrochemical series will have a tendency to corrode in acid solution by this mechanism. The anode areas, in this type of attack, are very large areas while the cathode areas are small areas or points.

- This is due to the fact that iron surface is covered with oxide film which causes difference in hydrogen overpotential at few points. Therefore, some areas act as cathode and some as anode.

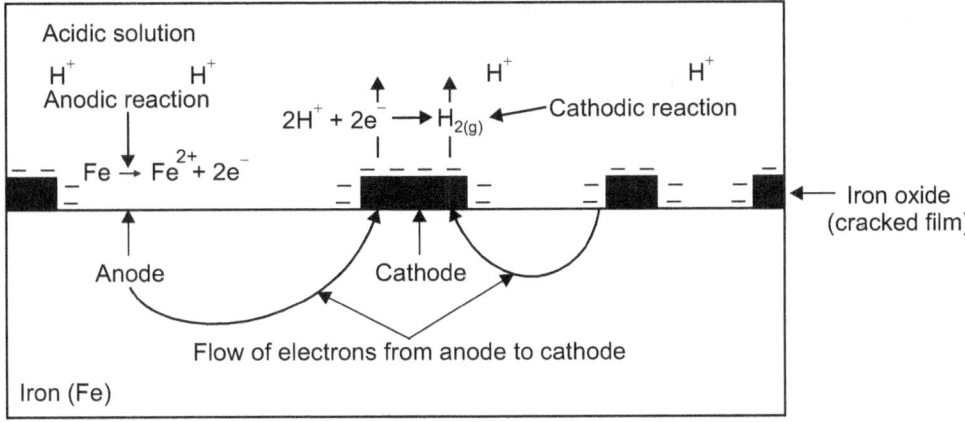

Fig. 4.8: Hydrogen evolution mechanism

The reactions taking place at anode and cathode areas are as below.

At anode, metal goes into the solution as ions

$$M \longrightarrow M^{+n} + ne^-$$

At cathode, elimination of hydrogen takes place

$$2\,H^+ + 2e^- \longrightarrow H_2 \uparrow$$

The overall reaction can be written as

$$M + 2nH^+ \longrightarrow M^{+n} + nH_2 \uparrow$$

Thus flow of electrons takes place from large anodic areas to small cathodic areas where hydrogen gas is evolved.

For example, a steel tank, containing acid industrial waste and small piece of copper scrap in contact with the steel, will undergo corrosion by hydrogen evolution mechanism. The portion of the steel tank in contact with copper is corroded most. The reactions are

$$Fe \rightarrow Fe^{++} + 2\,e^- \text{ (At anode)}$$
$$H^+ + e^- \rightarrow H \text{ (At cathode)}$$
$$H + H \rightarrow H_2 \uparrow \text{ (At cathode)}$$

Overall reaction: $Fe + 2\,H^+ \rightarrow Fe^{2+} + H_2 \uparrow$

The concentration of Fe^{2+} ions increases at anode and hydrogen overpotential at cathode which reduces the potential difference and the rate of corrosion. Hence severity of such type of corrosion is less.

4.11.2 Oxygen Absorption Mechanism

- Corrosion by this mechanism proceeds in mild acidic; alkaline or neutral environment (pH > 4) and when the dissolved oxygen is present in electrolyte. For example, iron and steel plate is corroded in neutral aqueous solutions of electrolytes (NaCl solution) in the presence of atmospheric oxygen.

- Consider a steel plate lying on the ground exposed to moist atmosphere. An oxide layer is formed on the surface of steel in due course of time, and drops of water may collect over the small cracks in the oxide film. Thus water acts as electrolyte, the cracks in oxide film as anode and the oxide-coated steel as cathode. The anodic area is restricted to small area of the crack while cathodic area is mostly the entire surface of the steel plate. Hence the total corrosion current is restricted to small area leading to a very strong localised attack on the exposed steel surface. The reactions at anode and cathode are as below

- At anode (crack): (not covered with oxide film)

$$Fe \rightarrow Fe^{++} + 2\,e^-$$
$$Fe^{2+} + 2\,Cl^- \rightarrow FeCl_2$$

- At large cathode (covered with oxide film): The electrons flow from anode which are intercepted by oxygen atoms of atmosphere. These in presence of water drop form hydroxyl ions as below

$$2H_2O + O_2 + 4e^- \longrightarrow 4(OH)^-$$
$$OH^- + Na^+ \longrightarrow 4(OH)^-$$

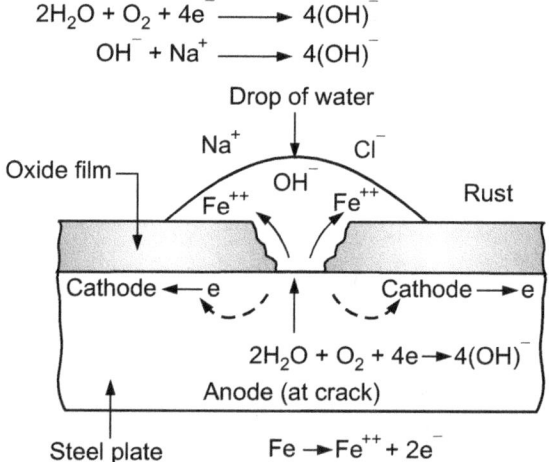

Fig. 4.9: Oxygen absorption mechanism

- Both anodic and cathodic products are water soluble and they diffuse towards each other. When they meet, $Fe(OH)_2$ (Brown) is formed; $Fe^{2+} + 2\,(OH)^-$ (∅ $Fe(OH)_2$; which in the presence of enough oxygen is converted to $Fe(OH)_3$ (Hard rust) which deposits as rust because it is less soluble.

- If the supply of oxygen is not sufficient then the corrosion product is black anhydrous magnetite Fe_3O_4.

- If anodic area is less then anodic current density is very high and under such conditions the process of corrosion is very rapid. If anodic area is covered by deposited rust, the process becomes slow or it stops due to repairing of film caused by deposition of rust.

4.12 FACTORS INFLUENCING THE RATE OF WET CORROSION

The rate of electrochemical corrosion is directly proportional to the electron flow from anodic area to cathodic area and this is further influenced by various factors as below

4.12.1 Factors Related to the Metallic Surface: The Factors Depending on the Nature of the Metal or an Alloy are

(a) Position of Corroding Metal in Electrochemical Series

- In the electrochemical series alkali metals or more active metals are at the top while the noble metals or less active metals are at the bottom. When two metals or alloys are in electrical contact in presence of an electrolyte (i.e. conducting medium), the more active metal (i.e. higher up in the series) suffers corrosion. However metals occupying bottom (i.e. having less tendency to lose electrons and form cations) possess little tendency to be oxidised to positive ions and hence, they are not easily corroded. The rate and severity of corrosion depends upon the difference in their positions and greater is the difference, faster is the corrosion of the anodic metal or alloy.

(b) Hydrogen Over-Voltage

- When two dissimilar metals are in electrical contact, certain extra voltage is needed to evolve hydrogen at a particular metallic cathode than that is needed to evolve hydrogen at platinum cathode. Depending upon the nature of cathodic metal, evolution of hydrogen is either slow or brisk. This evolved hydrogen forms a film around cathodic metal thereby developing back potential. The extra voltage is required to overcome this effect of back potential and is known as **"hydrogen over voltage"**.

- If the metal has impurities having high value of hydrogen overvoltage, a back potential will be set up and corrosion will diminish or even stop. For example, iron containing impurities like lead or tin corrodes much slowly as compared to iron having impurities like copper or platinum.

- Thus, the presence of impurities with low hydrogen over-voltage increases the rate of corrosion while presence of impurities with high over-voltage decreases the rate of corrosion of a metal.

(c) Relative Areas of Anodic and Cathodic Parts

- When two dissimilar metals or alloys are in electrical contact, the corrosion of the anodic part is directly proportional to the ratio of areas of cathodic and anodic parts. Corrosion is more rapid, severe and localized, if the anodic area is smaller because in such case the current density is much greater. Larger cathodic area demands great number of electrons which can be met by smaller anode area only by undergoing fast corrosion.

Thus anodic metal changes into metal ions more briskly, e.g. corrosion protective coating of Sn, Ni or Cr on Iron breaks even at few points, then the corrosion at these points is quite intense.

(d) Purity of Metal

- Impurities when present in a metal generally cause 'heterogeneity' thereby forming tiny electro-chemical cells (at the exposed parts). e.g. zinc metal with lead or iron as impurity undergoes corrosion of zinc around the impurity. The rate and extent of corrosion increases as the exposure and percentage of impurities increase. Hence corrosion resistance of a metal can be increased or improved by increasing the purity of the metal.

(e) Physical State of Metal

- The rate of corrosion is influenced by the physical state of a metal (such as grain size, uneven surface, stress etc.) The smaller the grain size of a metal or alloy, the greater will be its solubility and therefore, greater will be corrosion. This is called grain boundary corrosion.

- Presence of uneven surface increases the corrosion rate. In such cases, the crests having more contact with air behaves as anode while the troughs or crevices having comparatively less contact with air behaves as cathode. This creates a potential difference between crests or peaks and troughs or crevices resulting in corrosion at anode i.e. crests. This type of corrosion is called crevice corrosion e.g. at rivetted joints, irregularities at the two metal joint gets corroded.

- Similarly, the electrode potential of a strained metal is higher than that of annealed metal and hence, more strained (i.e. bent portion etc.) portion gets corroded.

(f) Nature of Surface Film

- In aerated atmosphere practically all metals get covered with a thin surface film (few angustrom thick) of metal oxide the thickness of which varies with the nature of the metal and environmental temperature. Metals such as Ca, Ba, Mg, Li, Na, K etc., form oxide films whose specific volume is less than that of the metal atom; hence the film formed will be porous.

$$2\,M \quad + \quad nO_2 \rightarrow 2\,M_2O_n$$

     (More volume)   (Less volume)

————————— Contraction —————→

- While metals like Al, Ni, W, Cr etc., form oxides whose specific volume is greater than the parent metal atom;

$$4\,M \quad + \quad nO_2 \;-\!\!\rightarrow\; \downarrow 2\,M_2O_n$$

     (Less volume)   (More volume)

————————— Expansion —————→

- Hence the resulting oxide film formed is impervious (i.e. non-porous). Such a film protects the metal from further corrosion (i.e. oxidation).

- Some metals like Al, Cr, Co, Mg, Ni, Ti etc., are passive metals. These metals exhibit high corrosion resistance than expected from their positions in electrochemical series or galvanic series. This is because of the formation of highly protective but very thin film (about $4 \infty 10^{-4}$ i.e. 0.0004 mm thick) of oxide on the surface of an alloy or metal. Further, the film is of self-healing nature (i.e. film if broken will repair or replenish itself) on re-exposure to oxidising conditions. The corrosion resistance of stainless steel is due to the passivating character of chromium present in stainless steel.

(g) Nature of Corrosion Product

- During corrosion of a metal or an alloy, films of corrosion products (e.g. oxides, carbonates, hydroxides of metals) are formed on the metallic surface. If the corrosion product is soluble in the corroding medium, it will be easily removed from the surface exposing the bare and fresh metallic surface for renewed attack by environment and this will increase corrosion. Whereas if the corrosion product is insoluble or sparingly soluble it can adhere to the metal surface thereby restricting further corrosion. Similarly, if the corrosion product formed interacts with the medium to form another insoluble product (e.g. $PbSO_4$ formation in case of Pb in H_2SO_4 solution) then the corrosion product will function as physical barrier thereby suppressing further corrosion.

4.12.2 Factors Related to the Environment

These are as follows

(a) pH of the Solution i.e. Electrolyte

- If the solution or electrolyte is neutral (pH = 7) or alkaline (pH more than 7) then the rate of corrosion is retarded and in acidic solution (pH less than 7) the rate of corrosion increases.

  For Example: The corrosion rate of iron in oxygen-free water is slow, until the pH is below 5. The corresponding corrosion rate in the presence of oxygen is much higher.

- At pH = 4 the corrosion rate is enhanced due to oxidation of ferrous (Fe^{2+}) ions to ferric [Fe^{3+}] ions by the dissolved oxygen at the anodic area. Consequently, corrosivity of materials which are readily attacked by acids can be reduced by increasing the pH of the solution. Thus, Zn suffers minimum corrosion at pH = 11. Al has minimum corrosion rate around pH = 5.5.

(b) Temperature of Electrolyte

- Ionisation and fluidity of the solution increases with rising temperature thereby increasing the corrosion rate e.g. caustic embrittlement takes place only at high temperatures in high pressure boilers.

(c) Humidity

- Humidity in air is also responsible for atmospheric corrosion. For example: Iron does not rust when exposed to dry air or moisture free air, but when exposed to humid or moist air iron undergoes rusting in a short time. The critical humidity (i.e. the relative humidity above which the atmospheric corrosion rate of metal increases rapidly) depends upon the physical characteristics of the metal and the nature of corrosion products. The corrosion of the metallic surface is rapid in humid atmosphere because atmospheric gases such as CO_2, O_2, H_2O (vapour) etc. get dissolved in water and produce an electrolyte which sets up an electrochemical corrosion cell.

- Further, the oxide film on the surface of a metal absorbs moisture though it is a solid body. In the presence of absorbed moisture on the surface, electrochemical corrosion is bound to occur. Rain water supplies moisture for electrochemical attack and at the same time washes away a part of the oxide film from the metallic surface causing enhanced atmospheric attack. Thus nature of source of mositure also plays an important part in electro-chemical corrosion.

(d) Presence of Impurities in Atmosphere

- The atmosphere in industrial area is contaminated with corrosive gases such as CO_2, H_2S, HCl, Cl_2, H_2SO_4 fumes etc. These gases increase the acidity of the liquid adjacent to the metallic surfaces so also electrical conductivity is increased. This increases the corrosion current flowing in the localized electrochemical cells on the exposed metallic surfaces. Similar in marine atmosphere, chlorides of sodium and other metal present in sea water increases the electrical conductivity of liquid layer in contact with the metallic surface; which results in increased and excessive corrosion of metallic surface.

(e) Presence of Suspended Particles in Atmosphere

- Solid particles suspended in air are also responsible for corrosion. For example, chemically active particles such as NaCl, Na_2SO_4, $(NH_4)_2SO_4$ etc., are capable of absorbing moisture and thus, act as strong electrolytes which lead to enhanced corrosion. Similarly, chemically inactive particles such as charcoal particles which absorb moisture as well as gases like SO_2, SO_3 etc., and thus slowly enhance the rate of corrosion.

(f) Formation of Oxygen Concentration Cell

- Differential aeration occurs when one part of the metal is exposed to a different air concentration than the other. The region where the oxygen concentration is smaller (e.g. oxide-coated part or less exposed part) becomes anodic; while more oxygen concentration regions [i.e. parts which are more exposed to air or oxygen] becomes cathodic. The more oxygenated and less oxygenated parts of metallic surface form "oxygen-concentration cell" in which the anodic part (less exposed) gets corroded. In other words, corrosion occurs where access to oxygen is least. This is known as "Differential aeration principle" given by Evans.

Some examples of corrosion by **Differential Aeration** are

- When a pipe-line layed under ground passes through dry soil as well as moist soil, that part of pipe line passing through moist soil has restricted access to oxygen or air and thus, behaves as anodic while that part passing through dry soil has more access to air or oxygen and thus, becomes cathodic. This results in corrosion of pipe passing through moist soil.

- Water line corrosion is common in case of ships, water storage steel tanks, etc., where a portion of a metallic surface is below water and remaining portion is above water. The metallic portion at the water surface is in contact with more-oxygenated water while the metallic portion which is well below the water surface is in contact with less-oxygenated water. This results in the formation of cell where metallic portion well below water is anodic while the metal surface in contact at water level is cathodic. Thus corrosion of metallic surface just below the water level takes place.

- Oil-pipe lines are corroded at the joints if these are leaking. The oil film at the joint restricts the access for oxygen to the inner part and thus, corrosion starts just below the oil film.

- When rivets or bolts used for fixing plates of a metal are not sufficiently tight, a film of moisture may spread under these. Due to restricted access for air under the bolts or rivets severe corrosion starts below the rivets or bolts.

- Iron corrodes under drops of water or a salt solution. Areas covered with drops have less access for oxygen and therefore, become anodic with respect to the other areas which are freely exposed to air or oxygen. Thus the portion of iron which is covered by water drops corrodes.

Table 4.4: Comparison between Dry and Wet Corrosion

Dry Corrosion	Wet Corrosion
1. This is due to direct chemical reaction.	1. This is due to electrochemical reaction.
2. It takes place in presence of atmospheric gases.	2. It takes place in presence of acidic, alkaline or neutral electrolyte.
3. Rate of corrosion is slow.	3. Rate of corrosion is high.
4. Product of corrosion is oxide, chloride, sulphide etc.	4. Product of corrosion depends on electrolyte and dissolved salts.
5. Anodic and cathodic areas not formed.	5. There is formation of anodic and cathodic areas.

4.13 ATMOSPHERIC CORROSION

The heaviest toll of corrosion of most metals and alloys in service is due to the atmospheric corrosion. The atmospheric corrosion is primarily due to the combined effect of (1) the oxide film formation, and (2) film breakdown.

Thus in atmospheric corrosion two types of reactions take place (a) Metal-gas type, and (b) Metal-liquid type.

The film formation is due to the oxidising action of air on the metal surface and if the oxide formed is continuous and protective the further attack is reduced. This follows the course of dry corrosion (oxidation corrosion).

The film break-down is due to electro-chemical action in presence of moisture or electrolyte on the metal surface. Cracks and discontinuities in the film produced will expose the fresh metal surface to the action of humid atmosphere. This will form localised corrosion cells. Then further corrosion will take place according to "Oxygen absorption mechanism" of wet corrosion.

The factors which decide the nature and extent of the atmospheric corrosion and corrosion products are as follows

- The chemical affinity between the metallic surface and the corrosive environment.
- The nature of the film or scale formed on the metallic surface.
- Critical humidity value of the metal.
- Suspended particles (solid or liquid) in the atmosphere.
- Atmospheric impurities (industrial waste gases e.g. SO_2, H_2S etc.)

The first two factors are already discussed under "Dry corrosion."

Critical Humidity Value

For breaking the film formed and electro-chemical corrosion to start, it is not necessary that dew point should reach. The reaction can occur far below the dew point, provided the critical humidity value is exceeded.

"The critical humidity for a metal is defined as the relative humidity above which rate of atmospheric corrosion of a metal sharply increases." This critical humidity value depends upon the physical characteristics of the metal as well as its corrosion products.

For example: Below 50 to 60 % relative humidity primary film of oxide gets formed on the iron surface. When relative humidity exceeds 60 % the primary oxide film on iron breaks and corrosion continues until a fine film of rust is formed on the surface of iron. This film is potentially active and therefore, if the relative humidity goes beyond 80 % there is a sudden increase in corrosion rate with the formation of usual red rust.

Suspended Particles: There are three types of suspended particles

- Essentially active (dissociating mineral salts) e.g. ammonium sulphate near towns and sodium chloride near sea.
- Essentially neutral but capable of absorbing active gases from the atmosphere such as various allotropes of carbon.
- **Neutral Particles Such as Crystalline Silica:** These have very little effect on corrosion because of their negligible capacity of absorption.

Industrial Waste Gases

SO_2 is the most active and affects the atmospheric corrosion to large extent.

It has a tarnishing effect on copper and silver articles. Nickel articles are fogged in presence of SO_2 of atmosphere if the critical humidity value for nickel exceeds. Due to fogging a creamy white film is formed on nickel surface.

SO_2 combines with the essentially active suspended particles (if present in atmosphere) which get settled on the metal surface. Thus, SO_2 can start the corrosion of iron at the second critical humidity value (i.e. 80 %).

Similarly, if second type of suspended particles are present in atmosphere, these absorb sulphur dioxide thereby increasing its local concentration on the metal surface. e.g., charcoal particles adsorb traces of sulphur dioxide and greatly increase the corrosion rate of iron articles.

4.14 IMMERSED CORROSION

When the metallic surfaces are dipped or immersed or put under the solution or electrolyte, the corrosion that takes place is called immersed corrosion. It takes the course of electro-chemical mechanism and corrosion rate is proportional to the electron flow. Thus electro-chemical cell is set up and anodic and cathodic areas are caused due to

- Physical difference which might have developed during fabrication.
- More than one phase if present in the metal.
- Due to differential aeration.
- Surface discontinuities due to crystal junctions etc.

Even very slight differences in the different parts of metal surface can start the electro-chemical corrosion.

The factors which influence the corrosion rate are as below

(a) Metallic Factors

- Electrode potential
- Ease of hydrogen evolution
- Presence of different phases in the metallic surface.

(b) Environmental Factors

- Temperature
- Rate of supply of oxygen
- pH of solution
- Metal-ion concentration
- Conductivity of solution

- Nature and distribution of corrosion products
- Relative movement of metal and environment.

The mechanism of immersed corrosion is mostly hydrogen evolution at cathode.

4.15 PITTING CORROSION   (Nov. 16)

When the corrosion is concentrated at some specific spots on the metal surface leaving the surrounding area practically unaffected, it is called **pitting corrosion**. It is called pitting because at the spots of attack pits, pin-holes or cavities are formed.

Pitting corrosion frequently ruins the tubes, pipes, vessels of various types.

It is due to the break-down of protective film on the metallic surfaces at some points. This forms a small anode and a large cathode and therefore, will follow the oxygen absorption mechanism. The protective film may break due to any of the following reasons

- Surface roughness,
- Scratches or cut-edges,
- Local straining,
- Sliding under load,
- Particular type of chemical attack,
- Presence of impurities such as sand, dust, scale etc. embedded on the metal surface.

Stainless steel and aluminium show pitting corrosion in chloride solutions.

Pitting tendency of stainless steel is decreased by the addition of 2 to 4 % of molybdenum.

4.16 UNIFORM CORROSION

In this type of corrosion a uniform decrease in volume of a metal takes place at a result of chemical action and soluble corrosion products are formed. In this type of corrosion, metal gets converted into soluble corrosion products at a constant rate which can be controlled to some extent. Under these conditions the useful life of a given material can be easily estimated and unexpected failure need not be feared. Uniform corrosive attack is rare, in practice. It is observed in metals like zinc, lead and aluminium.

4.17 GALVANIC CORROSION

When two dissimilar metals such as zinc and copper are electrically connected and exposed to electrolyte, the metal higher in the electrochemical series, i.e. zinc in the present case, undergoes corrosion and this type of corrosion is called **galvanic corrosion**. Zinc is higher in electrochemical series, hence forms anode and undergoes corrosion while copper, which is lower than zinc in electrochemical series, acts as cathode. The type of cathodic reactions depend on the nature of corrosive environment. The flow of electron current takes place from anodic zinc (undergoing corrosion) to the cathodic copper (remains unaffected).

At anode, $Zn \rightarrow Zn^{++} + 2e^-$ (Oxidation)

At cathode, $\underline{Cu^{++} + 2e^- \rightarrow Cu}$ (Reduction)

Net cell reaction $Zn + Cu^{++} \rightarrow Zn^{++} + Cu$

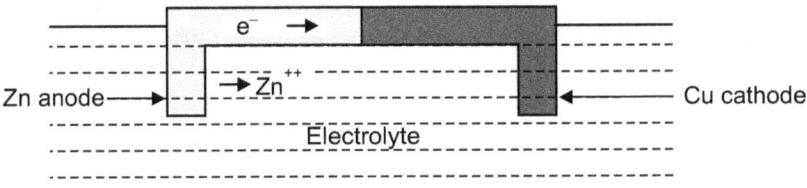

Fig. 4.10: Galvanic corrosion

Steel screws in brass marine hardware, a steel propeller shaft in bronze bearing and lead-antimony solder around copper wire are some well known examples of galvanic corrosion.

4.18 SOIL CORROSION

Corrosion by soils is very important in case of water mains, electric cables and other underground structures, which are embedded in the soil. The corrosiveness of the soil depends upon the following factors: (i) its acidity, (ii) degree of aeration, (iii) electrical conductivity, (iv) content of moisture and salt, (v) texture of soil, (vi) presence of bacteria and micro-organisms.

• The corrosion in soil depends upon the content of oxygen, moisture and soluble matter. The greater the contents, greater is the corrosion.

• Corrosion increases with increase in the concentration of H^+ ions.

• Greater the electerical conductivity, greater is the corrosion.

• Certain types of bacterias in the soil are responsible for the oxidation of organic matter and other oxidisable matter and produce gases which may cause corrosion.

• Presence of strong currents may also stimulate electrolytic corrosion.

• Soil corrosion is purely electro-chemical in nature. The texture of soil is determined by the percentage of particles of various sizes. When the particle size is small, the corrosion is more.

The mechanism of soil corrosion is similar to hydrogen evolution corrosion, if the solids are acidic in nature. The rate of corrosion in acidic soils, depends upon the pH or acidity of the soil, the presence of salts and the content of oxygen etc.

If air pockets are present in the soil, differential aeration corrosion may take place in different parts of the pipeline buried underground.

4.19 INTERGRANULAR CORROSION   (Dec. 12, May 17)

- This type of corrosion takes place because of loss of coherence between the grains. It occurs along grain boundaries and only where the material is highly sensitive to corrosive attack. When the grain boundaries contain material which has more solution potential than the grain centre, in the particular environment, the intergranular attack takes place and produces serious damage only at the grain boundaries and leaves the grain interiors unattacked or only very slightly attacked.
- Intergranular corrosion may be regarded as localised corrosion and depends upon the metallic structure as well as on the conditions that exist at grain boundaries, and other internal discontinuities such as slip planes.
- Intergranular corrosion follows the path of grain boundaries and takes place on microscopic scale without any evidence of intensive attack. Because of this, failures due to such corrosion occur without indicating any warning (due to loss of cohesion between grains).
- This type of corrosion causes brittleness or weakness in the underlying metal and is generally encountered in alloys.
- Such corrosion is observed in defective welding and heat treatment of stainless steels; copper and aluminium alloys. Microscopic examination can show intergranular corrosion. It also has adverse effects on the mechanical properties of alloys.

4.20 WATERLINE CORROSION

- This type of corrosion is also called as differential oxygen-concentration corrosion. It is generally observed that maximum corrosion takes place in a steel tank containing water along a line just below the level of water because access of oxygen is much less there.
- The area above the water line is highly oxygenated and hence acts as cathodic area. Consequently it is not corroded. However, little corrosion takes place when the water is relatively free from acidity. Waterline corrosion is also caused in marine ships and is accelerated by marine plants which are attached to the sides of ships.
- This type of corrosion can be prevented to a great extent by painting the sides of a ship by special anti-fouling paints.

At anode, $Fe \rightarrow Fe^{++} + 2e^-$

$$Fe^{++} + 2Cl^- \rightarrow FeCl_2$$

At cathode, $4e^- + O_2 + 2H_2O \rightarrow 4OH^-$

$$OH^- + Na^+ \rightarrow NaOH$$

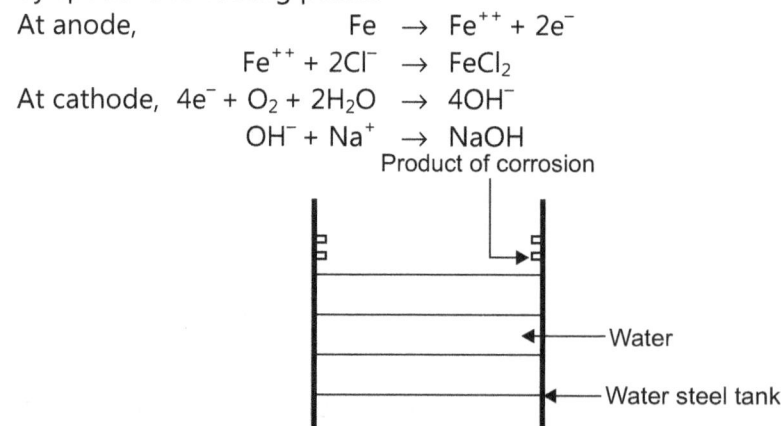

Fig. 4.11: Water line corrosion

4.21 CREVICE CORROSION   (Nov. 16)

It is a local corrosion usually created by dirt deposits, corrosion products, cracks in paint coatings etc. This is commonly observed near the gaskets, bolts, rivets, lap joints etc. Crevice corrosion is usually due to changes in acidity in the crevice, lack of oxygen in the crevice and concentration of detrimental ionic species in the crevice. Selection of resistant materials, proper design to minimize crevices and maintaining the surfaces clean are some of the control measures that can be taken to control crevice corrosion.

4.22 MICROBIOLOGICAL CORROSION

- This type of corrosion is caused by metabolic activities of various micro-organisms and hence it is known as **microbiological corrosion**. The micro-organisms are either aerobic or anaerobic which develop in an environment with or without oxygen. The various micro-organisms responsible for corrosion failures due to their activities are sulphate reducing micro-organism or bacteria, sulphur bacteria, iron and manganese micro-organisms, film forming micro-organisms etc.

- Sulphate reducing bacteria such as sporovobrio desulphuricous causes anaerobic corrosion of iron and steel as these bacterias grow in anaerobic conditions. They need oxygen as well as sufficient amount of sulphates for their growth. Their growth is maximum between pH 5 to 9 and temperatures of 20-30°C. The microbiological corrosion of iron under anaerobic conditions probably take the following course of reactions.

$$8\,H_2O \rightleftharpoons 8\,H^+ + 8\,(OH^-) \left.\right\} \text{(Anodic solution of iron)}$$
$$4\,Fe + 8\,H^+ \rightleftharpoons 4\,Fe^{2+} + 8\,H$$

$$H_2SO_4 + 8\,H \rightleftharpoons H_2S + 4\,H_2O \qquad \text{(Depolarisation due to bacteria)}$$

$$Fe^{2+} + H_2S \rightleftharpoons FeS + 2\,H^+ \left.\right\}$$
$$3\,Fe^{2+} + 6\,(OH^-) \rightleftharpoons 3\,Fe(OH_2) \left.\right\} \text{(Corrosion products)}$$

- This corrosion is localised as well as rapid and the main corrosion products are FeS (Black) and ferrous hydroxide, $Fe(OH)_2$.

- Iron and manganese micro-organisms are also aerobic in nature. They grow in running water as well as in stagnant water at temperatures between 5 to 35°C and pH ranging from 4 to 10 under aerobic (in presence of dissolved oxygen) conditions. They digest iron and manganese ions into their cells in presence of oxygen (aerobic) and form insoluble hydrates of iron and manganese dioxide (MnO_2). These products are thrown out of their bodies later on; which form a layer of corrosion product.

4.23 STRESS CORROSION

- This type of corrosion is produced by the combined effect of mechanical stress and a corrosive environment on a metal. This is also known as a stress cracking.

- Stress corrosion or stress cracking is common in fabricated articles of some alloys such as high zinc brasses and nickel brasses. It is due to the presence of stresses caused by heavy working like rolling, drawing or insufficient annealing. Stress corrosion is highly localized and the attack takes place when the overall corrosion is almost negligible.

- The corrosion agents are highly specific and selective in case of stress corrosion. For example, mild steel is stress corroded by caustic alkalies and nitrate solutions while brass is stress corroded by traces of ammonia. Stainless steel is stress corroded by chloride solutions.

- Stress corrosion is probably due to localised electro-chemical reactions, occurring along narrow paths forming local anodic and cathodic areas on the metal surface. Presence of stress gives rise to strain, which develops small localised zones of higher electrode potential. These zones become very reactive chemically and can be attacked even by traces of corrosive environment, resulting in the formation of cracks.

- The most important factors involved in stress corrosion are
  1. Magnitude and direction of stress.
  2. Specific environment and
  3. Structure and composition of alloy.

The magnitude required for this type of corrosion is about 50% of the yield strength. The stress may be applied externally or it may be residual stress resulting from cold working, unequal cooling, or volume changes accompanied by internal structural arrangement.

For stress corrosion, different environments are required for different alloys. For example, season cracking of brass takes place only in the presence of traces of ammonia or amines.

Season cracking due to stress corrosion generally takes place in copper alloys such as brass. Pure copper does not undergo stress corrosion, but presence of small amounts of alloying elements such as zinc, aluminium, arsenic, phosphorus, antimony etc. make the copper susceptible to stress corrosion.

4.24 VELOCITY RELATED CORROSION

4.24.1 Impingement Corrosion or Erosion Corrosion

- Erosion or impingement corrosion is due to the combined effect of corrosion and erosion i.e. abrasion produced by the impingement or strike of entrapped air bubbles, abrasive particles suspended in the liquid or turbulent flow of liquids. Impingement corrosion usually occurs in systems where fluid moves with high velocities. Failure of part in service may occur with faulty design and poor selection of construction materials.

- Due to the impingement of fluid with very high velocity on the metal surface local breakdown of the protective oxide film takes place. This makes the contact point (from where the protective film has been broken) anodic with respect to the unbroken protective oxide film which acts as cathode. The rate of impingement corrosion is usually very high since the fast moving fluid stream causes depolarization of local anodes (corroding areas) by sweeping away corrosion product and depolarization of the local cathodes (non-corroding areas) y brining a plentiful supply of dissolved oxygen to them. This makes the bare metal to be more anodic and increases the impingement corrosion.

- A few examples where impingement corrosion are corrosion in pumps, valves, turbine blades and tubes carrying sea water.

4.24.2 Cavitation Corrosion

- It occurs due to the formation and collapse of vapour bubbles or cavities on or near the metal surface. Cavitation corrosion occurs in systems which are subjected to rapidly changing pressures because liquid bubbles will form and collapse during low and high pressure cycles respectively. High impact stress will be produced due to the collapse of the liquid bubble on or near the metal surface. And this stress is responsible for cavitation damage because when corrosive liquid (electrolyte) comes in contact with these pits, the corrosion effect is further accelerated. The mechanism of cavitation corrosion is shown in stepwise in Fig. 4.12.

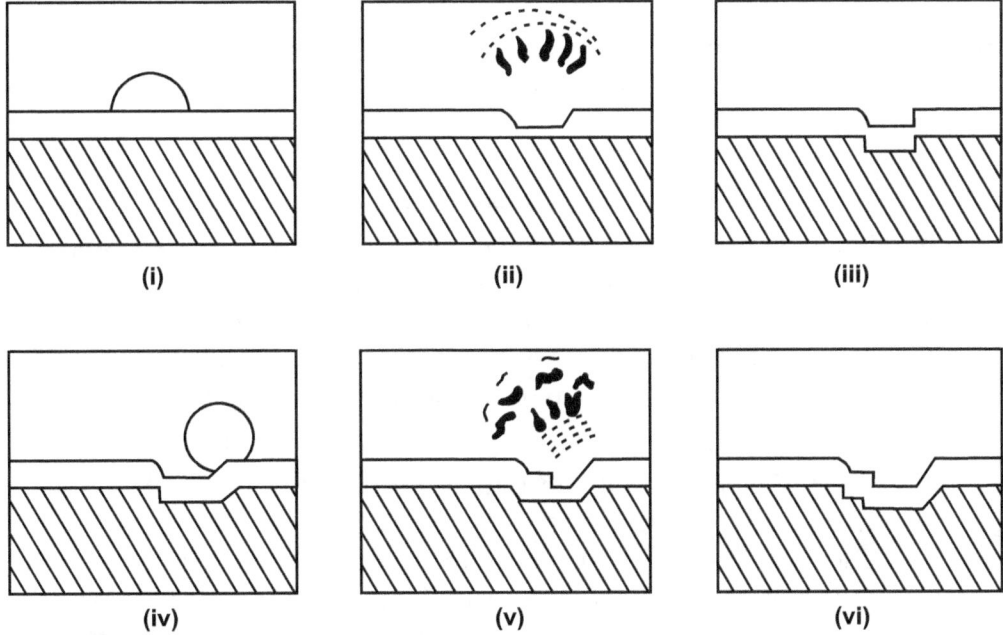

Fig. 4.12: Mechanism of cavitation corrosion

Fig. 4.12 (i) – the formation of bubble on protective oxide film.

Fig. 4.12 (ii) – the collapse of the bubble which destroys the film.

Fig. 4.12 (iii) – the corrosion of newly exposed metal surface and the film reformation.

Fig. 4.12 (iv) – the formation of a new cavitation bubble at the same spot.

Fig. 4.12 (v) – the collapse of new bubble and the destruction of protective film.

Fig. 4.12 (vi) – the corrosion of newly exposed areas and the reformation of oxide film.

A few examples of cavitation corrosion re corrosion in marine propellars, hydraulic turbines, pump impellars and diesel engine cylinder.

4.24.3 Fretting Corrosion

- This occurs at contact areas between two surfaces of materials which are subjected to vibration stresses. It is common at surfaces of clamped or press fits, keyways, engine bearings and bolted and rivetted joints.

- Metal surfaces are usually protected from atmospheric oxidation by the formation of thin protective oxide layer. When two metals parts are placed ion contact under load and subjected to relative motion, the protective oxide film breaks at high stress points causing the surface to expose to the atmosphere. The exposed metal surface, under the action of vibrational stresses and corrosive atmosphere, tends to oxidize which results in fretting corrosion. In the case of steel, patches of finely divided ferric oxide appears as a result of fretting corrosion. Soft materials are usually more susceptible to fretting corrosion than hard materials.

- Fretting corrosion destroys the dimensional accuracy of closely fitted parts, increases the susceptibility of fatigue of dynamically loaded machine parts and deteriorates the bearings surfaces, particularly the surface of ball roller bearing.

4.24.4 Corrosion Fatigue

- Corrosion fatigue is due to the combined effect of fatigue stress and corrosive environment. The fatigue of the metal occurs well below the normal fatigue limit. Due to corrosion fatigue cracks in groups appear on the surface of the metal. Corrosive environment reduces the fatigue life to a large extent. The environments which produce pitting attack on the surface of the material cause corrosion fatigue.

- A mechanism for corrosion fatigue takes places in two steps. In the first step due to corrosion, the pits of various depth are formed on the surface of metal. In the second stage, the cracks appear on the surface and further development of these cracks take place. This is due to the formation of concentration cell between the bottom of pits and the surface of the metal. Once a crack has been formed, it will spread rapidly due to the combined action of corrosion and alternate stress. Due to the applied alternate stress, the electrode potential of pit becomes more anodic than the electrode potential of the surface. And it is assumed that as the cracks increase in depth, the e.m.f. produced by the stress cells increases and the net result is the failure of metal by corrosion fatigue.

Damage Ratio (D.R.)

It gives the effect of corrosion of fatigue strength

$$\text{D.R.} = \frac{\text{Fatigue strength after corrosion}}{\text{Fatigue strength without corrosion}}$$

D.R. = 0.2 for carbon steels with salt water as corrosive medium

= 0.5 for stainless steels with salt water as corrosive medium

= 0.4 for aluminium alloys with slat water as corrosive medium

- For examples, where failure occurs due to corrosion fatigue are marine propellar shaft, super heater tubes, rock drill in mines and turbines.

- The most important protective measure against corrosion fatigue is treatment of the corroding medium and surface protection of the metal such as carburizing steel.

4.25 TESTING AND MEASUREMENT OF CORROSION

- Measurement of corrosion is usually done for (1) Monitoring the corrosion process taking place, (2) Evaluating the quality of the material being used, or (3) For studying the mechanism of corrosion.

- But one of the most difficult aspects of corrosion studies is the development of a means by which the relative resistance of different metallic surfaces to certain corroding media and conditions, can be evaluated. Since many variables are involved in the process of corrosion, it becomes practically impossible to devise a single test that will give results which are commensurable with service conditions.

The different methods generally used for the measurement of corrosion are

(1) Weight-Loss Method

- Often a test is set up in the laboratory to show relative corrosion resistance of material as measured by loss of weight. In this test, a clean metallic standard test piece is measured, weighed and exposed to corroding media for a known time. Then the piece is taken out, cleaned to remove the corrosion products and reweighed. The rate of corrosion, of the material piece is calculated by using the equation, $R = \dfrac{K \cdot W}{D \cdot A \cdot T}$

where K = constant, W = loss in weight in milligrams, D = density of the material in g/cm^3, A = surface area of test piece in sq. cm., T = time of exposure nearest to 1/100th of an hour. The results are generally expressed in millimeters per year [MPY] or milligrams per square decimeter per day [$mg \cdot dm^{-2} \cdot d^{-1}$]. Assuming that the surface corrosion was uniform, these units can be converted to depth of corrosion.

(2) Electrical Resistance Method

- This method is employed for materials to be used in the form of thin wire or strip and the property used is 'Electrical resistance increases as the corrosion decreases the cross-section of metallic material.' Hence, periodic or continuous measurement of the resistance between the ends of a specimen can be used to monitor the corrosion. The electrical resistance measurement has nothing to do with the electro-chemistry of corrosion reaction. Here, only the bulk property is measured which depends on the cross-sectional area of the material.

(3) Corrosometer Method

- Corrosometer measures the change in resistance of a standard probe as corrosion converts the metal to a corrosion product. A second reference probe covered with a highly corrosion-resistant coating is connected to a bridge arrangement. The ratio of the resistance of corroding test piece to the resistance of its non-corroding counterpart (reference probe) is directly related to the extent of corrosion.

- By this method, corrosion rates can be measured, without removing the metallic material from its position and without interrupting the process. Hence changes due to corrosion can be detected early and remedial measures can be initiated.

4.26 PROTECTION FROM CORROSION

- Because of enormous quantities of iron and steel rendered unserviceable by corrosion every year, the problem of preventing corrosion is important to metallurgists and engineers.

- Certain metals such as aluminium and magnesium withstand atmospheric corrosion well because of the formation of an impervious layer on the surface of the metal which prevents further corrosion. Iron rust, on the other hand, is a porous, loosely adherent mass which not only permits the corrosive attack to continue but also accelerates it by holding the additional electrolyte in its pores.

- Cold working accelerates corrosion. Surface of a drawn wire rusts quickly. If a metal contains punched rivet holes it corrodes rapidly near the holes because of the potential difference between the cold worked metal and the adjoining metal which has not been worked. Rivets should have the same composition as the metal or the contact will corrode rapidly.

- Considering all these aspects, one can conclude that the types of corrosion are numerous and the conditions under which corrosion takes place are also extremely varied. Hence diverse methods are to be used to deal with different types of corrosion phenomena.

4.27 METHODS FOR PREVENTION OF CORROSION   (May 17)

The different methods used for the preservation of metal and their alloys from the corrosive attacks of the environments can be considered under following general headings

- Proper design and material selection.
- Improving the characteristics of metal

        (a) Purification, (b) Alloying.

- Cathodic protection

        (a) Sacrificial anode method, (b) Impressed current method.

- Anodic protection

        (a) Potentiostat, (b) Anodizing.

- Modifying the environment

        (a) Deactivation, (b) Dehumidification, (c) Alkaline neutralization,

        (d) By using inhibitors.

- Application of protective coatings

        (a) Chemical conversion coatings, (b) Organic coatings, (c) Organic linings,

        (d) Ceramic protectives, (e) Metallic coatings.

4.28 IMPROVEMENT/CHANGES IN DESIGN

A proper design is capable of preventing the occurrences of in homogeneities in the metal and also in the corrosive environment. Such a proper design should avoid the presence of crevices between adjacent parts of the structure; even if the metals are same, because concentration differences are created due to crevices. Bolts and rivets are, therefore, to be replaced by butt-weld. If it is not possible to avoid crevices in a given design, efforts should be made to minimize the effects due to crevices. The accumulation of dirt or deposits of various kinds cause localized corrosion. Hence the design should allow adequate cleaning and flushing of those parts which are susceptible to deposits, dirt etc.

Sharp corners as well as recesses should also be avoided as these permit the formation of stagnant areas and accumulation of solids. The equipment when supported on legs will permit free access of air and prevent the formation of stagnant pools or damp areas.

While dealing with corrosive liquids, the design should permit uniform flow, because stagnant area on one hand and highly turbulent flow may result in accelerated corrosion.

Similarly, a design should prevent conditions which may subject some areas of structure to stress (e.g. cold working). If possible such equipments may be annealed in order to minimize residual stress to the lowest practical value.

The Important Cares taken during Design are

- Contact of dissimilar metals should be avoided in the presence of corroding solution. If this care is not taken then active metal undergoes corrosion more rapidly.

- If two dissimilar metals are in contact, then the anodic metal must have large surface area with respect to the cathodic metal. Small anodic area corrodes rapidly due to large corrosion current product from cathodic area.

- If two dissimilar metals are to be used then these must be close to each other in electrochemical series.

- An insulating fitting is placed during joining of two dissimilar metals.
- Any surface coating should be avoided for anodic metal.
- Texture of metal should be coarse grained.
- Metallic surfaces must possess smooth finish.
- Metals at anodic end in galvanic series will undergo corrosion rapidly.

4.28.1 Selection of Material

- Selection of the right type of materials is the main factor in controlling corrosion. The choice of the material should be made not only on the cost and structure but also its chemical properties and the environment should also be considered. The metallic materials should be used in their purest form as far as possible.

- Corrosion resistance as well as strength of many metals can be improved by alloying. e.g. (i) stainless steels containing chromium produce an exceptionally coherent oxide film which protects the steel from corrosive attack. (ii) Highly stressed 'Nimonic' alloys (i.e. Ni-Cr-Mo alloys) that are used in gas turbines are quite resistant to hot gases. (iii) Cupro-nickel [Cu: Ni:: 70: 30] alloys containing just 0.2 % of iron are extensively used for condenser tubes and bubble trays of fractionating columns in oil refineries.

- If two metallic materials have to be in contact then they should be so selected that their oxidation potentials are as near as possible. Further, the area of inactive metal i.e. more noble should be smaller than that of active or anodic metal.

- Wherever practicable, the metallic parts during storage should not come in contact with moisture. Therefore, while packing, the metal parts should be sealed in a low permeability plastic in presence of activated silica or alumina gel.

- Corrosion can be controlled by suitably adjusting the acidity or alkalinity i.e. pH of the environment. Every metallic surface has minimum corrosion at a specific pH. When control of pH is not practicable, corrosion can be reduced by using inert coatings or inactive metals.

- When contact of dissimilar metals is unavoidable, suitable insulators should be inserted between them to reduce current flow and attack on the anode.

4.29 IMPROVING THE CHARACTERISTICS OF METAL

(a) Purification of Metal

Impurities in metal make it heterogeneous thereby decreasing the corrosion resistance. Pure metals possess higher electro-chemical corrosion resistance e.g., Super purity Al (higher than 99.99 %) and chemical lead (99.998 %) are used in specific conditions. But in many cases this is not practicable because of the cost considerations and decrease in certain mechanical properties such as strength.

(b) Alloying

If metals are suitably alloyed both strength and corrosion resistance of most commercial metals can be increased. For maximum corrosion resistance to develop, the alloy should be completely homogeneous. In case of metals such as iron, nickel, copper, etc., the corrosion can be controlled by alloying because of their large capacity of solid solution.

Metals which are susceptible to corrosion can be made passive (Passivity is the lack of activity under conditions where normally a metal is expected to react readily) by alloying with one or more metals which are passive e.g. iron can be made passive by alloying it with the transition metal such as chromium, molybdenum, nickel etc.

4.30 CATHODIC AND ANODIC PROTECTION

If it is impracticable to change the nature of the corrosion medium then corrosion control may be achieved by cathodic protection or anodic protection.

4.31 CATHODIC PROTECTION

- The principle involved in this method is to force the metal to behave like cathode. Since there will not be any anodic area, the corrosion of the metal does not take place. The principle can be explained by considering the corrosion of a typical metal say 'M' in an acidic medium. The electrochemical reactions taking place in such a system are the dissolution of the metal and the evolution of hydrogen gas according to the following equation

$$M \longrightarrow M^{n+} + ne^-$$
$$2 H^+ + 2 e^- \longrightarrow H_2$$

- Cathodic protection can be achieved by supplying electrons to the metallic structure which is to be protected.

  There are two ways of cathodic protection

- By using galvanic or sacrificial anode i.e. galvanic protection.

- By using impressed current called as impressed current cathodic protection.

(a) Sacrificial Anode Method   (May 17)

- The metallic structure to be protected is connected by a wire to a more anodic metal. This results in concentrated corrosion at the more anodic (more active) metal; and this more active metal gets corroded slowly. The original metallic structure now behaves as cathodic and therefore is protected. The more active metal used for this purpose is known as **sacrificial anode**, which when gets consumed i.e. completely corroded is replaced by a new one. Mg, Zn, Al and their alloys are generally used as sacrificial anode. This method is used to protect buried pipelines, water tanks, underground cables, ship hulls etc.

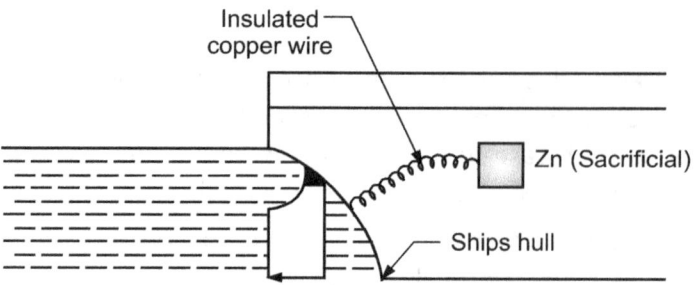

Fig. 4.13: Sacrificial anode

(b) Impressed (External) Current Method

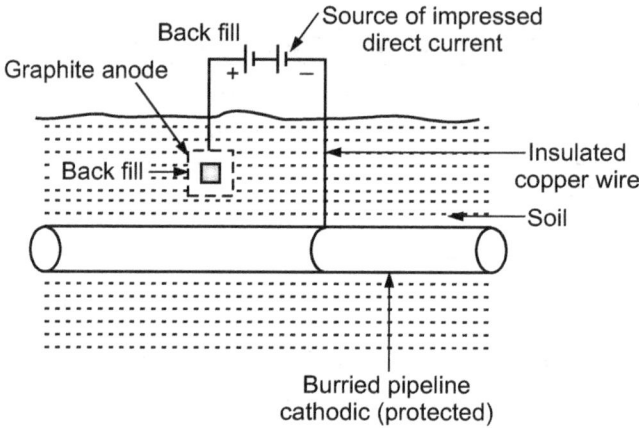

Fig. 4.14: Impressed current protection

In this method, an impressed current is applied in the opposite direction to counter-balance or nullify the corrosion current. The corroding metallic surface is thus converted (under the situation) from anode to cathode and thus protected. Generally, the impressed current is taken from a battery or rectifier using an insoluble anode such as platinum, graphite, stainless steel etc. This type of cathodic protection is useful in protecting box water coolers, water tanks, underground oil or water pipeline, transmission line towers etc.

Limitations of Cathodic Protection

- Capital investment and maintenance cost is high.
- Cathodic protection system which is protecting one pipeline may increase the corrosion of another adjacent pipeline or some metallic structure in the vicinity due to stray currents. This may lead to technical and legal problems.
- If the cathodic reaction produces hydrogen it may produce blisters on the protected metal itself. If a metallic surface (protected) is having a coating (protective) over it, then this coating may get peeled off i.e. will be removed.
- If a sacrificial anode metal is too active relative to the protected metallic surface or a too high potential as compared to open-circuit voltage for the metal/metal ion cell is used then problems associated with the evolution of H_2 or formation and accumulation of OH^- ions will be more.

Table 4.5: Comparison of Sacrificial Anode and Impressed Current Methods

Sacrificial Anode	Impressed Current
1. They are independent of any source of electrical power.	1. Requires mains supply or other source of electric power.
2. Their usefulness is generally restricted to the protection of well coated structures.	2. Can be applied to a wide range of structures including large uncoated structures.
3. They are relatively simple to install, additions may be made until the desired effect is obtained.	3. Needs careful design but it is easy to adjust the output.
4. They may be required at a large number of positions.	4. Small total number of anodes are required.
5. They are less likely to affect any nearby structures as the output is low.	5. Effects on nearby structures are required to be assessed.
6. Their output cannot be controlled but by selecting a proper material electrode, potential can be kept well below the damage point.	6. Controls are simple and even can be made automatic to maintain potential well below the damage point.
7. Their connections are protected cathodically.	7. Requires high insulation on connections to the positive side.
8. They cannot be misconnected so that polarity is reversed.	8. Requires polarity to be checked during commissioning because mis-connections may reverse the polarity and accelerate corrosion.

4.32 ANODIC PROTECTION

In this method, a metal is passivated by applying current in a direction that will render the metal more anodic. Anodic protection is based on the formation of a protective film on metals by externally applied anodic currents. For metals with active-passive transitions e.g. iron, nickel, chromium, titanium and their alloys, if a carefully controlled anodic currents are applied they are passivated and the rate of metal dissolution is decreased. To protect a structure anodically, a device called 'Potentiostat' is used.

(a) **Potentiostat** is an electronic device which maintains a metallic surface (to be protected) at a constant potential with respect to a reference electrode. Potentiostat has three terminals. Terminal 1 is connected to the structure to be protected. Terminal 2 is connected to auxilliary cathode usually of Pt or Platinum clad electrode. Terminal 3 is connected to reference (calomel) electrode.

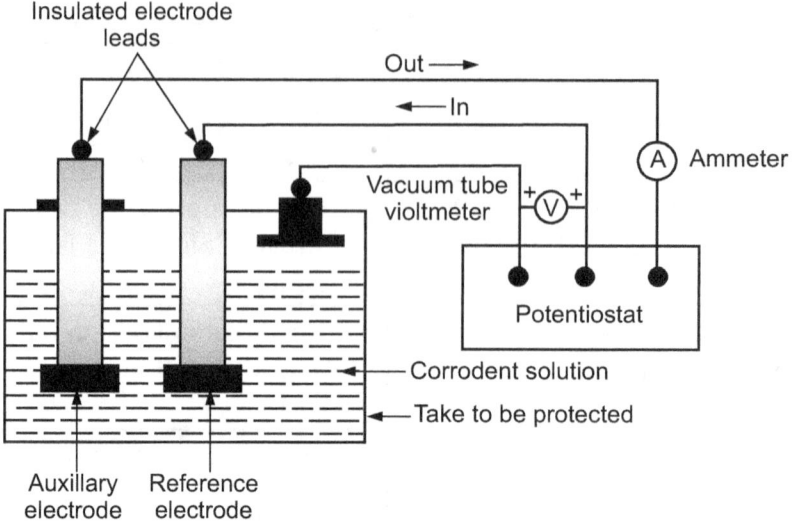

Fig. 4.15: Anodic protection

The optimum potential required for protecting a metallic surface is previously determined by electro-chemical measurements. The main conditions in anodic protection are (1) Potential range over which the metal is passive should be wider i.e. a range of about 50 mV. (2) The current density required to start the protection should be as low as possible. (3) Lower the passive current needed for maintaining the protection, lesser will be the operating cost of the device.

Advantages

- Low operating cost.
- Applicable to wide range of corrodents.
- Ability to protect complex structures.
- Few auxilliary electrodes are necessary.
- Feasibility of the process can be predicted in the laboratory by simulation.
- Protection current gives an indication of corrosion rate.

Limitations

- It is suitable for metal-corrodent systems which show active-passive behaviour.
- It has high cost of installation.
- If the system goes out of control, then there is a risk of high corrosion rate.

(b) Anodizing

- Metals like Al, Ti, etc. and their alloys form a thin oxide film on their surface when exposed to air. The oxide film for above metals is non-porous, adhesive and uniform in nature thereby providing better corrosion resistance to the base metal. However, the thickness of naturally formed oxide layer is very small and it does not protect the base metal properly. To overcome this problem, the thickness of existing oxide film is increased by electrolysis. The process is known as anodizing.

- Besides improving corrosion resistance, the anodized layer (oxide layer) also improves hardness, wear resistance, electrical insulation etc.

- In anodizing, the component to be protected is connected as anode in electrolytic cell, containing strong electrolyte such as conc. H_2SO_4. A small amount of current is passed which oxidizes the anode. The thickness of the oxide film is controlled by time and current density. The oxide layer formed is porous in nature which are then sealed by immersing the article in a bath of oil, wax, dye or boiling water etc. Then the anodized article can be put to actual use.

Anodic Oxidation of Aluminium

- When exposed to air, aluminium forms an oxide film of 0.01 μ to 0.1 μ thickness on its surface. If aluminium is made an anode in an acid electrolyte (H_2SO_4 ; oxalic acid or chromic acid etc.) the thickness of the oxide film increases to 10 to 20 μ. This increase in thickness is due to the formation of microscopic pores in the oxide film. The pores allow the electrolyte to penetrate deeper and form thicker film. The film so formed by anodic oxidation has open pores in the beginning, but these open pores are sealed immersion in boiling water. As a result of which, the oxide film gets converted into $Al_2O_3 \cdot H_2O$ (hydrated form) which occupies more volume thereby the pores are sealed. Alternatively, sealing can be done by immersing the component in boiling dilute sodium dichromate solution.

Table 4.6: Comparison of Anodic and Cathodic Protection

Anodic Protection	Cathodic Protection
1. Applicable to metals showing active-passive transition only.	1. Applicable to all metals.
2. More aggressive corrodents can be handled.	2. Used where no source of power is available by employing sacrificial anodes.
3. Though installation cost is high, operating cost is lower.	3. Lower installation cost.
4. Few electrodes are needed for replacement because of better throwing power.	4. Standard and well established method.
5. Feasibility can be predicted in laboratory and hence designing becomes easier.	5. Feasibility cannot be predicted in laboratory.

4.33 MODIFYING THE ENVIRONMENT

The corrosive effect of the environment can be reduced either by removing the harmful constituents or adding some such substances which will neutralize the corrosive effect of the harmful constituents of the environment.

(a) Deactivation: Quantity of dissolved oxygen in the environment decides whether oxygen concentration type of corrosion will proceed or not. By adjusting the temperature along with proper mechanical agitation the dissolved oxygen can be expelled from the environment. As the rate of corrosion decreases exponentially with the decrease of temperature, hence slight decrease in temperature would cause a pronounced decrease in the amount of corrosion product. This is known as deaeration. In deactivation method either sodium sulphite (Na_2SO_3) or hydrazine hydrate ($N_2H_4 \cdot H_2O$) is added to the liquid medium. Both the chemicals react with the dissolved oxygen readily, thus removing the oxygen from the site of corrosion and hence prevent corrosive action.

$$2\,Na_2SO_3 + O_2 \longrightarrow 2\,Na_2SO_4$$
$$N_2H_4 + O_2 \longrightarrow N_2 + 2\,H_2O$$

(b) Dehumidification: This involves reducing the moisture content of air well below the critical humidity limit for the metal so that the amount of water condensed on the metallic surface will not be sufficient to cause corrosion. For this purpose substances such as alumina, silica gel etc. are used. These substances can absorb moisture preferentially on their surface. This is applicable on economic considerations to closed areas such as air-conditioned places where steel articles are prepared.

(c) Alkaline Neutralisation: In this method the acidic nature of the corrosive environment is neutralized by using alkaline substances such as NH_3, $NaOH$, lime, sodium salts of petroleum phenols etc. These alkaline substances are injected in vapour or liquid form to the corroding environment (H_2S, HCl, SO_2 etc.) or its part. This method is used in refinery to control corrosion of equipment.

(d) By using Inhibitors: A small quantity of some substances when added to corrosive environment effectively decrease the rate of corrosion of metal. Such substances are called inhibitors. These are either organic or inorganic substances. These dissolve in the corrosive medium and form protective layer either on anodic or cathodic area. Those which cover anodic areas are chromates, phosphates, tungstates of transition elements, while those cover the cathodic area are amines, mercaptans, substituted ureas, etc.

They are divided into cathodic and anodic inhibitors on the basis of whether they inhibit anodic or cathodic reaction.

(i) Anodic and Cathodic Inhibitors

- As corrosion is electrochemical in nature, the inhibitive action of any substance is the result of control of anodic and cathodic reactions.

- Anodic inhibitors form soluble compounds with dissolved metal ions, which deposit on metal surface to form a protective film, which reduces corrosion of anode. They are oxidising agents like chromates, nitrates and ferric salts.

- In an acidic environment, evolution of hydrogen gas takes place at the cathode. Corrosion can be reduced by slowing diffusion of hydrated hydrogen ions to the cathode or by increasing the overpotential of hydrogen evolution. Antimony and arsenic ions deposit metallic film on the cathode and retard hydrogen-evolution reaction. In a neutral environment, cathodic reaction is the result of oxygen absorption and formation of hydroxyl ions. Sodium sulphite or hydrazine are used to remove oxygen from the solution.

$$2\,Na_2S_2O_3 + O_2 \rightarrow 2\,Na_2SO_4$$
$$N_2H_4 + O_2 \rightarrow N_2 \uparrow + 2\,H_2O$$

- Cathodic inorganic inhibitors like magnesium, zinc or nickel salts are effective in neutral and alkaline environment. They react with hydroxyl ions at cathode and form insoluble hydroxides. These get deposited on the cathode. Above inhibitors can also be classified as

(ii) Inorganic Inhibitors and Organic Inhibitors

- In neutral and alkaline solutions, chromates and nitrites act as anodic inhibitors. They are the most efficient inhibitors for controlling the corrosion of iron and steel in neutral and alkaline waters. Alkali inhibitors like sodium hydroxide, sodium carbonates and bicarbonates form metal hydroxides which serve as protective deposits. They are anodic inhibitors. Inorganic inhibitors do not give any protection in presence of acids and reducing conditions. For such conditions, polar organic compounds and colloidal organic materials are used as inhibitors. Their inhibitive action is because of physical and chemical adsorption of molecules on metal surface. They act as anodic, cathodic or mixed inhibitors. Due to physical adsorption of inhibitor, resistance to current flow at cathodic area increases. Due to chemisorption, co-ordinate covalent bond is formed between inhibitor and metal, so anodic polarisation takes place. Amines, heterocyclic nitrogen compounds, substituted urea and thiourea and metal soaps are used as organic inhibitors.

- Vapour-phase inhibitors are used to inhibit atmospheric corrosion of metals without placing it in direct contact of metal's surface. They possess high vapour pressure and are effective if used in close spaces like inside of packages. Some heterocyclic nitro-compounds, esters of carboxylic acid can be used as vapour-phase inhibitors.

4.34 PROTECTIVE COATINGS

Application of protective coatings is one of the oldest way to protect underlying material. A coated component is protected due to isolation of the component from the corroding environment. Depending on the type of metal, application, cost, etc. specific surface coating may be selected.

Whatever may be substance used for giving a coating on metallic surface for protecting it from corrosion, it must function as below

- It should physically isolate the underlying metal from the corroding environment.
- Under service conditions of temperature and pressure, the coating should be chemically inert to the environment.
- It should prevent the penetration of the environment to the material which it protects.

Some protective coatings in addition to above functions, impart certain specific mechanical and physical properties such as wear resistance, hardness, oxidation resistance, electrical and thermal insulating properties.

4.35 DIFFERENT WAYS OF SURFACE COATING

(a) Chemical Conversion Coatings

- These are inorganic surface barriers produced by chemical or electro-chemical reaction taking place at the base metal. These are used for increasing the corrosion resistance as well as decorative effect of the base metal. However, these are mainly used as base for paints, lacquers etc. The following are important conversion coatings
- Phosphate coatings which are produced by the chemical reaction of the base metal with aqueous solution of phosphoric acid and iron, manganese or zinc phosphate along with accelerators such as copper salts.
- Phosphate coatings are grey but can be turned into black by using bonderising as dye.
- Chromate coatings are used for zinc, cadmium-plated parts, aluminium and magnesium. These are produced by dipping the article first in acid potassium chromate and then in neutral chromate solution.
- Chemical oxide coatings are produced by treating the base metal with alkaline oxidizing solution or gases.
- Anodized coatings which are generally produced on Al, Zn, Mg and their alloys by electrolytic process in which base metal is made anode. Anodized coatings possess improved corrosion resistance as well as resistance to mechanical injury.

(b) Organic Coatings

- These are inert organic barriers such as paints, varnishes, lacquers and enamels which are applied on the metallic surface. The protective value of these coatings depends on (i) Its chemical inertness to the corrosive medium, (ii) Surface adhesion, (iii) Impermeability, and (iv) Proper method of application.
- These are mainly used when corrosion rate of an unprotected metal is less than 1.25 mm per year.
- The main drawback is that there is always a possibility of an abrasive and erosive action, which can easily destroy the continuity of a thin film thereby exposing the underlying metal to the corrosive action of the environment.

(c) Organic Linings
- Rubber and plastics are often used to protect the underlying metal from corrosion under highly corrosive conditions. The thickness of these linings varies from 3 mm to 6 mm depending on the requirements.
- The most widely used plastic for sheet lining is polyvinyl chloride. It has high chemical resistance and can be cemented rather easily to the metal surface.

(d) Ceramic Protectives
- These possess high resistance against oxidation even at high temperatures. They possess high chemical inertness to all corrosive environments except alkalis and HF. These are of two types, vitreous enamels and ceramic coatings.
- Vitreous enamels are glass-like materials which are fixed on the metal to provide the required protection. These are usually applied to cast iron and steel equipments such as tanks, kettles, pipings, etc.
- Ceramic coatings are similar to vitreous enamels but they possess higher refractoriness and hence are useful for metal protection against erosion, oxidation and intergranular corrosion at high temperature. These are applied to nozzle, motor tube lining, vanes and blades in gas turbines, tail pipe linings in ram jets, inner combustion chamber lining, burner parts, thermocouple tubes etc.

(e) Metallic Coatings
- Nearly all metals can be applied as protective coatings to the base constructional metal. These are divided into (i) Anodic coatings and (ii) Cathodic coatings.

(i) Anodic Coatings
For this purpose, the coating metal should have higher electrode potential i.e., anodic than the base metal (i.e., the metal on which coating is to be obtained). For example, more active metals such as Zn, Al and Cd are used as coating metals for steel as base metal. Zn, Al and Cd are anodic because their electrode potentials are higher than that of iron, the base metal. If at all pores, breaks occur in these anodic coatings, the underlying metal iron remains protected. Due to crack, a galvanic cell between Zn (if it is coating metal) and the exposed iron (i.e., exposed part of base metal) is formed. Zinc is anodic to iron therefore, zinc will dissolve anodically while iron being cathodic will be protected. Hence until all the zinc near the exposed iron is not consumed by anodic corrosion, iron will not be attacked by the environment. Thus, zinc coating protects iron sacrificially.

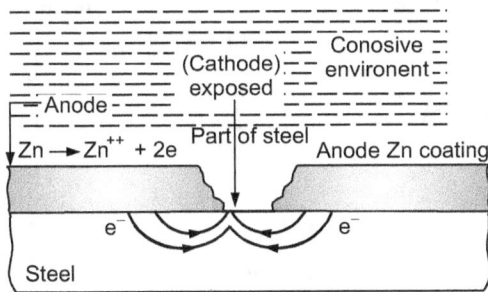

Fig. 4.16: Functioning of anodic coating

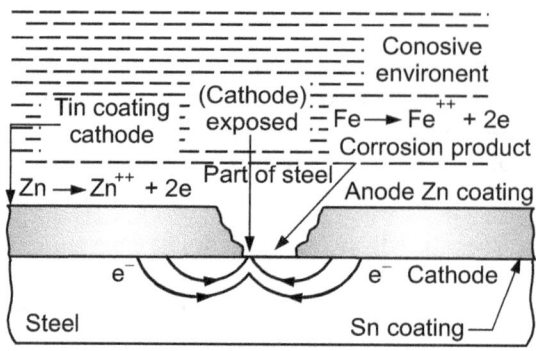

Fig. 4.17: Functioning of cathodic coating

(ii) Cathodic Coatings

This is obtained by coating more noble or less active metal (i.e. having lower electrode potential) than the base metal. Because of their higher corrosion resistance they protect the base metal. For the effectiveness of cathodic coatings, they should be completely continuous, free from breaks, pores or discontinuities. If such coating gets damaged or punctured, the base metal gets corroded to a large extent. The extent of corrosion in this case of the base metal, is much more than if it were not coated. For example, tin coating on iron sheet can provide protection only till the time the coating is continuous and intact. However, if the coating breaks, tin (being lower in electro-chemical series than iron) becomes cathode, while the exposed iron acts as anode. A galvanic cell is developed and extensive localized attack at the small exposed part takes place, thus causing severe pitting. At times the base metal, iron, will be perforated.

4.36 METHODS OF APPLYING METAL COATINGS

Before applying a protective coating on to a base metal, the selection of a proper coating metal and coating process is most important, so that effective protection will be obtained.

4.36.1 Selection of Proper Coating Metal

A proper coating metal is selected on the basis of following points

- Relative position of the base metal and the coating metal in the electro-chemical series or galvanic series is to be studied carefully.

- If the metal of which coating is desired is active metal than the base metal then essentially the coating metal should be higher (more anodic) in the electrochemical series than the base metal. In such combination, the base metal is protected electrolytically from corrosion. Such coating should be completely non-porous.

- While the cathodic (i.e. noble or less active) coating will form a barrier between the base metal and the environment and thus preserves it from the attack. The surface of such cathodic coatings should be essentially continuous because it is cathodic in nature and therefore, in the event of rupture of the film, instead of sacrificing for the base metal, it accelerates the attack on the exposed areas of the base metal.

- The metal of which coating is to be given should have sufficient resistance to corrosion.

- The coating should be sufficiently ductile and hard.

4.36.2 Selection of Proper Coating Process

A proper coating process should be adopted to meet the requirements of the job as well as it should be suitable for the coating and base metals. For this following points are to be considered

- Suitability for coating and base metals.

- Size and shape of the article to be coated.

- Optimum temperature suitable for coating metal and base metal.

- Physical properties required of coating for quality such as (a) Average thickness of coating, (b) Porosity or continuity, (c) Uniformity of coating, (d) Adherence, (e) Flexibility.

The different methods used for applying the protective metallic coatings are

- Hot dipping: (i) Galvanising, (ii) Tinning.

- Metal cladding.

- Cementation: (i) Sherardizing, (ii) Chromizing, (iii) Colourizing

- Metal spraying

- Electro-plating.

4.36.3 Preparation of Metal Surface for Coating

Whatever may be type of coating required to be given on to the surface of a base metal, it has to be prepared in a proper way so that the coating will have good adhesion. The preparation of the surface involves three steps

- The removal of grease and other surface contamination either by solvent degreasing, making the parts to be cleaned cathodic in alkaline solution at current density 1.0 amp. per sq. dm. etc.

- The removal of oxide scale and corrosion product either by abrasion or by acid pickling.

- Finally an etching treatment to secure adhesion or a buffing and polishing to improve the appearance of the applied coating.

4.37 HOT DIPPING PROCESS

In this process, the article to be coated is dipped in a bath of either molten metal or alloy of which coating is desired. After a sufficient time the article is removed with the adhering film of coating. The metal to be coated should have relatively low melting point [e.g. Zn (m.p. 419°C) and Sn (m.p. 232°C)] because high temperatures can cause following troubles

(1) Alter the mechanical properties of the base metal.

(2) Undue contamination of the bath by solution of the base metal.

(3) Too extensive penetration and alloying of the coating with the underlying metal.

For promoting adherence, some alloy formation at the interface between the base metal and the coating is desirable. The hot-dipping process is widely used for applying coatings of low-melting metals and alloys such as zinc (Galvanizing), Tin (Tinning), lead, terneplate (lead-tin alloy) etc.

4.37.1 Galvanizing

- Zinc coatings by hot dipping i.e., galvanizing is applied to base metals especially iron and steel when these are to be exposed to the atmosphere or soil. 'Sacrificial' electro-chemical protection to the base metal offered by zinc coating may extend for distance of 0.5 cm or more if the aqueous environment is fairly conductive.

Nature of Galvanized Coating

- Galvanized coating if properly applied consists of inner zones of iron-zinc alloy and an outer layer of almost pure zinc. The composition of iron-zinc alloy changes from outer layer to the surface of iron. The zinc content in alloy goes on decreasing as we go from outer layer to the base metal. Next to base metal, iron, there is a hard layer of $FeZn_3$ followed by $FeZn_7$, a layer responsible for adherence of zinc coating to iron. Next outer coating is $FeZn_{13}$ which limits the diffusion rate of zinc thereby controlling the rate of formation of zinc coating. Outermost layer is of pure zinc.

- The protective action of zinc coatings is best effective in the pH range 6.0 to 12.5. If the galvanized articles are subjected to corrosive environments within the above mentioned pH range then it can serve the purpose for many years.

Process

Galvanizing is Carried out in the Following Stages

(1) Preparation of Surface

Surface contaminations are removed in the following manner

- **Pickling Treatment:** The iron or steel article is pickled for 15 to 20 minutes in a pickling solution consisting of 7 % sulphuric acid at 60° C to 80°C.

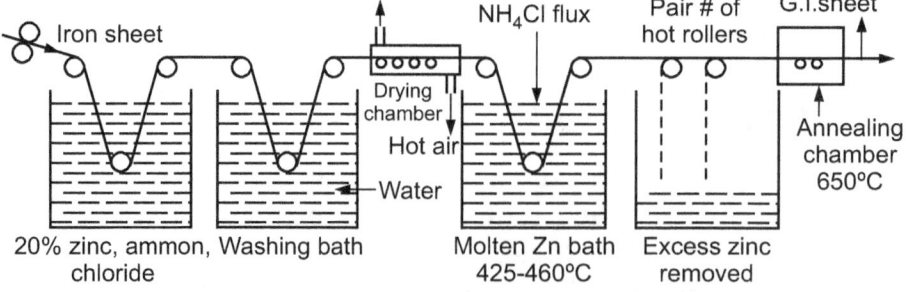

Fig. 4.18: Galvanizing of steel sheet

- **Preliminary Treatment:** The pickled article is treated with 5 % hydrofluoric acid to dissolve sand grains etc. if present on the surface of article. It is then stored under water to prevent oxidation.

- **Cleaning Solution:** Finally, before the article is treated in zinc bath, it is passed through about 20 % zinc ammonium chloride solution so as to clean any superficial oxide if formed during storage.

(2) Zinc Bath Treatment

- The article is then washed, dried and then dipped in a bath of molten zinc, maintained between 425^∞ C to 460^∞ C. During this zinc bath is kept covered with a flux such as ammonium chloride so as to avoid oxide formation. The article coated with zinc layer is then passed through a pair of hot rollers to remove excess of zinc and to produce uniform layer on the article.

(3) Finally the article is annealed at a temperature of $650°$ C and then slowly cooled.

Protective Action of Zinc [Galvanization]

- Thin coating of zinc in galvanized iron does not allow iron to come in contact with air and moisture, and hence protects it from rusting. Even when the protective zinc coating is broken, iron remains protected because standard reduction potential (S.R.P.) of Zn^{2+}/Zn electrode (– 0.76 V) is less than S. R. P. of Fe^{2+}/Fe electrode (–0.44 V). Hence the oxidation reaction $Zn \rightarrow Zn^{2+} + 2\ e^-$ (with lower S.R.P.) occurs preferentially. As such, it is zinc which tends to lose electrons, and not iron. Thus the reaction $Fe \rightarrow Fe^{2+} + 2\ e^-$ necessary for rusting does not take place.

- Zinc loses electrons and passes into the solution as Zn^{2+} ions at the anodic area. Hydrogen is discharged from the surface of iron in the cathodic area. Zinc is thus sacrificed in protecting iron. At areas where the surface coating is undamaged, zinc is protected from corrosion by firmly adhering layer of zinc oxide.

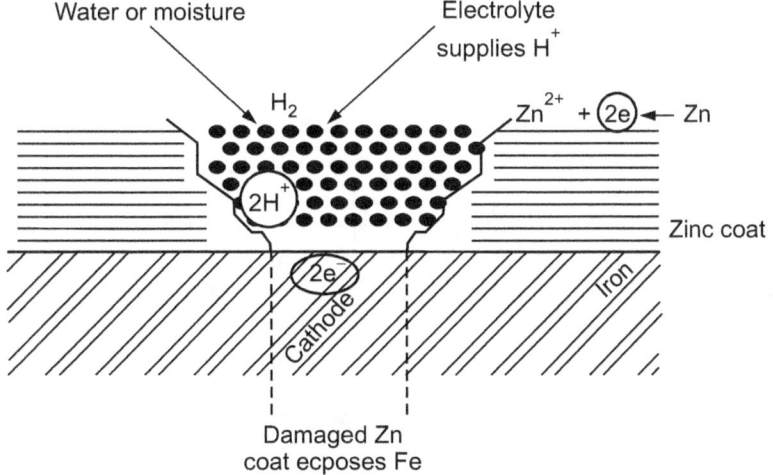

Fig. 4.19: Protective action of Zn in GI sheet

- Galvanized iron containers cannot be used for the purpose of canning food because zinc will pass into solution forming poisonous zinc salts which will poison the contents.

Applications

- The articles such as roofing sheets, pipes, wires, wire cloth, nails, pipe fittings etc. are protected from corrosion by them.
- Galvanized (zinc-coated) articles should not be used for preparing food, especially if acidic in nature.
- Zinc coatings are also effective on iron and steel articles exposed to sea water and other solutions high in chlorides.

4.37.2 Tinning

Tinning is similar to galvanizing. The essential differences are

(1) Zinc coating in galvanizing and tin coating in tinning are used.

(2) In galvanizing, the iron sheet after passing through molten zinc, directly comes out and then annealed while in tinning the iron sheet after passing through molten metal, passes through palm oil before it comes out.

Process

- First the steel sheet is pickled in dil. H_2SO_4 (4 to 8 %) at about 75°C for 3 to 5 minutes before tinning to remove the oxide film.
- After pickling, the steel sheets are made to pass by feed rollers in turn through the flux (a molten layer of zinc chloride, through the first compartment of molten tin at 300° – 340°C). Then the sheets pass through second compartment of molten tin at 238° to 243° C. The sheet coming out of second compartment passes through a series of rollers in palm oil bath. The palm oil keeps the tin molten as well as a thin layer of palm oil adhering to the tin layer protects it from oxidizing during solidification of tin in air.
- The palm oil is removed by saw dust or other similar material when the sheet comes out of palm oil. Then saw dust is removed and sheet is polished by dry flannel rollers.

This process produces a thin film of thickness 0.003 to 0.005 mm on the steel sheets.

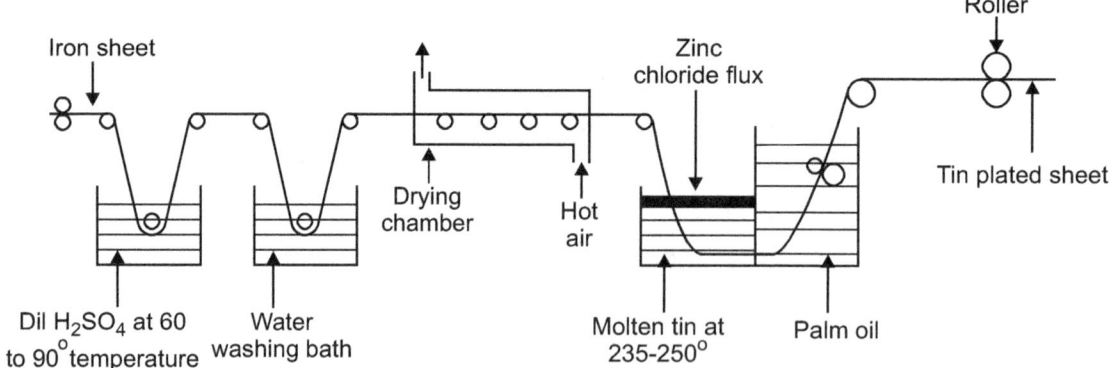

Fig. 4.20: Tinning of steel sheet

Protective Action of Tin [Sn]

- Tin is resistant to corrosion, hence a thin coating of tin over iron protects it from rusting. Tin coating, however, is not so durable as that of zinc in G. I. sheets. Moreover, when the layer of tin is broken and some iron surface is exposed, rusting is more rapid compared to unprotected iron piece. This is because S.R.P. of Fe^{2+}/Fe (– 0.44 V) is lower than S.R.P. of Sn^{2+}/Sn (– 0.14 V). Therefore, the oxidation reaction $Fe \rightarrow Fe^{2+} + 2\ e^-$ (with lower S.R.P.) is driven to the right. Thus, rusting is facilitated.

- [However, S.R.P. of Sn^{2+}/Sn electrode (– 0.14 V) is less than S.R.P. of Cu^{2+}/Cu electrode (+ 0.34 V). Hence Sn can protect copper as Zn protects iron.]

- In this case, hydrogen ions [H^+], originating from the solution of electrolyte, are discharged at the tin coating adjacent to exposed iron surface where dissolved oxygen acts as depolarizer. Electrons pass from iron (anodic area) to tin (cathodic area). Thus at the exposed iron surface (anodic area), ferrous ions pass into solution. These Fe^{2+} ions are oxidised to Fe^{3+} ions (ferric) by dissolving oxygen and produce rust.

- Tin plated containers are used in canning food. As long as the coating is not damaged, tin being more resistant to corrosion withstands the action of acids present in food. However, when the plated surface gets damaged, iron passes into solution but no poisonous tin compounds pass into the solution.

Applications

- Because of its non-toxicity, tinning is widely used for coating steel, copper, and brass sheets used for food containers.

- Copper wires are tinned to facilitate soldering.

- Tinned cans used for packing meat and some vegetables get blackened; while certain highly coloured fruits get bleached. To prevent this blackening or bleaching, the tinned cans should be lacquered or enameled on the inside.

4.38 METAL CLADDING

- "Metal cladding involves bonding firmly and permanently, a dense, homogeneous layer of a coating metal to the base metal on one or both sides."

- The thickness of the cladding metal usually ranges from 5 to 20 % of the composite plate. The cladding is accomplished for the following reasons

  ➤ To develop surface properties in steel sheets of more expensive, corrosion-resistant and high melting metals or alloys such as monel, stainless steel, copper etc.

  ➤ For combining the strength of steel wire with the high electrical conductivity of copper.

  ➤ For providing anodic protection to aluminium alloys.

- The choice of cladding material will therefore, depend upon the specific surface property that is to be developed or enhanced.

- One method of cladding consists of casting a duplex ingot with the coating material on the outside and subsequently rolling the ingot into sheet, bar or plate or drawing it into wire.

- In another method of cladding, the base metal sheet is sandwitched between two thin sheets of the coating material, which are then passed through rollers under the action of heat and pressure. This method is widely used in aircraft industry for manufacturing 'Alclad' sheets. Alclad is obtained by sandwitching Duralumin plate between two layers of 99.5 % pure aluminium.

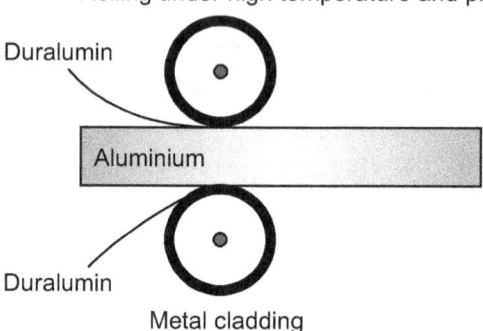

Fig. 4.21: Metal cladding

Generally metals such as nickel, copper, silver, platinum, etc., and alloys such as stainless steel nickel alloys, copper alloy etc., are used as cladding material while mild steel, aluminium, copper, nickel and their alloys are used as base metals.

Application

- In air craft industries for manufacturing of Alclad, it is obtained by sandwitching Duralumin between two layers of 99.5% Al.

4.39 CEMENTATION

- Cementation or diffusion coatings are obtained by heating the base metal in intimate contact with a powder of the coating metal. Diffusion of coating metal into the base metal takes place forming the layers of alloy of varying composition.

- This process is suitable for coating small articles of uneven surfaces and intricate shapes such as bolts, screws, threaded parts, valves and gauge tools, because the coatings obtained by cementation are uniform in thickness irrespective of the geometry of the treated surface.

- In cementation process, the base metal is usually iron or steel and the coating metals used are those which can alloy with iron e.g. Zinc, chromium and aluminium. The cementation processes are known as Sherardizing, Chromizing and Colourizing when the coating metals used are zinc, chromium and aluminium respectively.

(1) Sherardizing

➢ Sherardizing is cementation with zinc powder. First the article to be impregnated is cleaned and then packed with zinc dust in a light drum (to minimize the oxidation of zinc). The drum is then rotated slowly while it is being heated by gas or electricity. The temperature of the drum is kept between 350°C to 370°C. (Higher temperature leads to coarse crystalline coating of high iron content while lower temperature results in porous coating). The thickness of the coating can be controlled by changing the duration of treatment from 3 to 12 hours. At the end of the process, a minutely thin film of zinc alloy is obtained on the base metal. To get the best results, the purity of zinc dust used should be near 90 %.

➢ Sherardized coatings consist of one structural layer of $FeZn_7$ only. These coatings generally possess minute cracks because the coefficients of expansion of base metal and the coating i.e zinc-iron alloy are different. But these cracks do not affect the protective property of the coating as sherardized coating produces sacrificial electrolytic protection.

➢ As due to sherardizing very little change in dimension takes place therefore, it is used for protecting small steel parts such as nuts, bolts, washer etc. against atmospheric corrosion.

(2) Chromizing

➢ The base metal should be either low carbon steels (Carbon content 0.1 to 0.2 %) or carburized high carbon steels. Chromizing is carried out by packing the article to be chromized in a barrel along with a mixture of well-powdered chromium (55 %) and alumina (45 %) and is heated in an inert atmosphere at about 1300° – 1400°C for 3 to 4 hours. Alumina prevents the coalescence of chromium particles.

➢ The corrosion resistance of chromized coatings is comparable to that of ferrite stainless steels. Chromium forms solid solutions with iron with chromium content from 10 to 20 % depending upon the time and temperature of treatment.

➢ It is mainly used for gas turbine blades.

(3) Colourizing

➢ Colourized coatings are very much useful for protecting metals against high temperature oxidation.

➢ First the article is sand blasted and then heated in a tightly-packed drum alongwith a mixture of powdered aluminium, aluminium oxide and a small quantity (1 to 5 %) of ammonium chloride (acts as flux). The drum is heated to about 840° to 930°C for 4 to 6 hours while it is being slowly rotated. The thickness of iron-aluminium alloy (Al_3Fe) produced is 0.025 to 0.15 mm thick.

➢ To increase the penetration of aluminium by diffusion, the above treated article is held at 820° to 980°C for 12 to 48 hours in open. This reduces the aluminium content of the surface to 25 % as against 60 % in the above case, and the thickness of the alloy layer increases to 0.6 to 1.0 mm.

> ➤ Colourizing is applied to various surface parts, tubes of air heaters, radiant steam superheaters, pyrometric equipment etc.

4.40 METAL SPRAYING

- This is a process of obtaining a coating on the base metal by spraying the molten metal of which coating is desired, by means of a portable spraying apparatus.

Process

- First the surface of the base metal is prepared by sharp sand blasting for 1 to 3 hours so that a clean, fresh surface but highly roughened is obtained.
- Then the coating metal is sprayed on the prepared surface of the article either by Wiregun method or Powder metal method.
- Wire gun method, which is widely used for common metals uses a light weight 'pistol' which can be held in hand so as to direct the stream of metal at will. It consists of coaxial barrels. Through central barrel the coating metal is fed in the form of wire. The gaseous mixture acetylene and oxygen is supplied through the tube surrounding the wire barrel. The gas mixture is allowed to burn at the mouth of the barrel.
- This oxy-acetylene flame melts the protruding part of the wire.
- Through an outermost tube, surrounding the gas inlet, compressed air is admitted which atomizes the molten metal as well as projects it against the surface to be coated.
- In powder metal method, finely divided powder of a metal is sucked from the coating powder chamber into a blow pipe using either aspirator or suction pump.
- As this powder passes through the flame of a blow pipe it gets disintegrated into a cloud of molten globules. These are projected against the base metal and are absorbed on the surface of base metal. By this method, coatings of relatively low-melting metals like Zn, Sn can be obtained.

Nature of Coating

Molten metal particles after stricking the surface of base-metal, flatten into flakes and interlock with the surface irregularities. Sprayed coatings are continuous but porous to some extent.

Advantages

- Greater speed of working.
- Metal film is applied to the finished article or structure in place.
- Metal film can be applied to any desired spot.
- No further deformation of film as it is applied in situ.
- Particles of the sprayed coated metal form a work hard surface due to impact.

Disadvantages

- Adhesive strength of coating is comparatively low (as compared with hot-dipping or electro plated).
- Coatings are rather porous and hence have a tendency to catch soot and other forms of contaminations.

Applications

- Sprayed coatings can be applied even to non-metallic surface such as wood, plastic etc.

- Metal spraying is used for reclaiming the worn out machine parts.

- To protect the equipment in chemical industry.

- Coating by metal spraying can be used for giving the coatings of aluminium, brass, cadmium, copper, lead, monel metal, nickel, tin, zinc etc. on many articles.

4.41 ELECTROPLATING

- In principle, electroplating is the reverse of corrosion. In electroplating, metal is deposited from the solution while in corrosion, metal is dissolved in solution. When metals are electroplated for the purpose of protection against corrosion, care should be taken to verify the relative positions of the coating metal and the base metal in Galvanic series. A galvanic cell formed by the coating metal with the base metal should not increase the corrosion of the base metal. Hence the coating metal should be more anodic than the base metal.

- For protecting steel articles from corrosion, the coating metals used are zinc, nickel, chromium, tin and copper. At times alloys such as lead-tin, tin-copper, tin-zinc, and tin-nickel are also used.

- Nickel alone if used as a coating metal for steel, then sufficient thickness of the coating should be obtained because nickel is cathodic to iron. Thin coatings of nickel can serve the purpose for indoor atmosphere, while for outdoor atmosphere, first a thin copper coating and on that a nickel coating of sufficient thickness is obtained.

- Chromium coatings are used in automobile industry. Chromium coatings are generally thin and contain number of pores. As the thickness of coating increases so also the number of pores and the coating tends to crack. In commercial practice, 4 different coats are given on steel to safeguard it from corrosive attack, immediately above steel article surface is nickel - 0.005 mm, then copper - 0.013 mm, then nickel - 0.02 mm and finally chromium 0.003 mm, while on brass articles only two layers i.e. under coat of nickel - 0.03 mm and final coating of chromium - 0.003 mm is used. Chromium electroplated coatings possess very high corrosion resistance.

- In internal combustion engines, to increase wear resistance as well as running performance, electroplated chromium layer is used for certain parts which possess the required mechanical properties for their function but is readily corroded when subjected to working atmosphere.

- Electroplating is also used for temporary purpose in metal treatment. e.g. Steel parts are copper plated before carburizing so that undesired parts will not be carburized.

- In the process of hardening, portions of steel are protected from nitriding by electro-plating tin, or copper-tin alloys on such portions.

- The setup of electrolysis is as shown in Fig. 4.22. In electrolysis, article which is coated is connected to cathode and electrolyte consist metal to be coated on article surface. Here electrolyte undergoes ionization to produce metal ions. They are attracted towards surface of cathode, where it accepts electrons and deposits on cathodic surface. As the process of electrolysis goes on, the concentration of metal ion in an electrolyte decreases. To form uniform coating, it is necessary to add electrolyte or anode is made of coating metal. Therefore, it undergoes process of ionization and supplies metal ions continuously required for electrolysis. e.g. In electroplating of Cu, electrolyte used is $CuSO_4$ and anode is Cu metal. Following reactions take place.

    At anode, $Cu \rightarrow Cu^{++} + 2e^-$ (Oxidation reaction)

    At cathode, Cu^{++} (from electrolyte) $+ 2e^- \rightarrow Cu$ (Reduction reaction)

Application

- Electroplating in automobile industry, Electrodeposition in thin film formation.

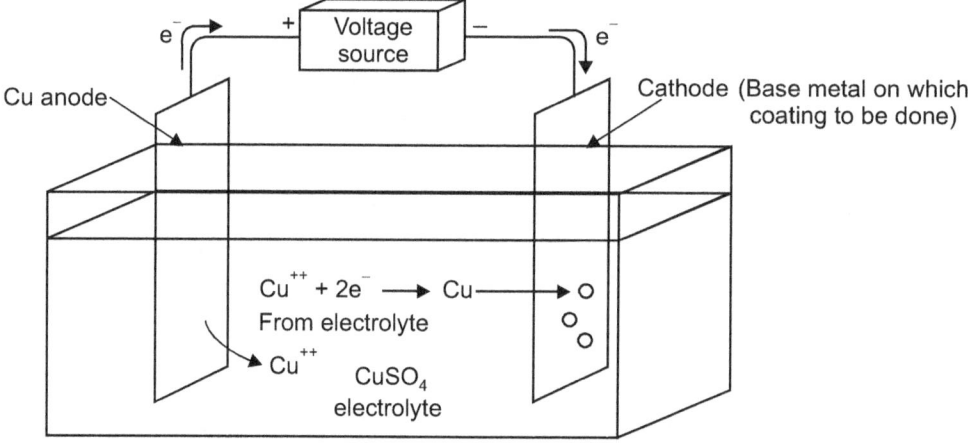

Fig. 4.22: Electrolyte bath in which deposition of Cu on cathodic surface going on

4.42 PAINTS AND VARNISHES

Organic coatings which are inert organic barriers such as paints, varnishes, lacquers, enamels etc. find wide applications under conditions where the corrosion rate of the unprotected metal does not exceed 1.25 mm per year. The coatings of paints and varnishes are applied on metallic surfaces and other constructional materials for corrosion protection as well as decoration.

The protective value of these coatings depend on

- Their chemical inertness to the corrosive environment,
- Their good surface adhesion,
- The impermeability to water, salts and gases and most important is
- The proper method of application.

(a) Paints

Paint is mechanical dispersion mixture of two or more pigments in a vehicle. The vehicle is a liquid, consisting of non-volatile, film forming material like drying oil and a highly volatile solvent called thinner. When paint is applied to a metal surface (usually by brushing or spraying), the thinner evaporates while the drying oil slowly oxidizes forming a dry pigmented film.

Characteristics of Good Paints

- It should be fluid enough to be spread easily over the surface.
- It should possess high hiding and covering power.
- It should form a quite tough, uniform and adhesive film.
- The film should not crack on drying.
- It should protect the painted surface from corrosions.
- It should form film, the colour of which is quite stable to the effect of atmosphere and other agencies.
- Film should be glossy and stable.
- It can be easily applicable with brush or spraying device and that it yields a smooth and uniform surface.
- It should possess high adhesion capacity to the material over which it is intended to be used.

Constituents of Paints

- **Pigment:** It gives colour to the paint e.g. White (Zn oxide), Red (Ferric oxide), Blue (Prussian blue).
- **Vehicle or Drying Oil:** It is film forming constituent of paint e.g. Glyceryl esters of high molecular weight fatty acids.
- **Thinners:** It reduces viscosity of the paint to suitable consistency e.g. Turpentine, mineral spirit, benzene.
- **Driers:** These are oxygen carrier catalysts. Oxidise oil rapidly. e.g. resonates, linoleates, tungstates etc.
- **Extenders or Fillers:** It reduces cost of product, increases covering power, help to reduce cracking etc. e.g. barite, talc, asbestos.
- **Plasticizers:** It provides elasticity to paint, minimizes cracking e.g. Tricresyl phosphate, triphenyl phosphate etc.

(b) Varnishes

It is a homogeneous colloidal dispersion solution of natural or synthetic resins in oil or thinners or both. There are two types of varnish

- **Oil Varnish:** It is a homogeneous solution of one or more natural or synthetic resins in a drying oil and a volatile solvent. This type of varnish dries up by evaporation of volatile solvent, followed by oxidation and polymerization. It takes comparatively more time for drying, but film produced is hard, lustrous and durable e.g. Copal varnish. They are used for exterior and interior work.

- **Spirit Varnish:** It contains a resin dissolved in a completely volatile solvent. Such varnish dries by the evaporation of the solvent. Spirit varnish dries rapidly, leaves behind film, which is brittle and so it has a tendency to crack or peel off. Moreover, the film is easily affected by weathering. e.g. spirit varnish is used for polishing wooden furniture.

Characteristics of Good Varnish

- It must form glossy, shiny and transparent film.
- Film must dry quickly.
- Film must be soft.
- It must resist wear and tear.
- Film must not shrink or crack on drying.

Constituents of Varnish

- **Resin:** Natural resins like shellacs, kauri, rosin, copal etc. and synthetic resins like phenol aldehyde, alkyds, urea formaldehyde etc. it provides an element of hardening, resistance to weathering, durability etc.
- **Solvents or Thinners:** e.g. Turpentine, petroleum spirit, kerosene etc. usually employed. It increases fluidity.
- **Driers:** It accelerates drying rate of oil e.g. resonates, naphthalene derivatives of Pb, Co, Mn etc.
- **Anti-skimming agent:** Like tert-amyl phenol, glycol etc. gives resistance to peeling of film.

REVIEW QUESTIONS

1. (a) What is corrosion ?
    (b) State the factors that influence the rate of electro-chemical corrosion.
2. (a) What is atmospheric corrosion ? Explain any two factors that cause the atmospheric corrosion.
    (b) Give a brief account of galvanic corrosion of metals.
3. (a) What are the pre-requisites of electro-chemical corrosion to take place and how are these satisfied in atmospheric corrosion of metals ?
    (b) Define immersed corrosion. Explain the mechanism of immersed corrosion.
4. What is chemical corrosion ? Describe its mechanism.
5. What is electro-chemical corrosion ? Explain its mechanism.
6. In practice, what factors lead to electro-chemical corrosion and how can you minimize the corrosion in each case ?

7. Explain what happens and why ?
   (a) If one surface of the metal is exposed to atmosphere while other is protected.
   (b) If two plates of the same metal are connected and dipped in neutral electrolyte while the other plate is exposed to oxygen.
   (c) When only one part of the metal is under stress and strain.
   (d) If iron, copper and zinc plates are placed in the moist atmosphere separately.

8. (a) Explain why corrosion occurs under a rivet ?
   (b) Discuss the factors affecting the rate of corrosion.
   (c) Describe the galvanising and tinning processes.

9. Describe 'wet' corrosion.

10. Explain the formation and growth of the oxide film on the surface of the metal by chemical attack of oxygen.

11. (a) What is the cause of corrosion of metals ?
    (b) Explain the economic importance of corrosion.

12. Explain the mechanism of hydrogen evolution and oxygen absorption in electrochemical corrosion. Give figures.

13. Give the experimental determination of rate of corrosion.

14. What is corrosion ? What are different types of corrosion ? Explain the mechanism of oxidation corrosion.

15. Explain the effects of nature of film formation on oxidation corrosion.

16. Give an account of different methods used for the measurement of corrosion.

17. Write note on differential aeration corrosion.

18. Write notes on (any four)
    (a) Galvanic corrosion, (b) Soil corrosion, (c) Waterline corrosion, (d) Crevice corrosion, (e) Microbiological corrosion, (f) Stress corrosion, (g) Factors influencing rate of corrosion.

19. Tin and zinc platings are used for prevention of corrosion. Which one is better and why ?

20. Write a note on cementation of metal surface with special reference to shearardizing.

21. Describe the hot dipping process of metal coating by either galvanizing or tinning.

22. What is the function of 'Cathodic protection' in corrosion control ?

23. Discuss the importance of design in corrosion control.

24. Write notes on
    (a) Cathodic protection   (b) Protective coatings

25. Give two methods of cathodic protection of metals.

26. Explain the importance of design and material selection in controlling corrosion of metallic materials.

27. Explain the following methods used for corrosion control (a) Sacrificial anode method, (b) Anodizing.

28. Distinguish between anodic protection and cathodic protection.

29. Give an account of different ways of surface coatings.

30. While applying a metal coating for corrosion protection, explain the importance of selection of (a) proper coating metal, and (b) proper coating process.

31. Give an account of hot dipping processes.

32. Explain the process of galvanizing with schematic diagram.

33. Explain the process of tinning with schematic diagram.

34. Give an account of cementation processes.

UNIVERSITY QUESTIONS

NOVEMBER 2016

1. One Assembly is made with nuts and bolts used for joining them. Where the probability of corrosion is more? Which type of corrosion is probable in this type ? Explain can it be avoided.   **[7]**
   [**Ans. :** Refer article 4.21]

2. Pitting corrosion is most dangerous amongst all types of corrosion do you agree with this statement? Justify your answer.   **[4]**
   [**Ans. :** Refer article 4.15]

3. In Anodic and Cathodic Inhibitors which is more protective, explain.   **[2]**
   [**Ans. :** Refer article 4.33]

MAY 2017

1. What do you mean by the term corrosion? What are the different ways to delay the destruction of metal under corrosion?   **[6]**
   [**Ans. :** Refer articles 4.1, 4.27]

2. Identify the type of corrosion for the following cases: **[4]**
   (i) Formation of cavities of small anodic area around which metal is relatively unattacked as compared large cathodic area.
   [**Ans. :** Refer article 4.10]
   (ii) Simultaneous effect of environment and cyclic fluctuation of stress.
   [**Ans. :** Refer article 4.23]
   (iii) The grain boundary phase or a region adjacent to the grain boundary becomes anodic and get preferably corroded due to precipitation of some phase.
   [**Ans. :** Refer article 4.9]
   (iv) An accelerated attack at the junction of two metals exposed to a corrosive environment.
   [**Ans. :** Refer article 4.11]

3. What is sacrifical anode ?   **[3]**
   [**Ans. :** Refer article 4.31]

✠ ✠ ✠

Unit V

SURFACE MODIFICATION METHODS

5.1 INTRODUCTION

Surface Engineering is the sub-discipline of materials science which deals with the surface of solid matter. It has applications to chemistry, mechanical engineering, and electrical engineering.

Solids consists two phases (i) Bulk phase and (ii) Surface phase.

The bulk material is covered by a surface. The bulk material in a solid is called the Bulk phase. The surface which bounds the bulk material is called the Surface phase. It acts as an interface to the surrounding environment.

The surface phase of a solid interacts with the surrounding environment. Due to this interaction degradation of the surface phase takes place over the time. Environmental degradation of the surface phase over time can be caused by wear, corrosion, fatigue and creep.

Surface engineering involves modification in the properties of the Surface Phase in order to reduce the degradation over time. This is accomplished by making the surface robust to the environment in which it will be used.

5.2 SURFACE MODIFICATION   (Nov. 16)

Surface Modification is the process of modifying the surface of a material by bringing changes in physical, chemical or biological characteristics of the surface of a material.

This modification is usually made to solid materials, but sometimes modification to the surface of specific liquids is also done.

The modification can be done by different methods. The purpose of it is to alter properties of the surface, such as: roughness, hydrophilicity, surface charge, surface energy, biocompatibility and reactivity.

Classification of Surface Modification Methods/ Techniques

The surface modification methods are broadly classified as

(i)   Mechanical surface treatments

(ii) Non-mechanical surface treatments

The non-mechanical surface treatments can be further classified as

- Thermal treatments
- Thermo-chemical treatment
- Plating and coating
- Implantation

The following list provides different surface treatments

1. Electroplating	2. PVD, CVD, IVD processes
3. Electoless Nickel	4. Composite
5. Thermal spraying	6. Surface welding
7. Ion Implantation	8. Anodising
9. Boronizing	10. Nitriding
11. Carbonitriding	12. Carburizing
13. Nitrocarburising	14. Surface alloying
16. Thermal hardening.	

The effectiveness depends on particular surface and modification technique.

The Fig. 5.1, illustrates different types of surface treatments and typical thickness of engineered surface materials produced by them.

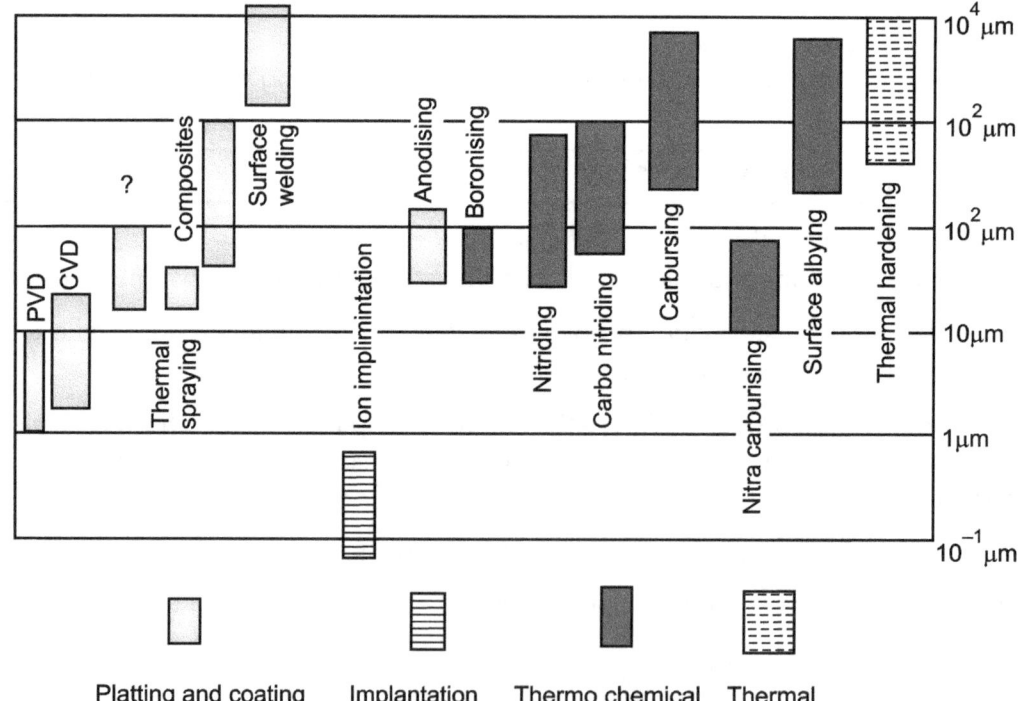

Fig. 5.1: Typical thickness of engineered surface layers physical vapour deposition

5.3 ELECTROPLATING   (Nov. 16, May 17)

Electroplating is the process of application of a metal coating to a metallic or other conducting surface by an electrochemical process. The article to be plated (the work) is made the cathode (negative electrode) of an electrolysis cell through which a direct electric current is passesd. The article is immersed in an aqueous solution (the bath) containing the required metal in an oxidised form, either as an aquated cation or as a complex ion. The anode is usually a bar of the metal being plated. During electrolysis metal is deposited on to the work and metal from the bar dissolves:

at cathode $\quad\quad Mz^+ (aq) + ze^- \rightarrow M(s)$

at anode $\quad\quad\quad\quad M(s) \rightarrow Mz^+ (aq) + ze^-$

Faraday's laws of electrolysis govern the amount of metal deposited.

The purpose of elecroplated is

- Enhancement in appearance;

- To provide a protective coating;

- To give the article special surface properties;

- To give the article engineering or mechanical properties.

The Process of Electroplating

- Electrodeposition is the process used in electroplating. It is similar to a galvanic cell acting in reverse.

- The part to be plated is made cathode of the circuit. In one technique, the anode is made of the metal to be plated on the part. Both components are immersed in a solution called an electrolyte containing one or more dissolved metal salts as well as other ions that permit the flow of electricity.

- A power supply supplies a direct current to the anode, oxidizing the metal atoms that it comprises and allowing them to dissolve in the solution.

- At the cathode, the dissolved metal ions in the electrolyte solution are reduced at the interface between the solution and the cathode, such that they "plate out" onto the cathode.

- The rate at which the anode is dissolved is equal to the rate at which the cathode is plated, vis-a-vis the current through the circuit.

- In this manner, the ions in the electrolyte bath are continuously replenished by the anode.

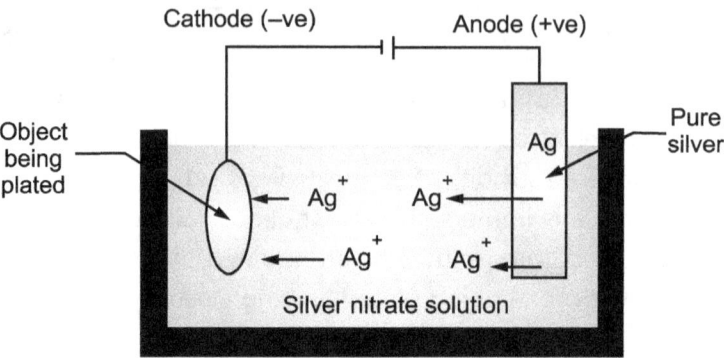

Fig. 5.2: Electroplating of a metal with silver

5.4 VAPOR DEPOSITION PROCESSES

In the vapor deposition processes, vapour of a material are made to deposite on the surface in order to improve its properties.

There are Two Categories of Vapor Deposition Processes

➢ Physical Vapor Deposition (PVD) and Chemical Vapor Deposition (CVD).

➢ In PVD processes, the work piece is subjected to plasma bombardment.

➢ In CVD processes, thermal energy heats the gases in the coating chamber and drives the deposition reaction.

5.4.1 Physical Vapor Deposition (PVD)   (Nov. 16, May 17)

- Physical Vapor Deposition (PVD) is a type of vacuum deposition methods which can be used to produce thin films.
- PVD uses physical process (such as heating or sputtering) to produce a vapor of material, which is then deposited on the object which requires coating.
- PVD is used in the manufacture of items which require thin films for mechanical, optical, chemical or electronic functions.
- Examples include semiconductor devices such as thin film solar panels,[1] aluminized PET film for food packaging and balloons,[2] and coated cutting tools for metal working.[3]
- Besides PVD tools for fabrication, special smaller tools (mainly for scientific purposes) have been developed.[4]
- In this process, the work piece or substrate is subjected to high temperature vacuum evaporation or plasma sputter bombardment to deposit thin films by the condensation of a vaporized form of the material onto substrate 16 surfaces.
- This process contains the three major techniques; evaporation, sputtering and ion plating. It produces a dense, hard coating.
- The primary PVD methods are ion plating, ion implantation, sputtering and laser surface alloying.

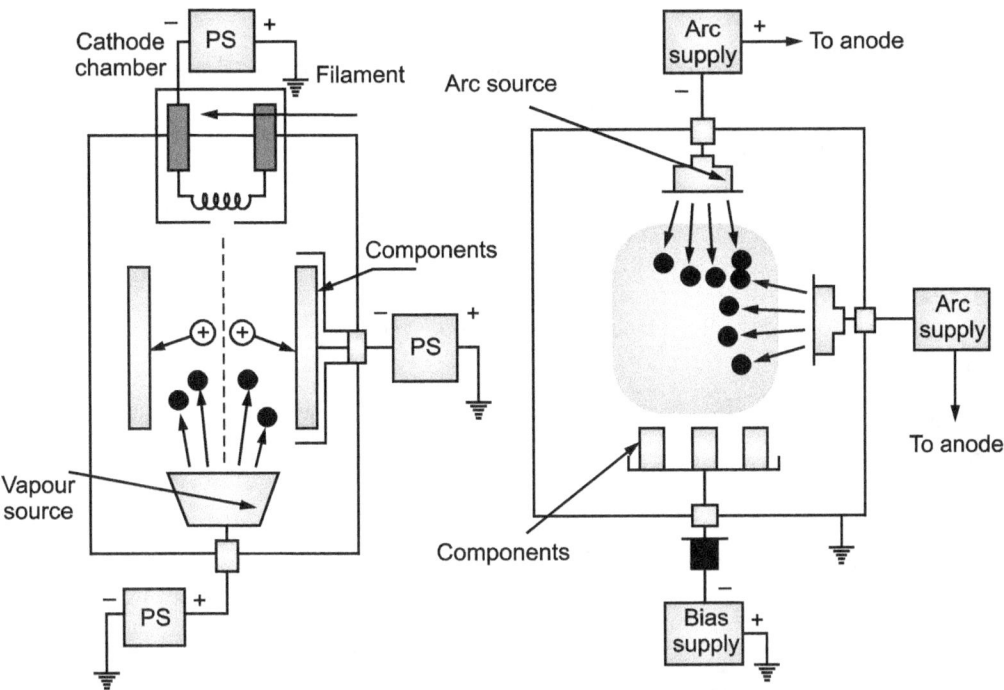

Fig. 5.3: PVD process using Plasma evaporation   Fig. 5.4: PVD process using are sputtering

- Common industrial coatings applied by PVD are titanium nitride, zirconium nitride, chromium nitride, titanium aluminum nitride.[5]
- The source material is unavoidably also deposited on most other surfaces interior to the vacuum chamber, including the fixturing used to hold the parts.

Advantages

- PVD coatings are sometimes harder and more corrosion resistant than coatings applied by the electroplating process. Most coatings have high temperature and good impact strength, excellent abrasion resistance and are so durable that protective topcoats are almost never necessary.
- Ability to utilize virtually any type of inorganic and some organic coating materials on an equally diverse group of substrates and surfaces using a wide variety of finishes.
- More environmentally friendly than traditional coating processes such as electroplating and painting.
- More than one technique can be used to deposit a given film.

Disadvantages

- It is not suitable for complex geometries.
- Some PVD technologies typically operate at very high temperatures and vacuums, requiring special attention by operating personnel.
- Requires a cooling water system to dissipate large heat loads.

Application

- PVD is used in the manufacture of semiconductor wafers, aluminized PET film for snack bags and balloons, cutting tools for metalworking and generally used for extreme thin films like atomic layers and mostly for small substrates.

- Aerospace

- Automotive

- Surgical/Medical [9]

- Dies and moulds for all manner of material processing

- Cutting tools

- Firearms

- Optics

- Watches

- Thin films (window tint, food packaging, etc.)

- Darts barrels

- Metals (Aluminum, Copper, Bronze, etc.)

5.5 CHEMICAL VAPOUR DEPOSITION (CVD)   (Nov. 16, May 17)

- In the broadest sense chemical vapour deposition (CVD) involves the formation of a thin solid film on a substrate material by a chemical reaction of vapour-phase precursors.

- It can thus be distinguished from physical vapour deposition (PVD) processes, such as evaporation and reactive sputtering, which involve the adsorption of atomic or molecular species on the substrate.

- The chemical reactions of precursor species occur both in the gas phase and on the substrate.

- Reactions can be promoted or initiated by heat (thermal CVD), higher frequency radiation such as UV (photo-assisted CVD) or a plasma (plasma-enhanced CVD).

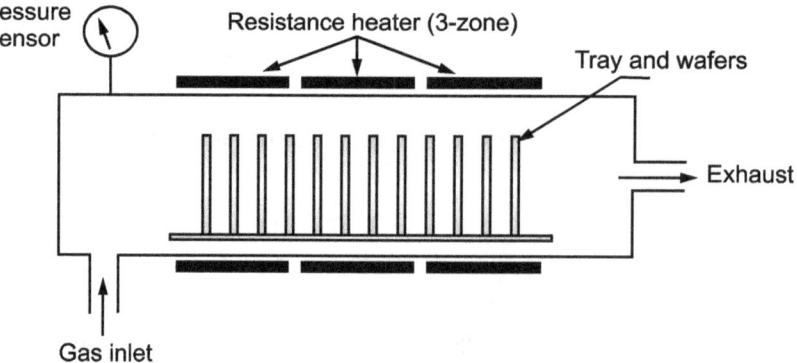

Fig. 5.5: Chemical Vapour Deposition (CVD)

- The variants of Chemical Vapour Deposition (CVD) are distinguished by the manner in which precursor gases are converted into the reactive gas mixtures.
- The gas called as precursor gas is usually in the form of a metal halide, metal carbonyl, a hydride, or an organ metallic compound.
- The precursor may be in gas, liquid, or solid form.
- Gases are delivered to the chamber under normal temperatures and pressures, whereas solids and liquids require high temperatures and/or low pressures in conjunction with a carrier gas.
- In the chamber, energy is applied to the substrate to facilitate the reaction of the precursor material upon impact and librated metal species are deposited upon the substrate to form coating.
- The lig and species is liberated from the metal species to be deposited upon the substrate to form the coating.
- Because most CVD reactions are endothermic, the reaction may be controlled by regulating the amount of energy input.
- Disadvantages of CVD, the precursor chemicals should not be toxic, and exhaust system should be designed to handle any reacted and unreacted vapors that remain after the coating process is complete.
- Other waste effluents from the process must be managed appropriately.
- Retrieval, recycle, and disposal methods are dictated by the nature of the chemical.
- For example, auxiliary chemical reactions must be performed to render toxic or corrosive materials harmless, condensates must be collected.

5.6 ION VAPOUR DEPOSITION (IVD)   (May 17)

- Ion vapor deposition (IVD) is a physical vapor deposition process for applying pure aluminum coatings to various substrates and components, mainly for corrosion protection.
- The process is carried out in a vacuum vessel that is available in various sizes.
- The process creates a clean, safe and environmentally friendly finishing system.
- It is a suitable alternative to cadmium plating processes, which are toxic and cause pollution.
- Because IVD aluminum is a replacement for cadmium plating, the largest use of IVD aluminum is for corrosion protection of ferrous alloy parts.
- The IVD aluminum-coating process is also qualified for use on copper-based, stainless steel and titanium-based alloys.

Benefits of IVD Include:
- Increases corrosion resistance
- Raises useful operating temperature
- Provides galvanic compatibility with aluminum structures
- Suitable for various substrates
- Environmentally safe for waste disposal

5.7 POWDER COATING   (May 17)

- Powder coating is the technique of applying dry paint to a part. It was first used in Australia about 1967.
- In normal wet painting such as house paints, the solids are in suspension in a liquid carrier, which must evaporate before the solid paint coating is produced. The final cured coating is the same as a 2-pack wet paint.

  In powder coating, the powdered paint may be applied by either of two techniques.
  - ➤ The item is lowered into a fluidized bed of the powder, which may or may not be electrostatically charged, or
  - ➤ The powdered paint is electrostatically charged and sprayed onto the part.
  - ➤ The part is then placed in an oven and the powder particles melt and coalesce to form a continuous film.
- There are two main types of powder available to the surface finisher:
  - ➤ Thermoplastic powders that will remelt when heated, and
  - ➤ Thermosetting powders that will not remelt upon reheating. During the curing process (in the oven) a chemical cross-linking reaction is triggered at the curing temperature and it is this chemical reaction which gives the powder coating many of its desirable properties.

Preparation

- The basis of any good coating is preparation. The reason behind failure of majority of powder coating is a lack of a suitable preparation.
- The preparation treatment is different for different materials.

  In general, **for steel the preparation for interior applications** may be:

Clean
Rinse
Derust
Rinse
Iron Phosphate
Rinse
Acidulated Rinse

- **For Exterior Applications:**

Clean
Rinse
Etch
Rinse
Grain Refine
Zinc Phosphate
Rinse
Acidulated Rinse

The Process

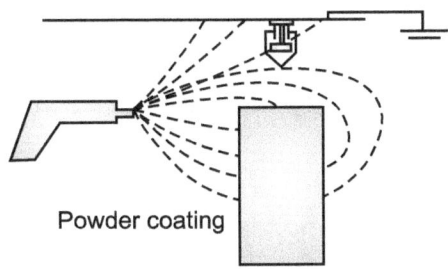

Powder coating

Fig. 5.6

• The powder is applied with an electrostatic spray gun to a part that is at earth (or ground) potential.

Before the powder is sent to the gun it is fluidized:

➢ To separate the individual grains of powder and so improve the electrostatic charge that can be applied to the powder and

➢ So that the powder flows more easily to the gun.

• Because the powder particles are electro statically charged, the powder wraps around to the back of the part as it passes by towards the air off take system. By collecting the powder, which passes by the job, and filtering it, the efficiency of the process can be increased to 95% material usage.

• The powder will remain attached to the part as long as some of the electrostatic charge remains on the powder. To obtain the final solid, tough, abrasion resistant coating the powder coated items are placed in an oven and heated to temperatures that range from 160 to 210 °C (depending on the powder).

5.8 SHOTBLASTING   (May 17)

Shotblasting is a method used to clean, strengthen (peen) or polish metal. Shot blasting is used in almost every industry that uses metal, including **aerospace**, **automotive**, **construction, foundry, shipbuilding rail**, and many others. There are two technologies used: wheel blasting or air blasting.

(a) Wheelblasting

Wheelblasting directly converts electric motor energy into kinetic abrasive energy by rotating a turbine wheel. The capacity of each wheel varies from approximately 60 kg per minute up to 1200kg/min. With these large amounts of accelerated abrasive, wheelblast machines are used where big parts or large areas of parts have to be derusted, descaled, deburred, desanded or cleaned in some form.

Often the method of transportation of the components to be blasted will define the type of machine: from simple **table machines** to integrated, fully **automatic manipulator** machines for full series automotive manufacturers, through to **roller conveyors** and **strip descaling systems**.

(b) Airblasting

Airblast machines can take the form of a **blastroom** or a **blast cabinet**, the blast media is pneumatically accelerated by compressed air and projected by nozzles onto the component. For special applications a media-water mix can be used, this is called wet blasting.

In both air and wet blasting the blast nozzles can be installed in fixed positions or can be operated manually or by automatic nozzle manipulators or robots.

The blasting task determines the choice of the abrasive media, in most cases any type of dry or free running abrasive media can be used.

5.9 ION IMPLANTATION

- Ion Implantation in the Ion Plating (IP) process, the target material is initially melted while the substrate is bombarded with ions before deposition to raise it to the required temperature.

- The coating flux ion is attracted to the substrate by biasing the substrate with a negative voltage.

- Thus sufficient ion energy is available for good inter mixing of coating and substrate at the interface Ion implantation is the introduction of ionized dopant atoms into a substrate with enough energy to penetrate beyond the surface.

- The most common application is substrate doping. The use of 3 to 500 keV energy for boron, phosphorus or arsenic dopant ions is sufficient to implant the ions from 100 to 10,000A below the silicon surface.

- The depth of implantation, which is proportional to the ion energy, can be selected to meet a particular application.

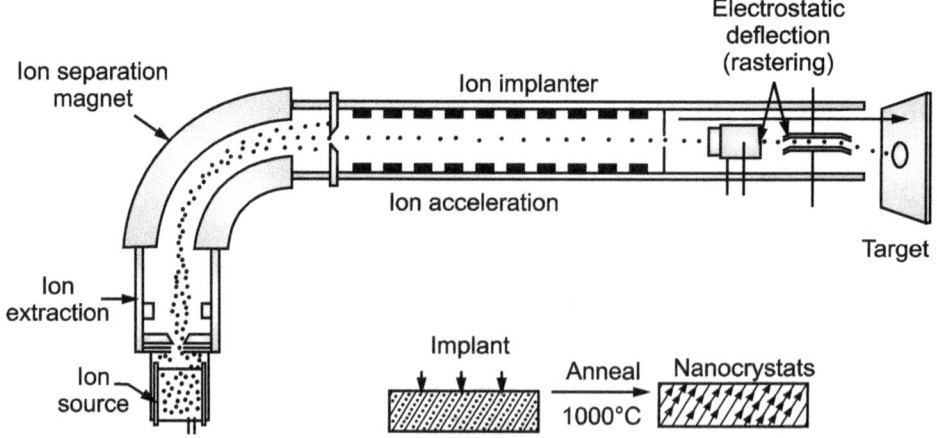

Fig. 5.7: Ion implantation

- The major advantage of ion implantation technology is the capability of precisely controlling the number of implanted dopant atoms.

- Furthermore, the dopants depth distribution profile can be well-controlled.
- Disadvantages of Ion Implantation are very deep and very shallow profiles are difficult, not all the damage can be corrected by annealing, typically has higher impurity content than does diffusion.
- Often uses extremely toxic gas sources such as arsine (AsH3), and phosphine (PH3) and expensive

5.10 PLASMA NITRIDING

Nitriding is a heat treating process that diffuses nitrogen into the surface of a metal to create a surface or case-hardened surface.

The three main methods used are: gas nitriding, salt bath nitriding, and plasma nitriding.

Plasma Nitriding

- Plasma nitriding is also known as ion nitriding, plasma ion nitriding or glow-discharge nitriding. It is an industrial surface hardening treatment for metallic materials.
- In plasma nitriding, the reactivity of the nitriding media is due to the gas ionized state. In this technique intense electric fields are used to generate ionized molecules of the gas around the surface to be nitrided. Such highly active gas with ionized molecules is called plasma. Hence it is called as **plasma nitriding**.
- The gas used for plasma nitriding is usually pure nitrogen, since no spontaneous decomposition is needed (as is the case of gas nitriding with ammonia).
- There are hot plasmas typified by plasma jets used for metal cutting, welding, cladding or spraying.
- There are also cold plasmas, usually generated inside vacuum chambers, at low pressure regimes.
- Usually steels are beneficially treated with plasma nitriding. This process permits the close control of the nitrided microstructure, allowing nitriding with or without compound layer formation.
- Not only the performance of metal parts is enhanced, but working life spans also increase, and so do the strain limit and the fatigue strength of the metals being treated.

5.11 ANODIZING   (Nov. 16)

- **Anodizing** is an electrochemical process that converts the metal surface into a decorative, durable, corrosion-resistant, anodic oxide finish. It is an electrolytic passivation process used to increase the thickness of the natural oxide layer on the surface of metal parts.
- The process is called anodizing because the part to be treated forms the anode electrode of an electrical circuit. Anodizing increases resistance to corrosion and wear,

and provides better adhesion for paint primers and glues than does bare metal. Anodic films can also be used for a number of cosmetic effects, either with thick porous coatings that can absorb dyes or with thin transparent coatings that add interference effects to reflected light.

- Anodic films are most commonly applied to protect aluminium alloys, although processes also exist for titanium, zinc, magnesium, niobium, zirconium, hafnium, and tantalum.

- Iron or carbon steel metal exfoliates when oxidized under neutral or alkaline micro electrolytic conditions; i.e., their on oxide (actually ferric hydroxide or hydrated iron oxide, also known as rust) forms by anoxic anodic pits and large cathodic surface, these pits concentrate anions such as sulfate and chloride accelerating the underlying metal to corrosion.

- Carbon flakes or nodules in iron or steel with high carbon content (high carbon steel, cast iron) may cause an electrolytic potential and interfere with coating or plating.

- Ferrous metals are commonly anodized electrolytically in nitric acid, or by treatment with red fuming nitric acid, to form hard black ferric oxide. This oxide remains conformal even when plated on wire and the wire is bent.

- Anodizing changes the microscopic texture of the surface and changes the crystal structure of the metal near the surface. Thick coatings are normally porous, so a sealing process is often needed to achieve corrosion resistance.

Coating

It is a process of applying a covering layer of a substance spread over a surface for protection or decoration.

5.12 SURFACE PREPARATION BEFORE COATING

- The basis of any good coating is surface preparation. The vast majority of powder coating failures can be traced to a lack of a suitable preparation.

- The preparation treatment is different for different materials.

- For steel, the preparation for interior applications may be:

Clean
Rinse
Derust
Rinse
Iron Phosphate
Rinse
Acidulated Rinse

5.13 SURFACE COATING DEFECTS

Sr. No.	Name of the Defect	Description	Probable Causes	Prevention	Repair
1.	Cracking	The splitting of a dry paint film through at least one coat to form visible cracks which may penetrate down to the substrate.	It is a stress related failure and can be attributed to surface movement, ageing, absorption and desorption of moisture and general lack of flexibility of the coating. The thicker the paint film the greater the possibility it will crack.	Use correct coating systems, application techniques and dry film thicknesses. Alternatively, use a more flexible coating system.	Abrade to remove all cracked paint. Correctly reapply the coating system or use a more flexible system and one less prone to cracking.
2.	Cracking At Welds	Paint coatings with visible cracks at weld seams which may penetrate down to the substrate.	Due to surface movement, ageing, absorption and desorption of moisture and general lack of flexibility of the coating.	Use correct coating systems, application techniques and dry film thicknesses or use a more flexible coating system.	Abrade to remove all cracked paint. Correctly reapply the coating system or use a more flexible system and one less prone to cracking.

Sr. No.	Name of the Defect	Description	Probable Causes	Prevention	Repair
3.	**Edge Corrosion**	Breakdown at edges resulting in corrosion.	Low film thickness, sharp edges, lack of stripe coats and flow away from the edges.	Ensure that all edges are radiused, stripe coats are applied and the coating has good edge retention.	Remove coating by abrading, radius the edges and reapply the coating system with adequate stripe coats.
4.	**Erosion**	Selective removal of paint films from areas or high spots.	The wearing away of the paint film by various elements such as rain, snow, wind, sand etc. Found to be more prominent on brush applied coatings because of the uneven finish.	Use a suitable coating system with resistance to surface erosion/abrasion.	Clean surface free from contamination and apply a coating system formulated and tested for the specific environment.
5.	**Abrasion**	The mechanical action of rubbing, scraping, scratching, gouging or erosion.	Removal of a portion of the surface of the coating or in severe cases removal to expose the substrate by contact with another object	Use of abrasion resistant coatings formulated with particular regard to resins and extender pigments.	Depends on the extent of the damage and could range from individual areas prepared by mechanical cleaning to the blast cleaning

Sr. No.	Name of the Defect	Description	Probable Causes	Prevention	Repair
			such as the use of metal chains for lifting, cargo, fenders, or the grounding of a ship.	With severe cases of abrasion the effects will only be reduced or limited by an abrasion resistant coating.	of large areas. Application of an abrasion resistant coating.
6.	**Adhesion Failure**	Paint fails to adhere to substrate or underlying coats of paint	Surface contamination or condensation, incompatibility between coating systems and exceeding the overcoating time.	Ensure that the surface is clean, dry and free from any contamination and that the surface has been suitably prepared. Use the correct coating specification and follow the advised overcoating times.	Depends upon the extent of adhesion failure. Removal of defective areas will be necessary prior to adequate preparation and application of correct coating system to manufacturer's recommendations.

REVIEW QUESTIONS

1. What is the surface engineering?
2. What is surface modification? Give it's classification.
3. Draw, sketch typical thickness of engineered surface layers physical vapour deposition.
4. Explain the process of electroplating.
5. Explain the stuttering process.
6. Explain advantages and disadvantages of PVD process (Physical Vapour Deposition).

7. Write a note on CVD.

8. Explain IVD (Ion Vapour Deposition) and their applications.

9. What is shotblasting and types of shotblasting.

10. What is Ion implantation? Working of ion implantation.

11. Write short note on plasma nitriding.

12. Write short note on anodizing.

UNIVERSITY QUESTIONS

NOVEMBER 2016

1. Explain with neat diagram physical vapour deposition. State its advantages, disadvantages and applications over other processes.   **[6]**

    [**Ans. :** Refer article 5.4.1]

2. What are different characteristics of surface improvements? Explain in brief.   **[6]**

    [**Ans. :** Refer article 5.2]

3. Write short notes on (any three)   **[12]**

    (a) Anodising :   [**Ans. :** Refer article 5.3]

    (b) Electroplating :   [**Ans. :** Refer article 5.3]

    (c) Ion implantation :   [**Ans. :** Refer article 5.9]

    (d) CVD :   [**Ans. :** Refer article 5.5]

MAY 2017

1. What are the properties of coating materials ? Which are affects surface quality? Explain any three surface cleaning methods.   **[6]**

    [**Ans. :** Refer article 5.7]

2. What is shot blasting?   **[3]**

    [**Ans. :** Refer article 5.8]

3. List out the factors affecting electro-deposition.   **[3]**

    [**Ans. :** Refer article 5.3]

4. Compare PVD and CVD coating.   **[4]**

    [**Ans. :** Refer articles 5.4, 5.5]

5. Explain the process of Ion vapour deposition (IVD) with principle of working advantages and disadvantages and applications.   **[6]**

    [**Ans. :** Refer article 5.6]

6. What is powder coating?   **[2]**

    [**Ans. :** Refer article 5.7]

✠ ✠ ✠

Unit VI

POWDER METALLURGICAL TECHNOLOGY

6.1 INTRODUCTION   (Dec. 11)

Powder metallurgy may be defined as the process of manufacturing components from metal powders by compaction and sintering. Many metal powders and their oxides are used in cosmetics, paintings and for decorative purposes for the last few centuries. Some of the components manufactured by powder metallurgical technique have unique applications, which may not be obtained by conventional processes.

Powder metallurgy (P/M) deals with,

(a) Powder manufacturing (b) Compaction and (c) Sintering.

Powder metallurgical parts find applications in the various areas such as

- Automobiles
- High temperature parts
- Superconducting materials and
- Aerospace
- Nuclear reactor parts
- Tool materials.

During the production of powder metallurgical parts, porosity cannot be avoided. However, this porosity becomes a unique property and is used in few applications like self-lubricating bearings. The final properties of the component depend upon properties of the metal powder as size, shape and sintering properties. Similarly, refractory materials like tungsten, molybdenum, zirconium etc. can be processed only by powder metallurgy technique. The applications of powder metallurgical parts are explained in detail at the end of this chapter.

6.2 METHODS FOR PRODUCTION OF POWDERS   (May 17)

Depending upon the final application of the powder, various methods of powder production are used. Each method produces powder with specific characteristics.

These methods are classified as follows

1. **Mechanical Processes**
   - Machining
   - Crushing
   - Milling
   - Shotting
   - Graining and
   - Atomization

2. **Physico-Chemical Processes**

- Condensation
- Thermal decomposition
- Reduction
- Electrodeposition
- Precipitation from aqueous solution
- Precipitation from fused salt
- Hydrometallurgical reduction
- Intergranular corrosion and
- Oxidation and decarburisation

6.2.1 Mechanical Processes   (May 10; Dec. 10, 13)

(a) Machining

- This method is mainly used to produce fillings, turnings, chips, etc. These can be pulverized by crushing and milling. Very coarse and bulky powders are obtained by this process.

- In this process, irregular shaped particles are produced. This is used for the production of magnesium powder (for pyrotechnic applications), beryllium powders, silver solders and dental alloys.

(b) Crushing

- This method is used for disintegration of oxides and brittle materials. Various crushing instruments such as stamps, hammers, jaw crushers etc. are used. The powder produced by this method is of angular shape for brittle material and of flaky shape for ductile materials.

- Titanium, zirconium, vanadium etc. can be powdered by this method. Some of the metals and alloys can be hardened first and then crushed for making powders.

(c) Milling

- This is one of the most useful method with which various fine grades of powders can be produced. Milling or grinding can be done by using ball mill, rod mill, impact mill, disk mill, vortex mill etc.

- In ball milling, the material to be disintegrated is tumbled in a container with a large number of hard wear resistant solid balls. These balls hit the material and break it. The speed and time of rotation of the container decides the nature of final product. The milling is carried out either in wet or dry condition. The ball mill container is of stainless steel or steel lined with hard alloy steel plates. The balls used are of white cast iron or hardened steel.

- The major disadvantages of milling are work hardening, excessive oxidation of the final powder, particle welding and agglomeration. Annealing in a reducing atmosphere eliminates these problems.
- This method is widely employed for carbide-metal mixture and cement materials to perform blending and particle size reduction.

(d) Shotting

- The method consists of pouring a fine stream of molten metal through a vibrating screen into air or neutral atmosphere like nitrogen.
- The molten metal gets disintegrated into a large number of fine droplets, which solidify as spherical particles.
- The opening of screen, its frequency for vibration and the melt temperature decide the properties of the powder produced. This method is mostly used for non-ferrous metals.

(e) Graining

- This method uses the same principle as above, with the only difference that the solidification is allowed to take place in water. Finally, pulverisation is used to produce fine powders.
- The metals like zinc, bismuth, tin etc. are pulverised by this method.

(f) Atomization   (Dec. 13; May 14)

- The principle of this method consists of disintegration of a stream of molten metal into the fine particles mechanically by using a jet of compressed air, inert gases or water (See Fig. 6.1).

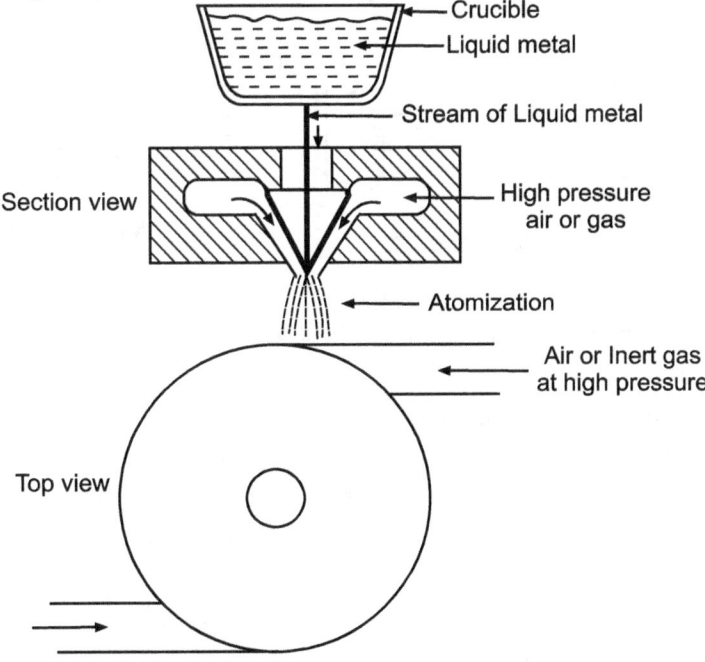

Fig. 6.1: Atomization for powder manufacturing

- Because of its various advantages, this method has wide applications. This method is mostly used for powdering of the metals such as tin, lead, zinc and aluminium, which have low melting points.

- Atomized products are generally sphere-shaped particles.

- By varying temperature of the metal, pressure and temperature of the atomizing gas, rate of flow of metal through orifice and nozzle decide the particle size, shape and distribution.

- It is a very flexible method, but not suitable for the refractory metals.

6.2.2 Physico-Chemical Processes

(a) Condensation

- This is a modification of usual distillation process. In this method, the volatile metal is distilled off and the vapours are condensed to produce powders (See Fig. 6.2). Metals like zinc, magnesium etc. are used to produce their respective powders. Zinc dust, at least 97% pure is produced in a very large quantity of tonnes by this way.

- Powders with very small particle size, less than 500 A° in diameter can be produced by this method.

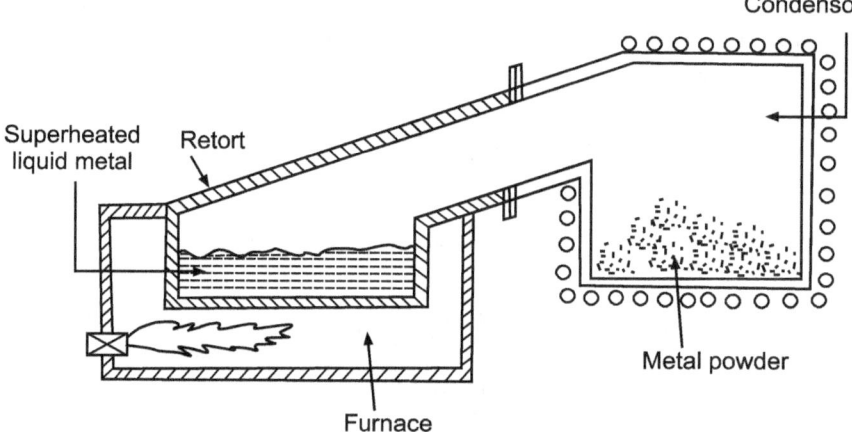

Fig. 6.2: Metal powder manufacture by condensation method

(b) Thermal Decomposition

- This method, termed as gaseous pyrolysis method is used for powdering of the metals like iron, nickel, zinc, magnesium, cobalt, chromium etc. The metal carbonyls are volatile liquids. They can be easily decomposed by forming powders.

  e.g. Iron pentacarbonyls $Fe(CO)_5$ can be thermally decomposed to form iron powder.

  $$Fe\,(CO)_5 \rightarrow Fe + 5\,CO$$

  Similarly, nickel tetracarbonyl $Ni\,(CO)_4$ gives nickel powder.

  $$Ni\,(CO)_4 \rightarrow Ni + 4\,CO$$

- These carbonyls may be produced by passing CO over a spongy or powdered metal at some suitable temperature and pressure. This process gives very fine powders. It is also economical as carbon monoxide can be recycled.
- Iron powders produced by this method are perfectly spherical and purest of all the commercial metals (over 99.5%). The iron-nickel powder produced by decomposition of their carbonyls is used for the manufacture of high permeability cores for long distance communication apparatus. Tungsten powder produced by this method is used for welding tungsten filaments.

(c) Reduction Method

- In this method, the metal powder is produced by reducing oxides or halides of metals, using a suitable reducing agent. This is one of the economical and flexible methods. It is extensively used for the manufacture of iron, copper, nickel, tungsten, cobalt powders.
- The process produces extremely fine and irregularly shaped particles with a considerable porosity. Normally carbon, hydrogen, ammonia and carbon monoxide are used as reducing agents.
- Large scale production of iron powders at low cost is possible by mixing high grade oxides with carbon and heating them in a ceramic container, because of low cost and availability of raw material. Metallic reducing agents are also used to reduce oxides

  e.g. chromium powder is produced by reduction of Cr_2O_3 with magnesium; zirconium powder by reduction of zirconium oxide with calcium and so on. Since, oxides are very brittle, fine powders are possible to be produced.
- W and Mo powders are prepared from WO_3 and MoO_2 by reduction with H_2 for their use in manufacture of incandescent lamp filaments, radiovalves, x-ray target etc. In most of the cases, irregular shaped fine powders are produced.

(d) Electrodeposition

- In this method, metal powders can be produced by electrodecomposition from aqueous solutions and fused salts.
- This method is a reverse of electroplating. In electroplating process, the parameters are adjusted to obtain adherent and continuous deposition, while in electro-deposition, coarse, loose and non-adherent deposition is required to recollect the powder.
- This technique is mainly employed for the commercial production of metal powders from copper, beryllium, iron, zinc, tin, nickel etc.
- Following three types of electrodeposition are practically used
  (a) Deposition as a hard and brittle mass, which may be ground to form powders;
  (b) Deposition as a soft, spongy mass, which may be powdered by light rubbing and
  (c) Direct deposition in powder form from the electrolyte, which drops to the bottom of the cell.

- The last two methods are used for production on the commercial line. However, the process is not suitable for production of alloy powders.

- Following conditions of electrolyte favour the powder manufacture

  ➢ High current density,

  ➢ Low metal-ion concentration,

  ➢ High acidity,

  ➢ Low temperature,

  ➢ High viscosity and

  ➢ Circulation of electrolyte

- The powders produced by this process are crystalline and dendritic having less flow rate in some cases. The purity as high as 99.9% in the case of non-ferrous metals may be reached.

(e) Precipitation from Aqueous Solution

- This process is based on the principle that less noble metal displaces more noble metal in the electromotive series, from an aqueous solution.

- This process produces very fine powders. For example, silver powder is produced from its nitrate solution by adding copper or iron; tin powder is precipitated by metallic zinc from stannous chloride solution.

- A very common method of producing copper powder is by precipitation from sulphate solution with iron.

- The precipitated metal powders are porous, but with excellent purity. This process produces dendritic shaped powder.

(f) Precipitation from Fused Salts

- Reactive metal powders are produced by precipitation from fused salts.

  For example, $ZrCl_4$ salt is mixed with an equal amount of KCl and some magnesium to produce Zr powder. Similarly, beryllium and thorium powders are produced.

(g) Hydrometallurgical Reduction

- Nickel, cobalt and copper powders are mainly produced by this method.

- The reduction of aqueous solutions or slurries of salts of these metals are made with hydrogen under controlled conditions of pressure and temperature.

$$M^{++} + H_2 \rightarrow M + 2H^+$$

- All metals must be washed to free from the traces of salts and then dried. This method is also used to produce composite powders.

- The process produces pure metal powders of spherical shape.

(h) Intergranular Corrosion

- Usually, grain boundaries of any metal corrode very fast than the grains. This is intergranular corrosion. In this method, the grain boundary area is intentionally corroded by suitable electrolyte. This process is used to produce stainless steel powder.

- Stainless steel is a type of alloy steel containing chromium and nickel. When stainless steel (particularly austenitic stainless steel) is heated in the temperature range of 500 to 800°C for a long time, the chromium combines with carbon and forms chromium carbides. These complex carbides get precipitated at grain boundary. The chromium, which is added to improve the corrosion resistance, thus, gets consumed with carbon and the corrosion resistance is drastically dropped. Such steel becomes sensitized in corrosive medium and intergranular corrosion i.e. separation of grain occurs.

- This network of carbide is preferentially corroded by boiling aqueous solution of 11% copper sulphate and 10% sulphuric acid. Rapid disintegration may be obtained using stainless steel as anode and solutions of copper sulphate and sulphuric acid as an electrolyte in a cell.

- These powder particles possess angular shape and the final particle size depends on the size of initial grain structure.

- This method was used in the past. However, atomization is more suitable now-a-days in view of mass production.

(i) Oxidation and Decarburisation

- This method is mainly used for the production of pure reactive metal powders, particularly niobium.

- The process consists of reacting metal carbide with metal oxide in vacuum at a higher temperature so that the oxygen and carbon are removed as CO and finally the metal remains in powder form.

However, due to its complexity, the process is not so useful on commercial footing.

6.3 CHARACTERISTICS AND TESTING OF METAL POWDERS

The method of production of metal powder decides its properties. The mechanical behaviour of the powder and its metallurgical component depends upon the characteristics of initial metal powder. So, it becomes necessary to test various properties of metal powders.

The main purpose of powder testing is to ensure, whether or not the powder is suitable for further processing.

The principal characteristics of a metal powder are,

- Chemical composition and purity
- Particle size and its distribution

- Particle shape
- Particle porosity
- Particle microstructure.

Other characteristics include

- Specific surface
- Apparent density
- Tap density
- Flow rate
- Compacting and sintering properties.

Sampling: The sample used must be a true representative of the entire batch produced. There are various methods used for making samples.

Coning and quartering method involves pouring of powder on a polished metal sheet and splitting up into four equal parts. This process is repeated till the required sample quantity is obtained.

The scoop sampling method consists in inserting a scoop into a thoroughly mixed powder in a container and then drawing it full of powder as a sample. Any sampling method can be adopted. It can be standardised as per individual's experience.

1. Chemical Composition

The chemical composition of any powder reveals the type and percentage of impurities it contains and determines particle hardness and pressing properties. Impurity refers to undesirable metal contents, which affect the mechanical properties of the component.

Insoluble oxides having more hardness than that of metal powder, increase abrasion of die and punch. Non-uniform pressing and sintering occurs due to these insoluble oxides.

The chemical composition of powder is determined by the well established techniques of chemical analysis. This includes,

- Gravimetric analysis,
- Volumetric analysis,
- Electrochemical analysis,
- Colorimetric analysis etc.

Oxygen content is determined by wet analysis. Some of the insoluble contents may be determined by dissolving the powder followed by filtering, igniting and weighing the residue.

2. Particle Size

Particle size affects mould strength, density of compact, porosity, dimensional stability etc. Particle size is expressed by the diameter of the spherical shaped particles and by the average diameter for non-spherical particles.

For all practical purposes, the selection of powder size for a specific application is usually based upon one's own experience. However, no doubt fine powder is always preferred to coarse one.

Metal powders are divided into three categories

- Sieve,
- Sub-sieve and
- Sub-micron or ultrafine.

A majority of metal powders employed in powder metallurgical industries vary in size from 4 to 250 microns. Very fine powders tend to be pyrophoric i.e. those which oxidise quickly in the atmosphere.

(a) Sieve Method   (May 17)

- This is the most popular and simple method. Different sieves are used for classifying powders. Standard sieves of different mesh sizes are used. This mesh size is standardised by the various international organisations.
- The opening of sieve is expressed by the number of meshes per linear inch. Woven wire sieves are made of copper, brass, nickel or even of nylon.
- Different mesh sieves are stacked over each other. The coarse sieve is at the top. The fineness goes on increasing towards the bottom.
- A sample of 100 gm metal powder placed on the top sieve is shaken or vibrated to provide two motions viz. circular and translating, for 15 minutes. The quantity of powder retained in each sieve is taken out and weighed accurately from these weights, size and size distribution can be found out.
- The particles, which pass through the sieve, are given minus number and the particles which are retained on the sieve, are given plus numbers of that sieve. The size distribution is expressed by weight fraction of powder retained on each sieve.
- The powders within the range of 44 to 840 microns can be successfully sieved.

(b) Microscopic Method

- Microscopic sizing or counting method depends largely on the skill. But, this is a direct method.
- It involves actual counting of particles and individual examination of a large number of particles on a glass slide. This is a time taking process, but one of the most reliable methods. Optical and electron microscopes are used for this measurement.
- As the powder is always of mixed sizes, a number of readings should be taken and an average may be mentioned for its particle size. Shape of the particles can also be visualised very easily.
- Optical microscope is used for the determination of particle diameters down to about 0.3 microns. An electron microscope is used for the particles in the diameter range of 10 to 0.001 micron.

(c) Sedimentation Method

- This is a method of classifying metal powders according to settling velocities in a fluid.

- Sedimentation involves suspending the powder sample by using a proper stirring in a fluid medium and allowing it to settle for a suitable time. The settling velocity in suspension is measured. The settling velocity of a spherical particle is proportional to square of the particle diameter.

- So particles having equal sizes can be separated as their settling time will be the same. The amount of particles settling at different intervals of time is measured. Irregularly shaped particle size is defined as the diameter of a sphere of the same material having the same settling velocity under constant conditions.

- Laboratory methods for sizing by sedimentation may be divided into two groups

  - ➤ The fractionating methods are use, when it is essential to separate individual size fractions for individual examinations.

  - ➤ Non-fractionating methods are used for determining size distribution and estimating specific surface.

- Following are some of the methods, which use the principle of sedimentation

  - ➤ Hydrometer or specific gravity method uses change in the specific gravity of suspension at various levels of depths.

  - ➤ Manometric method measures the change in the density of suspension by the change in the pressure at various levels of height.

  - ➤ There is one method called turbidimetric method based on change in intensity of transmitted light through dilute suspension at certain depth. However, the selection of test method depends on the various working parameters.

(d) Elutriation Method

- This method is used for sub-sieve powders.

- In this method, the metal powder is allowed to settle in a moving liquid or gas of constant velocity. The particles with settling velocity less than the velocity of rising liquid or gas are carried upwards, while those with higher settling rate fall in the column. By changing the velocity of the medium, the particles can be separated according to their sizes.

- This is a fractioning method and is used for the separation as well as determination of size fractions of the powders. This method is also useful to remove unwanted fine materials from the powder.

- Elutriation in air is widely used for metal powders.

3. Particle Shape

Various shapes of metal powders are observed according to the method of their production (See Fig. 6.3), e.g.

- **Spherical Shape:** Carbonyl iron, condensed zinc, lead, atomization, precipitation from aqueous solution by gases.

- **Rounded or Droplets:** Atomized copper, zinc, aluminium, tin, chemical decomposition.

- **Angular Shape:** Mechanically disintegrated antimony, cast iron, stainless steel by process of intergranular corrosion.

- **Accicular Shape:** Chemical decomposition.

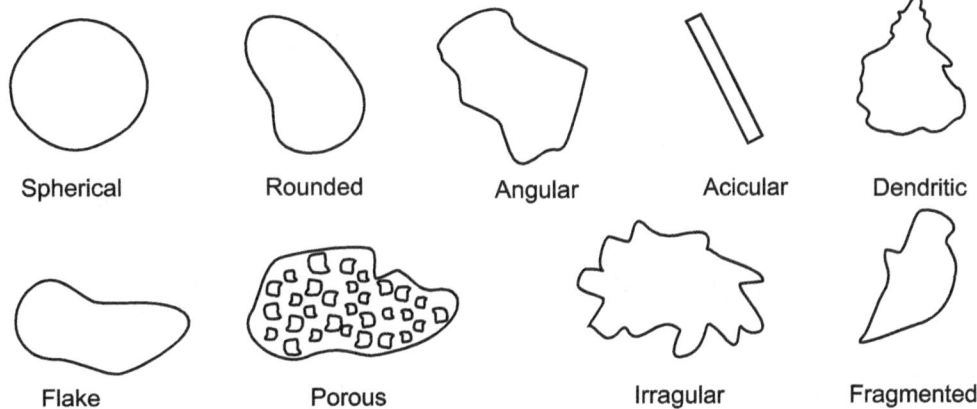

Fig. 6.3: Different shapes of metal powders

- **Dendritic Shape:** Electrolytic silver, copper.
- **Flake Shape:** Ball milled copper, aluminium.
- **Porous:** Reduction of oxides.
- **Irregular Shape:** Atomization, reduction.
- The packing capacity of powder depends on its shape. Irregular shaped particles give less density and flow rate with good pressing and sintering properties. Spherical particles have maximum density, flow rate and good sintering properties, but reduced pressing properties. Similarly, dendritic shaped powder shows less density and flow rate.
- For particle shape evaluation, optical or electron microscopic examination method is used. This is a direct method. It is also expressed by shape factor, which is the ratio of the length of particle to its breadth or surface area to size of the particle.

4. Particle Porosity

- The porosity of particles affects impact and fatigue strength as well as tensile properties of component. Porosity acts as a stress raiser, which is similar to nature of graphite in cast irons. It is practically impossible to produce P/M components without porosity. In fact, porosity itself becomes a necessary property in the case of self-lubricating bearings.

- The porosity may be present as,
  - ➤ Interconnected or
  - ➤ Separate pores.
- Porosity may be measured by mercury porosimetry (for interconnected pores). It consists of keeping P/M component with mercury in vacuum at the room temperature. The pressure of mercury is increased and the volume of penetrating mercury and density of porous material is measured.
- Porous parts can be studied similar to a metal sample (i.e. by following mounting, polishing and without etching).

5. Particle Microstructure

- For observation of microstructure, the same method of metallography i.e. polishing and etching is used. Smearing of surface layers during polishing may cover up the pores. So, extra precautions should be taken. After etching, the specimen should be thoroughly washed to avoid absorption of etchant in pores. So, electrolytic etching may be used.
- Metallographic examination reveals amount and distribution of porosity, phases, grain size, inclusion and heterogeneity in structure.

6.4 OTHER CHARACTERISTICS OF METAL POWDERS

1. Specific Surface

- The specific surface of powder may be defined as the total surface area of a particle per unit weight. The specific surface depends on size, shape, density and surface conditions of the particle.
- The specific surface i.e. contact area between powder particles strongly affects compacting and sintering properties. High surface area increases sintering rate as well as entrapment of air. This shows bridging effect, which causes cracks.
- Coarser powder with smaller contact area gives bad sintering and weak mechanical properties.

Specific surface may be measured by,

  1. Adsorption method and
  2. Permeability method.

- The permeability method is easy and quick. It may be used to control the process. This method involves measurement of pressure drop across the bed of packed powder particles contained in a chamber with relation to fluid flow. The surface area of powder can be calculated by measuring the resistance of a packed column of the powder to the flow of liquid.
- The specific surface can be calculated from the size distribution data either by graphical method or by numerical calculation.

Typical values of specific surface of iron powder are as follows

Powder	Particle Size (μ)	Specific Surface (cm²/gm)
Iron	65	510
	50	950
	6	5200

2. Apparent Density

- Apparent density is called as packing density or loading weight. It is defined as mass per unit volume of loose or unpacked metal powder. It includes internal pores, but excludes external pores. It depends on

  ➤ Chemical composition

  ➤ Particle shape, size, distribution and

  ➤ Method of manufacture.

- The apparent density decreases with decrease in size of particle and increase in the surface roughness. Coarse and spherical shaped powder shows good apparent density, while irregular and flake shaped powder shows poor apparent density. Very fine powder shows poor apparent density.

- It strongly affects pressing and sintering properties. Longer compression strokes are required for lower apparent density powders.

3. Tap Density   (Nov. 16)

- Tap density or load factor is the apparent density of the powder after it is mechanically vibrated or tapped until the level of the powder no longer falls. This becomes useful for storage, packing or transport of commercial powders. This shows a similar effect as that of apparent density on pressing and sintering properties. Tap density increases with reduced particle porosity.

4. Flow Rate

- This is one of the most important characteristics of powders. It measures the ability of powder to be transferred.

- It is defined as the rate at which metal powder flows under gravity from a container (called flow meter) through an orifice having specific size, shape and finish (See Fig. 6.4).

  Poor flow properties of powder result in slow and uneconomical feeding of a die.

- It is affected by particle size and distribution, absorption of moisture and coefficient of interparticle friction. Spherical powder shows maximum flow rate, while irregular and dendritic powders show poor flow rate. Hall flow-meter is used to measure the flow rate.

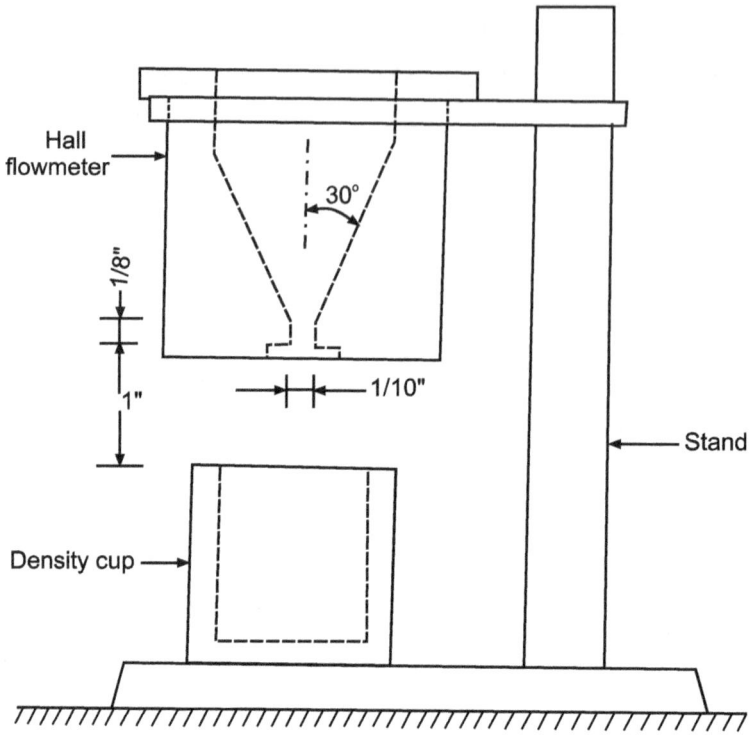

Fig. 6.4: Hall flow-meter

- It is accurately machined conical funnel made of brass with smooth finish having internal angle of 60°. The orifice situated at the bottom is either 1/8" (for ferrous powder) or 1/10" in diameter (for non-ferrous powder) and with length 1/8". The time required to flow the weighed sample of powder (around 50 gm) is measured and reported as flow rate in seconds or in gms/min in the case of non-standard weight of powder.

  Apparent density and flow properties are closely related.

5. **Compacting and Sintering Properties**

- These are represented by the following terms
  - ➤ Compressibility and
  - ➤ Compactibility.

Compressibility affects the density of P/M parts.

- It can be defined as the measure of ability of powder to get deformed under applied load. It can also be defined as, The ratio of green density of compact to the apparent density of powder (See Fig. 6.5) or

- The ratio of height of uncompacted powder in the die to the height of the pressed compact or

- The ratio of volume of the powder poured into the die to the volume of pressed compact.

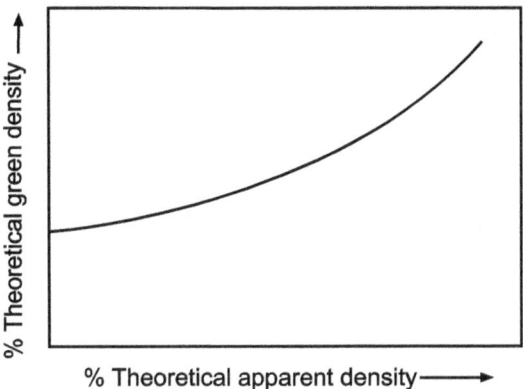

Fig. 6.5: Dependence of green density on apparent density of a metal powder

- This ratio is termed as compression ratio.

$$\text{Maximum compression ratio} = \frac{\text{True density of bulk material}}{\text{Apparent density}}$$

$$= 2 \text{ to } 8$$

Higher compression ratio increases friction between powder and the die wall.

- Compactibility is defined as the minimum pressure required to produce a powder compact of desired green strength.

  Both the above terms depend on
  - ➢ Particle size
  - ➢ Particle shape
  - ➢ Porosity
  - ➢ Hardness
  - ➢ Surface properties of powders

6. Green Density

- This is the density of a green compact i.e. density of compacted product; before sintering. It increases with

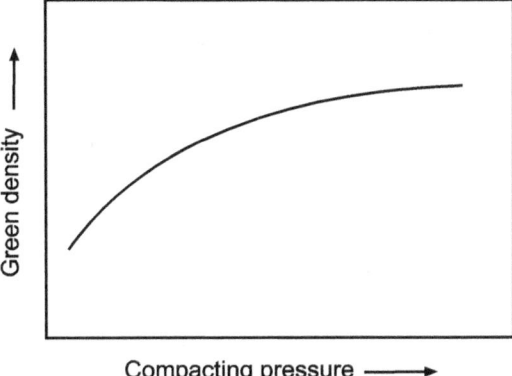

Fig. 6.6: Dependence of green density on compacting pressure

- ➤ Increase in the compaction pressure (See Fig. 6.6),
- ➤ Increase in the particle size,
- ➤ Less particle hardness and
- ➤ Low compaction speed.

- In the case of standard and regular shaped compacts (i.e. cubic, cylindrical), the green density can be calculated by its weight and dimensions. For irregular shaped compact, it is measured by weighing the sample in air and water. It is represented as gm/cc.

7. Green Strength

- It is referred as the strength of a green compact. It depends on compacting pressure. A P/M part gains green strength because of cold welding and mechanical interlocking of particles during compaction.

- *It is defined as the mechanical strength required for handling a green compact without any damage to its size and shape.* It is expressed in kg/mm^2.

- It depends on the size, shape, distribution, hardness etc. of powder. After compaction, the P/M parts are ejected from the die and transferred to a sintering furnace easily. So, green strength plays an important role.

The green strength may be tested by,

- ➤ Three point transverse rupture test or by
- ➤ Radial crushing test.

8. Green Spring   (Nov. 16)

- After ejection of compacts from the die, expansion of compact takes place. This expansion in size is both radial and longitudinal.

- The difference between the size of compact and the die is referred as green spring.

- As the compact is ejected, elastic recovery of particles takes place. When it exceeds the green strength of the compact, cracking occurs during ejection. During manufacturing of P/M parts with close dimensional tolerance, it is necessary to determine green spring.

- In many cases, the green spring is observed to be 0.2% on the diameter and 0.5% on the length.

The green spring depends upon

- ➤ Powder properties,
- ➤ Pressure of compaction,
- ➤ Elastic recovery of tools and
- ➤ Design of tools i.e. die and punch.

9. Sintering Properties

- **Dimensional Changes During Sintering:** Dimensional changes are observed, when sintering of a green compact is carried out. It is expressed as shrinkage.

$$\text{Percentage shrinkage} = \frac{\text{Change in length}}{\text{Sintered length}} \times 100$$

This is used in carbide industries, where dimensional change is of the order of 25%.

In the engineering component and bearing industries, the following formula is used for the calculation of shrinkage.

$$\text{Percentage shrinkage} = \frac{\text{Change in length}}{\text{Unsintered length}} \times 100$$

- **Sintered Density:** The method used to measure green density is used to measure sintered density also. It is related to the porosity of the finished products.

- **Porosity:** The total porosity present in sintered part can be calculated as,

$$p = 1 - \rho_p / \rho_s$$

where, p = Fractional porosity,

ρ_p = Density of sintered part,

ρ_s = Density of solid material.

It is not possible to produce P/M parts without porosity remaining after sintering. The porosity badly affects the mechanical strength.

The microstructural observation of a sintered part follows the same metallographic techniques.

6.5 POWDER CONDITIONING   (Dec. 12, 14; May 11)

The metal powders after production may not possess the required physical or chemical properties. Hence, powder conditioning is required, which involves mechanical, thermal or chemical treatments.

Powder conditioning can be explained as below

Heat Treatment

- Annealing heat treatment is used before mixing or blending. Annealing is carried out in reducing atmosphere or in vacuum. Annealing alters the mechanical properties.

- It eliminates Work hardening and Impuring content, also alters apparent density. High temperature heat treatment increases apparent density. This alteration in properties improves the sintering qualities.

- Annealing process forms spongy mass of metal powder and hence, pulverising and screening has to be carried out. If the powder has to be mixed with alloying elements, it is important to use the powder immediately after the annealing treatment.

Blending or Mixing

- It is an operation of thorough mixing of different powders of the same composition or of different compositions. The aim of blending is to obtain homogeneous mixture of powder.
- This helps to improve compacting and sintering properties. Additives such as binders or lubricants are usually included in these operations to control strength and porosities.
- It is very difficult to decide optimum mixing time. It must produce a homogeneous mixture in the least time.
- Various types of blenders and mills are employed for blending and mixing. Ball mills or rod mills are commonly used for mixing hard metals, but are less useful for soft metals.
- In general, double cone mixers or Y-mixers are used (See Fig. 6.7 (a) and (b)). Mixing may be either dry or wet. Wet mixing is used to produce more fine mixtures of powder particles. After this process, the powders are screened to remove unwanted material.

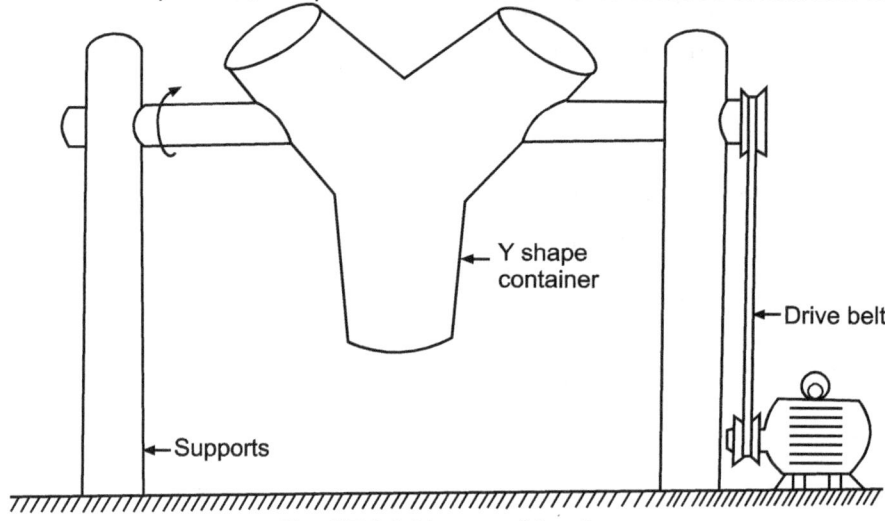

Fig. 6.7 (a): Y - cone blender

Fig. 6.7 (b): Double cone powder blender (horizontal type)

6.6 POWDER COMPACTION   (Dec. 10, 11, 12, Nov. 16)

- Powder compaction is the process of forming metal powder compacts of the desired shape. Following are the various methods of powder compaction
  - ➤ Pressureless shaping,
  - ➤ Cold pressure shaping and
  - ➤ Pressure shaping with heat.
- The aim of compacting is to consolidate the powder into desired shape, close to final dimensions. It also decides the porosity level.
- The pressure techniques involve die, isostatic, high energy rate forming, forging, extrusion, vibratory and continuous forming, while pressureless techniques involve slip casting, gravity and continuous forming.

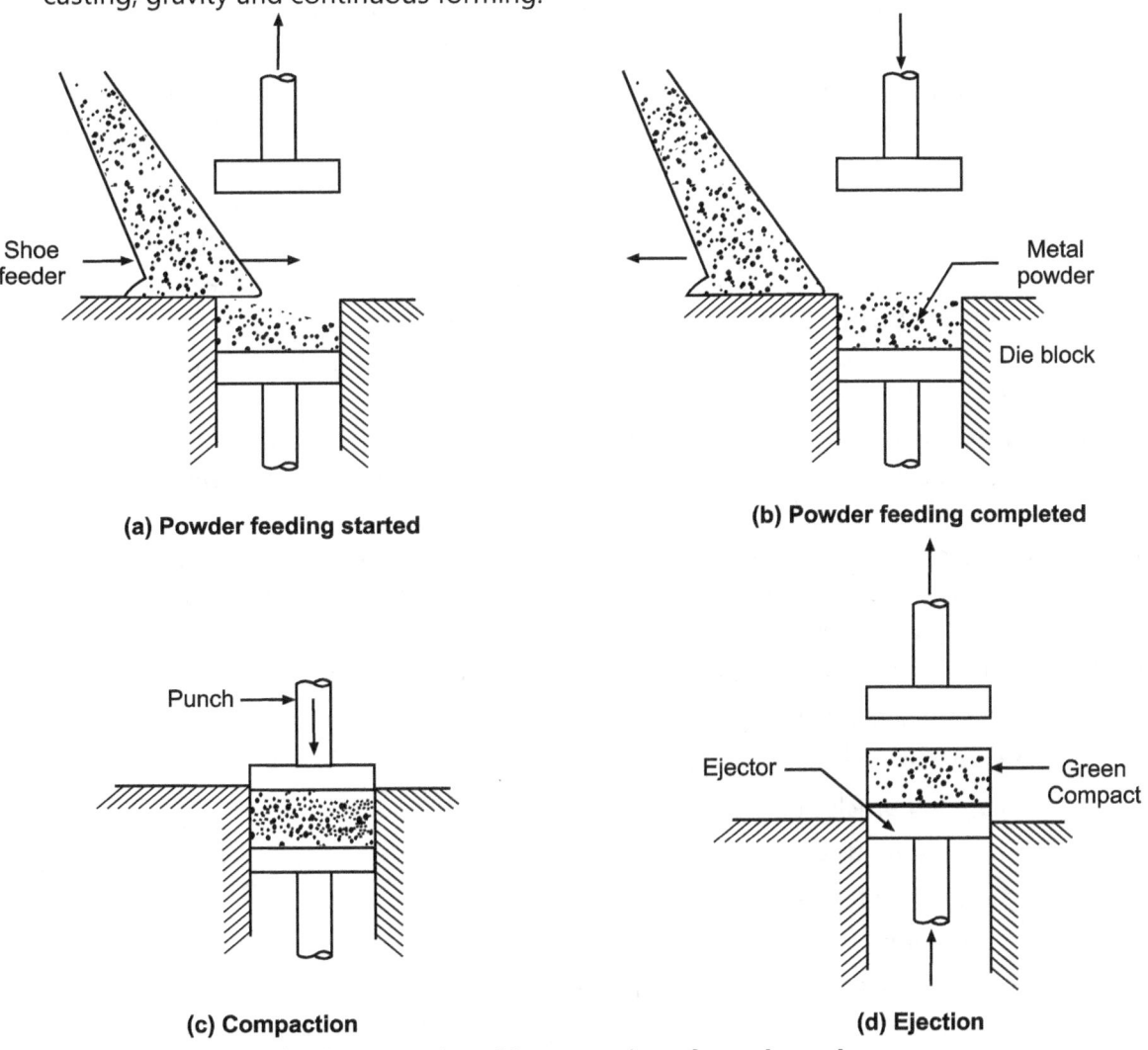

(a) Powder feeding started   (b) Powder feeding completed

(c) Compaction   (d) Ejection

Fig. 6.8: Steps in cold compaction of metal powders

- Die compaction is a general method used in industries. It consists of the following steps
  - ➤ Filling the die cavity with a definite volume of powder.
  - ➤ Application of required pressure by movement of upper and lower punches towards each other and
  - ➤ Ejection of green compact by lower punch (See Fig. 6.8).
- The loads used depend on cross-section of compact and required properties.

  The pressure may be obtained by using,
  1. Mechanical or
  2. Hydraulic press.
- Mechanical presses have high speed production rates, flexible design and economical operation. Hydraulic presses have higher pressure rating, but slow stroke speeds.
- The dies are usually made of hardened, ground and lapped tool steels. The punches are made of heat treated die steels, having less hardness than the die. The alignment of punches is very important.
- The isostatic compacting consists of application of equal and simultaneous pressure from all sides. A rubber mould immersed in a fluid bath within a pressure vessel is used. A uniform green density and other properties are obtained because of uniform application of pressure. This is used for ceramic materials.
- High energy rate process gives high pressure within a short time by using some sort of explosives.
- Forging and extrusion techniques are used for limited applications. These give high density compacts. Vibratory compaction uses pressure and vibration simultaneously. A very low pressure can give better densification in this case of compaction.
- Continuous compaction is used for simple shapes as rods, bars, tubes etc. Slip casting is also a familiar process used for ceramic powders. These are some of the compaction processes used in industries.
- Compaction pressure affects the various factors related to powders.
- Green density increases with
  - ➤ Increase in compaction pressure,
  - ➤ Increase in particle size and
  - ➤ Decrease in hardness.
- Better compacting technique
  - ➤ Reduces voids,
  - ➤ Produces adhesion and cold welding of powders,
  - ➤ Plastically deforms powder and
  - ➤ Increases contact area between powder and hence, density.

6.7 SINTERING   (May 10, 13, 17; Dec. 10, 11, 12, 13)

- This process is used to improve strength of green compact. Sintering is one of the essential last step in the manufacture of P/M part.

- It consists of heating the green compact at a temperature below the highest melting constituent. In some cases, the temperature is high enough to form some liquid phase,

  e.g. in the manufacture of cemented carbides. In this case, the sintering is done above the melting point of the binder material.

- During sintering, only surface diffusion of particles takes place. This reduces porosity and improves hardness and strength of green compact.

- Sintering may be explained by three steps as follows

  ➤ Surface diffusion of particles,

  ➤ Densification and

  ➤ Recrystallization and grain growth.

  Sintering is carried out in furnaces as

  ➤ Electric resistance furnace,

  ➤ Gas fired furnace or

  ➤ Oil fired furnace.

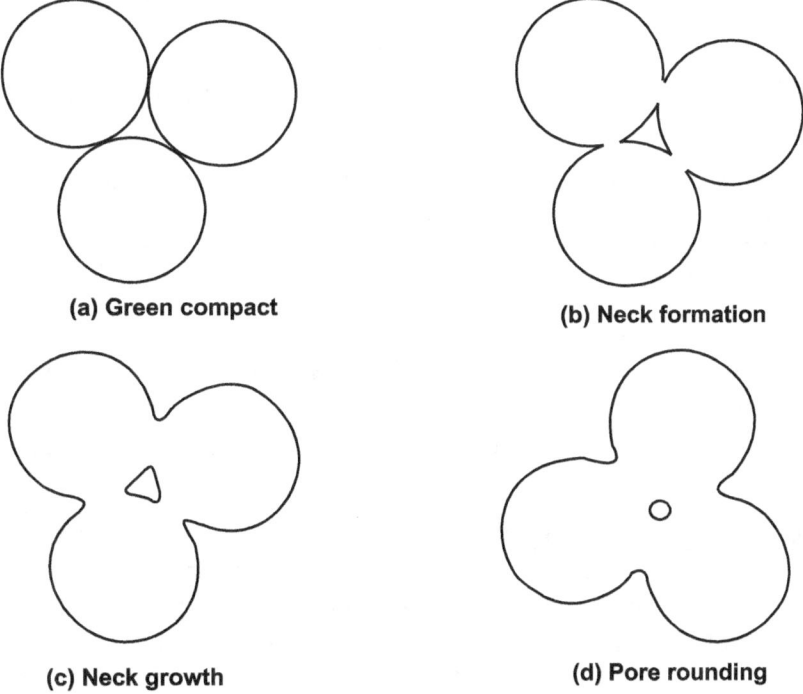

(a) Green compact   (b) Neck formation

(c) Neck growth   (d) Pore rounding

Fig. 6.9: Steps in sintering process

- Close control on temperature and atmosphere is necessary to achieve the desired properties. The formation of undesired surface films (as oxides) must be avoided as it affects the bonding between particles. So protective atmosphere should be used. The atmosphere should not contain free oxygen. It should be neutral or reducing.

- For sintering of refractory carbides and electrical contacts, a dry hydrogen atmosphere is used. Usually, for most of the commercial sintering operations, partial combustion of various hydrocarbons is used (e.g. natural gas or propane).

- The fundamental aspects of sintering involve

  ➢ Surface contacts,

  ➢ Neck formation and growth and

  ➢ Pore rounding (See Fig. 6.9).

Elevated Levels of Temperature Favour Sintering Process

- The sintering process starts with bonding between particles as the material heats up. Bonding consists of diffusion of atoms, where, there is intimate contact between adjacent particles.

- This leads to the formation of grain boundaries. This stage results in increase in the strength and hardness. The newly formed bond areas are called as *necks*. With time and at higher temperature, neck growth takes place followed by pore rounding. The last step in the sintering involves pore shrinkage and in rare cases, pore elimination.

- Depending on the temperature of sintering, it is classified as,

  ➢ **Solid Phase Sintering:** In this process, the compact is heated above the recrystallization temperature of low melting metal powder and

  ➢ **Liquid Phase Sintering:** In this process, the green compact is heated above the melting point of one of the alloy elements.

6.8 HOT PRESSING

In this process, the pressure and temperature is applied simultaneously. Moulding (or compaction) takes place at the same time. It reduces shrinkage and improves properties. This is used for limited applications such as for production of very hard cemented carbide parts. Another type is cold isostatic pressing in which only pressure is applied uniformly to give the desired size &shape to the powder.

6.9 SUPPLEMENTARY OPERATIONS

- This is used, where higher density or close dimensional tolerances are required. The sintered compact may show a slight size difference from designed one. This correction is done by placing the component in a master die and applying pressure. These operations are called as sizing or coining or repressing.

- Presintering involves interruption of sintering process at some temperature. This improves machinability. In some cases, resintering is carried out after re-pressing. This improves mechanical properties due to reduction in shrinkage.

- The post sintering heat treatment as stress relief or annealing may be used in some cases. Age hardening for non-ferrous and surface hardening for ferrous metals may be used. Various finishing operations as machining, shearing, broaching, deburring, grinding etc. are used.

- Impregnation is used to fill internal pores in sintered compact. This is carried out to improve antifriction properties. Various oils, waxes and grease may be used for impregnation. Impregnation with liquid lead is used to improve the specific gravity of ferrous metal compacts.

Testing of P/M Parts

The component should be tested for various properties as compressive and tensile strength, porosity, density, hardness, chemical composition and microstructure etc.

6.10 ADVANTAGES AND LIMITATIONS OF POWDER METALLURGY PROCESS

6.10.1 Advantages

Powder metallurgy process has several advantages over other conventional shaping processes.

These are summarized as below

- Without referring to equilibrium or phase diagram, components of any required compositions can be produced.

- A combination of metal powder and non-metallic material is possible.

- A close control on the amount of porosity is possible (See Fig. 6.10). This is required in production of filters, bearing and bricks etc.

- The production of refractory metals like tungsten, tantalum etc. and heavy metals is possible without melting.

- The production of components from metals, which are insoluble in each other during melting is possible by this process.

- Precise control on materials and properties is possible from starting step of production of powder to finishing step.

- From a single material, a range of densities can be produced simply by controlling pressure and temperature.

- High density parts can be produced.

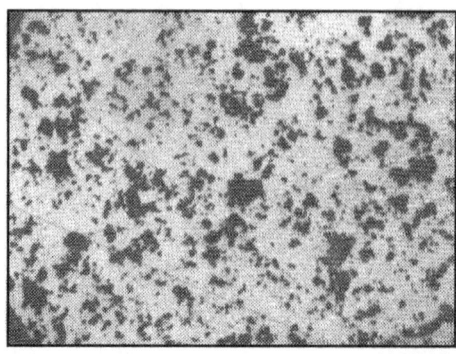

(400 X)

Fig. 6.10: Photomicrograph showing porosity (as black areas) in powder metallurgy component

- More complicated shaped parts as pinion can be satisfactorily made by this process.
- From single piece P/M component space saving and other design advantages can be obtained.
- It eliminates scrap.
- The powder metallurgical parts show good damping characteristics. This is used in air conditioning blowers.
- Practically, any desired material can be mixed.
- Composite and dispersion hardened materials can be produced.
- Production of cemented carbide tool is possible only by this process.
- Purity of metal powder can be retained upto final operations.
- It is an economical process for mass production. It is a very fast and smooth process.
- It gives excellent reproducibility.
- It can offer very complex shapes.
- It eliminates numerous machining operations.
- P/M parts can be welded, soldered or brazed easily, similar to conventional metal parts.
- Highly qualified or skilled worker is not required.

6.10.2 Limitations

P/M process show limitations as explained below

- The metal powders used in these processes are very fine. These fine powders tend to explode and cause fire hazards and oxidation during storing.
- It is very difficult to produce high purity powder. It is also expensive to maintain purity.
- Alloy powders such as stainless steel, brass, bronze are difficult to produce as simple method is not available.

- Very large sized components cannot be produced because of limitation of capacity of processes and furnaces available.
- For complex parts, the designing and machining of tooling is not easy.
- Components of theoretical density cannot be produced.
- Due to porosity, the specified mechanical properties are difficult to be obtained.
- Porous metals tend to oxidize rapidly.
- P/M parts show comparatively poor plastic properties.
- Higher investment is required for heavy presses and tooling (i.e. punches, dies etc.)

6.11 APPLICATIONS

The P/M parts find applications in the following areas

- **Refractory Metals:** Components produced by using refractory metals as tungsten, molybdenum and tantalum are used in electric light bulb, fluorescent lamps, radio valves, mercury arc rectifiers, x-ray tube etc.
- **Refractory Carbides:** These are very hard materials suitable for machining operations.
  - ➢ **Machining:** Lathes, drilling, knurling
  - ➢ **Instruments:** Gauges, indentors
  - ➢ **Wire Drawing:** Dies, blocks, jaws
  - ➢ **Deep Drawing:** Dies
  - ➢ **Mining:** Stone hammers, chisels, saws and also in chemical, textile and ceramic industries.
- **Automotive:** A large group of P/M parts are used in automobile industries. The application includes porous bearings, slide bearings, self-lubricated bearings, sintered and oil pump gears etc. Another important application covers the components like clutch plates, discs, electrical contacts, crankshaft drive or camshaft sprocket etc.
- **Aerospace Applications:** P/M parts are used in space applications in rocket, missiles, satellite etc. Tungsten parts are used in plasma jet engines at about 1850°C. Sintered bronze bearing and other bushing are used in explorer satellites, magnetic materials such as *Alnico* in communication system. Beryllium is used in gyroscope and heat shield for space capsules. Nickel is used in fuel cell for space electronic system. Be, Al, Mg and Zr are used in the form of solid fuels for rockets and missiles.
- **Atomic Energy Applications:** Various P/M parts are used in nuclear reactor. Dispersion strengthened materials are used in atomic reactors and rockets, magneto-hydrodynamic generators, high temperature gas turbine etc. Beryllium is

used as a fuel canning material for nuclear reactor. Uranium carbide, uranium dioxide are used as a fuel material, Be as moderator, Zr as cladding material.

- **Defense Applications:** P/M parts and metal powders are used in rockets, missiles, nose piece fuses, cartridge cases, fragile bullets etc.

- **Other Applications:** Metal filters are used in various chemical, sugar and pharmaceutical industries. Porous nickel electrodes are used in Ni-Cd batteries. Sintered friction materials are used as brakes in various applications. Electrical contacts are used in relays actuators, timers, switch gears etc. The typewriter contains various cams, gears and pawls made by P/M. Sintered tungsten carbide is used as ball on most of the ball point pens. P/M parts are also used as surgical implants.

6.12 MANUFACTURE OF SOME TYPICAL P/M COMPONENTS

6.12.1 Bearing Materials   (May 10, 11, 12, 13; Dec. 11, 13)

P/M techniques are extensively used in the field of bearing materials, which has porosity in the range of 15 to 30%. Among all these bearing materials, self-lubricated bearings are very famous. When a shaft rotates in a self-lubricated bearing, circulation of oil occurs around the shaft. This prevents the generation of heat due to friction.

This lubrication may occur by hydrodynamic process or boundary film lubrication.

There are various types of bearing materials. Oil impregnated porous bearings are discussed in this section.

Oil Impregnated Porous Bearings

- These are used under the conditions of dry friction. Porous bearings should have the following properties

  ➤ Enough porosity to hold the required amount of oil.

  ➤ The porosity should be interconnected.

  ➤ The bearing should possess the designed strength and dimensional accuracy.

- The basic advantage of these bearings is to work without lubrication and their resistance to corrosion. They do not require frequent maintenance. They are highly demanded in food and textile industries, where external lubrication is difficult and the lubricant should not go in the products.

- Porous bearings are usually made of bronze, brass, iron or aluminium powders with or without addition of graphite or other dry lubricant. Bronze bearings are most popular in this field.

- The various steps in the production of porous bearings include
  - ➢ Mixing of powders,
  - ➢ Cold compaction,
  - ➢ Sintering,
  - ➢ Repressing and
  - ➢ Impregnation with oil.
- Two types of bronze bearings are used as
  - ➢ Straight tin bronzes and
  - ➢ Leaded bronzes.
- The addition of graphite improves pressing properties, being a soft phase, but porosity increases. Large amount of graphite reduces strength.
- Copper and antimony powders are mixed with fine graphite powder to produce porous bronze bearings. Instead of using alloy powders, high purity annealed elemental powders are used to improve pressing and sintering properties.
- After blending or mixing, the powders are compacted in hydraulic or mechanical press at the pressure between 10 and 30 ton/in². The green compacts are sintered in a reducing atmosphere at a temperature of about 800°C for 90 Cu: 10 Sn bronze.
- A typical sintering cycle consists of holding the green compacts at about 450°C to remove lubricant and diffuse Sn into Cu. This is followed by further heating to 800°C. At this temperature, formation of tin rich liquid phase takes place.
- Re-pressing may be used to correct the distortions occurred during sintering. Sizing or machining can be done to adjust the pore size.
- The re-pressed or machined components are then finally impregnated with oil. This can be done by using pressure, vacuum or a combination of the both. For this purpose, the sintered component is held in oil bath at a temperature of about 90°C for half an hour. Such an oil impregnated bearing is called self-lubricating bearing as it does not require external lubrication.
- Porous iron bearings are manufactured by a similar method. Only higher compaction pressure and temperature is required. Iron-copper compositions with graphite are usually employed.

  Brass bearings are not in common use. Al-Sn mixtures are also used to produce bearings.
- The strength of bearing decreases with increase in porosity. So, the bearings having more oil holding capacity show less strength. But, they are suitable for higher speeds at less loads. Reversely, less porosity bearing may be used at lower speeds and higher loads.

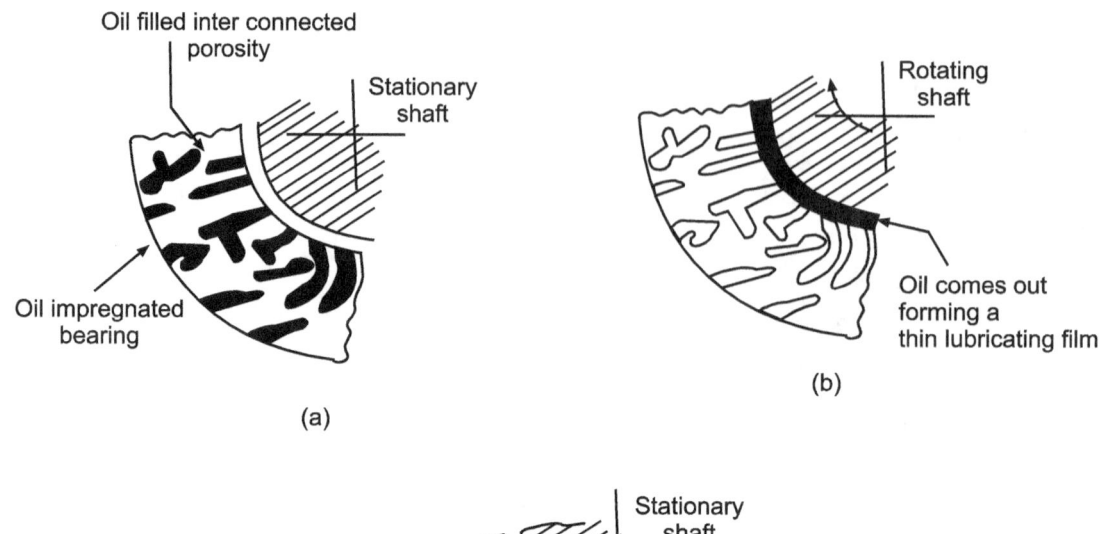

(a)

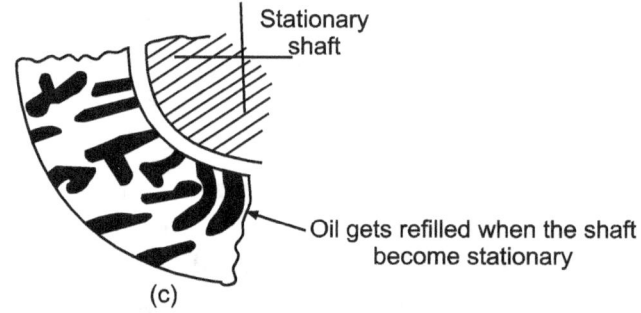

(c)

Fig. 6.11: Self-lubricated bearing. Exaggerated view of working principle

- The working of a self-lubricated, oil impregnated bearing is as follows (See Fig. 6.11)
- As the shaft speed increases, the temperature of bearing rises due to heat of friction. This decreases the viscosity and increases oil volume. So, the oil is pulled out from pores and is circulated alongwith the rotating shaft. Again as the speed of rotation decreases, the temperature drops down and oil goes back to pores by capillary action. This avoids wastage of oil as well as external lubrication.
- These bearings are used in pharmaceutical machinery, aviation, automobile, machine tools, food and textile industries.

6.12.2 Tool Materials   (Nov. 16)

- Various tool materials as cemented carbides, oxides, borides and diamond tools are manufactured by P/M process. The cemented carbide tools (See Fig. 6.12) are superior to other tools in respect of hardness, strength and abrasion resistance.
- The refractory metal carbides are also termed as hard metals. The principal constituents of the cemented carbides are metals and carbide powders. These are produced from carbides of refractory titanium, tantalum etc.
- These carbides exhibit red hardness i.e. retention of hardness at high temperatures. The carbides are very hard and brittle. They cannot sustain shock loads; however, Co, Ni, Cr etc. may be added to improve shock resistance.

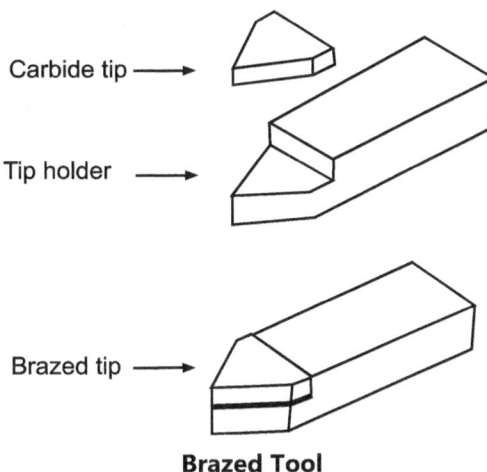

Brazed Tool

Fig. 6.12: Cemented carbide tipped tool

Following are the various steps involved in the production of cemented carbides

1. **Raw Materials**

- The carbide powders are manufactured by direct reaction of metal with carbon or reaction of metal oxides with carbon. The commonly used carbides are of tungsten and molybdenum.

- These are produced by direct metal carbon reaction. Tungsten carbide is produced by carburisation of metallic tungsten powder, which may be prepared by reduction of tungsten trioxide (WO_3) and tungstic acid (H_2WO_4).

2. **Milling**

- To obtain maximum hardness and minimum porosity, a very fine uniform distribution of carbide with cobalt is required. This can be obtained by ball milling. Wet milling can be carried out by using lubricants as paraffin wax dissolved in gasoline, acetone, alcohol, benzene etc.

3. **Compaction and Sintering**

- Carbide metal powders are compacted in hydraulic press to blocks or plates. The pressures used range from 35 to 45 kg/mm^2. Pre-sintering can be done at 400°C for a sufficient period to remove the lubricants by volatilisation. Sintering of these compacts is done in two stages.

- Initially, hydrogen atmosphere is used at about 900 to 1150°. After this stage, the compacts may be machined to obtain the desired shape and size. Final sintering is carried out in hydrogen atmosphere or vacuum at the temperature in the range of 1400 to 1550° for two hours. At this temperature, the bonding of particles occur by liquid phase formation. So, the carbides are cemented and hence, called as cemented carbides. A large amount of shrinkage occurs in this stage. The second stage sintering temperature decreases with increase in cobalt percentage. Cemented carbides may also be produced by infiltration of porous carbide skeletons with liquid cobalt.

4. Machining

- This step is required to be followed to achieve very close tolerances. The rough grinding is done by using silicon carbide grinding wheels and finally, metal bonded diamond wheels. Recently, electrospark or ultrasonic machining has been developed for threading, boring, engraving etc.

- A high degree of surface finish on cemented carbide parts may be obtained by lapping and polishing with diamond paste. The cemented carbide tools are used specially for finishing and machining operations on very hard materials as cast irons, super alloys, special alloy steels etc.

6.12.3 Cermets   (Dec. 2013)

Ceramics are characterized by high melting temperature, good creep resistance, greater chemical stability, abrasion resistance etc. On the other hand, metals possess high strength, ductility and resistance to thermal and mechanical shocks.

So, a combination of ceramic and metal called as CERMETS gives optimum properties. Ceramic powders are bonded by metallic powders. This is a composite material and hence, shows duplex structure.

Following are the three types of cement compositions widely used

- Oxide based cermets: e.g. Al_2O_3 with Cr or W.
- Carbide based cermets: e.g. TiC with Co or Ni and
- Boride, silicide and nitride based cermets.

Cermets may be formed by any suitable method as follows

- Slip casting
- Cold pressing
- Hot pressing and
- Extrusion.

Some of the cermets are also made by impregnation of a porous ceramic component with a metallic binder. The amount of binder varies in the range of 25 to 60%.

Applications of Cermets

- Flame holders and nozzles for jet propulsion,
- Flame protection rods, furnace muffles and tubes, pouring spouts,
- Container and control rod materials in nuclear applications,
- ThO_2-W cermets are used as cathode cylinders or electron emitting cathodes in magnetron valves,
- TiC cermet is used as cutting tool,
- Chromium carbide cermets are used as moulds, gauge, valve parts, seal rings and pumps.

6.12.4 Cemented Carbide Tipped Tools

- As the cemented carbides are costly and also very poor in shock resistance, full shaped tools are rarely used. So, the tools for lathes and shapers are tipped on cutting edge only, the rest of the tools being made of steel.

- A cemented carbide tip is placed on the tool and is brazed or mechanically clamped. These tools are superior compared to other tools in some properties such as hardness at high temperature, strength, abrasion resistance etc.

- They possess higher hardness upto 1500 VPN. They are mostly used for fast cutting of metals.

- The carbide tips are brazed with silver solder, electrolytic copper and copper-nickel alloys. The tool is first preheated and then brazed. After brazing, the tool is slow cooled to avoid cracks.

- The cemented carbide tips are tested for their density, hardness, hot hardness, transverse-rupture strength, impact strength etc. The metallographic examination also becomes necessary in some cases.

6.12.5 Diamond Impregnated Tools

- Diamond is the hardest known material. It is highly expensive and manufactured in small pieces. These are produced in a wide variety. They are suitable for precision boring, grinding, grooving and special forming. They can be used at higher cutting speeds. To overcome its brittleness, the diamond is used in the form of powder.

- The performance o diamond tool depends upon
  - ➢ Type, particle size and concentration of diamond grits,
  - ➢ Selection of bonding material,
  - ➢ Work piece material,
  - ➢ Cutting or grinding rate and
  - ➢ Surface finish required.

- These tools are produced from a mixture of diamond dust and powder of a bonding material such as mild steel, cobalt etc. Depending on operation, the diamond dust is used between 60 to 400 mesh. The amount of diamond dust in the tool may be expressed by a concentration number. 100 concentration means 25% by volume. The diamond tools are made with concentrations between 25 and 100.

- The technique employed for production of tool is cold compaction with subsequent sintering or infiltration, hot pressing and pressure sintering.

- Diamond powder is roughly mixed with metal powder as a binding material. Wet mixing and cold compaction is preferred. Vacuum or hydrogen atmosphere is used and sintering temperature is around 1000°C. To decrease porosity, hot pressing and pressure sintering may be used.

- In the infiltration technique, a prepressed component consisting of diamond dust and metal powder is infiltrated by using a low melting metal binder. This infiltration occurs by capillary action. Hot pressing is carried out in the temperature range of 600 to 900°C in reducing atmosphere.

- In pressure sintering, induction heating is used. In some cases, only the working face of a diamond tool is prepared by powder metallurgy technique, which is set in a metal shank. This can be done by soldering, brazing, sinter brazing, mechanical fixing etc.

- Diamond tools have found applications in cutting, drilling, shaping, sawing and finishing of various materials like concrete, rocks, glass, refractories etc. They are also used for various dies.

6.13 PRODUCTION OF REFRACTORY METALS   (May 13)

- The refractory metals are tungsten, molybdenum, niobium, platinum etc. These have high melting temperatures.

- They show higher reactivity with environment at elevated temperature. So, the production of these materials does not become economical on commercial scale by conventional casting or other manufacturing processes. Hence, they are manufactured by powder metallurgical process.

Production of Tungsten and Molybdenum

- For this process, hydrogen is used to reduce oxides or ammonium salts of these metals. Cold compaction with suitable lubricant is used.

- The presintering is done at around 1000°C using hydrogen atmosphere. This gives the required strength necessary for handling and clamping during main sintering.

- Final sintering is carried out by passing electric current through the ends of these compacts using water cooled clamps. Sintering is done in hydrogen or vacuum. Current densities are in the order of 1000 amp/cm^2.

- After this process, rolling, forging or swaging (at temperature 1300 to 1700°C for W and 1000 to 1400°C for Mo) is done to reduce porosity. Tungsten can be drawn in fine wires and used in filaments for electric bulbs. This is called ductile tungsten, which is thoriated. This thoriated tungsten finds application in electrical contacts, heating elements, radiation shields in nuclear reactors.

6.14 ELECTRICAL CONTACT MATERIALS

- The electrical contact materials include W - Mo, WC - Cu, W - Ag, W - Cu, Ni - Ag, Ag - graphite and Cu - graphite. These electrical contact materials are brazed or soldered on conductors. The conductor materials can also cast on contact materials.

- The electrical contact material should exhibit following properties
  - ➢ High electrical conductivity,
  - ➢ High thermal conductivity,
  - ➢ High hardness to resist wear and abrasion,
  - ➢ Less contact resistance and
  - ➢ Resistance to sparking.
- Normally, an individual material may not have all the above properties. So, more than one material is preferred as contact material.
- These can be manufactured by,
  - ➢ Pressing and sintering followed by mechanical working and
  - ➢ Pressing, sintering and infiltration.
- The first process consists of mixing of W or Mo with Cu or Ag (depending on application) in designed proportion and compacted in a press. The sintering of cold compacts is carried out in reducing atmosphere. The sintering temperature should be just below the melting temperature of the low melting metal.
- The properties of such compact can be controlled by controlling
  - ➢ Particle size,
  - ➢ Powder proportion,
  - ➢ Compaction pressure and sintering temperature and
  - ➢ Compaction process i.e. cold or hot type.
- Higher conductivity may be obtained by liquid phase sintering i.e sintering at a temperature just above the melting point of high conductivity metal.
- Infiltration process consists of infiltrating the porous refractory metal powder with high conductive metal. A very high density compact may be obtained by this process.

6.15 SINTERED METAL FRICTION MATERIALS   (May 17)

- Now-a-days, metal-nonmetal combinations are widely used to manufacture friction materials. These are used as clutch facing and brake linings. These materials consist essentially, a metallic matrix of copper or bronze for heat conductivity, lead or graphite to form a smoothly engaging lining during operation and silica and emery for frictional properties.
- Such a friction material should exhibit the following properties
  - ➢ Better coefficient of friction,
  - ➢ Optimum wear and abrasion resistance,

➤ Good thermal conductivity,

➤ Good corrosion resistance and

➤ High temperature strength.

• The raw material consists of copper, tin, lead, graphite, silica and iron. The blending or mixing is done in double cone or Y-cone blenders. The compaction pressures are not very high (less than 40 kg/mm^2).

• The sintering is carried out in the range 750 to 850°C using protective atmosphere. The supplementary operations like sizing or re-pressing and any machining may be given to obtain exact size and shape.

• Now-a-days, more weightage is given on ceramic and powder metallurgical projects, as these are giving unique results. However, an extensive research is still required to find new applications. Even in space lab, some of the microgravity experiments in which two powders with higher density difference can be mixed in non-gravitational or micro-gravitational conditions, are becoming successful.

REVIEW QUESTIONS

1. State whether the following statement are *true* or *false* and justify your answers.

   (a) Melting of all constituents is necessary in powder metallurgy techniques.

   (b) Porosity can be eliminated completely in P/M parts.

   (c) Refractory metal can be cast easily than powder metallurgy process.

   (d) Powder metallurgical process is useful to produce light weight components.

   (e) Density of compact is increased by increasing compaction pressure.

   (f) Self-lubricating bearings are more suitable in food industries.

   (g) A protective atmosphere is must for sintering.

   (h) Powder shape decides its compaction properties.

   (i) Stainless steel powder can be produced by intergranular corrosion.

   (j) Cermets are produced by mixing ceramics and metals.

   Ans.:

(a) False	(b) False	(c) False	(d) True	(e) True
(f) True	(g) True	(h) True	(i) True	(j) True

2. Why the factors like particle size, shape and distribution have importance in the packing of powder ?

3. Discuss the effect of powder production method on powder shape.

4. Suggest suitable metals and the production process for the following

    (a) Friction materials,

    (b) Electrical contacts.

5. Explain why P/M process is unsuitable for certain components. Give 3-4 such components and justify.

6. List (do not discuss) the various applications of P/M process.

7. Explain any four powder production processes.

8. Discuss in general the process of powder metallurgy with respect to the following points

    (a) Powder production,

    (b) Compaction and

    (c) Sintering.

9. What are the important characteristics of metal powders ? How are they evaluated ?

10. Discuss the advantages and disadvantages of powder metallurgy.

11. Suggest suitable metals and the production process for the following

    (a) Self-lubricated bearings,

    (b) Cutting tools.

12. Write short notes on:

    (i)   Cemented carbides

    (ii)   Atomization

    (iii) Advantages of power metallurgy

    (iv)   Particle size and its distribution

13. Explain about segar cones and Tempil sticks.

14. Write note on powder conditioning.

15. Describe the steps involved in manufacturing powder metallurgical component.

UNIVERSITY QUESTIONS

DECEMBER 2013

1. Explain atomization process with neat diagram used in powder production.   **[4]**

2. Describe with a suitable flow chart manufacturing of cemented carbide tool.   **[4]**

3. Explain the mechanism of sintering, and what is liquid phase sintering.   **[4]**

4. Describe with a suitable flow chart manufacturing of oil impregnated bearings.   **[4]**

5. What is sintering? Explain the stages of sintering.   **[4]**

6. What are the disadvantages of powder Metallurgy over other conventional Process?   **[4]**

7. What is mint by green strength of a compact?   **[1]**

MAY 2014

1. Explain the process of impregnation of self lubricating bearings.   **[4]**

2. Draw a flow chart for the production of cemented tools.   **[5]**

3. Explain the terms :   **[4]**

   (1)   Flow rate   (2)   Apparent density.

4. Describe the steps involved in manufacturing of powder metallurgy component.   **[5]**

DECEMBER 2014

1. What are the major steps in manufacturing of component by Powder Metallurgy ?**[6]**

2. What are the advantages and limitations of Powder Metallurgy ?   **[7]**

3. Draw the flow chart for manufacturing of cemented carbides ?   **[6]**

4. List down the steps involved in production of sintered structural components.   **[3]**

5. What is conditioning of metal powders ?   **[4]**

MAY 2015

1. Define the term 'powder metallurgy' with steps of processing and classification of powder manufacturing processes.   **[5]**

2. What do you mean by the term 'sintering' ? Explain the stages of sintering.   **[4]**

3. Explain the role of powder metallurgy' for manufacturing of 'cemented carbide'.   **[4]**

4. Explain powder metallurgy with characteristics of metal powders, advantages, disadvantages and areas of applications.   **[5]**

5. What do you mean by conditioning of metal powders ? Explain with purpose and different processing stages.   **[4]**

6. What is a 'self-lubricated bearing' ? Explain the role of powder metallurgy for manufacturing of 'self-lubricated bearings'.   **[4]**

NOVEMBER 2015

1. Discuss about particle size, shape and size distribution and its effect on the properties of the final sintered compact.   **[6]**

2. Using flow sheet explain manufacturing of cemented carbide tools by powder metallurgy.   **[7]**

3. Discuss production of Iron powder by reduction process.   **[4]**

4. What is compaction ? List the defects of compact and their remedies.   **[5]**

5. What is sintering ? Explain the stages of sintering.   **[4]**

MAY 2016

1. Define the term 'powder metallurgy' ? List out its various applications specifying example for each of them.   **[5]**

2. What are the various properties of powder material that should be evaluated in powder metallurgy process ?   **[4]**

3. What are the steps involved in the production of a 'refractory materials' using powder metallurgy ?   **[4]**

4. Explain the classification of various processes used to manufacture the powder in powder metallurgy process.   **[5]**

5. What do you mean by sintering of metal powders ? Explain with purpose and different processing stages ?   **[4]**

6. What are the steps involved in the production of a 'diamond impregnated tools' using powder metallurgy ?   **[4]**

NOVEMBER 2016

1. What is the best suitable process for manufacturing of oil impregnated bearings? Explain its advantages over other manufacturing processes.   [7]

    [**Ans. :** Refer article 6.12.1]

2. Explain importance of sintering with its different stages to get required strength to green compact.   [6]

    [**Ans. :** Refer article 6.7]

3. Define the following: [4]

    (i)   Green Spring

    (ii) Tap density.

4. Write flow-chart of production of Tungsten cemented carbide tool.   [3]

    [**Ans. :** Refer article 6.12.2]

5. What are the different techniques used for compaction? Explain Isostatic compaction in detail.   [6]

    [**Ans. :** Refer article 6.6]

MAY 2017

1. Explain the basic steps of powder metallurgy process.   **[4]**

    [**Ans. :** Refer article 6.2]

2. Explain the role and function of lubricants and binders in Powder Metallurgy.   **[6]**

3. Why is sintering important step in Powder Metallurgy?   **[3]**

    [**Ans. :** Refer article 6.7]

4. Sieve analysis method is used in determination which property of powder metallurgy? Explain it with neat diagram.   **[5]**

    [**Ans. :** Refer article 6.3]

5. Write flow chart of production of friction material.   **[4]**

    [**Ans. :** Refer article 6.15]

6. Explain Carbonil process for powder manufacturing.   **[4]**

✠ ✠ ✠

MODEL QUESTION PAPER – I

End-Sem Theory Examination

Time : 2 Hours   **Marks : 50**

Instructions to the Candidates:
1. Figures to the right indicate full marks.
2. Use of electronic pocket calculator is allowed.
3. Assume suitable data, if necessary.

---

1. (a) Differentiate between hot working and cold working. [4]
   (b) Explain elastomers [4]
   (c) Sketch within a cubic unit cell the following planes:
       (100), (110), (111) and (011). **[4] OR**
2. (a) Define the term polymer? Explain with types, characteristics and applications. [4]
   (b) Explain work hardening on the basis of dislocations. [4]
   (c) Derive the expression for deformation of single crystal by slip? State the condition for geometrical hardening and geometrical softening. [4]
3. (a) Explain fatigue fracture in detail with a neat diagram. [4]
   (b) What are the non-destructive applications of eddy current testing? [4]
   (c) Define Hardness of the material? Explain any four testing methods for checking the hardness of the material. **[4] OR**
4. (a) Write short notes on :
       (1) Durometers.
       (2) Erichson cupping test [6]
   (b) Explain piling up and sinking effects on surface of test piece found when conducting Brinell Hardness test. [6]
5. (a) What is atmospheric corrosion? Explain any two factors that cause the atmospheric corrosion. [5]
   (b) Write a note on cementation of metal surface with special reference to sheearardizing. [4]
   (c) Give an account of hot dipping processes. **[4] OR**
6. (a) What is the surface engineering? [4]
   (b) Write a short note on plasma nitriding. [4]
   (c) What is ion implantation? Also give working of it. [5]
7. (a) Discuss about particle size, shape and size distribution and its effect on the properties of the final sintered compact. [5]
   (b) Explain the role of powder metallurgy' for manufacturing of cemented carbide? [4]
   (c) What do you mean by the term 'sintering' ? Explain the stages of sintering. **[4] OR**
8. (a) Explain atomization process with neat diagram used in powder production. [5]
   (b) Explain the process of impregnation of self lubricating bearings. [4]
   (c) What is conditioning of metal powders? [4]

MODEL QUESTION PAPER – II
End-Sem Theory Examination

Time : 2 Hours   **Marks : 50**

Instructions to the Candidates:
1. Figures to the right indicate full marks.
2. Use of electronic pocket calculator is allowed.
3. Assume suitable data, if necessary.

---

1. **(a)** Explain classification of engineering materials. Explain in brief thermoplastic and thermosetting polymers. **[4]**

(b) What is role of dislocation in the plastic deformation of metal? **[4]**

(c) Define space lattice? Write any three imperfections in crystals / lattices with example of each. **[4] OR**

2. **(a)** Differentiate between slip and twinning. **[4]**

(b) Explain the strain hardening with curve. **[4]**

(c) Derive the expression for deformation of single crystal by slip ? State the condition for geometrical hardening and geometrical softening. **[4]**

3. **(a)** What is endurance limit ? Explain fatigue fracture with suitable figure. Also state the applications where fatigue strength is necessary. **[6]**

(b) What is the concept of True stress and True strain ? Derive the relations between them also find out the condition for necking. **[6] OR**

4. **(a)** Explain the methods of magnetization and demagnetization of component during magnetic particle inspection. Why the demagnetization is necessary after testing? **[6]**

(b) What is the purpose of 'Impact Test' ? Explain with and the factors affecting the impact values of the component, **[6]**

5. **(a)** State the factors that influence the rate of electro-chemical corrosion. **[4]**

(b) Write note on differential aeration corrosion. **[4]**

(c) Explain the process of galvanizing with schematic diagram. **[5] OR**

6. **(a)** Write a note on CVD. **[4]**

(b) What are the surface coating defects? **[4]**

(c) Draw typical thickness of engineering surface layers physical vapour deposition. **[5]**

7. **(a)** What is compaction ? **[2]**

(b) What are the advantages and limitations of Powder Metallurgy ? **[7]**

(c) What is a 'self-lubricated bearing'? Explain the role of powder metallurgy for manufacturing of 'self-lubricated bearings'. **[4] OR**

8. **(a)** Explain any four powder production processes. **[7]**

(b) Explain about segar cones and tempil sticks. **[6]**

✠ ✠ ✠

UNIVERSITY QUESTION PAPERS

DECEMBER 2013

Time : 2 Hours   **Max. Marks : 50**

1. (a) What is work hardening? Explain the property variation with proper graph before and after work hardening.   **[6]**

    (b) Explain the advantages of composite materials over conventional materials with suitable example.   **[4]**

    (c) Differentiate between thermoplastic and thermosetting polymers.   **[2] OR**

2. (a) Differentiate between slip and twinning.   **[4]**

    (b) Show the self explanatory diagram for point defects.   **[2]**

    (c) Explain any one method of polymer processing, with suitable diagram.   **[4]**

    (d) What are Cirmets ?   **[2]**

3. (a) With a neat diagram explain fatigue fracture in detail.   **[4]**

    (b) Define toughness, Notch sensitivity.   **[2]**

    (c) What is mint by transducer, explain the respective NDT method makes the use of sound waves.   **[4]**

    (d) What are the advantages of Dye Penetrant test over the other NDT methods.   **[2] OR**

4. Write true or false and justify your answer.   **[12]**

    (a) Creep fracture is a transgranular fracture.

    (b) Erichson cupping test is used for sheet metals only.

    (c) For checking the hardness of phases in metals, Rockwell C scale is used.

    (d) In a brass component subsurface defect can be easily determined by magnetic particle test.

5. (a) Explain atomization process with neat diagram used in powder production.   **[4]**

    (b) Describe with a suitable flow chart manufacturing of cemented carbide tool.   **[4]**

    (c) Explain the mechanism of sintering, and what is liquid phase sintering.   **[4]**

    (d) What is spring back.   **[1]OR**

6. (a) Describe with a suitable flow chart manufacturing of oil impregnated bearings.   **[4]**

    (b) What is sintering? Explain the stages of sintering.   **[4]**

    (c) What are the disadvantages of powder Metallurgy over other conventional Process.**[4]**

    (d) What is mint by green strength of a compact.   **[1]**

7. (a) Write short note on :   **[12]**

    (i)   Biosensors.

    (ii) Shape memory alloy.

    (iii) Nano material and their applications

    (iv) Soft and Hard magnetic materials.

   (b) Suggest suitable material for the replacement of heart valves.   **[1] OR**

8. **(a)** Piezoelectric materials are smart materials explain in detail.   **[4]**

   (b) What are the property requirements in the materials / metals used for cryogenic application and suggest the suitable materials for the same.   **[5]**

   (c) Define following (any two) :   **[4]**

      (i)   Biomaterials.

      (ii) Superconductivity.

      (iii) Super alloy.

MAY 2014

Time : 2 Hours   **Max. Marks : 50**

1. **Solve any three:**

   (a) Differentiate between cold working and hot working.   **[4]**

   (b) What is role of dislocation in the plastic deformation of metal.   **[4]**

   (c) Explain how engineering materials are classified. Explain in brief thermoplastic and thermosetting polymers.   **[4]**

   (d) Explain elastomers.   **[4] OR**

2. **Solve any three:**

   (a) What is recrystallization? Explain the factors affecting recrystallization process.   **[4]**

   (b) Explain the strain hardening with curve.   **[4]**

   (c) Explain hybrid composites.   **[4]**

   (d) Write short note on ceramic materials.   **[4]**

3. **(a)** What is endurance limit ? Explain fatigue fracture with suitable figure. Also state the applications where fatigue strength is necessary.   **[6]**

   (b) Write short notes on :   **[7]**

      (1) Poldi hardness test   (2) Compression test.   **OR**

4. **(a)** Which type of test is carried out at high temperature of metal sample under test. Also explain the related curve obtained. (Draw suitable figure).   **[7]**

   (b) Write short notes on :

      (1) Erichson cupping test   (2) Durometers.

5. **(a)** Explain the process of impregnation of self lubricating bearings.   **[4]**

(b) Draw a flow chart for the production of cemented tools. **[5]**

(c) Explain the terms : **[4]**

(1) Flow rate   (2) Apparent density. **OR**

6. **(a)** Describe the steps involved in manufacturing of powder metallurgy component. **[5]**

(b) Explain the automization process of powder manufacturing with neat sketch. **[4]**

(c) Write a short note diamond impregnated cutting tools. **[4]**

7. **(a)** Classify different magnetic materials, and explain any one in detail. **[6]**

(b) Give classification of different biomaterials, and explain any one in detail with proper applications. **[6] OR**

8. **Write short notes on (Any three)** **[12]**

(1) Carbon nanotubes

(2) Smart materials

(3) Behaviour of metal at low temperature

(4) Soft and hard magnetic materials.

DECEMBER 2014

Time : 2 Hours **Max. Marks : 50**

1. **(a)** Sketch within a cubic unit cell the following planes :

(100), (110), (111) and (011). **[4]**

(b) Differentiate between slip and twinning. **[4]**

(c) Explain the classification of composites. **[4] OR**

2. **(a)** The planes in a crystalline solid intersect the crystal axes at (2a, 2b, c). (2a, b, 2c) and (a, b, c:). Calculate the Miller Indices of this plane. **[4]**

(b) Explain any two Imperfection in Crystal (or Lattices) from the list given below:

(i)   Edge Dislocation

(ii)   Stacking fault

(iii) Low angle boundary. **[4]**

(c) A glass fibre reinforced epoxy matrix composite contains 60 volume percent of continuous glass fibre. Determine Young's modulus of the composite assuming longitudinal loading condition. Modulus of elasticity for glass fibre is 72 GPa and that of epoxy is 2.4 GPa. **[4]**

3. **(a)** The following observations are made during tension test carried out on a 15 mm diameter plain carbon steel rod

Yield load = 68 kN

Ultimate tensile load = 105 kN.

Find the yield strength and ultimate tensile strength of the steel rod.   **[4]**

(b) Which non-destructive test is suitable for the following situations ?   **[4]**

(i)   For detection of surface cracks on brass components.

(ii) For detection of slag inclusion of welded joint.

(c) What are the non-destructive applications of eddy current testing ?   **[4] OR**

4. (a) Explain fatigue test.   **[4]**

(b) Explain piling up and sinking effects on surface of test piece found when conducting Brinell Hardness test.   **[4]**

(c) Explain the principle advantages and limitations of Radiographic test.   **[4]**

5. (a) Briefly explain Bio-material and its classification ?   **[6]**

(b) What are Nano-materials ? Explain any three properties of Nano materials.   **[7] OR**

6. (a) Briefly explain Biosensors and its application.   **[6]**

(b) Write advantages of Cryogenic materials.   **[3]**

(c) Explain Shape Memory Alloys (SMA).   **[4]**

7. (a) What are the major steps in manufacturing of component by Powder Metallurgy ? **[6]**

(b) What are the advantages and limitations of Powder Metallurgy ?   **[7] OR**

8. (a) Draw the flow chart for manufacturing of cemented carbides ?   **[6]**

(b) List down the steps involved in production of sintered structural   components ?   **[3]**

(c) What is conditioning of metal powders ?   **[4]**

MAY 2015

Time : 2 Hours   **Max. Marks : 50**

1. (a) What do you mean by the term 'Unit Cell' ? Define various lattice parameters.   **[4]**

(b) Differentiate between cold working and hot working according to temperature, variation in mechanical properties, grain formation and areas of application.   **[4]**

(c) What is composite material ? Explain with classification and types.   **[4] OR**

2. (a) What do you mean by the term polymer? Explain with types, characteristics and applications.   **[4]**

(b) What do you mean by the term 'ceramic' ? Explain with types, properties and application.   **[4]**

(c) Derive the expression for deformation of single crystal by slip ? State the condition for geometrical hardening and geometrical softening.   **[4]**

3. **(a)** What is the concept of True stress and True strain ? Derive the relations between them also find out the condition for necking. **[5]**

   (b) What do you mean by the term 'Hardness of the material' ? Explain any four testing methods for checking the hardness of the material. **[4]**

   (c) What do you mean by 'non-destructive testing'? Explain ultrasonic method of testing with working principle, advantages and drawbacks. **[4] OR**

4. **(a)** Identify the methods of NDT in the following cases : **[5]**

   (i) Cavities, cracks or region of variable density for the metal/ non-metallic components manufactured by casting, welding and forging etc.

   (ii) To sort out dissimilar metals and detect differences in their composition, microstructure etc.

   (iii) Detecting internal defects such as cracks, porosity and laminations in Metallic and non-metallic components during or after production.

   (iv) Various kinds of flows in ferromagnetic components made from various welding, castings and forging etc.

   (v) Invisible cracks, porosity and other similar defects on the surface of components made up of metal, non-metal, plastic, glass etc.

   (b) Explain with working principle the material test for the component which shows a plastic deformation under constant stresses for a longer time at high temperatures. Draw the type of possible microstructure during this test. **[4]**

   (c) What is the purpose of 'Impact Test' ? Explain with and the factors affecting the impact values of the component. **[4]**

5. **(a)** Define the term 'powder metallurgy' with steps of processing and classification of powder manufacturing processes. **[5]**

   (b) What do you mean by the term 'sintering' ? Explain the stages of sintering. **[4]**

   (c) Explain the role of powder metallurgy' for manufacturing of 'cemented carbide' ?**[4] OR**

6. **(a)** Explain powder metallurgy with characteristics of metal powders, advantages, disadvantages and areas of applications. **[5]**

   (b) What do you mean by conditioning of metal powders ? Explain with purpose and different processing stages. **[4]**

   (c) What is a 'self-lubricated bearing' ? Explain the role of powder metallurgy for manufacturing of 'self-lubricated bearings'. **[4]**

7. **(a)** Explain the following terms (any two) **[4]**

   (i) Piezometric materials

     (ii)   Soft and hard ferrites

     (iii) Super-conductors.

(b) What do you mean by the term 'biomaterials' ? Explain with different types ? **[4]**

(c) Explain the concept of 'shape memory alloy' with advantages, disadvantages and applications. **[4] OR**

8. (a) Explain the following terms (any two) : **[4]**

     (i)   Cryogenic applications of smart materials

     (ii)   Modern materials for high temperature applications

     (iii) Dielectric materials.

(b) Explain the concept of nano-science and technology. **[4]**

(c) Explain 'Biosensors' with principle, advantages and applications. **[4]**

NOVEMBER 2015

Time : 3 Hours   **Max. Marks : 50**

1. (a) Show that the atomic packing factor for BCC crystal is 0.68. **[4]**

(b) Explain any two point defects with the help of diagram. **[4]**

(c) A continuous and aligned glass fiber reinforced composite of 40 volume % of glass fibers having a modulus of elasticity of 69 GPa and 60 volume % of a polyester resin that, when hardened, displays a modulus of 3.4 GPa. If the cross-sectional area is 250 mm^2 and a stress of 50 MPa is applied in this longitudinal direction, compute the magnitude of the load carried by each of the fiber and matrix phases. **[4] OR**

2. (a) Derive linear density expression of FCC [100] and [111] directions in terms of the atomic radius R. **[4]**

(b) Explain the following processing methods of ceramics : **[6]**

     (i)   Cold isostatic pressing

     (ii)   Slip casting.

(c) Explain work hardening on the basis of dislocations. **[2]**

3. (a) A cylindrical specimen of steel having an original diameter 12.8 mm is tensile tested to fracture and found to have an engineering fracture strength of 460 MPa if its cross-sectional diameter of fracture is 10.7 mm, determine :

     (i)   Ductility in terms of percent reduction in area.

     (ii)   True stress at fracture. **[6]**

(b) What is fatigue ? Draw S-N curve for Mild Steel and Aluminum and explain Endurance limit. **[6] OR**

4. **(a)** Explain the methods of magnetization and demagnetization of component during magnetic particle inspection. Why the demagnetization is necessary after testing? **[6]**

(b) Differentiate between dye penetrant inspection and fluorescent penetrant inspection. **[4]**

(c) Explain Moh's hardness scale. **[2]**

5. **(a)** Discuss about particle size, shape and size distribution and its effect on the properties of the final sintered compact. **[6]**

(b) Using flow sheet explain manufacturing of cemented carbide tools by powder metallurgy. **[7] OR**

6. **(a)** Discuss production of Iron powder by reduction process. **[4]**

(b) What is compaction ? List the defects of compact and their remedies. **[5]**

(c) What is sintering ? Explain the stages of sintering. **[4]**

7. **(a)** Define nano-material and give application. Write a note on carbon nano-tubes. **[6]**

(b) Give the classification of bio-material. Describe properties and application of Nickel alloy as bio-material. **[7] OR**

8. **(a)** Explain the use of Ni base and Cobalt base alloy for high temperature application. **[4]**

(b) Explain the properties of superconductors. Briefly explain any two applications of superconductors. **[6]**

(c) Discuss the effect of Cryogenic heat treatment on steel alloy. **[3]**

MAY 2016

Time : 2 Hours   **Max. Marks : 50**

1. **(a)** What do you mean by space lattice ? Write any three imperfections in crystals/lattices with example of each. **[4]**

(b) What is plastic deformation in materials ? Differentiate between slip and twining. **[4]**

(c) What do you mean by isostress and isostrain condition in composite materials ? Calculate the composite modulus for polyester reinforced with 60 volume % E-glass under isostrain conditions. (Take young modulus for polyter 6.9GPa and fir glass it is 72.4GPa). **[4] OR**

2. **(a)** What do you mean by the term 'Polymer' ? Differentiate between Thermoplastic and Thermosetting polymers. **[4]**

(b) What do you mean by Composite Materials ? Explain with its types and classification. **[4]**

(c) What do you mean by "True stress and True Strain in materials" ? Derive the relationship between both of it. **[4]**

3. **(a)** What is the difference between Hardness and Toughness of the material ? Explain any two testing methods for checking the hardness of the material with their principal of working and mathematical formula for calculation ? **[5]**

(b) What is Notch toughness in Impact Test ? List out the factors by which the Impact values of materials get affected. **[4]**

(c) What do you mean by 'Non Destructive Testing ? Explain Radiography method of testing with working principal, advantages and applications ? **[4] OR**

4. **(a)** Identify the methods of material testing in the following cases : **[5]**

   (i)   To measure hardness of cast components, heterogeneous materials like cast irons and porous powder metallurgy components.

   (ii)   To measure the properties like electrical conductivity, magnetic permeability, grain size, heat treatment conditions, hardness and physical dimensions.

   (iii) To test large sized, uniform thickness and one/many components at the same time.

   (iv)   In quality control test for detecting internal defects such as cracks, porosity, and laminations in metallic and non-metallic components during or after the production.

   (v)   Materials working for a continous high temperature service under stressed conditions such as jet engine components, gas and steam turbines, nuclear reactors and tungsten filaments for electric bulbs.

(b) Explain the working principle of fatigue test machine ? What are the different protection methods of fatigue life ? **[4]**

(c) What do you mean by the term 'creep fracture' ? What are the requirements for creep resistant materials ? **[4]**

5. **(a)** Define the term 'powder metallurgy' ? List out its various applications specifying example for each of them. **[5]**

(b) What are the various properties of powder material that should be evaluated in powder metallurgy process ? **[4]**

(c) What are the steps involved in the production of a 'refractory materials' using powder metallurgy ? **[4] OR**

6. (a) Explain the classification of various processes used to manufacture the powder in powder metallurgy process. **[5]**

(b) What do you mean by sintering of metal powders ? Explain with purpose and different processing stages ? **[4]**

(c) What are the steps involved in the production of a 'diamond impregnated tools' using powder metallurgy ? **[4]**

7. (a) Explain the following terms (any two) **[4]**

    (i)   Biomaterials

    (ii) Shape memory alloy

    (iii) Superconductors.

(b) What do you mean by the term Piezometric materials ? Explain with types. **[4]**

(c) Explain the magnetic material ? Differentiate between hard and soft magnetic materials ? **[4] OR**

8. (a) Explain the following terms (any two) : **[4]**

    (i)   Nanomaterials

    (ii) Biosensors

    (iii) Dielectric materials

(b) Explain the concept of smart materials and its Cryogenic applications. **[4]**

(c) Explain 'The Modern materials for high temperature applications' ? **[4]**

NOVEMBER 2016

Time : 2 Hours   **Total Marks : 50**

Instructions to the candidates :

    (1) Answer Q. 1 or Q. 2, Q. 3 or Q. 4, Q. 5 or Q. 6, Q. 7 or Q. 8.

    (2) Neat diagrams must be drawn wherever necessary.

    (3) Figures to the right indicate full marks.

    (4) Use of calculator is allowed.

    (5) Assume suitable data, if necessary.

1. (a) Show the following planes on a cubic cell (222), (110). **[4]**

(b) Define the following : **[4]**

    (i) Co-ordination number

    (ii) Hot working

(c) Materials like Al shows more plastic deformation by the slip mechanism than twinning. Explain in detail. **[4] OR**

2. (a) No. of atoms per unit cell in FCC metal is 4 explain with mathematical proof. **[3]**

   (b) What is Polymer and how its molecular structure is different than metals? Explain. **[3]**

   (c) What do you understand by crystal imperfection ? Explain the Edge dislocation with a neat diagram. **[6]**

3. (a) Compare and contrast between. **[6]**

   (i) Dye penetrant test and ultrasonic test

   (ii) Brinell harness tester and Rockwall hardness tester.

   (b) One Assembly is made with nuts and bolts used for joining them. Where the probability of corrosion is more? Which type of corrosion is probable in this type ? Explain can it be avoided. **[7] OR**

4. (a) Draw the self-explanatory diagram for the following: **[4]**

   (i) Stress-strain diagram for Cast Iron.

   (ii) S-N diagram for Cu.

   (b) For checking internal defects in brass component which NDT methods are used, justify your answer. **[3]**

   (c) Pitting corrosion is most dangerous amongst all types of corrosion do you agree with this statement? Justify your answer. **[4]**

   (d) In Anodic and Cathodic Inhibitors which is more protective, explain. **[2]**

5. (a) Explain with neat diagram physical vapour deposition. State its advantages, disadvantages and applications over other processes. **[6]**

   (b) What are different characteristics of surface improvements? Explain in brief. **[6] OR**

6. Write short notes on (any three) **[12]**

   (a) Anodising

   (b) Electroplating

   (c) Ion implantation

   (d) CVD

7. (a) What is the best suitable process for manufacturing of oil impregnated bearings? Explain its advantages over other manufacturing processes. **[7]**

   (b) Explain importance of sintering with its different stages to get required strength to green compact. **[6] OR**

8. (a) Define the following: [4]
   (i) Green Spring
   (ii) Tap density.

   (b) Write flow-chart of production of Tungsten cemented carbide tool.   [3]

   (c) What are the different techniques used for compaction? Explain Isostatic compaction in detail.   [6]

MAY 2017

Time : 2 Hours   **Max. Marks : 50**

N.B. :- (1) Neat diagrams must be drawn wherever necessary.

(2) Figures to the right indicate full marks.

(3) Use of Calculator is allowed.

(4) Assume Suitable data, if necessary.

(5) Answer Q. No. 1 or Q. No. 2, Q. No. 3 or Q. No. 4, Q. No. 5 or Q. No. 6, Q. No. 7 or Q. No. 8.

1. (a) Calculate atomic packing factor for BCC and FCC crystal structure.   [6]

   (b) What is strain hardening and how does it affect plastic deformation? Explain theory of dislocation on the basis of rotation of slip planes during plastic deformation.[6] **OR**

2. (a) What do you mean by the tern "Miller Indices"? Explain the procedure and determine the Millar indices for plane (111)   [4]

   (b) What makes ceramics different than polymers with respect to properties?   [2]

   (c) What are different classifications of imperfections is crystal structure? Explain the point imperfection in detail.   [6]

3. (a) What is the basic difference between destructive and non-destructive testing? Explain the purpose of the following testing methods:
   (1) Tensile test
   (2) Ultrasonic
   (3) Creep test.   [7]

   (b) What do you mean by the term corrosion? What are the different ways to delay the destruction of metal under corrosion?   [6] **OR**

4. (a) Identify the type of corrosion for the following cases: [4]
   (i) Formation of cavities of small anodic area around which metal is relatively unattacked as compared large cathodic area.

(ii) Simultaneous effect of environment and cyclic fluctuation of stress.

(iii) The grain boundary phase or a region adjacent to the grain boundary becomes anodic and get preferably corroded due to precipitation of some phase.

(iv) An accelerated attack at the junction of two metals exposed to a corrosive environment.

(b) What is sacrifical anode ?   **[3]**

(c) What is the basic difference between hardness and toughness of the material? Explain the method to determine the toughness.   **[6]**

5. (a) What are the properties of coating materials ? Which are affects surface quality? Explain any three surface cleaning methods.   **[6]**

(b) What is shot blasting?   **[3]**

(c) List out the factors affecting electro-deposition.   **[3] OR**

6. (a) Compare PVD and CVD coating.   **[4]**

(b) Explain the process of Ion vapour deposition (IVD) with principle of working advantages and disadvantages and applications.   **[6]**

(c) What is powder coating?   **[2]**

7. (a) Explain the basic steps of powder metallurgy process.   **[4]**

(b) Explain the role and function of lubricants and binders in Powder Metallurgy.   **[6]**

(c) Why is sintering important step in Powder Metallurgy?   **[3]OR**

8. (a) Sieve analysis method is used in determination which property of powder metallurgy ? Explain it with neat diagram.   **[5]**

(b) Write flow chart of production of friction material.   **[4]**

(c) Explain Carbonil process for powder manufacturing.   **[4]**

www.ingramcontent.com/pod-product-compliance
Lightning Source LLC
Chambersburg PA
CBHW080955020726

47505CB00009B/2211